Luna *and* Sol

A FORBIDDEN LOVE STORY

A. M. Kusi

ISBN-13: 978-1-949781-02-1
ISBN-10: 1-949781-02-X

Published by A. M. Kusi 2018
amkusinovels@gmail.com
Visit our website at www.amkusi.com
Editing: Editing by C. Marie & Emerald Eyes Editing
Proofreader: Sara Wilkins
Sensitivity Editing by: Renita McKinney of A Book A Day
Cover design and formatting: Archangel Ink

To all who encouraged our writing, with a special thanks to Mom and Nana.

To our daughters Ellyson and Emelynn.

Sign Up to Get New Releases

The best way to get updates about new releases, giveaways, and more is by joining our newsletter.

Visit the website below to join:

www.amkusi.com/bookfans

Coming soon

The Orchard Inn

Contents

*"I have seen your darkest nights and brightest days and
I would want you to know that I will be here forever
loving you in dusk."*

-Atticus.

CHAPTER 1

"Luna? Wake up. Luna?"

Luna awoke with a start, hearing the whispers of a ghost. The room was black except for a few small rays of dim sunlight peeking through the cracks in the doorway. She sat up and rubbed her eyes then felt around for her cloak. When she found it, she wrapped the soft fabric around herself.

Luna stood and walked to her bedroom door; she opened it and stepped outside to the common room. This was where she and her father shared meals or sat and talked by the stone fireplace. Gannon was still sleeping, and Luna wanted to take a walk before she greeted him. She splashed some of the room temperature water on her face from a bucket on the table then grabbed a twig from a wooden bowl, chewing on it as she walked out the door, bucket in hand.

The sunrise was a bright purple-pink. The air was cool for a morning in the middle of summer, but Luna didn't mind it. She walked around the many huts in her village where most were still sleeping. As she made her way to the outer wall her father had built soon after her mother's death, she nodded to the men who were posted as guards. Luna passed through the entrance of the wall toward the river for fresh water. Safety was the reason her father had said they should erect the stone wall, but Luna never felt unsafe outside it. She couldn't remember a time when the Nets or the Dabney tribe to the east had instigated violence toward them.

Gannon had changed after that fateful morning of her mother's death, and he seemed to grow angrier as time went on. He forbade Luna and the rest of the Barden tribe from seeing or even speaking to the Nets. Luna couldn't remember much of her mother, but she remembered that day so very clearly. She remembered that her mother was friends with the Nets, which made her confused, because Gannon blamed them for Terra's death. Luna knew that was not true because *she* was the reason her mother had died, and she was sure of this. She could never gather the courage to tell her father what happened. She could never tell him his wife and son had died because of his own daughter, because of her.

Luna knew her father had wanted a son, and whenever he had the opportunity, he reminded her that she was to produce him an heir to help him conquer the Nets. Why this all seemed to depend on her ability to produce a male heir she didn't understand, except that her father was a very superstitious man who depended on the wisdom from his shaman.

Luna supposed she would be joined with someone of her father's choosing at some point, though she much preferred to be alone. She had hurt enough people and felt she was unworthy of love. She knew she was not good enough for her father, and she doubted she would be enough to please a man. Luna couldn't help but think her size also had something to do with the lack of interest from so many of the tribesmen. Luna was larger than her mother had been with thick, strong, muscled limbs, but she also carried extra weight in her stomach. The other women were fair and thin with lighter features. Luna contrasted with them in almost every way with her dark curly hair and brown eyes. The only thought that brought her comfort when she looked at her reflection was that her hair was like her mother's.

Luna reached the outer edge of the forest, collecting raspberry leaves, as her mother had taught her, and sticking them into her pockets. She walked along the path toward the river and gathered broadleaf plantain as well as a few sprigs of wild mint. Luna filled the bucket with fresh water from the river and sat there for a moment, taking in the burbling sounds it made. The birds were just beginning to wake up and look for their breakfast. The sun was higher now, almost fully above the mountains to the east.

Suddenly, Luna heard a noise from across the river. She watched in stunned silence as a brown Net woman filled her own bucket opposite Luna. The woman was older, her grey hair dreaded with beads strewn throughout. The tunic she wore was pale yellow, which contrasted with her dark skin beautifully.

The woman kindly greeted her, "Good morning child."

Luna froze. She knew her father would be livid if she spoke to the woman, but she didn't fully understand why. Luna felt no danger, but she had been wrong before, and she didn't trust her own intuition anymore. Luna simply nodded quickly, picked up her bucket, and left.

On the walk home, she gazed admiringly at the rising sun and the various colors of all the plants and wildflowers in the fields that surrounded the walls of her village. The corn had grown to be almost taller than she was. She walked back through the gate, nodding to the guards before making her way to her home. The wooden door was open when she returned. She could see her father was smoking a pipe, his mouth surrounded by a once red but now fully white braided beard; it was his morning routine. Gannon sat on a small stool outside their part-stone, part-wood home, heating a pot of water over a small fire pit. Gannon was a tall man with broad shoulders and thick arms, and he wore a long light brown sleeveless tunic that showed off his various tribal tattoos. Thor's hammer was one that stood out on his tricep in faded ink. A leather belt encircled his waist and created a short kilt that ended just above his knees. His hair was braided to match his beard, and his face was serious, always solemn. His eyes were a sad, stormy grey-blue.

"I've got the chicory root in there. What did you bring from the fields?" Gannon asked without looking up at his daughter.

Luna reached into her pocket and pulled out the herbs she had gathered. "Raspberry leaf, wild mint, and plantain." He didn't respond, so she lifted the lid off the pot and dropped the medicinal plants in. Luna went inside and placed the bucket of fresh water on the wooden table, and then she went to her room and changed into a cream-colored tunic. Next, she grabbed the jar where she stored her charcoal black paint. She painted her skin with a thick line across her face, between her eyes and nose, the symbol of a Barden noble, of a chief's daughter.

Luna tied a leather belt around her waist and secured the small dagger she always carried behind her. The belt had a sheath for her weapon at the base of her back and one pouch, which she carried flint and other small necessities in. She looked around the dim room for a moment. She put her hand out and felt for the wooden latch to open the small window, letting in a pocket of sunlight and instantly brightening the dark space. She found her quiver immediately. Luna preferred to heal with her herbs rather than take a life, but make no mistake, she was capable of using her bow. She simply preferred not to unless it was absolutely necessary. She grabbed the items and made her way back out the front door.

Her father had just poured her tea into a handle-less

clay cup. Luna set her bow against the side of the house before taking a seat on the low empty stool next to her father. The earthy taste of the hot tea was comforting to Luna, prepared just the way she liked it.

"I used the last of the honey, so maybe you could find some for us today," Gannon said before he took another sip. A lone drop of tea escaped his lips and slid down his braided beard, suspended for a moment on one of the ends.

"I will find some today," Luna assured him.

"Be careful and don't go too far. Thamos saw some black bears in the south end near the berry bushes. Take the horse," he instructed as he stood, tea in hand.

"Then I'll head north, up the mountain," she agreed.

"Good girl," he replied then entered the house, shutting the door behind him.

Her father's approval gave Luna some comfort, although she felt no more confident than before. Gannon had left Luna to herself since she had reached her age of maturation. The event was marked by an intricate and painful tattooing ceremony with the elder women of the tribe. On her light olive-toned chest was a dark black circle. She liked to think of it as a new moon. It had five lines radiating from it, like the points of a star, representing the five elements. The four lower lines were more like dash marks. The top line was solid and ran from the black circle all the way up her neck and chin, stopping just before her bottom lip. She remembered it was the one that had hurt the most. The geometric triangular symbols for air and water lay directly under the tattooed dash marks across her clavicles, not quite to the ends of the tattoo but aligning directly in the middle of each line. The symbols for earth and fire were at the top of her breasts, just to the sides of her cleavage, and out of sight with her tunic on. Spirit was the only symbol not tattooed on her body.

Luna finished her tea, nodding her good mornings to the tribe members who passed by on their way out to the river for their own fresh water. She unhooked a leather strap from a notch on the wall of the house. The long belt had several drawstring linen bags on it to contain whatever she foraged that day, something she had made herself. Some of the bags were empty, and others carried supplies she might need. Luna grabbed her bow and quiver before going to the makeshift corral to get her horse, Willow. Luna saw the golden-brown mare from a few yards away, happily grazing. She led Willow out into the humid summer morning, put the leather strap over the mare, and secured it before pulling herself onto the horse. She loved to ride bareback. She had spent so much time with her horse that she didn't even need to use a rope to direct her. Luna patted Willow's golden brown shoulder before grabbing hold of the horse's matching mane.

"Let's go, Willow!" She gave a light nudge with her feet and off they went at an easy and steady pace.

Luna made her way north, past the raspberry bushes

where she had just picked the leaves for their morning tea. She had to duck under branches as she and the horse weaved their way into the woods. She stopped a few times in the duration it took to reach her destination, using the small knife she'd brought to gather wild medicinal mushrooms. She placed them in one of the cloth bags she had brought with her before continuing on her usual route. Finding the tree where the wild honey bees had made their hive, she slipped effortlessly off her horse. She collected a piece of bark from a tree and placed a few tiny twigs and dried leaves on it. Next, she took out the pieces of flint she carried in the pouch on the leather belt around her waist. Striking the rocks together, she created enough sparks to make a little fire, and eventually it produced enough smoke for what she intended.

She was quiet, her bare feet stepping on the soft ground carefully, trying not to alert the bees that she was there for their treasure trove of golden honey. Luna blew softly at first, sending the smoke into the hole of the great oak tree where the bees had made their hive. The buzzing got louder, so she blew harder, enveloping them in the smoke. The dull buzz let her know she could do her work. Setting the smoking bark on the ground out of the way, she grabbed her dagger once more. Luna was careful to carve out just enough of the honeycomb to last her and her father a couple weeks. Some of the bees started crawling on her hand that held the dagger, and she quickly and calmly retreated back to the horse. She placed the honey in a jar she kept in one of the linen bags. Her hand stung with itching pain and she swatted the bee. She watched the dead insect fall to the ground as she scraped her dirty fingernail across the site of the sting, pulling the stinger out.

Luna looked around until she spotted what she needed: a broadleaf plantain. She plucked one of the leaves and put it in her mouth, chewing until it formed a paste. She spit the green slime onto the sting site of her right hand. Next, Luna ripped off a piece of her tunic and wrapped it around her wound until it was secure. She emptied the smoking bark and leaves onto the ground, covering it with fresh dirt to make sure the fire didn't grow.

Willow waited patiently, grazing nearby on spots of green grass. Luna climbed back up onto her horse, deciding to head deeper into the woods and up the mountain. The woods made her feel at home; the forest made her feel close to the spirit of her mother. She could tell the trees and plants her secrets, and they wouldn't betray her. She went along her usual way, looking for more medicinal plants and fungi. The path was worn from her frequent trips, but today she saw something that was not usually there: footprints, specifically large bear footprints, and they were fresh.

"Hmmm. I think we will avoid our normal route today, Willow. It seems the gods would have us adventure along a new path," Luna said out loud as she used her feet to direct the horse to move further north instead of cutting west toward the river.

They carried on, weaving in between the tree branches and downed trees. As they got farther in, Luna slid off the horse, leading the mare on foot as far as she could. The forest grew dark and thick as she trekked up the mountain. She had never been this far up the north mountain before and could hear the rushing sound of water, sparking her curiosity. Luna took a rope out of one of the linen satchels and placed one end around Willow's neck, the other around a large pine tree. She untied a linen bag from the leather strap, attaching it to the belt on her hip before heading deeper into the woods, the bow and quiver still strapped across her back.

The smell of wet earth grew stronger as she continued. The ground grew softer under her feet as the path she chose was nearly bare except for pine needles, roots, and patches of stubborn moss that willed itself to live. The sound of the water emptying into itself drew her closer. The trees looked much bigger and older here. Some had fallen, their decaying rusty colors contrasting with the bright green leaves springing forth, the offshoots of new trees growing on top of the dead, signaling the growth that comes from death and the cycle of life. Red squirrels chattered as they scurried from the ground around ferns and other forest flora to a nearby tree, as if to say her very presence was a nuisance. The loud sound of the rushing water drew her on.

The thick forest gave way as Luna pushed branches out

of her path and stepped through. Moss covered the ground where she took soft steps, getting closer to the rush of the water. All around her was a light mist that smelled of the moist earth with hints of pine and notes of green from the lush thick forest behind her. She took careful steps as the ground turned to dark dirt and finally stone before ending abruptly.

She now stood on a cliff ledge. Looking down, she could see a large waterfall that was preceded by a series of smaller ones. The edge of the cliff was lined with a few tall cedar and evergreen trees. There were several smaller lichen-covered boulders, but the ground was bare except for some reddish-brown mushrooms that lined the edge, just a little farther out than Luna was comfortable reaching for at that height. She looked to her right and saw a boulder-filled river lined by forest on either side with not much warning of the sudden drop down to the falls.

Luna followed the cascading water to the left with her eyes and saw that there was a clearing next to a large deep pool at the base of the waterfall. She saw a way of climbing down but decided it would be easier to go back into the woods and make her way down then cut back to the open space.

Once she took the first steps into the clearing, she took a deep cleansing breath in. It was the exhilarating smell of freedom. *Paradise*, she thought to herself. It had been a while since she went exploring deep into the woods, and never had she gone this far before. It was worth it. This would be her new favorite spot. She looked around, taking in the full sight. The waterfall fell straight down into a large green pool with sizeable boulders covering either side. She could see the ledge where she had first spotted this site from above. Part of her wished she could live there, just her, the water, and the forest. The waterfall was brilliant. The sound of the rushing water was loud, and she imagined it was almost deafening in the spring when all the snow melted. It was a truly magnificent sight.

The pool from the falls emptied into a smaller river carved in between the large boulders from years of erosion, making smaller waterfalls. Farther down the river, it was more like a wide stream, and the river rocks were smaller. The moss and lichen-covered boulders were fewer and farther between, and there were spots of light in the river where the sun broke through the thick canopy of trees. Some boulders had trees sprouting on top of them, and others near the edge of the river were included in the trees' root systems. A few of the boulders had ample covering of moss and young trees growing upon them. Life had found a way to grow even though its roots were planted on solid rock, and others had worked their way through the darkness of crevices.

Out of the corner of Luna's left eye, she saw a large birch tree with peeling bark. She almost didn't recognize it as a birch tree because it was covered with moss, and the bark was darker on the side facing the river. It was more like three birch trees with moss-covered roots intertwined, forming what looked like one giant tree, much greater than any of the three could have been on its own.

Luna took a step closer to examine the magnificent sight then recognized the dark brown growth on the side of one of the trees. She pulled out her dagger and struggled to cut off the conk of chaga mushroom. It was the biggest one she had ever found, and this great tree had more than one growth spot. Just as Luna put her knife away and placed the beautiful mushroom in the linen bag at her hip, the sound of splashing in the river caught her attention.

She jolted to face a very large buck that was staggering and breathing heavily across the shallow part of the river. She watched as it barely made its way out of the water before it stumbled to the ground with a bleat. The sight of the arrow sticking out of its right side now made it clear that this deer was someone's prey. Luna's eyes darted to the other side of the river, searching for the hunter. Her hands pulled the bow and one of the arrows from her back as she walked closer to the suffering animal. She waited a minute, then two. Nothing. What if the hunter came to collect his deer? Luna knew the animal had come from the west side of the river, knew the hunter would be a Net tribe member. The animal was on her side of the river, though, and crossing the water would start a war between the two tribes.

Luna bent down, setting the bow on a large stone and the arrow back in her quiver. She used her knife to end the animal's suffering without hesitation. As she leaned over it, thanking it for its life, her mind wondered what she would do if the hunter didn't come. Would she leave the animal there to rot? There was no way she could drag it to where she had left Willow tied up. That was at least two miles away, and the forest was too thick for the horse to make it through.

Before she could come up with a viable solution, she felt the presence of someone else. Her eyes darted back across the river, and striking green eyes stared at her. Luna momentarily froze with fear and held her breath. Their gazes locked as they scrutinized each other. Luna grabbed her bow from the stone, standing to show him she was ready to defend herself. His eyes were an intense and radiant grey-green. His brown hair was short, tracing the shape of his head. A trimmed beard lined his strong jaw, shadowing his already dark brown handsome face. His nose was wide and his lips were full. Luna noticed he wasn't wearing a shirt, and his muscles were toned and defined. He held a dark red bag in one hand, and the other hand was empty. The young man wore knee-length short pants made from a beautifully woven bright blue fabric, the same color her mother had worn the last day she had seen her. There was a leather belt with a knife sheathed in it across his waist, and a bow and quiver across his back as well. Luna's eyes made their way from his face down to his bare feet before going back to those mesmerizing eyes that did not seem to pose her any threat. The expression on his face was not welcoming, but Luna felt he meant her no harm. That tiny voice inside her—the one she usually ignored in favor of following her father's rules—pushed her farther forward.

At first, the stranger took a step back. Standing still, he watched her as she placed her bow on her back again. Luna grabbed the animal's antlers and began to pull the deer across the shallow river to the man with the piercing green eyes, her body disobeying the screaming voice of her father in her mind. The water was cool and sent an initial shock to Luna's already adrenaline-fueled body. The able-bodied young man watched, not making any attempt to help her. Luna struggled with the heavy animal, dragging it across the cool river. The deer's smell was repugnant, especially since it was wet. Luna dropped it at the edge of the stranger's side of the shallow river, careful not to step onto the dry ground. Then she backed away, slowly retreating to her side once more. The man hesitated, so Luna washed her hands in the water and found a soft piece of earth to sit on at the edge of the forest on a beach of small river rocks.

Luna's cheeks were flushed red, partly from the exertion of dragging the deer by herself, and partly because she could not fathom why she would do such a daring act. Just a few hours ago she hadn't even been able to say good morning to the Net woman in yellow, and now here she was dragging an animal to the other side of the river for one of them. Her father…what would he think of this? What would he say about her actions? Only the forest would know. It gave her comfort and confidence to be in the woods. *Maybe that's why I did it*, she convinced herself. She wouldn't let herself believe it was because of the mysterious stranger with the luminous green eyes who showed no malice, even though his body language seemed unwelcoming and guarded.

Luna watched as the captivating man slowly proceeded toward the deer, taking out a large knife before cutting into the animal. She saw him carefully remove the valuable organs, placing them in wooden containers he took out of the red bag he carried. He rinsed the deer's empty cavity with water from the river before heading back into the woods. He was gone for a few minutes, and Luna wondered if he was going to return. He did several moments later, leading a brown mare with white spots covering its body. Luna watched as he lifted the deer almost too easily with his compact yet muscular frame and laid it across the horse. He had already tied the red bag onto the mare. After securing the deer with rope, he brought one of the wooden bowls with a lid into the river toward Luna. She stood quickly upon the mystery man's approach. He made his way to the middle of the river and set the bowl on a boulder. Looking at Luna, he nodded once before heading back into the woods with his horse.

Luna waited to see if he was going to return, but he

didn't. She wondered if he had left the bowl for her. She wondered what was inside it. Curiosity got the best of her, and she retrieved the container from the boulder in the river. She waited to examine its contents until she was back on her side. She opened it gingerly, not knowing why she was feeling so timid. She saw the dark red of a deer heart inside. She smiled with a mixture of relief and inquisitiveness. Luna gathered up the linen bag with the mushroom along with the bowl before heading back into the woods toward Willow. She was not able to get the man or his eyes out of her head the whole way through the forest. Knowing the contents of the bowl answered one question but created so many others. Who was this man? Why had he left the deer heart for her? The walk back took less time than she'd expected, and she placed her items in the leather strap on the horse, which was neighing and pulling at the rope.

"I'm here. I'm ready to head back. Shhhh," Luna said out loud, patting her horse.

She led the animal back the way they'd come until the forest was clear enough for her to ride. She would cook the heart for dinner, and her father would be none the wiser. If he asked, she would make sure to omit the details of how she got it. Once she reached the edge of the woods and the familiar sight of the mostly stone wall reached her eyes, she couldn't help but look out toward the river that separated the Net tribe and hers. She wondered about the handsome stranger with green eyes who'd made her feel a tangled mess of emotions she couldn't yet make sense of. She wondered if she would see him again. Luna stuffed down the confusing ball of anxiety inside her as she swallowed hard.

CHAPTER 2

Sol made his way southwest toward his tribe, leading his horse on foot.

He couldn't get the woman at the river out of his mind. Her eyes were a rich dark brown, accented by the black paint underneath them. Her loose curly hair had blown wildly in the wind as she leaned over the deer, ended its suffering, and softly spoke her thanks to the animal, something Sol had thought would be above the Barden tribe. She'd surprised him on many accounts in their short meeting. How could so much be said without any words being spoken? Sol had seen the tattoos on her chest, her tunic comfortably fitted against her curvy body. Her thighs, he noticed, were thick and strong. She knew her way around that dagger she carried with her too, he guessed. Why would she risk so much and bring him the deer?

His thoughts were momentarily interrupted as he exited the woods and saw his sister. A smile broke out on his usually serious face as he joyfully announced, "Akiiki! The gods have been gracious today. We will have fresh meat for dinner!"

"Ahhh, my brother, that is good news. The baby has been wanting some meat," she said, patting her small pregnant belly.

Sol took a minute to admire his sister. Akiiki had long lanky arms and legs and was taller than him. She wore a long bright yellow tunic with intricate white beadwork at the ends. Akiiki had on several necklaces of wooden and clay beads, sea glass, and feathers, all beautifully arranged. Her hair was a neatly shaped large afro.

"So, does that mean you will also cook this dinner?" Sol asked with a chuckle.

"Mmmmm, I think we both know the answer to that, dear brother." Akiiki laughed a loud but gentle laugh. "Ask Bomani—he loves to cook!" his sister said, pointing to her husband a few hundred yards away, busy working under the shade of few maple trees.

"All right." Sol led his horse toward Bomani. When he got closer, he could see his brother-in-law was carving another beautiful spoon from a piece of solid oak.

Bomani spoke before Sol got the chance. "Brother, what do you have there? Did you find this sick deer lying in the forest? Are you trying to kill us with bad meat?" He laughed at his own joke.

Sol made a clicking sound with his tongue before answering with a large smile that showed off his white teeth. "You know I have some luck every now and then."

"Luck? You? Ha! I suppose you want my help to hang the animal, huh?" Bomani asked, motioning toward the deer with his carving knife.

"Thanks for the offer. Your wife said you were going to cook it for us too," Sol said, trying to sound serious.

"I bet she did. Ha! Well you know me, brother—if it will make my queen happy, I will do it." Bomani smiled and looked lovingly at his wife in the distance. Even though they were joking around, Sol knew Bomani meant that last part with all his heart.

Bomani put away his carving knife and blew the wood chips off the half-carved spoon before standing up. He gathered his tools and patted the lingering bits off his light green tunic and matching pants. When Bomani stood, he was at least a foot taller than Sol, and his shoulders were very broad and muscular—a gentle giant. He also wore his hair a bit longer in a short afro.

"Well, I'll follow the great hunter." He motioned with his hand for Sol to lead the way.

Sol laughed as he led the horse on. They talked and joked as they traveled to their destination. The area was mostly clear except for some established trees that grew with large gaps of space in between. There were several wooden dwellings built in the vicinity and some longhouses. Sol found a rope waiting for him at the butchering area they had set up. There was a large, thick, weathered wooden table that had several knife marks going in all directions across the dark surface, and it was surrounded by wooden stools. There was already a bucket full of water someone had set up, as well as several different-sized wooden bowls. They untied and lifted the deer off the horse, setting it on the table. Bomani tied the deer's hind legs with one end of the rope then Sol helped him tie the other end around a sturdy branch of the nearby elm tree. They hoisted the deer up high enough to skin it.

"I'm going to wash my horse. Can you start?" Sol asked.

"Sure, sure. I have to clean the animal *and* cook it! The life of a chieftess's son is too easy—you have your brother in-law do all your hard labor," Bomani joked as he got to work.

Sol laughed again. He had such a joyful boisterous laugh, but usually only those closest to him got to hear it. Sol removed the red bag from the horse and placed the jars on the table, opening their contents. He emptied the water into one of the larger wooden bowls and placed the organs inside to soak. He would rinse them off when he returned.

Sol led his horse to the river until he was knee deep in the refreshingly cold water. Using the empty bucket, he rinsed the mare's bloodstained coat, revealing once again the pure white spots that covered her light brown coat. The horse drank some of the water before Sol pulled her back out to the river's edge where some tall grass grew in the meadow clearing. He filled the bucket with fresh water before sitting to watch the gurgling water. He took a long inhale then let out an equally long exhale. Sol's eyes wandered to the other side of the cool green-toned river. He wondered about the Barden woman at the waterfall, unable to get her face out of his mind.

After a few minutes, he shook his head, trying to jar the thoughts away. He stood and brought the horse back to its grazing pasture then returned to Bomani with the water. Bomani had already expertly taken the hide off with his knife. They washed the animal hair off the carcass before beginning their work, carving and cutting the meat off the bones until they had fully butchered the animal, laughing and joking together all the while. The bones were placed in a large pot to be boiled down into broth over the next few days. The meat was cut into portion-sized hunks, and the organs were separated on the table with the tongue and eyes. Bomani put the skull in another pot to boil before putting one hand on his hip, exaggeratedly scratching his head with the other. "Brother? Where is the heart?" Bomani moved one of his hands around the organs in the bowl, searching.

Sol felt a surge of panic. "I already gave it away."

Bomani laughed. "I'm sure you did. How is Layla today?" Bomani winked at Sol.

Sol felt a flood of relief. "I don't know. Why don't you ask her." It was a statement, not a question.

"I'll start cooking the evening meal," Bomani said as he grabbed the deer liver and a few hunks of meat from the bowl for his wife, Sol, and their family.

"Good, because I'm hungry," Sol admitted.

"I don't know why you are so hungry—you don't do any work. Ahhh, the life of the chieftess's—"

Sol cut Bomani off before he could finish. "You are her son now too. Don't you forget, dear brother."

Bomani shook his head as he laughed loudly and walked away. Sol placed some pieces of cloth over the bowls to keep the bugs away. He knew the rest of the tribe would be by to take what they needed for their dinners.

The summer night was as typical as any other for the members of the Net tribe. The families ate outside around a fire where they had conversation. The air was filled with a chorus of voices and laughter. Some serious conversations were had around the different fires in hushed voices. Children played freely. Some children as young as five practiced their carving skills on a stick they'd found while others watched in awe of the storytellers. Some of the children danced to the drums, others played. The night was filled with firelight and contentment.

Sol ate with his sister and brother in-law. His younger twin brothers, Ata and Atsu, were also there, poking fun at each other's expense. Sol's younger brothers' handsome facial features and mischievous eyes were similar, but Ata left his hair short while Atsu had his longer and braided. The twins were similar in height, both taller than Sol but shorter than their older sister. Sol's mother was sewing a cloak in a wooden chair by the firelight. Her long braids were starting to turn silver, her brown eyes warm and wise, her face bearing many lines from years of laughter and worry. Sol watched his family enjoy their dinner. It gave him satisfaction to know he'd brought something to contribute to the tribe. He enjoyed hunting every now and then solely for that reason. Usually, Sol would be found working with wood, carving or building.

The Nets were a joyful, warm, and inviting people. Sol wondered about the woman because she didn't fit what he thought of the Barden. He could vaguely remember a time when the river had not been such an enforced boundary and he could play on both sides. He remembered the time when his mother came to him and told him they could not cross anymore, the day the river became a boundary line. She had looked worried and sad. Sol had brushed it off, as he had so many of their rules back then, back before he knew better, before his propensity for rule-breaking cost him his father's life.

Sol said his good nights to his family and walked the rest of the way to the lean-to where he liked to sleep during the nights of the year it was warm enough to do so. The shelter faced the ocean, and he liked to listen to the sound of the waves hitting the rocks and washing up on the sandy shore. The salty sea air was welcoming to Sol. He liked the way the moon reflected off the waves and how many stars he could see from his wooden shelter. There wasn't much except a bucket of water, a wooden chest with his clothes, and some furs laid down for a bed, but it was quiet and it was his. Sol fell asleep quickly with no one close enough to hear his light snoring.

* * *

Luna returned home in time to start the evening meal. She had stopped by the field on her way home and picked some dark leafy greens, tomatoes, yellow squash, and zucchini from the giant gardens. She prepared dinner, trying to think of something else, anything but the mysterious stranger and his piercing green eyes, a man she was forbidden to speak to or communicate with. As she cut up the embezzled deer heart for her and her father's dinner, she couldn't get the encounter with the stranger out of her mind. She heated the leftover mint and raspberry leaf tea from the morning while humming a melody. Suddenly, she heard the door open, interrupting her forbidden thoughts. Luna was surprised to find her father's sister in the doorway instead of him.

"Hello, Luna. Mmmm, it smells good." Alice set down the jar she was holding on the wooden table. She took a long inhale of the pot Luna stirred before giving her niece a hug.

"Hello, Aunt Alice. Are you staying for dinner?" Luna asked as she smiled, grateful for the distraction from her secret thoughts.

"Well, since you have invited me, yes," Alice replied, the right side of her mouth curving into a half-smile. Alice was tall and thin. She had silver wiry hair and bright sky blue eyes. She wore a plain light purple tunic that was long and fit loosely. Alice was all Luna had for a close female influence since her mother had passed away. Alice showed her the amount of warmth and love she was capable of, not being a naturally maternal woman. Her aunt did not have any children of her own. Alice's lover had died tragically from the venom of a snake bite, and she had never found another she wanted to bind her life to. Alice would remind her niece from time to time as she grew up that if she ever found the mate to her soul, with a real knowing and raw love like she'd had, to hold on to it with all her might. Alice was also the closest thing Luna had to a friend. Luna just didn't seem to click with the other young tribeswomen; they were mostly thin and of fair beauty. They were also much more interested in finding husbands and too concerned with the activities of other people, in Luna's opinion. She much preferred the silence of the forests and meadows in solitude.

"I've brought you some salt. I went over to the Dabney lands to trade some of my tinctures, and I thought you could use some." Alice motioned to the jar on the wooden table. Their tribe was on reasonably good terms with the Dabney tribe to the east. Luna's tribe, the Barden, celebrated turning the wheel of the year with the Dabney tribe, and bartering was common between the two bordering tribes since they seemed to have a lot in common with each other. The tribes looked so much alike that it was hard to tell just by looking at a man whether he was Barden or Dabney. Their culture and society were similar in the way they viewed the division of men as superior and women inferior.

Luna's eyes lit up. "Oh! It is just what this dinner is missing! Thank you, Alice."

Alice found a seat on a wooden stool, fanning herself as she enjoyed the breeze from the open door. "What did you do today, child?"

Luna hesitated. "Oh, I…um…I found some honey, and some chaga—the biggest chunk I have ever seen! Do you need some?" she asked, purposefully avoiding the details that followed finding the mushroom as she added a few pinches of salt to the pot she was stirring. It felt wrong not to tell her confidante the thrilling events of her afternoon. Luna struggled, not wanting to upset her aunt, who would surely tell her father. Alice was close with Luna, but she suspected her aunt was loyal to her father first. Luna decided it best to keep it a secret for now. Alice and Luna passed the time talking about the dinner, tinctures, and the bartering Alice had done that day. They made a mental list of all the wild herbs they needed to harvest in the coming months to dry out for winter or tincture in the strong ferment they got from the Dabney. The women lit candles to light the room as the sun set, and just as Luna finished her plate of deer heart and vegetables, her father's silhouette darkened the open doorway.

"Smells good," he said as he made his way into the

house. He hung his leather pouch on one of the wooden pegs that stuck out of the wall behind the door then he shut it.

"Tasted good, too!" Alice said, giving Luna a wink. Luna filled the bowl she had used with the stew once more and handed it to her father. He sat down on the wooden stool by the empty fireplace out of habit.

"I found honey today, and a large piece of chaga." Luna unwrapped her treasured brown mushroom from the linen bag.

"Woah! You were not joking when you said it was big!" Alice's eyes grew wide as she slapped her knee.

A disinterested groan was the only response Luna received from her father.

"You will be happy when this keeps you from getting sick as the cold weather and snow come." Alice narrowed her eyes at her brother, cautioning him.

"If the gods decide I should get sick, there is no plant on this land that will help me," Gannon replied, focusing his eyes on his dinner. "Is this deer heart?"

Luna stood up from the stool where she was sitting, hoping her father didn't notice the color that flushed her cheeks. "Yes." She let out an exaggerated yawn. "Well, I'm really tired. I'm going to head to bed now. Good night, father. Good night, Alice." She kissed her father on his temple and gave her aunt a quick hug before retreating to her bedroom after grabbing a candle off the mantle.

Luna closed the door behind her with relief. After using the candle she held to light a few more in her room, Luna set it on the small wooden table by her bed. She picked up a piece of cloth and wet it with a bottle of ointment then washed her face with it. She used the bucket of warm water and another piece of fabric to wash her feet before blowing out the candles. She slipped out of her tunic in the darkness. It was too hot to wear anything. She knew at some point she would reach for the thin woven blanket by her feet, but for now, she would enjoy lying naked on the linen-covered furs and animal hides that made up her bed on the floor. She enjoyed the darkness. She could hear her father and aunt making small talk in the other room, but her thoughts drifted to the waterfall and all its magic. She thought of the stranger with those unforgettable eyes. Did he go there often? Was that his secret paradise? She wanted to go back, but she knew she shouldn't. She definitely should not go that way again…but she hadn't had time to fully explore the waterfall and all the plant life and fungi growing that far up the mountain. *It would only be for foraging purposes*, she thought to herself as she fell asleep.

The next morning, Luna woke early and went through her usual routine. She got fresh water, and this time there was no one else at the river. She gathered more fresh herbs for their tea. Next, she painted her face and changed into a black tunic before heading out to enjoy the hot cup of tea that waited for her with little conversation from her father.

"Where will you be foraging today?" he asked.

She wondered if he asked out of responsibility or because he truly cared. Her father wasn't one for small talk, so she would assume the former. Luna had the feeling of fluttering in her stomach as she answered, "I'll head back up north. I saw some mushrooms I didn't get a chance to inspect." *At least that much is true*, she thought as she took the last sip from her tea.

"I'll be going to speak with Bale about the trade of goods for fish, so I won't be home in time for the evening meal," he told her as he got up and went back in the house, his tea in hand.

"Okay," Luna responded, knowing full well her father would be out very late talking to the chief of the Dabney tribe and would most likely stumble home just a few hours before the sun came up. The Dabney had a gift for their fermented drinks, and Gannon would fully partake every so often.

Luna set her cup down by the pot, grabbing her bow and supplies before heading to get her horse. As she walked to the pasture where Willow grazed, her heart thudded with excitement and anxiety. She led Willow out and put the leather strap around her with the various linen bags. She brought all her usual supplies with the addition of the bowl the stranger had gifted her. *I should return it*, she rationalized to herself. That was the reason she should see him again. Even for a wooden bowl, it was intricately designed with the carving of Neith, the goddess of hunting. There was also an inscription carved into it: *The sacrifice of one gives life to another*. Luna ran her fingers over the words before putting the bowl into one of the bags. She mounted her horse, nudging it north with the heels of her bare feet.

Once she reached the thick part of the forest, she tied the horse to a tree near the river and removed a couple bags from the leather strap. Luna peeked inside the one with the bowl, more so out of hesitation, as her body hummed with a storm of anxious energy. The air was already hot and humid, and it was still hours before noon. As Luna made her way up the mountain through the thick brush, she wiped beads of sweat from her brow. The sound of the rushing water grew stronger. *At least it is cooler in the forest*, she thought to herself as the trees changed to more pines and evergreens than maples, birch, and elms.

As she walked the two miles to the waterfall, she had con-flicting thoughts. Everything she had been told about these people should have made her want to run in the opposite direction, yet something inside her pushed her on. A foreign energy drew her up the mountain. Was it curiosity? Yes, Luna admitted to herself—she was so damn curious about the stranger with the vibrant eyes. *I will return the bowl and that will be it*, she told herself just as the forest cleared. The waterfall came into her vision. She immediately scanned the other side of the river for any signs of the man. Nothing.

Luna decided it was best to keep busy than stare into

the forest on the other side of the falls, so she left all but one of her bags in the clearing near the birch trees with the giant chaga mushroom growing on them, along with her bow and quiver. Next, she got to work looking for other fungi and useful plant life. The hours trickled by slowly, and Luna had given up hope that the Net man would return.

She snacked on a wild apple and a piece of dried venison she had brought with her as she sat on a giant boulder overlooking the waterfall. The rush of the water was almost deafening up that close. The coolness of the rock and the spray of mist in the shade of the canopy of trees lining the river refreshed her, but she was still hot and sticky in the humidity. Luna tossed the core of the apple into the water downstream and watched it being carried off until it went down the smaller falls out of sight. She walked to the water's edge and untied her leather belt, dropping it to the dry ground. Next, she slipped off her black tunic until she was fully naked, feeling the hot sunlight on her exposed light olive skin. She stepped into the refreshing water. The rocks made way, moving under her naked feet. She wanted to feel the ice-cold water that promised relief from her anxiously buzzing mind. She could just let all her worries wash away and flow down the river. The water grounded her. It called to her.

Luna walked forward until she was up to her waist in the deep green pool. She dunked her black tunic that was already wet from her sweat and washed it before wringing it out and laying it on a small boulder in the sun to dry. She took one more glance around at her surroundings and then swam in, covering the rest of her body in the icy liquid. It was a welcome sensation on such a hot day. Luna tried to swim to the base of the waterfall, but the current was too strong. She held her breath and tried to see what was in the blue-green waters below her. She came up for air after finding it too difficult to see the bottom and guessed it was very deep. Luna floated on her back, enjoying the cool water. It made her feel alive. Above, she could see a ledge on either side, and it looked like a giant stone doorway covered in moss and lichen. She felt at peace. Luna flipped over and started to swim back when a black shape caught her eye to the side where she had left her things near the birch trees.

A large black bear now stood between her and the only sizable weapon she could use to defend herself. The bear was tearing apart the bags, probably smelling the honey from the previous day, but it hadn't noticed Luna yet. She was stuck naked in the pool with a bear blocking her only access to her bow—her single line of defense—and to her path home. She quietly waded behind the rock where her tunic was drying, trying to think of what to do. Just then another dark figure caught her eye to the right, and she felt a strong hand grab her arm. The stranger pulled her naked body out of the water quickly and quietly while putting his other hand up to his full lips to signal her to remain quiet. She looked in his grey-green eyes and nodded.

CHAPTER 3

ol pulled Luna into the woods, out of the water, and away from the bear onto Net tribal lands. They stopped, squeezing behind a large pine tree when they were far enough into the brush to be hidden from the animal. They both turned their faces in its direction, making sure it had not seen their escape. The bear was still tearing apart the linen bags, licking and crushing the contents.

When Luna was satisfied her life was not in immediate danger anymore, she realized her naked wet body was pressed against the warm figure of the stranger. With each rapid breath, her firm breasts grazed his muscled chest. She glanced down at herself in embarrassment and could feel her cheeks blush red.

His eyes met hers. "You can't go now. You will have to wait the bear out." His voice was deep and firm. He took off his blue tunic and handed it to her as he turned, forcing himself to look away. Even though the woman's body was cold from being in the river, her touch warmed him with desire, a feeling that was quickly stifled as flashes from his past attacked his consciousness. Sol's body grew tense and his breathing quickened.

Luna gladly accepted his gift and pulled the tunic over her head. It was a bit snug on her breasts and quite short, but at least she wasn't naked anymore.

"Thank you," she said.

Sol just nodded his head.

She couldn't help but notice the defined corded muscles that covered his back and arms. He seemed tense to her. Was he…in pain?

Sol's traumatizing memories came back to him, drowning him in violent visions like a giant wave. His mind was no longer at the waterfall with the Barden woman but there in the meadow with his father fifteen years before. He could smell the bear and hear the screams as well as see flashes of the mauled flesh of his father, Jabari.

Luna placed a hand on his arm, the scorching heat yanking him back to reality. He turned to face her again and saw her lips moving, but he couldn't formulate a response just yet.

"Are you okay?" Luna asked again, genuinely concerned.

Sol was so shocked by the flashback that he felt like he needed to steady himself and did so against the tree with one of his hands. He nodded his head and took a few deep breaths.

Luna looked in his eyes, which now seemed more grey than green, sensing something was different in them. She felt like she needed to fill the silence.

"I'm Luna."

"Sol," he answered.

"You look like you are in pain, Sol. Are you hurt?"

"No. The bear…" He was more distracted by the way his name sounded coming off her lips than the flashback now.

"I don't know what I would have done if not for your quick thinking. My weapon is over there being destroyed right now," Luna said, then wondering if she should have admitted her vulnerability to him.

Sol watched her as she glanced toward the bear and then back to him. It was as if they had known each other before. He recognized her in some way.

"A bow isn't a great match for a bear when you're by yourself. I would know." Sol looked down in shame. He noticed just how short his tunic was on her and admired her strong thighs and ample hips. His garment was a bit snug on her voluptuous body, which he liked.

"Why?"

Sol's eyes moved upward to her face once again. Her lips were full. Her eyes were a warm brown, highlighted by the black tribal markings under them. He could sense pain in her eyes, which he could relate to. She had a few freckles but an otherwise smooth complexion. She was not stunningly beautiful, but she did have a natural beauty about her.

"Why what?" he asked.

"Why would you know?" Luna asked curiously.

"My father was killed by a bear. He was protecting me

when I was a boy."

"Oh, I'm so sorry. That must have been… He must have really loved you." Luna empathized. She knew full well what it was like to lose a parent.

"It was because of me that he died." Sol didn't know why he admitted it out loud to this stranger, a woman he didn't even know. He hadn't talked about the events of that fateful day since it had happened so many years earlier and now he was telling a stranger, and an enemy of his tribe, no less. He had a proclivity for being guarded, but his walls didn't seem to stand a chance around her, and that scared him. His usually closed-off self was now telling her his deepest hurt. Sol usually followed rules strictly since that day when he'd broken them to venture into the meadow looking for berries. His father had warned him not to because they had seen bears in the area. He'd vowed he would never break the rules again, and now here he was taking a Barden onto their tribal lands.

"You were just a boy. A man and his young son are no match for a bear," Luna said comfortingly, interrupting his self-flagellation.

Sol could feel a small sense of consolation from her words, even though he did not believe them just yet.

"We have to wait out the bear before you can go back."

We. She liked the sound of it as it left his lips.

"Okay," Luna replied. "How long were you here before you saw the bear?" she asked suspiciously.

Sol's gaze was unwavering. "Long enough."

Luna's cheeks flushed pink once again as she caught his meaning.

"Why did you bring me the deer yesterday?" Sol asked the question that had burned in his mind the whole trek up to the waterfall, which he'd made in hopes of catching a glance of the woman again. He had wanted to study her and had done so for a couple hours, out of sight in the forest. He had watched her as she gathered plants and mushrooms and figured she knew her way around plant medicine. He watched as she ate her lunch on the boulder. When she pulled off her tunic, he couldn't look away. Her body was like a magnet, drawing his eyes to every curve. The sun reflected off the sweat on her olive-toned body. He could see the full tribal tattoo that covered her chest, admiring her pointed breasts as she turned to look around her before jumping into the pool of water. He remembered he thought she had seen him for a moment. Then he saw the bear. He knew he couldn't leave her to be torn apart like his father had been, but he didn't know why the thought of leaving her to fate bothered him so much.

"It wasn't mine to keep," she answered.

"But, it died on your land. You ended its life. It was yours."

"No, I just ended its suffering. I thought you wouldn't retrieve it since it was on our land and that could…incite a war…" Luna said worriedly, now realizing her own geography in that moment. She was on their land.

Sol saw her glance around him at the forest and then back to him.

"I won't say anything," he promised.

"Why did you pull me out of the river?"

"You needed help," he answered, wondering why she would ask a question with such an obvious answer.

"Are all the people of your tribe like you?"

Sol's faced squinted in confusion. "What do you mean?"

"You seem kind and caring," Luna replied honestly.

Sol backed up a step. Looking her up and down, he felt his anger rise before declaring, "We are kind and caring. It is you Barden who are selfish, arrogant, and obsessed with power." His voice rose with each word.

Luna searched for the bear and saw it look their way before it stopped sniffing at the river's edge. Sol quickly stepped in front of her, pushing her back against the tree with his body touching hers, once more hidden from the bear. He peeked around to watch the animal. The bear seemed satisfied and went back to searching for food along the river, content with the damage it had caused to Luna's belongings.

It was suddenly harder for Luna to breathe. Having Sol's body so close to hers ignited a yearning deep within her for something she didn't recognize.

"I didn't mean..." Luna whispered, finding it hard to speak. "I just meant you are not what I was told your people are like."

"Neither are you," Sol replied, his gaze so intense she thought he might kiss her. The closeness of their bodies made her aware of her growing desire. Her breathing grew deeper in an effort to calm her carnal appetite, but his natural scent was tantalizing at that proximity. His chest and abdomen were toned and muscular but not overly large. He was different in so many ways, and that piqued her fascination and fueled the thirst she felt deep within her body.

Sol couldn't help but notice how their bodies fit together so perfectly behind the pine tree. He could smell the floral scent of her hair, like fresh roses. His hands were on the bark behind her and he let them drop slowly past her shoulders, down to the curve of her waist. He felt his breathing quicken with desire as their bodies pressed against each other's. Her lips were enticing and her eyes inviting. He felt his body starting to respond and released his hold, backing up a step to give them both a little more space.

"Why did you come back?" he asked her.

Luna swallowed hard, trying to regain her composure and remember why she had dared to do such a thing. "I…I brought your bowl. It's beautiful. Did you carve it?"

Sol nodded. "You surprise me too, Luna."

Luna liked the way her name sounded coming out of his full brown- and pink-tinged lips. Sol checked on the bear again, just in time to see the large animal making its way back into the woods.

"It's leaving," he told her as he walked slowly toward the river.

Luna let out a large exhalation, partly out of relief but mostly to calm her active imagination before following Sol. She took notice of his nicely shaped backside before she walked over and retrieved her black tunic, which had dried almost completely in the hot sun. Luna glanced at Sol, who politely turned his back so she could change into her clothes. She handed him his shirt when she was done and retrieved her belt from the dry river stones, tying it back on. They looked at each other for a moment, both wondering what they should do next.

"Your bowl," Luna said before she made her way to the mess the bear had made. The quiver was intact, though all the arrows had spilled out. The bow had bite marks but was otherwise unscathed. The linen bags were ripped to shreds, and the contents, including the wooden bowl, were half-smashed, half-eaten by the bear. Luna collected the wooden fragments that were left and carried them back across the river to Sol, careful to keep her feet on the neutral ground of the riverbed this time.

"I'm sorry, but it's destroyed."

He took the pieces from her. "I'll make another. I didn't expect you to bring it back to me anyway."

Luna bit her lip, not wanting to leave but not sure what to say. They just stared into each other's eyes, knowing they could never go back to their lives and forget about each other after this meeting.

"Do you come to the waterfall often?" Luna asked, hoping he would see her efforts and drive the conversation. She was not yet ready to part ways.

"Yes. There are a lot of strong trees that fall during the storms that I can use for my craft," Sol said, motioning to the forest.

"I just found it, but there are a lot of medicinal plants here that would be useful for me. Would you make me one of your bowls in exchange for some healing arnica salve you can use for your muscles? I mean…I'm sure working with wood requires a lot of physical…and you get sore… umm…" She motioned to his chest.

"Okay," Sol agreed, ending the awkwardness she felt.

Trading had been common among all the tribes in the past, but now only the Dabney tribe would trade with the Nets. The Dabney wanted to keep the Barden chief happy since the produce that carried them through the winters came from Barden farmland. Sol was friendly with Aidan, the son of the Dabney chief, which helped keep the trade going.

"Okay," Luna echoed.

"Tomorrow?" Sol asked.

Luna's heart skipped a beat with surprising excitement at his request.

"Tomorrow," she agreed.

She watched as Sol went back the way they had just come from, disappearing into the green and brown of the forest. Luna gathered her bow and placed the scattered arrows into the quiver before adjusting them across her back. She would want to be careful on the walk back to her horse, keeping a watchful eye out for any sign of the bear. Luna found Willow still tied to the tree where she had left the mare, happily drinking the cool water from the river.

"Let us journey home," Luna said as she led the horse south, weaving through the trees.

As Luna broke free from the forest, the sight of the wall reached her vision. She had always thought it was there to keep things out and protect her, but on this day it seemed it was there to keep her in. Sol seemed genuinely kind, and he had risked his life for her, a stranger. Luna didn't overlook the fact that she was also the daughter of the man who had ended all communication with his tribe. Things just didn't make complete sense to her, and her curiosity grew. She had to know more about Sol and his people, if only to mend the wounds she felt she was responsible for due to the death of her mother. She believed she could restore trade with them at the very least. She could see he was talented, and she remembered the beautifully woven fabrics his tribe was known for. *First, though, I will go home and make myself some dinner*, she thought as her stomach growled from hunger.

Luna returned the horse to its pasture before stopping by the gardens for some lettuce, tomatoes, cucumbers, and a pepper to make a salad for dinner; the weather was too hot to be cooking over a fire for very long. She nodded her greeting to the tribesmen guarding the wall on her way home. They were placing bets on a game they were playing. Luna got to her house and set the vegetables on the table before grabbing a medium-sized clay bowl and a piece of honeycomb that she then placed in a smaller clay jar. She made her way into the center of their village and stopped in at the home of one of the tribeswomen who would frequently have chickens and other fowl butchered and already plucked. Luna found a large chicken breast she wanted and offered the woman the small jar in exchange.

"No, you take it. My gift to the chief," the busty woman said from behind a table of select cuts.

"You have already given us so much. Please take the honey," Luna pleaded.

She nodded as Luna placed the jar in her hands and walked out with the chicken breast in the spare bowl she had brought with her. Some of the other tribe members were out making their rounds and gathering up the ingredients needed for their dinners. They would all nod to her out of respect for her father, but she felt their watchful eyes. She had heard the rumors and all their expectations of her producing an heir for her father's bloodline. The people of the tribe didn't seem to see her worth for more than what her womb could produce. Luna didn't feel special in that regard either, because that was how the value of all the young women in her tribe was perceived. The young tribeswomen would be trained in how to raise children, how to care for a home, and also how to defend it. As the daughter of the chief, Luna was given much more freedom to roam about as she wished, as long as she was contributing something and kept house for her father. The only exception to this rule was Luna's Aunt Alice. She was a childless woman who had reached a higher social standing in their tribe, and Luna guessed it was because of Alice's close relationship with Luna's father, Gannon.

Luna reached home as the sun was beginning to set and started her dinner. When she was finished, she poured herself a cup of tea that had been left in the pot since the morning then made her way out toward the torch-lit wall and past the night guards who were just starting their shift. Their job seemed silly to her for the first time in all her life, and the thought surprised her. As she made her way through the meadow that was alive with fireflies in a glowing dance as they searched for their mate, Luna knew the chances of her finding her own perfect mate seemed dubious. She knew her father would probably arrange a match for her eventually. Crickets chirped and cicadas made their long, loud vibrating noises, taking turns in a chorus. Bats chirped overhead, and she occasionally spotted them in the moonlight that lit the way for her. As she got closer to the river, the sound of bullfrogs and tree frogs let her know just how alive the land was. She saw the glistening water of the river reflecting the glow of the moonlight. Luna removed her belt but kept her tunic on this time as she waded into the cold waters, feeling instantly cooler.

"Thank you for this gift, Mother." Luna spoke to the waters and the land, that which gave all things, her goddess.

After sitting to fully immerse herself, Luna left the cool waters and retrieved her belt before making the walk home. She enjoyed the sounds of summer and felt more alive than she had in a long time. She made her way to her bed and slept soundly, alone in the quiet house.

* * *

Sol left Luna in the forest and made his way back to his horse, which was tied up a few minutes' walk from the waterfall. He made his way home and thought about everything that had been said between Luna and himself, as well as what had gone unsaid. The feeling of her naked body against his had made the already hot weather seem sweltering. His mind wandered, remembering the feeling of her waist under his hands and that look in her eyes. He could tell she shared his forbidden attraction, and the thought brought him an exhilarated excitement that he tried to push down.

Sol made his way into the clearing where his tribe resided and a beautiful woman approached him.

"Sol. I have been looking for you," she said.

He dismounted his horse before replying, "Well, Layla, you have found me."

Layla stood in front of him now, blocking his path with her muscular arms crossed. She stood at his height with a thin and athletic body. She had long wavy hair with colorful feathers sticking out from a beaded headband across her forehead. Her eyes were a seductive dark brown. She had white paint dotted above her eyebrows with more white dots of varying sizes mixed with small vertical lines down to the middle of her nose. One thin horizontal line spanned from the inside corner of her right eye across her nose to her left. The last small vertical line traced the bottom of her plump pink lips and went partly down her chin. Layla was breathtakingly gorgeous. Her figure was draped in a bright purple wrap with matching turquoise beaded earrings and a chunky necklace.

"Bomani keeps teasing me about a deer heart," Layla said, pretending to be bothered.

Sol felt the complications mounting. "What about it?"

"He said there was no reason to keep denying what everybody already knows to be true," Layla answered, moving her hands to her hips.

"That's just Bomani making jokes and trying to get you worked up. It seems to have worked." Sol forced a nervous chuckle and nudged his horse on.

"Well, I thought he was trying to tell me something you were maybe too afraid to," she challenged.

Sol stopped and faced Layla. "If I wanted to say something to you, I would say it. I am not afraid of saying anything." His face was serious and his eyes showed her he meant what he said.

"Well, you have a talk with him then. I don't need anybody wasting my time," Layla warned as she watched Sol continue to the horse pasture. She liked the sight of him walking away. *Someday*, she thought to herself. Someday, he would be hers.

Sol left his horse in the pasture and opted for a quiet dinner by himself. There was much to think about. Sol made his way to his lean-to with the remains of the wooden bowl. He started a small fire and threw the broken pieces in. The smell of salty air mixing with the smoke brought a feeling of contentment to him. Watching the waves grow larger, he got up and made his way to the shoreline. There was a rope attached to a wooden peg buried in the sand. Sol pulled it slowly, and he could see splashes breaking the water thirty yards away. He pulled the rope faster until the net was within reach. He found one large red fish and one smaller striped bass. Sol grabbed the striped bass by the gill and pulled it out of the netting. He placed the fish on the sand and the netting with the red fish next to it. Next, Sol pulled his knife out of its sheath on his leather belt to cut the fish into large chunks after thanking it for giving its life to him. He removed the red fish from the netting by its gills and replaced it with the chunks of bass.

Sol brought the red fish up the sandy beach to his hut near the fire pit. He set it on a nearby stone before heading back to retrieve the net. He threw the netting with the fresh bait back out to sea and checked to make sure the wooden peg was secure, burying it in the sand. Sol cleaned the fish by descaling it after throwing its belly contents back into the water. He found the sharpened stick he had used before by the small fire pit and speared it through the fish's mouth to its tail. Sol placed the fish on a makeshift rotisserie and made his way to the ocean water once more. As he pulled the blue tunic off over his head, his nose detected the smell of roses. He inhaled deeply with the tunic up to his nostrils this time, recognizing the scent as Luna's. Sol tossed the shirt onto the dry sand and walked into the ocean for a short swim. It was a humid summer night and he was hot for more than one reason.

As the fish slowly cooked over the fire, Sol watched the stars appear one by one until they were innumerable. The moon made him think of Luna and their meeting. He couldn't help but remember the feeling of her soft naked skin against his body, the curve of her waist under his fingertips, and the fiery hunger it had built inside his body. The memory of her exposed figure entering the green pool at the waterfall filled his mind, and his imagination wondered what it would be like to be naked against her. Logic told him seeing her again was entirely the wrong thing to do, but another voice that grew increasingly louder nearly drowned out his usually cautious instinct. He would see her again the next day.

CHAPTER 4

Luna dreamt she was running, screaming, "Mama!" as her five-year-old self searched frantically through the village. Luna ran to the meeting house and opened the door. She looked inside in the almost empty space and saw her mother's carefully dressed body. Terra's nearly translucent hand was holding her stillborn child. The baby was still wrapped in the green woven blanket from earlier, tucked into Terra's arm, his cold cheek touching the soft fabric on the breast he would never suckle from. Terra's now porcelain skin was cleaned of blood. Her hair had been brushed and left to surround her face. Little Luna knew her mother's friend Mama Dalila must have washed her and put the bright blue tunic on her. Terra's brilliant green eyes were still shut. Was she just sleeping? Luna reached out and touched her mother's hand, shocked by how cold it was.

"Mama…" she whispered.

She heard her father's voice close outside and instinctively decided she should hide. She went under a table that had a long cloth hung over it. She could see the men's bare feet as they walked in and stood around the table she was hiding under.

Gannon came into the room of the meeting house with the shaman, a man a little older than Gannon who had a white beard and a few strands of white hair sticking out at odd angles from his mostly bald head. His thin body was covered with a loosely draped red tunic that had embroidered beadwork down the middle. He had satchels surrounding his belt, and his face was painted with white stripes and dots, the sign of a wise man. Luna heard him empty the contents of one of the bags onto the table above her.

"I want to know why the gods would do this to me!" Gannon demanded furiously.

Luna's heart thudded in her chest as she sat frozen under the heavy wooden table.

"The runes don't always give you the answer you want, but they do give the answers you need." The shaman spoke calmly, but his voice held surprising strength.

"Just read them," Gannon muttered, giving in.

"I see a new life…yes, a child. I see darkness and light. I see two great forces, two tribes joining together as one," the shaman replied after picking up some of the pieces off the table.

"Your runes tell a lie, shaman! My wife is dead and there will be no more new lives," Gannon shouted angrily at the wise man before him.

"The runes do not lie, though they may tell you something you do not want to hear. Your bloodline has not ended. You have a daughter."

"My daughter is a child! How will she help me conquer the Net tribe and get the revenge I deserve? They will pay for taking the life of my wife and my son—my heir! I told her they were not to be trusted!" He slammed his fist on the table, making Luna jump, but she stayed quiet.

The shaman firmly replied, "Children do grow up, Gannon. You shall see—the runes do not lie."

Luna jolted upright from her bed, drenched in sweat, interrupting the flashback of the living nightmare she had experienced as a child. She clutched her chest and tried to calm her heavy breathing and racing heartbeat. She wondered what the gods were trying to tell her.

Luckily, it was dawn, so she quietly made her way into the common living space. Luna heard loud snoring coming from her father's room. She hadn't heard him come in, and it surprised her that she had slept so soundly. She grabbed the bucket and a small basket before heading to the raspberry bushes. After collecting the herbs she needed for her morning tea ritual, she returned to boil the water herself. She knew she would have some solitude this morning as her father slept in, and she was glad for it. Luna finished her tea and cleaned up the kitchen area before packing her food and supplies for the journey back to the waterfall, back to Sol.

Luna decided to walk the whole way there this time. She didn't know when Sol would meet her, and she knew time would inch by as she anxiously waited. It was better that she keep busy, and walking helped Luna clear her mind anyway. So, she set off with her bow and quiver full of arrows. She chose a leather satchel from her room to carry the supplies. It had been her mother's, and the satchel was the one thing Luna cherished more than anything, the solitary piece of her mother that she had left. Luna set out on her long trek up the mountain, to the waterfall. Her eyes relished the beauty of the summer meadows full of yellow, white, and purple wildflowers that were alive with buzzing pollinators. The cicadas still sang their long, loud vibrations. The butterflies floated gently, disappearing and then reappearing in the tall green grasses. The sky was blue with not so much as a single cloud, and the weather was hot for a midsummer morning. At the edge of the farthest meadow, she crossed into the forest.

She noticed the coolness of the air as soon as she was under the shade of the trees, making her way through the ferns and other fauna. Luna found a few mushrooms she knew she could put to use, and also some large broadleaf plantain leaves. She placed them in her satchel and continued through the ever-thickening foliage, weaving under low branches and through thick brush. She soon found her way to the edge of the clearing by the waterfall. The rushing sound of the water brought her comfort and a new surge of excitement. She wondered how long Sol had watched her from the woods the previous day. She was curious if he had liked what he saw, feeling the hot flush of her cheeks at the embarrassing thought. A man like Sol would never be interested in her. Even if he were by some trickery of the gods, once he found out what she had done, he would see just how unworthy of any affection she truly was.

* * *

Sol had woken to the sound of birds feasting on the small crabs and marine life the tide had left behind. He went for a swim to wash his body before beginning his day, and the salty water refreshed him. Sol changed his clothes and gathered his tools before heading to his mother's house. He didn't feel very hungry, but he knew he had a long day ahead of him and he needed sustenance.

When he arrived at his mother's house, he could smell the mouthwatering meal she was already cooking. He saw her sitting outside her longhouse, stirring a large pot over the outdoor fire. He wondered to himself what she would think of all of this. He set his things on the ground and took a seat on an empty wooden chair.

"Almost ready," she said. After a few moments of silence, she asked, "Did you sleep well, my son?"

Sol realized he had been staring at nothing in particular and blinked a few times before responding. "Yes. The sea air does me good."

"Is something on your mind? You didn't share the evening meal with us last night." Sol's mother placed a scoop of the steaming vegetables and venison broth into a plain wooden bowl.

He took it gladly, his hunger now apparent. He took a sip, careful not to burn his mouth, before answering her. "Have you ever thought you knew who someone was but then discovered something that made you question everything you thought you knew?" he asked her.

Sol's mother smiled, assuming her son had begun falling for someone. She also assumed she knew who it was.

"Yes."

"What did you do about it?" he asked her after taking another drink from his already half-empty bowl.

"I was open to it. I asked questions and observed until I could make sense of it." She poured a few more bowls with the steaming broth before collecting one for herself and sitting next to her son.

Her wise words made sense to Sol, and he decided to take them to heart. Sol's younger twin brothers came out of the longhouse, one after the other, rubbing the sleepiness from their eyes. The young men had seen twenty full turns of the wheel, only three less than Sol. Sol drank the rest of the broth from his bowl before using his hand to pick out the remaining bits of meat and vegetables. The soup was comforting and filling.

"Atsu, did you boil the eggs from yesterday?" their

mother asked as she finished her bowl, licking her lips.

"Yes, Mama. They are just there," Atsu said, pointing back into the longhouse.

"Good. You can all take some for your midday meal," she said.

He listened to his brothers and mother discussing how they would separate the duties for the day. Sol knew his sister Akiiki and his brother in-law Bomani would be along soon, so he decided it was best for him to be on his way. He went to retrieve two eggs from the longhouse before grabbing his things and heading toward the waterfall. Sol loaded his horse with his wood carving tools and a chunk of strong oak he had been saving.

Along the journey, he thought about what his mother had said. He knew he had trouble keeping an open mind sometimes, and this would be an excellent time to practice the skill. He wasn't sure what to make of Luna yet. She was different than anyone he had known, but also similar at the same time. She made him feel things he never had before; he felt completely mesmerized by her, an overwhelming interest he felt powerless to resist. The contradiction of what he knew about her people and what he had experienced with her made his usually focused mind swirl with conflict. He needed answers to the questions that had emerged from his meetings with her.

* * *

Luna had assumed she would be the first one at the waterfall but was pleasantly surprised to see Sol already at work burning a piece of partly carved wood across the river.

"Is that for me?" she asked as she made her way to one of the giant boulders in the river closest to him, careful not to step onto Net land again.

Sol's eyes shot up in her direction the moment she started speaking. He took notice of how the light grey tunic she wore fit around her shapely figure. He realized he liked the sight of her. A feeling of knowing took over his body.

"Yes," he answered.

"I'm glad you came," she admitted as she pulled a few items from her satchel.

"Where did you get that?" he asked, recognizing the leather bag.

"It was my mother's." Luna ran her fingertips over the elaborate design on the front flap.

"It looks familiar. My father worked with leather like that." Sol wasn't sure why he offered up the information to her; whenever he was around her, he seemed to become a sieve of personal facts. He drew his attention back to his craft, scraping the burned embers out of the wood.

"Do you?" she asked.

"Do I what?"

"Work with leather?" Luna wasn't sure where to start or what it was she wanted to achieve in their meeting today, but in some newly awakened part of herself, she knew it felt right to be there. She wanted to know more about Sol because everything about him contradicted the image she had formed based on the stories her father had repeatedly told her growing up.

"No. I work with wood mostly," he answered, shaking his head.

Some time passed in comfortable silence as they each got to work. Luna looked up from the beadwork she was sewing, admiring him as he sat cross-legged working at his craft. He carved the hunk of wood, slowly developing a hollowed curve inside. The brightly colored yellow tunic he wore was cut off at his shoulders, contrasting his dark skin as well as highlighting the muscles on his arms as he worked. She could see beads of sweat developing on his brow. His eyes met hers, and she realized she had been caught staring at him. Luna refocused on the beadwork in her hands and tried to not look back up.

Sol had seen her watching him and decided it was his turn to ask a question. "Your father is the chief?"

Luna paused her sewing. "Yes."

"He is okay with you being here?"

"No. I mean, he doesn't know. I didn't tell him," Luna answered, flustered.

"Why?"

She was a bit surprised by the intrusive question. "I…I don't know. I didn't want him to tell me not to come I guess."

"Where does he think you are?" Sol asked out of genuine concern for his safety.

"I didn't get the chance to tell him where I would be today. He was sleeping off a late night of fermented drinking when I left. I usually tell him if I am headed to the north woods, or that general direction." Had she said too much? She wasn't sure, and she focused back on her beadwork. Her speech seemed to come out jumbled around Sol.

"Well you are a woman now, anyway." He looked up after once more igniting the fire in the developing belly of the bowl.

"What does that mean?" Luna asked defensively.

"I mean you are grown. You are free to roam about as you please…right?" Sol asked, a little confused.

"No. I am not married and therefore still under my father's house until I am joined with another," Luna explained, relieved and somewhat comforted by his meaning.

"What? You're under his house? I don't understand."

"I have to be submissive to him until I am hand-fasted to another man." Luna nearly choked on the word 'submissive'. She hated that her father and her tribe thought she was somehow inferior to a man because she had been born female.

Sol's facial expression was part confusion and part disgust. "That doesn't make any sense. Wait, then are you in line to be chieftess? Can women in your tribe rule, or is it only the men?"

It gave Luna comfort that Sol seemed as revolted by the patriarchal notion as she was. This had been her life, though. Everyone in her upbringing lived by this way of thinking, and no one had questioned it, at least no one to her knowledge. It felt good to have someone else validate her thoughts on the subject.

"No. Never."

"So, what happens if your father dies? Who would rule your tribe?"

"It would be for the shaman and the male elders to decide, unless I produce a male heir," Luna answered.

Sol shook his head, not sure what to say but not liking the sound of Luna being forced to make a child with another man. He was surprised by the protectiveness he felt for her. He had to remind himself she was still very much a stranger.

"Do women rule in your tribe?" Luna asked, suddenly very curious.

"My mother is the chieftess. In my tribe, as soon as a girl becomes a woman, even when she is still in her parents' home, she has the right to do as she pleases, as long as she is not causing harm to another. It is the same for all people in my tribe. There are no real distinctions between man and woman," Sol explained.

Luna felt like she connected with Sol now more than ever. She hadn't realized there was a man out there—let alone a whole tribe—who valued *all* people as equals. She wished it could be the same for the Barden, but the impossibility of the idea of her father even entertaining such a thing was an instant discouragement to the thought.

"What is your family like?" Luna asked, suddenly wanting to know more about Sol and his tribe's way of living.

Sol was quiet for a moment as he emptied the coals from the burned wood onto the river stones, not sure what information he should reveal to Luna. He quickly decided no harm could be done by telling her about his family's personalities and way of living as he would simply be sharing his culture.

"My mother is strong and kind. She is the best person on this land, and the wisest," Sol started.

Luna set down her beadwork, deciding it was better to be face to face for this conversation. She liked the way Sol's usually serious face seemed to light up when he talked about his mother. She could sense his love and the deep respect he had for her.

"She sounds wonderful," Luna said, and she meant it.

Luna's words made Sol feel connected to her. He felt like sharing more, so he did. "My older sister, Akiiki, she is pregnant and has a strength about her...she is not afraid to be herself, but in a gentle way. She will be a great mother. Her mate is one of my closest friends. He is always so joyful, constantly smiling and joking. They are a great match. They complement each other's strengths and weaknesses very well."

"What's his name?" Luna asked.

"Bomani."

"That's an interesting name," Luna said admiringly.

Sol continued, "I have two younger brothers, Ata and Atsu, and they are twins. They like to start trouble with each other, but they have a close bond between them. They help my mother with her herbs and whatever needs to be done."

"Oh, your mother knows about plants?"

"Yes."

"I can offer you something for the bowl instead of the salve if you don't need it," Luna said, suddenly worried what she'd offered to barter with would not be as valuable as she had thought.

"No, I will still trade for what we agreed." Sol noticed he was neglecting the oak and grabbed a chisel before continuing.

"Well, I do add other things to it. It's my own recipe, so maybe it will be a little different. Do you live with your brothers and mother?" Luna asked, trying to change the subject back to Sol.

"No—at least, not right now. I like my space. While it is warm enough, I sleep in a small lean-to by the ocean."

That piqued her curiosity. "The ocean?"

"Someday I want to have a home there," Sol answered then suddenly worried he'd shared too much.

"What is the ocean like?" Luna asked, intrigued.

Sol stopped the chisel and looked back into Luna's eyes before asking, "You have never seen the sea?"

"No," Luna replied.

"It is unlike anything else in the land. Nothing can be compared to it. The waves grow very large during storms, a strength no man or beast could conquer. It moves farther and closer to the shore throughout the day, like it is breathing. The smell is…salty. I guess I don't really know how to describe it. I'm not very good at that sort of thing," Sol answered honestly.

"It sounds amazing and magical. Maybe someday I can see it," she hoped out loud, though she realized it was impossible.

They decided it was a good time to stop, stretch their limbs, and eat something. They both took out food they'd brought from their provisions. Sol ate the eggs and some carrots while Luna ate the bread she'd packed with some berries mashed and spread on it. The breeze blew, providing them with a perfect temperature. It wasn't too hot by the waterfall, and the rays of sunlight that broke through the canopy of the forest above danced in the water, highlighting the mica in the river stones. Luna and Sol spent the rest of the afternoon talking about their tribes and their lives on their separate sides of the river. They both felt that they were getting to know so much about each other in such a short amount of time. It seemed fast, but also like it was meant to be that way. The more they talked, the more they felt the connection developing between them.

"I have to head back. My father will be wanting his dinner," Luna said as she reluctantly packed her satchel back up with the items spread across the boulder.

"Your father doesn't cook?" Sol asked, still surprised at how incapable the men of her tribe seemed.

"No. I mean, not since I have been old enough to," Luna explained.

Sol shook his head. "Will you come tomorrow?"

Luna's heart beat faster at his request. "Yes," she answered, trying not to sound too emphatic in her response.

"Until tomorrow then, Luna." Sol stood to say goodbye, feeling like he wanted to reach out and hug her before parting ways. He thought better of it and restrained himself.

She liked the way her name sounded coming out of his mouth. She bit her lip, afraid of what her body wanted.

"Until tomorrow," she echoed.

Sol watched her walk away, admiring the sway of her hips. He'd gotten so many answers to his questions that day, but he didn't feel like he had made any more progress on making sense of things. In fact, with all the new information he had, his world seemed to be spinning more out of control than before. He wanted the next day to be there already.

Luna made the long walk home through the forest thinking of the conversations they'd had that day. The miles went by quickly as she enjoyed replaying the way Sol described the ocean and the way his face lit up when he talked about his family. She enjoyed seeing that part of him. When the wall around her village came into view, the dark clay slathered across the different sized rocks seemed increasingly ugly to her. She realized the builders seemed to have done their work hastily, and the many imperfections were beginning to show through with cracks. Luna quickened her pace, suddenly not very interested in conversing with any tribe members. As she made her way through their doorway, she was surprised to see her father was already home.

"Where have you been all day?" he asked abruptly.

Luna was caught off guard. "In the forest. I was looking for plants to—"

"You are not going to find a husband in the forest."

Gannon slapped his hand on the wooden table, making a loud sound. Luna jumped. Gannon was usually grumpy after a night of drinking but seemed even more rigid tonight. Luna was speechless. Her father's eyes fell to the leather satchel across her body. He had given it to her after burning everything else Terra owned with her body on the pyre.

"You are too much like your mother. I have given you too much freedom."

"Father, I—"

"You will come with me to the trade with Bale tomorrow. He will meet us at the border of our lands."

Luna knew it wasn't a request. She nodded her head and took her things to her room. She blinked back tears before she swallowed hard, trying to stop the surprising emotions from overpowering her and escaping. She still had to get through dinner with her father.

Just then she heard him speak loudly through her closed door. "I'm going out."

She heard him leave, slamming the front door behind him. The tears flowed freely then. She threw herself onto her bed and buried her face in it to muffle the sounds of her crying. Luna was surprised at her own emotions and reaction to her father's words. He had been stern with her before, but she had never reacted so strongly. Luna realized it was the thought of missing her meeting with Sol that was so hard for her. She sat up and wiped her eyes. The black paint from her face had rubbed off on her hands. She swung open the bedroom door and used the bucket of water to clean her hands and face. If she'd had a mirror, she would have seen the redness of her face and the puffiness of her eyes. What would Sol think when she didn't show up? Would he ever come back? Would he be angry that she had wasted his time? Why did she care so much about what he thought?

Luna waited until her face was cooled before she draped a cloth over her head to partly veil it. She left her house seeking out her aunt's advice. Alice lived on the other side of the village, and Luna could easily find her way there in the growing darkness as she had traversed it many times. Luna stopped to listen at the door before entering, and in the seconds that followed, she was happy she did so. Luna heard her father's voice inside, speaking with her Aunt Alice.

"I just don't know what else to do with her. I have given her more freedom in the hope she would naturally see that the woods are no place for her," Gannon admitted in a defeated tone.

As Alice responded, Luna moved out of sight, into the shadows to the side of the doorway so no passerby could see her spying.

"Gannon, Luna belongs in those woods. They are all she has left that connects her to her mother. They bring her value, even if you may not see it."

Luna strained to hear her aunt's muffled voice.

He sighed. "She is old enough, and I need an heir."

"You want her to be cared for too, don't you?" Alice asked him.

"Of course. She is my daughter, after all. I'm getting older and I need time to prepare an heir, but she doesn't even put herself out there for the opportunity," Gannon argued.

"Well, I think taking her with you to the trade tomorrow is a good idea, but you also have to let her have her freedom. I think there is a compromise to be had here," Alice explained, trying to keep the peace between them, as she always had.

"I suppose you're right," he agreed.

"It takes a woman to know a woman," Alice said as the

front door opened abruptly.

Luna held her breath as she watched a stream of water come pouring out the doorway and splash on the ground. The door was closed again and Luna let out a sigh of relief that she had not been caught spying. She decided to not test her luck a second time and hurried home.

Luna decided to eat bread with dried venison for her dinner. She kept to her room as she ate, afraid of facing her father again that night. She knew she had to go with him in the morning and hoped he would leave her alone after that. Luna thought about the conversation she'd overheard between her father and aunt. He'd said he wanted her happy; that was something, at least. She had never heard him speak so openly with anyone else in his life, and certainly not with her. She thought all he cared about was an heir, but a small part of her wanted to believe he loved her and wanted her to find happiness as well as being cared for. Luna wished she could be the heir, not because she wanted the power of leadership, but because she didn't want the pressure of having a child. Luna did not feel ready to become a mother in any sense of the word, but she couldn't tell her father that because to him, motherhood was her birthright. She wasn't even sure if she wanted to be a mother any time soon, and no one had ever asked her. She was told she was ready, was told she would be a mother, and that was that.

Luna changed into a long white tunic to wear to bed

before blowing out the candles. Her chest was heavy with anxiety. Would Sol be disappointed when she didn't show up in the morning? Would he be angry? She thought about the picture of his family he had painted with his words. They seemed so loving, and at the same time, fiercely strong—two things her father had gotten very wrong when he described the Nets to her. The conversations were rare now, but they had been far more frequent when she was a child, when the wounds were still fresh. He said the Nets were deceptive and unintelligent. He said they were subhuman and didn't even take care of their own children. Everything she had been told about the Nets seemed like a lie after her meetings with Sol. The questions incited an anger within her, but she wasn't sure who she should direct that rage at. How could so many things about them be completely misunderstood? Luna decided if her father had the chance to really get to know the Nets, he would fall in love with their culture and family dynamic like she had. She realized just then that she was admitting to herself that she was in fact falling for them…maybe even for Sol.

CHAPTER 5

Luna awoke suddenly from a nightmare. It was too early to start the day, but she knew she wouldn't be going back to sleep. She lay in her bed, attempting to calm her breathing as she remembered the dream that had plagued her fitful night's sleep. In the dream, Luna was being chased by a bear, and she had woken up abruptly as she was overtaken by it. She convinced herself it was because of the black bear that had surprised her and Sol just days ago. The previous night's events now came rushing back to her at the thought of him. The argument with her father had sent her into a tailspin. Having heard her father say the words 'She is my daughter' reminded Luna that like it or not, she did have a duty to her people. She had to put her own happiness aside and make an attempt. Maybe her father would recognize her efforts. Maybe then she would be good enough for him, she hoped.

Eventually Luna got up and went about her usual routine, needing some time outside the walls, which were becoming more and more suffocating as the days progressed. She needed time in nature to ground herself for what was expected of her that day. The woods beckoned her with the rustle of leaves from the intensifying winds. The sky mirrored what she felt inside, dark and gloomy with a brewing anger. It would storm, she was sure of it.

Luna took her time going back to her house to face her father. Her mind worried about what Sol would think of her not showing up for their meeting. Maybe the storm would give him a reason not to be angry with her. Why did she care so much about what he thought? She didn't want to face the answer to that question yet. So, Luna walked past the guards at the gate and went straight home. Her father was waiting outside in his usual spot, heating the pot of water for tea. Luna dropped the herbs in, adding to the already ground chicory root that was steeping inside. She sat quietly, waiting for her father to speak first, keeping her eyes on the empty mug.

"What did you find today?" Gannon asked, like it was any other day.

Luna was not surprised as her father never apologized or discussed conflicts they had. He just pretended like nothing had happened.

"Calendula flowers and stinging nettle," Luna replied, not taking her gaze off the cup.

She watched as her father filled it with the tea. Luna was thankful to have something to do with her hands and took the cup. She inhaled deeply, smelling the earthy tea before releasing her breath in an attempt to cool it down before taking a sip.

"Looks like rain. We will take the wagon and leave before it starts," Gannon said as he got up and headed into the house.

He didn't wait for a response, so Luna didn't bother with one. Luna knew what was expected of her. She took her time finishing the tea, relishing the quiet of the morning before heading into her room to get dressed.

"Wear the one that is for tribal celebrations," Gannon ordered as he took a puff of his pipe and walked back out the door to prepare the wagon.

Luna didn't bother to ask why and did as she was told. She found the white dress carefully folded in a wooden chest in the corner of her room. The fabric was soft and decorated with colored thread at the seams. Luna washed under her arms with a salt crystal before pulling the dress over her head. It had been almost a year since she had worn it last, and it fit pretty much the same. The cut across the front of her chest was much lower than that of her other tunics, showing off her cleavage and generous bust line. The sleeves split at her shoulders, joining again at her elbows and creating a draping effect. The dress showed off her legs with slits that came up to mid-thigh in the flowing fabric.

Overall, the dress didn't leave much to the imagination. Luna felt sick to her stomach as she laced up the black sandals on her usually bare feet. She preferred not to wear shoes. Luna painted her face in her usual fashion, signifying her place as daughter of the chief. She felt as though she was about to be put on display, and she didn't like it. Everything in her body screamed against it, but Luna felt she owed her father at least this much since she had taken his wife and son away from him. Luna left her hair down. Her curls were wild, and if that was the only thing she could keep the way she liked, that would have to be it. Luna walked out to meet her father. The wind was increasing in strength, but it was warm. Luna climbed into the front seat of the wooden wagon next to her awaiting father.

"Good girl," he said, slapping the reins against the horse's back, and they were off.

* * *

Sol woke to the sound of distant thunder. He saw the storm out in the distance over the choppy grey waves moving toward him. He quickly wondered if the weather would prevent Luna from meeting him. The fact that she was his first thought didn't escape Sol as he quickly changed into a fresh blue tunic. Next, he folded the skins he slept on and the remainder of his clothes into the wooden chest in an attempt to keep them dry when the storm reached the small lean-to. Sol headed to his mother's place where the familiar smell of soup led him to find his sister stirring the large communal pot when he arrived. She poured the broth and its contents into the same wooden bowls from the day before and gave one to Sol before helping herself to another.

"What are you planning today to keep dry, brother?" Akiiki asked.

She had noticed he seemed a little different at their evening meal the night before and wanted to talk with him about it when no one else was around.

"I was going to go into the forest actually," he answered truthfully before drinking some of the broth.

Akiiki had a surprised look on her face. "With this storm coming? What is so terrible that you have to keep hiding in those woods day after day? Risk your life for what, oak?" she asked inquisitively.

"I am not hiding. I work with wood, and wood grows in the forest," Sol answered.

"What is going on with you? Something seems different in you."

Sol took a large bite of the venison from the soup, buying himself time. "What do you mean? Am I different in a bad way?"

"No. You just seem quieter these days. Something is on your mind. I know you. I know you will tell me when you are ready," she said before drinking the soup from her bowl.

Just then, Bomani rounded the corner with an armful of wood for the fire.

"Sol! Are you eating all the food again? Save some for the baby, eh?" he teased as he dropped the wood in a pile in the nearly empty wooden box where they kept it. Bomani gave his wife a kiss on her lips and then one on her growing belly before grabbing his own bowl of soup and finding a seat next to her.

Sol finished his soup before heading into the longhouse. He grabbed a couple apples and boiled eggs from inside the dark space before he went back out to the fire.

"I better get going," he announced as he gathered his tools.

"Where are you going? It is going to storm you know, or are you blind? Eh?" Bomani laughed.

Akiiki came to his rescue. "Let him be, Bomani."

"Stay dry," Sol said as he headed to his horse.

Sol could hear Bomani echo his last statement and then chuckle to himself as he made his way to the pasture. The horses were unsettled with the energy from the approaching storm, and Sol decided it best that he leave the animal. Was he crazy to risk being exposed in a storm like this in hopes that Luna was just as crazy as he was and showed up to meet him? Maybe, but there was only one way to find out. Sol set off as fast as he could to beat the storm to the waterfall, and hopefully to Luna.

* * *

Luna and Gannon arrived at the designated meeting spot directly on the border where the two tribe lands met.

The Dabney chief, Bale, was sitting on a chair in a small tent they had set up for this very occasion. Bale looked like he could have been a brother of Gannon's. They were both big, burly men with long white braided beards and hair.

"Old friend," Gannon greeted him.

"You speak as though you haven't seen me in ages, like you weren't just in my own house drinking all my fermented barley drink! Ahhh, get off your high horse and let's get this over with before we get hit by Zeus's lightning bolts, would yah?"

Luna had only ever heard Bale speak to her father with such authority as that, but it still surprised her. She knew he was the only one who could get away with it. Luna looked at her father to gauge his reaction.

"You made out pretty well? with the load of produce I brought over, so don't act like you got taken advantage of," Gannon replied, giving it right back to Bale as he got down off the wagon.

Once he had gotten off, Bale realized Luna was there too. She had been hidden behind her father's large frame.

"Luna! What a delightful surprise. Why would you bring such a beautiful creature out in a storm like this? You are a fool, Gannon. Look, you have even angered the gods and brought this storm upon us," Bale said, pointing to the ever-darkening heavens as he stood to greet her.

"You old fool, that doesn't even make any sense. Have you already started drinking this early in the morning?"

Gannon challenged his friend.

"Nahhh, mead doesn't count because it is made with berries. It's a morning meal." Bale laughed. "Aidan! Aidan? Come here, boy!" he called to his son.

A tall, broad-shouldered, handsome young man came running from another nearby tent Luna hadn't noticed before, about a hundred yards away, just inside the tree line. He had dark black hair and blue eyes. When he reached them, he offered his hand to Luna, and she accepted it. She noticed how big his hand was compared to hers and how small she felt standing next to these three men, unlike how she usually felt.

"Hello Luna. I remember you from the fertility feast in the spring," he said with an alluring air about him.

"Yes, I remember," she replied, breaking her gaze to look toward her father.

Aidan kept his eyes fixed on Luna and took in every captivating inch. *He's bold*, she thought to herself, feeling his eyes undress her while her father was busy talking to Bale about terms of trading. They were giving each other a hard time, trying to drive a hard bargain. Gannon wanted fresh fish from Bale in exchange for some of his harvest.

"Let's take a walk while they talk business. It isn't that interesting anyway." Aidan suggested, and Luna obliged.

He was nice to look at, she had to admit, but Luna didn't feel the same with Aidan as she had next to Sol. She realized she was comparing the two men and let the thought pass.

She hoped Sol was somewhere safe and warm.

"What do you do, Luna? Besides looking ravishing all the time, I mean."

Luna smiled out of nervousness. "I make herbal remedies and use plant medicine."

"That sounds…interesting. You must know a lot about how the body works then," Aidan said suggestively.

She ignored his remark. Luna wished she could have been back at home at the very least if she could not be with Sol as she had promised.

"Not nearly as much as my Aunt Alice," Luna answered, hoping he would rein in his aggressive flirting. It made her feel uncomfortable.

She felt conflicted because she enjoyed the attention from Aidan, but she didn't appreciate the way he gave it to her or the way he looked at her. He made her feel like an object.

"I'm sorry, you are just the most beautiful woman I have ever laid eyes on. Let's start over," he said as he turned to face her, his eyes meeting hers.

"Okay," Luna agreed.

After that he made polite small talk as they walked around the clearing, his arm linked with hers. They arrived back to where their fathers were and saw that they had indeed agreed upon terms and had amused smiles on their faces.

"Time to get you back before the storm gets here," Gannon said as he reached his arm out for his daughter.

"It was really nice to see you today, Luna. I hope I can

see you again sometime soon." Aidan bowed low as she took her father's hand and got back into the wagon after nodding politely.

"Boy, you are something else!" Bale teased his son, smacking his arm. "I'll see you later, Gannon."

After they were out of sight, Gannon asked Luna about her time with Aidan. He asked what she thought of him. Luna had never had her father ask such a personal question of her, and she felt bewildered.

"He seemed kind," was all Luna had to say to him about it after being paraded in front of the two men and then molested by Aidan's eyes.

After Aidan had apologized, he'd stopped the bold flirting and remained polite, though the way he looked at Luna went unchanged. She wasn't sure what to make of him. The ride back was quiet after that until they reached their home. As soon as they were inside, the sky opened up and the rain poured down. The thunder was loud overhead and shook the ground. The wind whipped through the cracks in the door, creating a pool of water on the ground.

Luna and her father ate their midday meal in the candlelight while the storm raged outside. Hours had passed by the time the thunder and lightning lessened. The rain had let up but still persisted.

"Now that the storm is gone, I have some things to attend to in the village, and then I will be with Bale. I won't be back until tomorrow sometime."

Luna wondered what kept her father away so frequently, but she was thankful for the solitude. Luna watched him leave and made sure he was out of sight before she started the journey to the waterfall in the rain. Luna didn't bother to bring anything with her this time or even change out of the white dress. She couldn't stand the waiting one minute more. She had to know. Luna jogged the four miles to the waterfall in the gentle but steady rain on the path that was beginning to form from her trips up the mountain. The forest offered her some protection from the weather. Luna realized how crazy she was for going out in this weather, now soaking wet, heading farther from home as the sun was beginning to set. Just then she reached the clearing by the waterfalls. The river was rushing faster and louder than usual.

"Sol?!" Luna yelled. She wasn't sure if she hoped he would be there or that he was home warm and dry, assuming only a lunatic would go out in weather like this. Luna didn't see him, and she was now shivering cold and completely soaked. She realized the lunacy of her trek. If he had come by, it was so late in the day, he would have been long gone by now. She searched along the river's edge for some sign of shelter. Suddenly, a flicker of light caught her eye.

* * *

Sol had reached the waterfall and searched for any sign of Luna earlier that morning, before the storm rolled in. He knew he better not risk the trek back through the storm and sought shelter. He scanned the edge of the river and saw a dark space between two of the giant boulders. There was a small cave between them with the earth and overgrowth of tree roots above. It was perfect. He got to work gathering some wood for a small fire for light and to ward off any animal that would try to seek a break from the rain there as well. Once Sol was comfortable in the cave, he had nothing left to do but wait it out and think of Luna. Hours went by as the storm came and went. The rain was still coming down steadily, and he decided he would try to wait it out, hoping for a break before he made his way home. His lean-to was probably no dryer than this small cave, and he didn't welcome the idea of staying in his mother's house to be pestered by questions from his well-meaning family. Just then Sol heard a voice as Luna's figure appeared in front of the small shelter. She looked naked, the white dress she was wearing now completely see-through from the rain.

"Sol! I didn't think you would be here. I hoped…" Luna trailed off, shivering.

"You look like you're freezing," he said as he got up.

He could stand up, hunched over in the cave if he was directly in the middle of it. The boulders joined near the top, creating a peak. The ceiling of the boulders was dark earth and stringy root systems from the ledge above, creating just enough space for them to keep dry in the storm. It wasn't until then that Luna was aware of how she must look. Her wet curly hair stuck to her body, which was now on full display for the second time in front of Sol. His eyes were once again glued to her nearly naked figure, but then his gaze met hers. She looked into his fire-lit eyes, not sure what she was searching for, but the small voice inside her told her she had found it. He took off his tunic once again and turned to sit down as she changed into it.

"Come here," he said.

She did after placing her dress on the moss- and river-stone-covered ground near the fire to dry. Luna sat by him, their bodies pressed against each other's. She felt the cold all the way to her bones, but his body was hot and it brought her warmth. Sol wrapped his arm around Luna, rubbing it up and down her shoulder in an attempt to warm her up faster.

"We have to stop meeting like this," he said, feeling an insatiable desire mounting once again due to the closeness of their bodies and the visual of her naked fresh in his mind.

Luna felt a rush of panic. "Oh," she managed, thinking he meant he didn't want to see her again.

"Your naked body is bewitching," he admitted, surprising himself as well as Luna.

She realized he had not meant he wished to discontinue their waterfall meetings, which brought her sudden and revelatory relief. Sol found her attractive, and once she understood that, she felt her body immediately grow hot. She looked in his eyes, so close to hers. She felt his body shift to face her better.

Sol knew this was forbidden, but he didn't care anymore as something more than carnal took over him. She felt his body pressing closer to hers, his hands moving around her waist, pulling her closer.

Luna felt the magnetic pull of his lips, and she put one of her hands on his chest to halt him.

Sol stopped, waiting for her to make the next move.

Their eyes met. She decided to lay her head down and snuggle into his warm naked chest. Luna was afraid of the feelings and desires he evoked in her body. He held her and they watched the fire burn in the small cave as the rain persisted. Part of her hoped the storm wouldn't end so they could stay like that forever. The thought surprised her as she had only spoken with him a few times. The quickened pace of her trust in him scared her. She had to admit she liked the feeling of lying on his muscled chest. It felt safe. It felt like home.

They woke to the sound of birds chattering and the steady rush of the waterfall. They had fallen asleep in the cave, wrapped in each other's arms after a long night of talking as they waited out the rain. Luna was thankful her father had been out for the night as well so she hadn't had to rush home when the time for their evening meal came or explain she had disobeyed.

Sol was happy he'd had some food for them to share. When the dawn came, reality also came with it. Sol needed to head home because he knew his family would be worried about him. Luna wanted to change before her father saw her still in the previous day's clothes and assumed the worst.

Luna had never been this close to a man before. Sol had given her the emotional intimacy and friendship she had desired for what seemed like all her life. He satisfied a craving deep within her that she hadn't even known she had. He was confident, but not cocky. He seemed to know what he wanted in life, and she hoped she would be part of that life. He saw her as an equal, and he didn't push her to do things she didn't want to do like all the other men in her life had. Luna knew her feelings for him had grown, and she was terrified about what that meant. Luna changed into her dress after Sol stepped out of the cave to stretch his body.

Luna handed him his shirt, and he knew it would smell like roses long after she left. He knew his initial infatuation with her was turning into something else, something deeper. He didn't know what it was, but he knew this perfect stranger was now someone he cared for, someone he felt connected to. Sol felt a satisfaction even though they had not been physically intimate.

Luna floated all the way home with her head high in the clouds, dreaming of the what-ifs and replaying their conversations in her mind. She remembered the way it felt to lie on his bare chest. His smell had been intoxicating. She remembered listening to his heartbeat as she fell asleep. She had felt herself hold her breath in suspense between beats, praying to the gods it would continue. Now, she thought herself silly for it. Luna made it home to find no sign that her father had been back yet, and she sighed with relief. She changed her tunic for the day and set out toward the river to wash the white dress.

* * *

Sol returned to find his family abnormally quiet while eating their morning meal. The relief that spread across their worried faces said everything.

"Why would you go out in a storm like that? Where are your brains? Are you trying to kill me with worry?!" Sol's mother scolded him.

"Mama, I—"

"Where is your head at these days? You are never to do that again, do you hear me? Sol, I'm not joking, I will kill you myself if that happens again."

"Yes, Mama," he agreed, still not regretting the choice he had made.

"Did you stay in the woods all night long?" Akiiki asked out of concern.

"I found a cave for shelter," Sol explained.

"You know who lives in caves? Animals, that's who. Are

you an animal or a man?" Bomani asked, being serious for once.

"I can see you were all very worried. I am sorry, and I swear it will not happen again," Sol promised.

Ata and Atsu were enjoying their brother being scolded instead of them for once.

"What is in those woods that is so important?" The question came from Layla behind him. Sol turned and saw she was coming around the edge of the longhouse.

Sol made a clicking sound with his tongue. "You involved the whole tribe in your worry? I didn't know I was so important," he joked, trying to make light of the situation as well as avoid the question.

"Not the whole tribe, just me," Layla answered.

Sol was sure he didn't want to ask why and changed the subject. "I better go make sure my lean-to is still standing and see how my things fared. I'll be back soon Mama. I'll help you around here today if you wish."

"I do wish," she answered firmly.

He took that as his opportunity to escape all the questions, many of which he didn't quite know the answer to himself. Some questions he was afraid to answer, especially now that his mind was able to think logically. The closeness of Luna's body had filled his own with yearning that had clouded his judgment the previous night. His mind wondered what would have happened if she hadn't stopped his advances.

CHAPTER 6

Luna returned from washing the white dress and made herself something to eat. She tried to keep herself busy and made a large batch of the arnica salve. Of course, that only made her think of Sol and the salve being slathered all over his corded muscles, which only made the day drag on slower. Luna decided it was best she got out of the house, so she grabbed her things and headed out to see her aunt. The quick walk there took her no time at all, and she was delightfully surprised to find her aunt outside to greet her.

"Luna! What can I do for you?" Alice asked. She was picking small elderberries off a clustered stem and dropping them into a bowl. Her hands were purple.

Luna sat beside her aunt, quickly picking up some of the berries to busy her own hands. "Oh, I just didn't know what to do with myself. Father told me to stay home and there wasn't much to do," Luna admitted.

"Give him some time. He will calm down and you will be back in the woods soon," Alice encouraged, not looking up from her work.

"I hope so."

A few moments of quiet passed before Alice asked, "Is something on your mind?"

Luna hesitated, not sure how to formulate the words. She wanted to tell her aunt everything, but something held her back.

"What does love feel like?"

Alice thought long and hard after glancing toward Luna's awaiting gaze before answering. "Love is not so much a feeling as it is an action. Love…is something you do." She struggled to find the words. "I can only tell you what it was like for me. My love and I just fit together perfectly, in every way." Alice smiled. "Our love went beyond feelings and words into action. The way we *were* was love. Does that make sense?" Alice asked, pausing her work momentarily.

Luna nodded her head.

"Why do you ask? Is there someone you want to tell me about?" Alice probed, continuing to retrieve the berries.

Luna bit her lip. "Not yet. I mean, I don't know yet."

It was Alice's turn to nod her head. After that she told Luna she had an extra rabbit hanging behind the house that she should take for their dinner as she didn't want it to go to waste. Luna helped her finish the elderberries, making small talk, and said her goodbye after retrieving the hare. Luna stopped to gather some vegetables from the gardens before bringing the rabbit home and cleaning it for their evening meal.

As Luna started preparing their dinner, Gannon came home. He walked in and retrieved his well-used wooden pipe out of his room. He placed dried herbs inside, bringing a small flame to them. He puffed on the end a few times and sat by the fireplace. Luna didn't say anything, waiting for him to take the lead.

After several minutes, Gannon began, "Where did you find the rabbit?"

"Alice."

He nodded his head as he took a long inhale from the pipe and released the smoke into the room. "What did you do today?"

Luna felt the panic of her secret being found out fill her body as she stirred a few pinches of salt into the meal she was cooking. "I made salve then went to see Alice and helped her with the elderberries. I also went to the gardens and got what we needed for this." She motioned to the pot of steaming rabbit meat and vegetables.

The aroma from the cooking meal filled his nose and made his mouth water. Gannon could see his daughter was unhappy and uncomfortable. He wished her mother were still there; she would know how to talk to her and tell her everything a mother is supposed to. The anger began to rise in him, but the shaman's words were seared into the back of his mind. He needed an heir, *the child,* and then he could put his plan of revenge against the savages into action. Gannon thought he had figured out just how to make that happen, which brought a small amount of relief to him in that moment.

Luna had many questions she wanted to ask her father. She wanted to ask about the Nets. She wanted to ask about her mother. She wanted to ask for permission to go back to the waterfall so she could see Sol. She hoped she could see him again soon. Something was missing from her life, and it was Sol. In that instant, Luna realized she felt homesick for Sol. She missed him.

Luna finished making dinner and they sat in silence, enjoying the flavorful dish. After it was cleaned up, she pulled out her beading project and worked on it by firelight until it was an acceptable time to go to bed. Gannon sharpened his knife and pulled out a map that was drawn on a piece of tanned hide with several markings to the sides. Luna didn't pay much attention to it, but Gannon was so focused on it he didn't even realize she had gone to bed.

In the morning, Luna took her time at the river getting ready for the day before meeting her father for tea. She sat and gladly took the cup he had poured for her.

"What part of the woods will you be in today?" he asked, just like it was any other morning.

Luna's stomach flittered with butterflies of anticipation. Had she heard her father correctly? She answered, trying not to seem overly enthusiastic, but she couldn't hide the small smile that creased her lips due to receiving his permission.

"North."

"Make another rabbit for dinner tonight," he said before getting up and heading into the house.

Luna forced herself to stay put until he was out of sight. Once the door was closed, she no longer tried to hide the large smile that now adorned her face. She was going to be able to go back to the woods that day. She was going to be free. She was going to see Sol.

* * *

Sol had checked his lean-to, and after he was satisfied that no real damage had been done, he went to his mother's, as promised. She had a long list of things she wanted him to do, and he did them without protest. By midafternoon, she had relaxed, and they were able to have some conversation.

"Mama?"

"Yes, my son?"

"Why are the Barden against us?"

The question caught his mother by surprise, and she took a moment to formulate an answer. "Gannon, their chief, is a very angry man. He thinks we are to blame for his misfortune and all that is wrong in this land. He wants what we have, and he wants to rule over us. Why do you ask?"

"I wanted to understand why crossing is forbidden and trading is nonexistent," Sol answered honestly.

"I want to know what is going on in that head of yours.

You have been different the last few days. You have to ask yourself: are you running from something, or are you running to something?"

Sol accepted his mother's question and knew she didn't mean for him to answer it out loud. They spent more time on various projects she had for him then she took him on her rounds to meet with tribe members and hear about their needs.

Ata and Atsu had taken their turn and gone hunting for their tribe. This time, the brothers brought back a large doe. Sol helped them butcher it and took his turn to cook dinner for the family. He decided cooking was a good way to make amends for worrying them all. He was surprised when Layla showed up to their family meal, and he was thankful she didn't say a word to him. After dinner was done and their conversations wound down, Sol said good night and headed for his respite by the sea. Halfway home, he heard his name called from behind him; it was Layla.

"Sol, you really had me worried last night."

"There really wasn't anything to worry about," he said, annoyed.

"Easy for you to say," Layla replied, feigning hurt—*or is it genuine*, Sol wondered.

"Why?"

"Because you don't worry about anyone other than yourself and your mother," she answered.

"No one else gives me reason to worry," Sol said, being

honest.

Layla stepped closer and put her hand on his chest. "I guess I will give you a reason to worry about me then."

Sol backed away from her advance, not sure what to say.

She pointed at him. "We belong together, Sol, and the sooner you realize that, the better your life will be." She turned to walk away, her hips swaying from side to side.

Sol shook his head incredulously as he turned and continued home. Layla was beautiful, but Sol didn't think of her like that. He didn't think of anyone like that, except… Luna. He realized he missed Luna. Sol had spent the whole day busy with his mother and his family, but every now and then she had come into his thoughts. He wondered what she was doing, wondered if she had gotten in trouble again. He remembered when she told him about the meeting with Aidan and Bale. He could tell Aidan made her uncomfortable. He knew how Aidan was and felt anger rise when he thought of Luna's father pushing her into a situation like that. It wasn't jealousy, he told himself, just concern for the lack of respect she was given.

Sol reached his lean-to and went straight to sleep after a late-night swim in the salty waters. When he awoke the following morning, he remembered the events with Layla and what she had said to him. He hoped she wouldn't show up at his family's morning meal and was glad when she didn't. Sol grabbed his tools and the partially complete bowl before heading up to the waterfall, hoping Luna would be able to meet him there. He had already decided he would wait all day.

* * *

When Luna got to the waterfall, she saw Sol was already there working on the almost complete bowl to trade. She walked quietly, careful not to betray her arrival. He was busy carving by the edge of the river, working with a small chisel and mallet. Luna made her way to the boulder where she had sat before, quietly sat down, and waited. After a few moments passed, she saw Sol look up toward her side of the river. He saw her out of the corner of his eye and quickly turned to her. She saw a look of surprise and then a smile cross his usually serious face, another new experience for her.

"How long have you been there?" he asked with his deep voice.

"Not long," she answered.

"I didn't know you could be so quiet," he joked with a smile. *Another first*, she thought.

"What is that supposed to mean? Do I talk too much?" Luna asked, pretending to be offended.

"No, no. I just don't get surprised that often."

"I guess I'm the exception," she said, remembering their first conversation.

"I guess so." Their eyes lingered on each other's.

"Sol, tell me more about your people. Does someone in your family hunt for you?" Luna asked, adjusting in her seat to get more comfortable.

"All members of the tribe take turns hunting. Someone gets the deer or whatever animal it is, and then a few people will help to butcher the animal. Those that help with that part get to pick their pieces before the rest of the tribe. Everyone knows where to go to get what they need for their immediate and extended families. We eat our meals together in the morning and the evening. We also take turns cooking in our families, so both the men and the women cook," he explained.

"Do only the women rule in your tribe?"

"No, my father was chief and my mother is chieftess. They led in partnership. When he died, she was just the only one left. When my mother passes on to the spirit realm, my older sister will be chieftess and her husband will rule by her side. It is the oldest child who is next in line to be chief unless they do not wish to bear the burden. In that case, the next child has the opportunity."

"Wow. That sounds so different than my tribe," Luna remarked.

"How so?" Sol asked.

"Well, there are usually only a few people in our tribe who hunt or raise the fowl. We barter with them for their services if we do not wish to hunt on our own. We grow large fields of foods, which most of the tribe members take care of. Those who take care of the land get to enjoy only what they need for them and their families. My father gets what he needs as chief, and I do as well because I am his family. We have a shaman and healers, like my Aunt Alice. The women are the only ones who cook, unless the man is without a wife or daughter. Men are the only ones who can govern. We have the chief and then elders. Women have to be under their fathers until they are passed on to a man as his wife. Then she is under her husband." Luna's brow furrowed as she explained the differences.

Sol shook his head. "That does not make sense to me, how your tribe treats its women."

"It used to make some sense to me when I was younger. Now, not so much. I feel trapped sometimes. I feel like I am always trying to prove my worth to my father." Luna stopped and looked at Sol, realizing she was getting more personal with him than she had with anyone else in her life, even Alice.

"What do you believe happens when someone dies?" Sol asked, asking her to go deeper.

"I was taught that they should be burned and returned back to the ground, back to nature. I searched the sky after my mother was burned for a sign that she was up there, shining her light amongst the other stars. I feel her in the forest. I believe her spirit is in the animals and the trees, the river and the wind," Luna explained.

"We are similar in that, except we place the ashes in the

ocean as well as the forest," Sol said.

"Where do you feel your father?" Luna asked.

Sol looked away from her gaze and closed his eyes momentarily before replying. "I feel him when I am in the sea and when I do any of the tasks he taught me: hunting, butchering, and carving." He motioned to the bowl in his hands and then continued. "I also feel him when I am with my family, hearing their laughter together over a warm meal and a fire."

"Your family sounds so wonderful. They sound like such special people," Luna said.

"They are," he agreed.

Sol and Luna passed the day learning about each other and their respective tribes. They stayed separated, him on his side of the river and her going no farther than the boulder she sat on. They kept the distance partly because of the treaty, and partly because the growing physical attraction between the two of them scared her. If another Net knew Luna had crossed onto their land, his family would have the right to attack, being that the boundary had been crossed without permission from the chieftess. Luna guessed his family would not be as eager to do such a thing as her father would, but she didn't want to test her theory just yet.

They spent their day together before parting reluctantly. One day turned into two, and then before they knew it, almost a month had gone by with daily secret meetings at the waterfall. Luna felt enchanted by Sol and his world. She wanted to be a part of it so completely.

Sol felt intoxicated by Luna's presence. She consumed his thoughts when he wasn't with her, and he yearned for her closeness when she was present. He was glad she kept her distance, coming no closer than the boulder, because when she was close to him, his whole body ached to be a part of hers. He had never felt the way he did around Luna before, and he guessed he never would again.

"The sun is getting low," Sol said.

"The day went by fast," Luna admitted. She stood with her feet in the river and her back leaning against the boulder, tucking a stray curl behind her ear.

Sol blew the last of the wood chips off the finished oak bowl before walking to meet Luna in the river for the first time. She adjusted herself, standing straighter as he approached. She could feel the fluttering in her stomach that had become commonplace during her visits with Sol. He picked up her hand and placed the bowl in it. His touch stirred the longing she felt for him. The icy river suddenly didn't feel so cold to Luna as her body came alive with the scorch of his fingertips against her skin.

He watched her as she slowly took the bowl and admired it, avoiding his eyes.

"Sol, it is so beautiful. I didn't know this kind of intricate design could be done on wood," Luna said as she turned the bowl in her hands so she could see every inch.

The oak bowl was smooth except for a realistic-looking bear carved on one side and then a small sun on the bottom, his signature.

"The bear is so…fitting," she said as she looked in his eyes. "I brought the salve for you too." She turned to set the bowl on the boulder behind her and pulled a clay pot from the leather satchel.

Sol's body was begging him to press closer to her, but he resisted the urge.

"Let me know if it works," she said, handing him the jar as she turned around to face him once again.

Luna wanted to be in his arms again, like they had been that night in the cave. She wanted to have his arms around her and talk and laugh as they had then. She felt frozen though, unable to move.

He took it but remained where he stood, so close. He knew in that instant he wanted to see her face light up again, as it had with the bowl. He wanted to give her another gift. His mind screamed not to, but he couldn't help himself.

"Luna?" he asked.

His face was so close she could smell his sweet breath. "Yes?" she managed, almost in a whisper.

"Do you trust me?" he asked.

It took her a minute to respond. "Yes, I think so," she admitted.

"Will you meet me tonight at the southwestern-most point where all three lands border? After your father and your village are asleep, will you meet me there by the river?"

Luna was confused and then intrigued and excited all at once. "Why?"

"I have something I want to show you."

"Yes," Luna answered, still having trouble formulating words with his body so close to hers.

He smiled. "Good. Until tonight then." He turned to go, but Luna reached her hand out to his to stop him, and he felt a bolt of electricity enter his body from where she touched him.

"Wait, how will I find you?" she asked worriedly.

"It will be a full moon. I will find you, Luna," he said, and with that they picked up their things and went their separate ways.

Luna's head was still reeling from the feeling of excitement and nervousness coursing through her body. She was fascinated by all that was Sol, and the fact that it was forbidden just added to the temptation. *He* was forbidden. Sol provoked feelings and sensations in her that she hadn't even known existed, and now she had just agreed to sneak out in the middle of the night to meet him in secret. It was a thrilling thought, and she admitted to herself that her curiosity was getting the best of her once again.

Luna made it through dinner with her father, the time inching by. She did her best to not seem anxious. She stopped her leg from bouncing frantically up and down on two occasions before giving up and telling her father she was going to go for a walk before bed. He informed her that he would be going with Bale for most of the night after he finished his dinner, and that brought her a wave of relief. She didn't care why he had been staying there a couple nights a week, coming home in the wee hours. Luna was just glad for the solitude and the privacy, especially on this night. Luna went for a walk outside the house by the wall while there was still some light left in the sky. She figured she better find an easy area to scale the wall rather than have the night guards ask her about where she was headed at the odd hour, or worse, report it to her father. Climbing the wall was her best chance. Luna made it home after her father had gone and she spent time organizing the things in their living space before doing the same in her bedroom by candlelight.

She sat in the silence of her home, listening as the villagers grew quieter. She opened the latch of the wooden window and peered out into the darkness. She watched the moon get higher in the sky as the shadows moved. Luna changed into a black tunic, better for hiding in the dark, she thought. The moon was full and bright. Luna splashed her face with water, washing the black markings off like she usually did at night. She blew out the candles and lay there in her bed, still and quiet, her heart pounding in her ears until she couldn't stand it any longer. She quickly and quietly left all her belongings in the room except the belt with the small knife she wore around her waist, and she shut the door to her bedroom. Luna crept outside, carefully shutting the front door behind her. Next, she retraced her earlier steps and found where she would cross the wall. After crouching to avoid some passing villagers and checking to see if anyone was around, Luna began her ascent over the crumbling stone wall. Once she made it to the other side, she crept through the tall grass of the field, keeping as low as possible. The chorus of the night insects and animals urging her on, she made it to the cornfield. Luna felt relief as she was finally able to stand up, knowing the tall corn would hide her from the luminous moonlight. Her heart still raced with anticipation.

At the edge of the cornfield, Luna trekked on until she reached the river. She followed the edge of it south to where she would meet Sol and waited.

* * *

Sol hadn't planned to ask Luna to meet him, but he didn't regret it either. He wanted to show her something and he knew she would love it. He knew it would bring her joy, and for once he thought it was something worth breaking the rules for. Sol made it through dinner with his family, trying not to seem too distracted. He made his way to his lean-to and waited for dark. He would get there early to be on the lookout for her. Thoughts swirled in his head, and he needed to calm them down. He took off his clothes and walked into the crashing waves of the ocean. A late-night swim was just what he needed to feel calm and refreshed. He could now consider his plan with a more logical mind, and he still thought it was a good idea. Sol changed into a white tunic shirt and shorts before heading out to his destination.

Once he was there, looking eagerly across the river to where both the Barden and the Dabney tribe lands met, he searched for Luna. She wasn't there yet, so he would wait. He waited an hour and then he saw her walking along the edge of the river toward him. She stopped directly across from him, her face glowing in the moonlight. She didn't have on the black paint that usually decorated her skin, and it gave him the chance to see her naked face for the first time. She was truly beautiful. His attraction had grown in surprising ways since they first met. He saw her look around nervously and realized he had been ogling without letting her know of his presence.

"Luna." She heard Sol call her name from across the river and watched him walk out from behind the shadow of a tree, his white clothing contrasting with the night.

"Sol." She breathed a noticeable sigh of relief.

"You came."

"I said I would," she answered in a loud whisper.

Sol walked down into the middle of the shallow river. She saw him reach out his hand toward her, inviting her to come forward. She did.

"Do you trust me?" he asked her for the second time that day.

"I'm here aren't I?"

"This isn't the part you have to trust me for," he said, her curiosity increasing with each second.

Luna hesitated and felt as though she was at a crossroads. She didn't know which way was up and which was down in that moment, but she knew one thing without a shadow of a doubt. "Okay, I trust you," she told him.

Sol took her hand and she felt a slow hum of electricity start to build. He led her to his side of the river and stepped onto it, pulling her beside him. Luna followed his lead and stepped out of the river onto Net tribal land.

CHAPTER 7

Sol led Luna in the moonlight, through the woods and grasslands further southwest until the dirt and grass gave way to fine sand and clusters of tall stiff salt grass on either side of them. Once they had reached the top of the small sand dune, Luna felt a blast of salty air assault her senses. It was like nothing she had ever seen before. The giant waves clapped and boomed as they toppled over and spilled onto the beach, the tide coming in and reminding her of thunder. The rushing ocean water was rhythmic, like breathing, just as Sol had described. Luna was overcome with gratitude, excitement, and wonder as she studied the black sea water under the brightness of the light from the full moon.

"Sol!" was all she could manage.

He had been watching her intently the whole time, trying to memorize her reaction to his surprise. She certainly was not disappointed, and neither was he.

"This is amazing! This is the best thing I have ever seen!" Luna finally managed. A single tear escaped her eye.

Sol watched her wipe it away and asked, "Are you okay?

Are you sad?"

"No, I'm not sad." She looked in his eyes, the moon shining on his concerned face. "I am the happiest I have ever been in my entire life with a man who has the most beautiful heart, a man I am not supposed to speak to, in a land I am forbidden to enter. Even if I never experience the love I feel right now again in my lifetime, even if I am found out, I would never take this back. I am so undeserving of this kindness, and yet I am so very grateful!" she exclaimed, knowing at that moment that she loved him, that she had loved him for a long time. Even though they had only been acquainted for a month, it felt like she had known him for far longer. She knew her life would never be the same.

Her raw honesty struck him to his core. Though he tried to formulate a response, none came to him. There was so much to process from her words. She was the most deserving person, and it bothered him that she thought so little of herself.

"What do you mean you're undeserving?" he asked.

Her eyes welled with tears as she looked away from him toward the ocean again. "It's complicated."

"Let's walk along the beach and you can tell me," he offered, taking her hand in his and leading her west toward his lean-to.

Luna had never told anyone the story of the day her mother died. She felt safe with Sol, and she knew she needed to be honest with him. *Luna? Wake up. Luna!* Her mother's words seemed to whisper through the darkness over the drum of the waves, encouraging her to begin.

"My mother woke me up to go collect herbs early in the morning. The moon was still up. She wanted to go for a walk with me before the baby came. She was so excited, knowing that the day was upon her when she would get to meet her son. I was excited, too." Luna swiped the tears that began streaming down her cheeks from the memory.

She continued, "I remember the warmth of her hug around her pregnant belly, her green eyes, and sometimes I see flashes of her beautiful face. She would call me her *little bear*." Luna paused, smiling at the memory.

Her face fell as she recounted the next part. Sol wrapped his arm around her shoulders. "I asked her to go for a walk, running into the forest. We would always explore new parts of the woods. She taught me which plants would be useful for what, which mushrooms were poisonous, and which bark made a great tea or tincture, for common ailments."

Sol said, "So that's where you get your love for plant medicine."

Luna nodded and continued. "I climbed an ash tree effortlessly, making my way up into its strong branches. My mother didn't caution me as my father would have. She trusted me, even though I was only five years old. From what I can remember, and what my aunt has told me, my mother didn't agree with everything my father and our tribe believed about how women should behave, or us being weaker in every aspect. I remember my father arguing with her several times about me running wild as a child. My mother would say, 'Wildness is just what she needs, because in her wildness is where she will find her freedom and strength'. I didn't care, as long as I got to run about as I pleased."

Luna took a breath, preparing herself for the next part of her confession. "I was so excited because I found a bird's nest in the tree. I barely heard her caution me when my tunic got stuck, and I yelled for help. I remember the ground suddenly feeling a lot farther down. I thought I was going to fall to my death. She reached me so fast, even with her large belly. My mother unhooked my tunic, and we made our way down the tree. I jumped off, holding her hand and turned in time to see her final descent. She jumped the last bit off the tree and grabbed her belly in pain. I asked her if she and the baby were okay. She assured me they were. My mother had already been through three miscarriages, so we were worried when she was with child."

Sol could sense where Luna's story was going, and he gave her shoulder a squeeze of encouragement.

"We walked toward home along the river after that, stopping to let her rest on a rock. I could tell she was in pain, but she assured me it was the baby coming. We heard a voice from across the river. A Net woman, who was my mother's best friend."

Sol was surprised. "Someone from my tribe?"

"Yes," Luna answered before continuing. "My mother said the time was upon them, and the Net woman offered to help my mother to her own home, as it was closer. My mother sent me to get my father. I didn't want to leave her; I felt protective of her. We were like a team, and it felt wrong to break that up. But, I also knew my mother needed my help and for me to be strong. I ran to get my father, seeing his big red beard in the distance. I yelled to him, telling him where my mother was. That was the last time I saw him so excited." Luna's gaze fell.

"He picked me up and twirled me in a full circle before we rode on his horse to your village. I watched my father pace back and forth outside the dwelling where my mother was laboring. She had gone that far along in her pregnancies only once, when I was born, so we were hopeful that everything would be fine this time. My father wanted a son so that he could raise him to be the tribe's next chief after he was gone. He prefers the ruler of our tribe stay in his bloodline. He wanted his son to rule and did not want to rely on my future husband," Luna explained.

Sol didn't like the thought of anyone else becoming so close to Luna. He wondered why the men in her tribe thought themselves so much better than those who brought life into their world.

"I wanted to go inside and be with her, so I did just that. I trusted my mother was in good hands. The women didn't seem to mind me being in there, so I made my way to my mother's free hand and took it in my own. She smiled at me, giving my hand a squeeze. I sat there mesmerized by the chanting. The women worked together in unison. I watched as my mother's usually light olive face flushed red surrounded by her curly brown hair. I remember thinking she was the most beautiful person in the world. Then everything started to go wrong. She let go of my hand and crawled onto all fours. I watched part in horror and part in amazement as my little brother was birthed. My mother had spoken to me about the process, but seeing it firsthand was both frightening and exciting. The cord was wrapped around the baby's neck. They tried to help him, but it was too late; he never took a breath." Luna looked out to the ocean, remembering each detail that was seared in her memory.

"I watched as the features on my mother's face turned from hope to awestruck grief. She started crying and called me over to her. She wrapped her arms around me, holding me close. She told me my brother decided it was best to stay in the land of the gods. I knew then that it was my fault. I was worried for my brother, my mother, and what my father would do when he found out.

The women started acting worried, making my mother drink tea and pressing on her stomach. My mother never looked away from me, but I could see the fear in her eyes. She said, *Luna…little bear, I love you. Remember how much I love you. I need you to be strong. I need you…to take care of yourself…* I was too frozen in fear to answer. There was so much blood. I watched in horror as the women pushed and pulled on her stomach. She yelled at me to get my attention, forcing me to look in her eyes rather than the carnage. She said something to me, but I can't remember what it was. I remember her face right before she died. She looked peaceful and calm as she stared into my eyes, deciding the single most important thing to tell me. Her last words were, *I love you, little bear.* I watched as her light olive skin turned as pale as the clouds. Her brilliant green eyes suddenly went empty, and the hand that held mine grew heavy and lifeless."

By the time she was done sobbing in his arms, they had reached his dwelling. Sol built a small fire. They sat next to each other, her hand still in his, fitting together perfectly.

"My father blamed your people for killing my mother. He forbade any contact after that, and he built the wall. I went to the meeting house and found her body while they set up the pyre. I looked at her holding my brother against the breast he would never suckle from. All because of me. I should have never climbed that tree. If I hadn't, my mother would still be alive, as well as my brother. If I had only listened and done what my father had wished."

"Oh, Luna. That was not your fault. It sounds like a complication that was out of everyone's control. I have unfortunately seen it before. My mother helps deliver babies in my village. It doesn't happen often, but it does happen."

Luna wasn't ready to part with the guilt she had carried for sixteen years, but his words did bring her comfort.

Sol knew she was worthy of happiness. He knew she was worthy of love, even. He took her face into his hands gently but firmly, looking deep into her soul. "You are deserving of my love."

She gazed into his eyes, not able to look away as she felt her body melt. Luna did something more brazen than she had ever imagined herself doing before: she moved her other hand to the back of his head, pulling it forward. She pushed her lips onto his, their mouths meeting for the first time. A flood of heat ignited every inch of her body. She hadn't intended to kiss him, hadn't intended to fuel the fire of desire that now burned hotter inside her, but now she couldn't resist.

Her kiss was soft and strong, her lips fitting perfectly with his. He felt her grow limp, melting in his arms. He moved his hands from her face to her hips, pulling her closer to him. The softness of her body met with the hardness of his, and they stopped kissing all at once. Gazing into her eyes, panting heavily with anticipation, he searched for permission.

"If I don't stop now, I don't know if I will be able to," he admitted voraciously, waiting to follow her lead.

Luna thought about the man in front of her. She had just given him her first kiss, and now contemplated giving him everything. There was no question in her mind; she was ready. "I don't want you to stop," she said, her voice a throaty whisper with unabashed pent-up need.

Their lips met again, the feeling of his warm mouth closing over hers making her feel like she was leaving her body and meeting him both in the physical and the spiritual realm. Luna's heartbeat grew rapid, her curiosity taking place of any shyness, her hesitancy turning into urgency. They gave in to each other, exploring each other's bodies, leaving no area untouched. Luna felt like she had been struck by lightning, her body emitting a vibrating energy. There was so much pleasure, so much passion as they gave themselves to each other for the first time with the ravenous wanting and desire that had been building since they first saw each other.

Sol's hands left tingling sensations wherever he touched. Luna felt as though some part of her had been set free, as if she was completely herself for the first time in all her life. She raked her fingers over his rippled chest, caressing every hard muscle. Her hands felt Sol's response. Luna felt powerful knowing she was the cause of his reaction. She moaned in pleasure, hearing Sol groan in ecstasy.

As their bodies intertwined and then merged together, they each felt complete for the first time in their lives. Baring their naked souls to each other unashamedly, their love for each other was finally physically manifested.

CHAPTER 8

They lay together by the flickering fire. Luna's head lay on Sol's warm chest, listening to the sound of his heartbeat between the sounds of the rushing waves. Their legs intertwined as they watched the fire dance under the canopy of stars and listened to the steady sound of the water. They enjoyed the euphoric relaxation that now settled in their bodies.

"That was…beautiful," Luna said, her hand finding his. "Is it always this amazing?" she asked.

"I wouldn't know. I hope so," he answered honestly.

"I'm hungry," she admitted.

Sol sat up, the fire illuminating his toned naked body. He grabbed a nearby pot of water and placed it by the fire before standing up. "Come on," he said with his hand extended, inviting her.

Luna stood up, the moon shining on her bare figure. He thought she was stunning.

"Wait, I need my clothes," Luna said, suddenly feeling self-conscious.

"Not where we're going." He led her to the wooden peg

in the sand.

Luna watched as Sol pulled up the netting. She could see movement in the net but didn't quite know what to make of it. He carried the netting back toward the fire and she followed.

"What is it?" she asked.

"Crab. Only the best," he answered, noticing the look of uncertainty on her face.

Luna had seen them before, but they had been red in color and already dead as they had traded for them from the Dabney tribe. Her father didn't care for crab, so she had only eaten it once.

There were four crabs in total inside the netting, and Sol set to work grilling them over the fire. Luna sat on the furs and watched him. He was careful but still got pinched by one of the crustaceans. Luna laughed at the sight of him jumping from the pain.

"Here I am risking my life to cook for you and you laugh at me!" he joked.

"You should have seen your face!" Luna laughed again.

"I see how it is," he said.

The crabs were cooked, and he brought them to her on a wooden platter. The steam billowed out as he split one of the crabs open and showed her how to pound the claws with a stone to get to the meat.

"Mmm. It's sweet," she commented after taking a bite.

"It's my favorite."

"I think it will be my favorite now, too." Their eyes met and she smiled. "Tell me about your father," Luna requested.

Sol's face grew serious for a moment as he pulled a piece of shell from his teeth before answering. "His name was Jabari, and he was fearless. He loved my mother and our family. We were everything to him…" Sol trailed off, watching the waves.

"How did it happen?" Luna asked directly.

The question brought Sol's eyes back to hers. "Because of me."

"A bear attack is not in your control," she told him gently.

"He told me not to go to the meadow because others had seen fresh signs that a bear had been hanging around. I didn't listen and went ahead. I was a stubborn child. I was oblivious to the bear's presence until I heard my father scream for me to run. I didn't even know he was there until I heard my father raise his voice, which he very rarely did. That's how I knew something was not right. I turned and was confused at first because I saw a large brown furry figure between my father and me. Then I realized it was a grizzly bear that had been following me. With my father's shout, the bear turned and went bounding over to him where he stood with a bow aimed—a true warrior. I wanted to run to him, and at the sound of the roaring giant bear, I wanted to run home to safety in the same instance. There was no time, and I felt crippled by fear. I heard him scream out one more time for me to run. I did, but only as far as the tree line, where I turned, fully expecting to see him behind me." Sol turned to face the fire, but instead of the orange flames, he saw the agonizing memory play out in the silhouette of billowing smoke. He continued after a slight pause. "Then, I saw the carnage. His face…was… gone. There was so much blood. I had killed my father. I thought about giving my life to the bear as well, to pay for my disgrace, but I was weak. I ran home to tell my mother and my family what had happened."

Luna felt a pull to hold Sol in her arms again. She put down the crab and hugged him. She knew he was battling feelings of guilt, and she also knew her saying it wasn't his fault again wouldn't bring him the comfort he needed.

Luna offered a new perspective instead. "Your father sacrificed everything so you could have a future. The best way to honor him is to live for him, to live a life your father would be proud of."

Sol heard her words, really heard them, and they made sense. If he was going to live when his father could not, he should do more to make him proud. He would live an honorable warrior's life so his father's death would not be in vain. Sol looked down at Luna, her arms still snugly around him.

"Thank you," was all he said as he lifted her chin so their lips could meet again.

They finished their dinner and Sol brought the bucket

of shells and dirty water to empty its contents into the ocean. After he returned, he took Luna's hand and led her to where the sea washed onto the sand. The water was cool and cleansing. Luna stood there and was enjoying the waves when she felt something move under her foot. She yelped and Sol caught her just before she flopped onto the ground.

"It's just the sand moving under your feet from the sea waves," he explained.

Luna let out a noticeable sigh of relief. "I thought there was a creature in there!" They both laughed.

Sol took her hand and led her deeper in the cool sea water. Once they were waist deep, he pulled her close. Their naked bodies met amidst the waves, their figures highlighted by the full moon.

"I wish I could stay here forever," Luna admitted.

"Me too," Sol agreed as he kissed her again.

After the late-night swim, they felt clean and tired. The moon was getting lower and they both knew the sun would be up soon, which meant their utopia must come to an end. Sol and Luna got dressed and sat by the dying fire. He held her in his arms, wishing this could be their life. He knew he could not go back to the way things were before meeting Luna. He wasn't sure how having her in his world would be possible, but he decided not to think about that right then. For the time being, he would enjoy their stolen moments together.

Luna felt herself relax in the warmth of his strong arms.

She wanted to stay there and not go back home. She loved her father and her aunt, but she decided in that moment, if she had to choose, this was where she would want to be. She felt herself slowly drift off.

He watched her sleeping in his arms, studying the shape of her face, wanting to kiss every part of it again. He stayed awake, enjoying just being close to her. When the time came, he gently woke her. "Luna…Luna, the sun will be up soon."

Every part of her body resisted the thought of waking up. Sol pulled her arm up gently, and she gave in. Luna stood, still half asleep, and wrapped her arms around him.

"I love you," he whispered in her ear.

The words jolted Luna awake as she felt a tingling, warm wave of love wash over her body. She looked in his eyes, saying it out loud for the first time. "I love you, too."

Sol and Luna walked side by side, holding each other's hand until they reached the edge of the river. They parted ways as the reds and yellows of the predawn sky began to make their appearance, sealing their goodbyes with a kiss that tasted sweet, like the unforgettable memories they had just made together.

Luna walked home, careful to climb back over the wall as to not draw suspicion from the guards at the wall. She reached her home as the fiery red horizon started to give way to a brilliant orange sunrise lined with purple hues at the edge. Luna made her way inside to her dark bedroom, removed her belt, and lay down, falling asleep quickly. She slept late, waking just before the midday meal, but still felt groggy. Luna made her way into the common room and searched for any sign that her father had been there. Thankfully, there was none. Her secret was safe. Luna washed her face and changed her clothes. As she went about her morning routine several hours later than usual, her mind replayed the events of the previous night. She missed Sol already.

The afternoon was hot and she was ready for another swim in the ocean, but she would have to settle for the river. Luna made her way through the village, past the wall, and along her usual route to the waterfall. She rode her horse this time since she was getting a late start, and she also brought the satchel she had left from her mother. When Luna arrived, she found Sol sleeping on a fur he'd laid on the bed of river stones. She snuck up quietly and fell next to him less than gracefully to give him a kiss. Sol's reflex kicked in as he was jolted awake. Before he realized what was going on, he found that Luna was now in front of him—or under him, as it were. He shook his head as she laughed.

"You're not so hard to sneak up on, you know that?" she asked jokingly.

"Someone kept me awake all night."

"Was it worth it?" she asked shamelessly.

"Absolutely," he replied before leaning down to meet

her lips with his.

Luna wrapped her arms around him, pulling him closer. Sol understood her invitation and let his hands explore. They gave in to their hunger and reached for the divine once again. After they made love by the river, they lay together breathlessly, their bodies sticky with sweat.

"How about a swim?" Sol asked.

"Okay."

Sol followed her lead, enjoying the view as she made her way into the pool by the falls. Once Sol and Luna were fully immersed in the water, they swam to the middle. The water was cold, perfect for the humid summer day.

"I have to gather some herbs tomorrow, but I could be here in the afternoon," Luna said.

"I have some projects I have been neglecting at home too. Tomorrow afternoon it is," Sol said before splashing Luna and swimming out of reach.

She swam after him, reaching the shore a little too late. He was just out of splashing distance.

"Just wait until I sneak up on you next time," she joked, feeling the kiss of the sun on her skin. A gentle breeze sent goose bumps all over her body as she reached for her clothes.

They got dressed and sat together on the large boulder where they talked while the hours passed.

"Let me see your satchel," Sol asked, and Luna handed him the leather bag without hesitation. Sol flipped it open and looked inside, his suspicions were confirmed.

"What is it?" Luna asked.

"My father made this satchel."

"What? You're joking," Luna said in disbelief as she took the bag from him to see the familiar mark of a sun. "You have the same mark as your father?"

"I adopted it."

"Oh. Sol, you should take it, as my gift," she offered.

"Absolutely not. I know how much this bag means to you." He pushed the satchel back to her.

Luna thought about it for a moment. "I think it is a fair trade—your father's leather satchel for your heart."

Sol looked back and caught her sly gaze.

Luna saw his confused look and continued, "After all, you gave me your heart that first day you met me in the woods. Remember, in the bowl the bear destroyed?"

Sol smiled as he erupted into laughter.

"I won't take no for an answer, and if you refuse my gift, well, it could be seen as a grave disrespect. You would not want to disrespect the Barden chief's daughter would you? That could incite war. So, you see, Sol, the very balance of peace and war—life and death, really—rests on your decision to accept this gift or not." Luna finished making her case.

Sol had not seen this side of her, and he liked it. He saw the assertion and fight that began to emerge from her like a flower slowly budding. Sol was enchanted as he happily admitted defeat. "Okay. I'll take it, for now."

It was Luna's turn to smile now as she emptied the satchel's contents into a linen bag she'd also had inside it before handing her most beloved possession over to the man she loved.

"I better head back. Dinner needs cooking," she said.

"I look forward to tomorrow," he replied.

Luna kissed him, and her body pleaded with her to stay. "Until tomorrow then." She forced herself to leave Sol at the river but did allow herself a quick glance back at his handsome face before entering the forest.

Once she was near her village, Luna gathered a handful of vegetables she needed for dinner. She dropped them at home and headed for one of the villagers who provided meat to pick out a piece of venison before going home to cook it and wait for her father's arrival. Gannon came in the door just as Luna had filled herself a bowl and sat down to enjoy it. She got back up and filled another bowl for him as he set down his tools. Luna didn't usually ask her father questions, mostly because her father wasn't much for answering them, but this night was different. Maybe it was the fact that she was still feeling bold from the passion that had filled her night and afternoon, or maybe it was the fact that she felt a spark of hope.

"Father?"

"Hmmm?" he grunted as he ate the venison stew.

"I was thinking about what you said. I was wondering

if you had ever considered a marriage between two tribes as an option? I mean, it could solve some of the issues between the Net tribe and our own."

Gannon stopped eating and stared at his daughter. A delighted look appeared across her father's usually serious and glum face. Luna remembered a time when his face used to look like this more often, before her mother died. She had wanted his features to return to those of happiness, but something about the glee in his eyes made her shift uncomfortably in her seat.

"I think you are finally starting to think like a grown woman—like a chief's daughter."

She is my daughter. The memory of the words he had spoken to her aunt came back to her. A flutter of hope filled her belly and she could not contain her smile. They finished their meal in silence. Luna could not wait to tell Sol about the encouraging conversation.

* * *

Sol had left shortly after Luna, collecting some fallen branches for lumber. He didn't know what he would use them for yet, but the way the wood twisted was beautiful to look at, and he knew he could create something with it. Sol made his way into the village, saying hello to his brothers, who were wrestling on a patch of green by the tree line of the woods to the north. Sol brought the branches to a bigger lean-to type of shed outside his mother's longhouse.

His mother heard the sound of the wood being dropped and peeked her head around the edge. "Sol, you are back." It was more of a statement than a question.

He walked over to where she sat mixing herbs at a small wooden table.

His mother looked him up and down, her eyes catching sight of the leather satchel across his shoulder. A look of recognition crossed her face. Sol's mother felt as though she had been hit by a rogue wave. At once, it all made sense to her.

CHAPTER 9

Luna spent the next morning collecting medicinal plants and fungi she needed for her salves, tinctures, and herbal medicines. She made her way to the waterfall to meet Sol with a smile on her face and an expectant flutter in her chest. When she reached it, he was not yet there, so Luna busied herself with the chaga mushroom on the birch tree before wading through the cool water and setting up her beadwork on the boulder. She stood on slippery river stones, leaning against the rock. She closed her eyes, feeling the cool water on her feet, and took in the sounds around her: the burble of the river, the rush of the waterfall, the wind moving through the trees causing them to creak and sway, and finally, the birds chirping on the sweeping branches above. This was the closest she felt to the land of the gods, but she still felt something was missing. She knew the homesick feeling that accompanied Sol's absence would immediately dissipate once he arrived to meet her.

* * *

Sol woke up that morning, enjoying the sound of the seabirds feasting on shellfish and crustaceans. The air was misty, so he couldn't see the sunrise. He stood up and walked the length of the beach to where the low tide waves met the brown sand with a kiss. He rinsed his body in the cool sea water before walking the coastline, not completely sure what he was searching for. He walked, smelling the saltiness of the seaweed and brine until a small purple shell caught his eye. Sol picked it up, inspecting his treasure, and saw the small hole near the bottom. *It's perfect*, he thought to himself, now sure of his plan for it. Sol went back to his lean-to and dressed for the day in a bright blue tunic and black knee-length shorts. Sol searched for his tools and remembered he'd left them at his mother's by the wood he had collected in the forest on his way back from meeting Luna. He also remembered that his mother had seemed more quiet than usual. Sol pushed the thought out of his mind as he bounded through the forest toward her house.

He arrived to see her heating soup over the fire. He could tell by the aroma that it contained fish of some sort. He walked up next to his mother and looked inside the large pot. He licked his lips and wrapped his arm around her as he said, "Mmmm, it smells delicious, Mama."

To his surprise, she set down the spoon down she had been stirring the soup with and turned to give him a full hug. She squeezed him tight and then released him to look into his eyes, not letting him go.

"What is it? Is something wrong?" he asked with a look of concern crossing his handsome features.

"Have you found the answers to the questions that plagued you before?"

Sol searched for the memory of their previous conversation before answering, "I think so…not completely, but many of them."

Sol's mother released him and turned her attention back to the pot of soup. She used the wooden ladle to pour two large scoops into a bowl for him. She made sure to scoop him some of the crab bits and fish eyes, as she knew they were his favorite.

His reply didn't seem to give her full relief, but she didn't look quite as concerned as before either.

"Are you worried, Mama?" he probed.

"All mothers worry about their children. When you become a mother, you become a worrier."

Sol wasn't sure what to say. He wanted to tell her about Luna, but he feared his mother's reaction. If she told him to stop seeing Luna, Sol would have to choose between the woman who raised him and the woman who had his heart. He loved both women differently but fiercely; of that he was certain.

"I am going with Bomani today. We are going to work on building a home by the sea for me."

"It's about time," she said, nodding her head.

"What do you mean?" Sol asked incredulously.

"My son, your veins are filled with sea water. It has been that way ever since you were a little boy. You need a better place to stay, somewhere you can start a family and not freeze in the cold season," she answered, her mood seeming a bit lighter.

"I say I am building myself a lodge and you jump to me starting a family." Sol laughed.

"A mother knows, my son. We worry and we know."

Sol finished his breakfast as his brothers woke to join him and his mother. Bomani and Akiiki came shortly after, and Sol made plans with his brother-in-law for the large task they were starting. Sol had been gathering large pieces of lumber and unique branches for the past couple years, not knowing what they were for exactly but feeling confident he would be able to put them to use somehow. The idea had come to him when he ate dinner with his family the previous night. He would build himself a cabin by the sea. He would build it high off the ground for when the storms came and the waters rose. He'd used the charcoal from the fire to draw his idea on a piece of leather to show Bomani. The idea was different than any of their buildings, but Sol knew it would work. Bomani laughed at his plan but agreed to help.

Sol grabbed his tools and the branches he had left at his mother's longhouse the night before then headed back to the beach. Bomani followed behind with his wife at his side. The two men worked the morning away into the afternoon, making conversation with Akiiki, who sat watching them.

"My brother, you seem different," she stated.

"I am still me, Akiiki," he answered as he paused, out of breath from splitting the long tree he had felled.

"I mean, you seem happier," Akiiki clarified.

"I am happier," he admitted.

The rest of the morning passed quickly as they worked to gather all the pieces needed to build the foundation of the beach cabin. At midday, they stopped to eat and then parted ways. As Sol made his way through the village, he caught sight of Layla. She smiled at him, and he nodded to her as he set off into the forest to meet Luna.

* * *

Luna didn't have to wait long for Sol. She heard a rustle of leaves parting and turned to see him making his way toward her.

"Were you trying to scare me?" she asked with a smile.

"No." He shook his head, but the white toothy grin betrayed his intentions. Sol walked up to Luna and pulled her in for a hug before releasing her enough to kiss her.

"I have to tell you something," she said excitedly.

"What is it?" he asked, curious.

"I had an idea. I want to be with you and not have to worry about someone finding us. I want to be able to show everyone that your people are not what we have been led to believe. I want to be with you, Sol."

"I want to be with you too, Luna, but I don't see how that can happen without destroying our families and inciting a war," Sol responded.

"That's where my idea might work. I talked to my father last night—"

"You told him about us?"

"No." Sol seemed relieved with Luna's answer, so she continued, "I asked him about a marriage to resolve the issues with your tribe."

"What did he say?" Sol asked cautiously.

"He seemed very happy with the idea. I was surprised, but he seemed elated about the concept." Luna looked at Sol as she waited to hear what he thought about her idea, which was essentially her proposal of being hand-fasted together.

Sol thought long and hard about Luna's words. He knew he wanted Luna to be a part of his world. In the short time he had known her, he felt much closer to her than anyone else he had ever known. He loved her, and he couldn't imagine his life without her anymore.

"I can speak to my mother and see what she thinks," he answered.

Luna's grin widened into the biggest smile he had seen since she had seen the ocean for the first time. With that thought, Sol remembered what he'd brought for her.

Luna watched Sol pull something small and purple out

of his pocket. There was a string tied through a small hole on one end.

"I found this today on the beach. I figured if I couldn't bring you to the ocean, I could bring the ocean to you." He held up the necklace so she could see it.

Luna touched the brightly colored shell, admiring it. "It's beautiful. I'll never take it off. It will remind me of you," she said as he tied it around her neck.

They kissed, sealing their agreement before enjoying each other again by the river. Sol and Luna passed the afternoon together, delighting in each other's company and conversation. He told her about his plans for the house on the beach, and she imagined herself happily living by the ocean. They agreed that Sol would try to talk to his mother before they met again the following afternoon. Luna and Sol parted with a kiss before returning to their respective tribes.

Luna stopped to gather vegetables from the garden, some for her dinner and extra to trade for rabbit. She collected the rabbit and cooked her father dinner. She anxiously awaited nightfall because sleep helped time pass faster. She wanted the next day to come so she could hear of Sol's conversation with his mother. Finally, the time came for her to sleep, and she let it claim her.

* * *

Sol made his way home, seeking out his mother when

he arrived in the village. When he reached her longhouse, he saw she was talking with another tribeswoman in the distance. Sol waited by the fire pit until she was done. Sol's mother saw him and waved before she walked toward him.

"How is your house coming along?" she asked.

"Good. We are just making the pieces we need for the foundation today, but we got a lot done this morning."

"That is good news."

"Mama, I wondered if I could ask you something." Sol patted the empty seat next to him.

"Of course." She accepted his invitation and sat by her son.

Sol wasn't sure where to start. "I was thinking about what you said, about why the Barden hate us. I wondered if you thought a joining of sorts between the two tribes would work to bring peace." Sol looked at his mother as he waited patiently for her response.

She sat quietly thinking for a long time. "What do you mean by a joining?" she asked for clarification.

A jolt of panic filled Sol as he considered how best to answer. "I mean, I don't know, like an agreement of peace…for a marriage." Sol studied his mother's reaction to the mention of marriage.

She seemed unfazed and responded, "I suppose a marriage would be a good way to join the tribes, but I don't think their chief would agree. His hate runs deep."

"So, you would be open to the idea as long as the Barden chief agreed?" Sol asked, trying to clarify.

"If it was what the people of the tribe wanted, then yes. It would have to be done with the Barden chief's blessing though. Otherwise, it would be a declaration of war instead of a hand-fasting ceremony," his mother answered, her warning clear.

Yes, the people would very much want this, Sol thought to himself with excitement at the possibility.

"Which two people do you have in mind?" his mother asked.

"Oh, no one in particular. I just wanted to know if it was even possible and if you would support an idea like that." Sol felt a tinge of guilt about partially lying. He had never lied to his mother. Even when she'd asked how her husband had been killed, he had admitted his fault.

"I'll help you cook dinner," he offered.

Sol ate dinner with his family and said his good nights. He went back to his lean-to and thought about his plans for the house, his mother's words about having a place to start a family, and her agreement to a marriage between the tribes. He let himself dare to hope as he watched the tide come in. He fell asleep in his lean-to replaying every detail of the night Luna had met him at the ocean.

* * *

Luna awoke before the sun in her anxious excitement for the day. She visited the river for water and the edge of the woods for herbs as she usually did to pass the time then enjoyed her tea with her father. She wanted to ask him what the next steps would be to forge the joining of tribes but restrained herself. He seemed in a better mood since their conversation two nights before, and that was something she had going for her. After she finished her tea, she packed her things and headed to her aunt's house.

"Do you need help today, Alice?" Luna asked as her aunt came into view.

Alice was sitting outside her house, enjoying her tea as she boiled herbs in a pot. "I can always use extra hands," Alice said before taking the last sip of her tea.

Luna helped her aunt process some of the fresh herbs and plants that were piled on the kitchen table, separating them into bundles and tying them to hang so they would dry properly. Luna spent the morning with her aunt. She had learned almost everything she knew about herbal medicine from her, with the exception of what she remembered from her mother.

"You know almost as much as me, child. I think you may surpass me soon," Alice told her.

"I don't know about that, Alice. The plants don't seem to speak to me as they do you."

"Well, I've got to have something going for me. You got the looks."

Luna laughed. "I suppose you have to tell yourself that."

"I didn't notice your necklace before—is that a shell? I

have never seen one that color," Alice asked as she reached out to touch it.

Luna blushed and panicked momentarily, not knowing how to respond without betraying herself. She said nothing.

"I was going to go into Dabney tribe lands to trade some of my elderberry elixir. Would you like to join me?" Alice asked.

Luna looked down at the food she was preparing for the midday meal while she answered, "No, I think I will go into the forest and see what adventure the gods have in store for me today."

A look of confusion crossed Alice's face. "Okay. Have you been in the south woods lately? I saw a whole patch of raspberries growing there and they are the biggest ones I have seen in many years."

"No, not lately. I will have to check them out tomorrow," Luna answered, feeling discomfort at the question.

She finished her lunch and said her goodbye as she made her way home to drop off some of the items Alice had given her. She retrieved her bow and other supplies she needed for the afternoon.

Luna made her way through the forest to where the air smelled like wet earth, and she heard the rush of the waterfall. Sol was waiting for her on the boulder where she usually sat, facing her direction so there would be no chance of surprising him. He saw her and smiled before walking in the stream of neutral ground to meet her.

Luna smiled back and greeted him with a soft passionate kiss and a tight embrace. She had been waiting in anticipation all day, and she could not bear one more second. "What did she say?"

Sol laughed before answering, "She agreed."

Luna's mouth fell open as her stomach seized with flutters of excitement. "What do you mean? What did you ask her?"

"I asked her if she would approve of a marriage to join the two tribes, and she agreed as long as the people involved wanted to and the chief of the Barden approved. She was doubtful he would, which is why she made it clear that he had to be in agreement. Otherwise, it would start a war." Sol was serious with his reply, but he recapped his conversation with his mother with a smile on his face.

"So, what's next?" Luna asked.

"Now, we wait a bit. Let's give your father some time to think."

"Okay," Luna agreed, looking in Sol's eyes.

"Okay." He smiled before picking her up in a bear hug and spinning her around while they both laughed.

They were hopeful, and that was enough.

Sol and Luna spent the days of the next month filling their time apart with their duties and anticipation. They spent their afternoons hurrying to the waterfall to meet each other, stealing their secret and forbidden moments. The weather had started to turn cooler as the crisp smell of autumn's approach became apparent. The leaves had begun to turn, some vibrant red, some yellow and deep orange. Some of the trees were so bright, they looked as if they were going up in flames. The days grew shorter, and it started to get darker much earlier than the month before. Luna had also noticed other changes that started as the season approached.

Luna met her father for tea, and Gannon said, "I'm going to the Dabney lands for trading later to make preparations for the harvest feast. Do you want to join me?"

Luna was surprised at the broken silence, as well as the invitation. "I wanted to get a few things done this afternoon. Can I go next time?"

Gannon looked a little confused. "I have thought about your request of a marriage between the tribes, and I am making some preparations."

Luna nearly choked on her tea. "What is the next step?" she asked, trying to hide her true excitement.

"I will need to make the final arrangements and speak to the boy."

"Oh, I see," Luna said, wondering how she would arrange such a meeting.

"Where are you going this afternoon?" he asked suspiciously.

"To the—"

"North forest," he interrupted, finishing her sentence.

"Yes," she admitted, not sure if she should tell him

the truth. She figured if he was arranging her marriage plans, he would have some idea that she had been meeting someone. How else would he know there was a specific man he needed to speak to? Her father stood up and entered the house, signaling the end of the conversation.

Luna made her way to her aunt's house with a bowl full of fruit she'd picked from the wild apple trees they had found and cultivated. Some of the fruit on the trees were just beginning to ripen enough to be eaten.

"I bring gifts from the goddess Ceres," Luna said as she placed the bowl at her aunt's feet.

"Oh, I do love these kinds of gifts," Alice admitted as she stopped the basket weaving she was doing and picked an apple to consume.

Luna helped Alice pour tinctures and make salves until midday.

"After the meal, I was going to work in the gardens, harvesting," Alice stated, implicitly inviting her niece to join her.

"Oh, I have some things I need to finish for myself this afternoon." Luna drank the warm vegetable- and chicken-filled broth as quickly as she could.

"All right," Alice said as she stood up and gathered her basket, a shovel, and a sharp knife. She walked Luna to her home before heading to the gardens to begin her work.

Luna gathered her bow and a few linen bags before heading out of the village toward the waterfall. Alice watched her niece with increasing curiosity from one of the giant gardens as Luna headed north, disappearing into the forest.

After Luna arrived at the waterfall, she crossed the now icy water in the brisk air. It sent a chill down to her core. Luna reached the boulder where she and Sol had spent the last month sitting together with their arms wrapped around each other. There, they had discussed their plans for the hand-fasting ceremony, as well as their life together. It had been a wonderful and hopeful month.

As Luna replayed the conversation with her father in her head, a familiar feeling of anxiety and excitement rose in her chest for several reasons. There was so much to tell Sol. She wanted him to help her make sense of what her father had said to her as well as getting his opinion on another matter that seemed entirely more important than she would have thought in that moment. She now waited with uncertainty on the boulder, yearning for Sol's warm embrace to chase the chill from her body.

Suddenly, Luna felt an electric presence behind her. Before she could turn to see who was there to greet her, she felt two strong hands roughly clasp her neck from behind and squeeze viciously.

CHAPTER 10

Luna jolted upright, trying to pull away from whomever was behind her. She turned as she thrust forward, and her attacker lost her grip but dug her fingernails into her neck, drawing blood. Luna saw a woman. She was stunning and beautiful, even with her face in an angry snarl. She wore a bright blue wrap with chunky turquoise jewelry. Her arms were adorned with bracelets, and her hand now held a knife she had concealed on her thigh.

Luna backed away in the cold river, trying to retreat back to her land as she said, "I don't want to fight you."

"It's too late for that, whore!" she cried out as she charged forward, knife raised.

Luna put her arm up to block the woman's swipe. "I wasn't on your land!" she screamed before the woman struck her mouth with her fist.

"This isn't about my land! You Barden people are always taking what isn't yours. You crossed the wrong Net woman this time!"

The woman lunged at Luna. Luna grabbed for the hand

that held the knife and slammed it into the nearby boulder with her own weight. Both women were knee deep in the river, struggling. Luna repeatedly slammed the attacking woman's hand against the rock, managing to loosen her grip enough for the knife to fall and sink into the river.

Luna's hand found it quickly and she threw it across the river, out of reach. As she did so, the wild, angry woman exploited the weakness and swung at Luna's face again, this time striking her square in the jaw. Luna yelped and stumbled back to the river's edge. The woman jumped on top of her, seizing her opportunity, and began to choke Luna once again. Luna reached for the woman, swinging her fists, but the attacker's face was out of reach. Luna clobbered her fists into the woman's arms. When that didn't work, Luna tried to pry her hands free from her neck, digging her fingernails in as deep as she could. Luna tried to kick and squeeze her legs, but her attacker was relentless.

Up until that point, Luna had thought she would be able to reason with the woman. As she stared into the hate-filled eyes above her and the wicked smile that twisted in horrid delight, she realized she had misjudged her attacker. Luna remembered the knife that was tied in her leather belt, but it was behind her, and she couldn't reach it while she was pinned on her back. Dark spots started to cloud Luna's vision. Her arms dropped to the riverbed in defeat as her lungs burned for air.

* * *

Sol made his way to the waterfall. He was excited to tell Luna about the progress he had made on the house. He wondered if she could sneak away and risk meeting him again so he could show her. A strong crooked branch caught his eye on the forest floor. He slipped down from his horse to inspect it and thought it must have fallen in the last storm. Sol decided it would prove useful so he would tie the branch to his horse. As he picked up the tree limb, he noticed a fresh set of footprints next to it that hadn't been visible before. As far as he knew, he was the only one who ventured this far into the north woods. He inspected them closer, and a jolt of panic shot through his body when he realized the footprints were leading straight to the waterfall. Sol dropped the branch and mounted his horse, kicking his heels into the animal, urging him to run.

Sol got as far as he could on horseback, and when he was close enough he pulled the reins to slow the horse just enough so he could jump off. He stumbled as he landed but regained his balance and ran for the waterfall just in time to see a familiar figure hunched over Luna's body.

"STOP! STOOOOOP!" Sol yelled with his palm open, signaling the words he spoke as he ran as fast as he could toward the women.

* * *

"You will die here alone! And when Sol comes to find us, I will tell him you attacked me!" the woman spat out, leaning closer to Luna's ear so she was sure to hear.

The words were muffled by the sound of Luna's heartbeat thudding in her ears. Luna thought of Sol. She thought of their beautiful moments together. She wondered how his tribe would be punished once her father found her dead body. Then she thought of her mother. The darkness that filled her vision shifted to an image of Terra in a field of lavender. She wanted to be with her mother in that moment. She wanted to run toward her and join her in the afterlife.

"Little bear…little bear! It is not your time. Fight, my daughter. It is not just yourself you are fighting for! Fight, my warrior!" Her mother's words sent a warm shockwave through her body.

Luna's hand gripped a large river rock and she swung at the woman's head with all her might. Luna heard a sharp thud and a crack. The woman's grip immediately loosened, and Luna shoved her off. She gasped for air, rolling onto all fours. It hurt to breathe. Luna's whole body ached.

An arm grabbed Luna. She turned and swung instinctively, punching Sol in the face. He yelped from the smack and staggered backward from the force. He covered the sore spot with one hand and held the other out.

"It's me, Luna! It's Sol! You're safe!" Once he saw that Luna recognized him, he approached her with his arms open, offering comfort.

Luna gave herself to his warm embrace. Her lungs were still burning with fire, and her body dripped from the icy river water and cool breeze, sending goose bumps all over her as she shivered and shook.

Sol squeezed her tighter to his body, trying to warm her. He looked her over and saw that her skin was torn around her neck, her arms, and her face. Luna's lip was bloody, her eye swollen. He glanced over at the woman who had attacked her, now lying at the river's edge with blood coming from the side of her head. He recognized her immediately. *Layla.*

Sol wanted to know what had transpired, what had led to the fight. "What happened, Luna?"

Luna's heavy breathing had slowed to normal but painful breaths. "I was waiting for you, and the coward grabbed me from behind. I told her I didn't want to fight." Luna's breathing quickened again as her body started to shake, not from the cold but from the shock of it all.

Sol pulled her closer. "Shhh. It's all right. It will be okay. Are you hurt badly anywhere?"

Luna pulled away enough to look at him. "I will be fine. Is she dead?"

Sol let go of Luna and walked over to Layla. "No. She's still breathing, but she needs the healers or she might die soon. I have to get her back."

"Do you know her?" Luna asked.

He nodded his head before answering, "Layla."

"Why would she attack me? I thought you said your people were peaceful?!" Luna felt herself starting to unravel.

"She wanted me, and I refused her. She probably blames you. I can't believe she would risk so much," he answered honestly.

Luna struggled to remember the details. "She said my people were always taking what isn't theirs." Luna's anger rose as she recalled the woman's words.

"Luna, I want to stay here with you and make sure you are okay, but I also need to get her help," Sol explained, feeling torn.

Luna looked into the eyes of the man she loved and nodded her agreement.

Sol kissed her forehead then walked back over to the woman. He picked up Layla's limp body and carried her across the river, disappearing into the forest.

Luna waited a few minutes to see if he would return, but he didn't. She felt so many emotions all at once—anger, sadness, jealousy, fear, and so many questions. Then Luna remembered the clear picture of her mother in the moments before she thought she would be taken by the gods.

Terra's words rang clear in her mind: *Little bear…little bear! It is not your time. Fight, my daughter. It is not just yourself you are fighting for. Fight, my warrior!* Luna knew what her mother's words meant.

Luna took a drink of water from the cold river. It burned her throat and hurt to swallow, but the icy water also brought her some relief. Suddenly, Luna felt her stomach drop. She hunched over and vomited into the river. She wiped her bloody lip with one hand before scooping up some clean water to wash out her mouth. The feeling passed, and she painstakingly stood up. She had to get home, but she had no idea how she would explain her blood and bruises to her father. She had to think of something or he would march on the Nets that very night for revenge.

Suddenly Layla's threat came rushing back to Luna. Layla had said she would kill her and she would tell Sol Luna attacked her. *I should have killed Layla*, she thought to herself as she made her way south through the forest. She quickly regretted the thought, though. An unfamiliar emotion had driven the notion, and she wasn't sure why she felt a stab of jealousy. Luna wished she had remembered this fact when Sol had asked her what had happened. Why would that woman attack her, risking the tentative peace agreement between the tribes? All because of Sol? How had Layla known Luna knew Sol? Sol had described his people as so loving and kind, not violent and antagonistic. Luna wondered how Sol's tribe would react. She wondered how he would explain it to his mother, especially if Layla woke up and told the lie she'd planned.

Luna reached the forest's edge, still having no clear idea how to explain her situation. She knew Alice would be her best chance, but she also knew Alice's loyalties lay with Gannon. Luna tore off a piece of her tunic large enough to wrap around her head and hide her face. Instead of walking through the gates, she would climb the wall near her aunt's house. Luna was hurrying out of the woods toward the gardens when a voice from her far left caught her attention.

"Luna!"

Luna turned quickly to see her aunt standing nearby with a basket full of raspberry leaves. Luna walked over to Alice, careful to keep her head lowered.

"My child, what's wrong?" Alice asked worriedly.

"Alice…I need your help." Luna unwrapped the torn cloak from her face, and her aunt gasped.

"Luna, what happened to you? *Who did this?*"

"Alice, I have never asked you for anything in my life. I need your help now. I need you to hide me for a few days. I don't want my father seeing me like this."

"Days? Luna, have you seen yourself? This will not be gone in just days. What happened, and who are you protecting? Why are you always going into the north woods? What is going on? Tell me the truth. I deserve that much if I am going to go behind my brother's back and hide you for a few days."

"I just don't want him to see me right now. I need some time and some herbs to take the swelling and bruising down. I was attacked. I have been meeting someone, and he was late. A woman came and surprised me. That is the truth. I just don't want a war to start because of me."

Alice nodded as she listened to Luna. She saw there was truth in her niece's words, and she wanted to keep the peace as well. "Okay. Come to my house. I will tell your father you are not feeling well and will be with me for a few days. He can fend for himself for that long."

"Oh, thank you Alice!" Luna sighed in excited relief.

"After those three days, you will have to tell your father," Alice warned.

"I will," Luna agreed.

Alice followed Luna to the wall and helped her climb over then took her into her house. She helped Luna change into clean, dry clothes. Alice made her some tea before applying arnica to Luna's bruised muscles and healing salves to her open wounds. Alice worked in silence, and Luna was thankful for it. Luna just wanted to rest, and she fell into an exhausted sleep upon Alice's bed.

Luna awoke the next morning later than usual, and she couldn't believe she had slept so much. She sat up in her aunt's bed with every muscle aching. The house was quiet, but she saw her aunt sitting at the table in her common room.

Luna spoke in a hoarse voice. "Good morning." Her jaw ached from the movement, and her throat burned.

"A fine morning it was—it's nearly midday," Alice answered as she picked up the pot and poured Luna a steaming cup of tea in a clay mug.

"Did you speak to my father?" Luna asked worriedly.

"Yes." Alice paused before going on, taking in the swollen eye and purple and red splotches in the shape of handprints on her niece's neck. Luna looked much worse than she had the day before. "I told him you were not feeling well and needed to stay with me but would be back in a couple days. I think he plans on going to stay with Bale until then. If it is a Dabney woman who attacked you, you should tell him that, Luna. Is his life in danger?"

"No, he is safe. It wasn't a Dabney who attacked me," Luna admitted, her throat feeling a little better from the tea.

Alice's eyebrows rose and her eyes widened. "A Net woman attacked you? Are you sure?"

"Yes, I'm sure."

"Why?"

"I was on their side of the river," she lied.

"Why would you do that? You know better!" Alice scolded.

Luna looked at the floor.

"Luna, there is something you are not telling me."

"Aunt Alice, you told me if I was ever to find a love that was real and raw, I should hold on to it with everything I had. That is what I have done."

Alice stood and walked over to the fire. Luna wasn't sure if she was angry with her or not.

"You're right, I did say that. Your father is not going to take this well," she warned.

"I asked him about a marriage, to make peace between

the Nets and us. I asked him what he thought about that and he liked the idea. I was surprised too, but——"

Alice shook her head almost violently. "Luna, you have no idea what you have done. Your father…that is not what he heard from your conversation. Do not tell him about the Net man."

Luna was surprised at her harsh words and even more shocked that her aunt was telling her not to be completely honest with Gannon. "What do you mean?"

"It will destroy him. We will figure something out, but you need to forget this man. Forget for his own good. If you tell your father, he will slaughter this man and his tribe." Alice walked over and firmly grabbed Luna by her shoulders as she looked into her confused eyes. "You must never see that man again, for his own good, for the love you have for him. If it is real, you will be willing to do this *to save his life*."

Luna shook her head in disbelief.

Alice rattled her shoulders and Luna winced in pain. "Luna, think about what I said. Wait a couple days and then go back to tell him goodbye. That is something I wish I'd had the chance to do." With her final words of advice, Alice let go of Luna's shoulders and left her house.

Luna crumpled in a defeated pile on the floor. The tears came, washing over her face. Her tears became sobs, and it was suddenly harder to breathe. Luna felt an invisible weight on her chest as she struggled to inhale and exhale.

Panicking, she drew too many breaths too quickly. The room darkened and Luna blacked out.

When Luna awoke, she was still on the floor by the fire. She guessed she hadn't been there for too long and decided to retreat to the bedroom. She had to see Sol. She wanted to know how they would solve this problem, if he would run away with her. She wanted to ask him how it had gone with Layla and his tribe. She wanted to know if the woman was in fact dead. The thought brought mixed feelings to Luna. She grabbed her belt with the knife and tied it back on. Luna grabbed a head covering before opening her aunt's door to go to the waterfall.

"Where do you think you are going?" It was Alice.

"I…I am going to say goodbye," Luna answered, surprised by her aunt's appearance.

"Not today you aren't," Alice said. "You need another day to recover, at the very least. If you are attacked again, you need to be able to defend yourself and see out of that eye. Those woods could be crawling with Nets," Alice whispered.

Luna nodded and turned back into the house, closing the door behind her. Everything was a complete mess, and it was all her fault. Was this the price she must pay for her wrongdoings as a child? She had known all along that she was unworthy of Sol's love, and now everything was falling apart as she had feared it would the whole time. She hoped not; she didn't want to believe it. Maybe that was selfish of her, not to take the universe's punishment, but something small inside her rebelled at the thought. Luna made her way over to the tea and poured herself another cup.

Luna passed the day slowly, trying to sleep. Her aunt came in twice to help her reapply the salves to her wounds, and she heated up a rabbit soup for dinner. Luna drank the delicious broth, and her body welcomed the warmth. She had felt a chill in her bones since that afternoon at the waterfall. Luna fell asleep and slept fitfully through the night. Her dreams were plagued with nightmares. Sol was walking away from her in one dream, and he was killed by her father in another. She searched for her mother in the dreams but didn't find her. Instead, there was a bear in her last dream, the one from the waterfall. This time, Luna walked over and faced the bear. The bear watched Luna and then nudged the unbroken bowl Sol had made. Luna picked it up and saw that it was the newer bowl Sol had made for her with the image of the bear.

Luna woke with a start. She rubbed her eyes and stretched her muscles, which still ached, though they hurt a bit less than the day before. She pushed the dreams out of her mind as she changed into a burnt yellow tunic her aunt had retrieved for her. Luna got ready and met her aunt at the table for tea.

Alice looked up at Luna as she walked into the dim room. Her eye was less swollen than the day before, and her bruises had improved some. There were dark brown scabs around her neck, across her arms, and in the split of her lip. "Take that with you." Alice motioned to the spear against the wall, as well as Luna's own bow and quiver. Alice saw her niece's questioning glance and answered, "I see you must have had a meeting with a bear."

"He saved me," Luna explained.

Alice nodded her head in understanding. "Take these with you, just in case. Say your goodbye, and come home safely. You can wait until tomorrow to speak with your father." Luna nodded and collected the weapons as Alice stood to pull a linen wrap around her shoulders. "It's cold out today. Drink some tea before you leave."

Luna did as her aunt instructed and drank the warm herbs. Although Alice had added honey, the tea tasted bitter. Luna drank it and opened the door to leave.

"Thank you for everything you have done, Alice." She wondered if it would be the last time she spoke to her aunt.

"You're welcome, my child."

Luna climbed over the wall after saying her goodbye and made her way to the north woods. Luna carefully weighed her options. Would she have to run away? Was she really going to leave the man she loved? Alice's words rang in Luna's mind, the warning to save his life. Her stomach twisted in knots, and she felt it drop then seize again. She stopped by the edge of the giant cornfield, clutching her stomach. She vomited on the ground by the garden. Her nerves were so tied up, she didn't know which way was which. She just needed to get to the waterfall, just needed to be in Sol's arms again then everything would be okay.

"Luna!" An angry voice boomed behind her, and she turned to see her father's face shift from a look of questioning to one of horror, and then it became red with rage as he demanded, "What happened to you?!"

CHAPTER 11

Sol had left Luna soaking wet and bloodied as he found his horse and laid Layla atop it. He tied her so she would not fall off as he led the mare down through the forest to his tribe. He wanted to stay with Luna, but he knew he had a duty to his people as well. Luna was okay; she had said it herself. Luna had said Layla surprised her and attacked first. He believed Luna but wondered why Layla would do this. Over him? The thought seemed incredulous. Was Layla more calculating than he realized? Sol had known Layla ever since he was a child. He wanted her to explain to him why she would attack Luna.

Sol couldn't get Luna's bloodied and broken image out of his mind. Suddenly, he panicked. What would Luna tell her father? Would his tribe be in danger of an attack? He should tell his mother, if only to have her prepared for an invasion of retaliation. Sol wondered how he was going to explain this to his tribe, and to his mother. How could he have been so stupid? How could he tell her this was all his fault? How could he face her again, explain he had broken the agreement and put all of their lives in danger? Hadn't he learned *anything* from his father's death? Sol continued to berate himself.

Sol led the horse until he reached the edge of the tree line. He saw that there were several tribe members around and took a deep breath before leading the horse through them. He felt their eyes upon him. Some of the people gasped and approached.

"Who is that?" asked one.

"Layla!" answered another.

"What happened? Who did this?" asked many others.

"Get my mother, and get the healers," Sol commanded, and two of the men ran off.

Sol led the horse to the healing tent just as Bomani came rushing up to him.

"Sol!"

"Help me bring her in," Sol demanded.

Bomani helped to untie the ropes and carefully carried Layla into the dimly lit tent. There were healers there waiting for them. Sol backed up and watched them get to work on her immediately. They checked her breathing and her wounds. First, they washed the blood from her head and saw that the cuts from the rock were not deep, but it was swollen and bruised. They applied some herb pastes another healer had just ground up, and another got to work cleaning the wound.

Just then, Sol's mother burst into the tent. "What happened? They said you found a tribeswoman beaten."

His mother saw it was Layla, and a look of realization crossed over her face.

"I only saw the end of it," Sol answered truthfully. "Mama, can I speak to you alone?"

"Yes, my son. Let's go home." She left the tent, and he followed obediently.

When they reached her longhouse, he saw his brothers Ata and Atsu sitting by the fire with questioning looks. Sol's mother walked into the home and Sol followed. His brothers knew their mother's face meant business and they should stay outside.

"My son," his mother said firmly, breaking the silence. "I let you keep your life and your choices to yourself, but now this is affecting others. Now, you must tell me everything. Tell me, why her?"

"I honestly don't know why Layla went up there."

"No. Why would you choose the Barden chief's daughter?"

Sol was absolutely shocked at his mother's words. How did she know? He was speechless.

"Sol, you know the risks, and still you chose this woman?"

"Mama…" His voice faded as he searched for the right words. "It just happened."

"Things like this do not just happen. Tell me from the beginning."

"How did you know?" he asked.

"Never mind that right now. Just tell me," she answered.

"I was hunting and the deer ran to her side of the river before collapsing. I happened upon her as she cut its throat. She dragged the deer to our side of the river but stayed in the water. I gave her the heart in gratitude."

His mother nodded as she followed along without interruption. Sol continued, recapping the last couple of months to her, making sure to omit bringing Luna onto their land to see the ocean and the fact that they had been physically intimate on several occasions.

His mother took a few moments before responding, "Do you truly care for this woman? Do you truly love her? Is she your soul match?"

"I believe so," he answered truthfully.

"The answer is far from simple now, my son. A woman is badly beaten and unconscious in the healer's tent. I am assuming this woman is also in similar shape, which means her father will see her and take this as an opportunity to retaliate. I have to notify the tribe to be on alert, and I must post warriors to look out for any sign of the Barden. In the meantime, we will wait for Layla to wake before convening a tribal meeting. She has to tell us her side of things." After explaining, she walked out of the longhouse, leaving Sol alone in the dimness.

The full weight of the consequences of his decisions now fell heavily on Sol's shoulders as he dropped to kneel on the ground. He lifted his hands to his face as he took several deep breaths.

"What have I done?" he groaned aloud.

Just then Akiiki walked in and found her brother on the ground.

"Brother, what has happened? They said Layla was in a fight. Was it the Barden?" she asked, putting her hand on his shoulder for comfort. When Sol didn't answer, his sister pressed, "Sol, something is going on with you. I am always here to listen. You shouldn't carry all of this on your shoulders alone."

Sol looked up at her. "Yes I should. It is all my fault, and I am the one who should be suffering—not Layla, not our tribe, *me. I* broke the laws again! I should not be trusted! I have caused so much damage! I am not worthy of love!" He pounded his chest with clenched fists.

Akiiki knelt down beside her brother so they were eye level. "My brother, you have always been hard on yourself. This can't be all your fault. Did you beat Layla?"

"I might as well have. I think she followed my path," he answered, speaking cryptically.

"What is wrong with her following your path?" Akiiki asked in disbelief.

"I went to meet someone in the woods, near the waterfall. Layla got there before me yesterday." Sol looked down at his feet.

Akiiki looked confused as she glanced from side to side, replaying his words. "Is this person why you have seemed happier these past months?"

"Yes."

"Sol, I trust you, and I've seen the positive change in you since you met this person. I also know Layla. I know she has wanted you as a husband for a very long time, at least since Bomani was joined with me," Akiiki explained, looking at Sol's grave face.

"What is that supposed to mean?" he asked.

"It means whoever this person is, they were able to help you come out of the shell you have been in ever since Daddy died. It means I know Layla can be a jealous person. This person you were meeting could be who Layla took her frustrations out on," she answered.

"I just don't understand *why*. That doesn't make sense to me. I have made no positive responses to her advances. I made it clear that I wasn't interested."

"Did you make it clear? Did you tell her directly that you were not interested in her in that way?"

"Yes, I mean…I think so…I guess not that directly," Sol answered as so many new questions swirled in his head.

"We just need her to wake up and give us answers," Akiiki said.

"If she doesn't wake up, we could have a bigger problem on our hands."

Akiiki patted his shoulder and stood up carefully with her growing belly. She asked, "What's her name?"

Sol looked up at Akiiki before answering, "Luna."

Akiiki turned and left the longhouse after nodding her head.

Sol wrestled with the thought of what to do before finally deciding to wait outside the healing tent for Layla to wake. He thought it would be better to keep his hands busy so he grabbed a few tools and a chunk of maple before heading to the tent. Once he arrived, he saw there was already a small crowd outside. They didn't bother asking him any questions, the look on his face was serious and uninviting. The small crowd started to disperse throughout the hour as they all had things that needed to be done. Layla's mother was inside the tent, chanting her prayers to the gods and goddesses. Sol waited until the sun started to set and fires began being lit. He could smell the fragrance of several dinners being cooked, but he was not hungry. He started a fire outside the healing tent so he could work by the light. He was carving the wood into an animal shape.

Healers came in and out of the tent to exchange places with other healers, making sure they met their families' needs and their own needs for rest. Sol's mother came several times to check on Layla but didn't say another word to Sol. She had placed warriors by the river to take turns watching out for any sign of the Barden. Sol felt like this disruption of normalcy and of their safety was all his fault. In that moment he thought of Luna. How was *she?* Was *she* safe? He wished he could go check on her but knew without a doubt that was impossible.

Sol woke with a start, seeing one of the healers run past him. He didn't even remember falling asleep. He stood gingerly and stretched his stiff body. His muscles were sore from carving and sitting outside the tent all night. Sol looked down at his feet and saw a wooden bear. He wasn't sure why he would choose such an animal to carve with his history, but he had. Sol opened one of the flaps and called in to announce his presence. "It's Sol."

"Come in," said a voice from within.

He walked in and saw Layla lying on the bed of furs and green linen. Her eyes were open and focused intently on him. One of the healers was tipping her head and helping her drink a few sips of tea.

"She had a fever all night, but it broke this morning. She just woke up," the healer explained. "We sent for the chieftess."

Just as the woman finished her words, Sol's mother walked into the tent.

"Layla, can you speak?" his mother asked.

Layla tried to nod her head but winced in pain from the motion. "Yes," she answered instead, her eyes squinting.

"Do you remember what happened to you?" Sol's mother asked, and Sol knew enough to be silent.

"Yes. I was walking in the forest to the north. I was searching for Sol." She paused, taking a breath and refocusing her eyes on him.

"What happened next?" Sol's mother prodded.

"I remember standing on the edge of the river by the waterfall and seeing a woman, a Barden woman, on our tribal lands. I tried to talk to her and ask her why she had crossed the border. She just laughed at me and said she was the chief's daughter and she could go wherever she wanted. She attacked me. I had no choice but to defend myself. I remember being hit with something hard and then waking up here." Layla looked to her chieftess.

Sol didn't think Layla's story aligned with what he knew of Luna.

"I see. Convene a meeting with the elders of all the families outside my home," Sol's mother ordered one of the healers. The woman left right away to do as she was told. The chieftess very rarely issued any orders or used her authoritative voice so when she did, everyone knew not to second-guess her.

"Layla, I will tell the council what you said since you are not well enough to move on your own. Is that agreeable?" Sol's mother asked.

"Yes," Layla answered, knowing better than to nod her head this time.

"Sol, come with me. You must give them details of what you saw too." Sol's mother led him out of the tent, but before he turned to follow her, he saw Layla shoot an intense and unsure glance at him. She must have not known he had seen anything. Sol followed his mother out without another word. They arrived at her home where the elders had almost completely gathered. Sol heard the drumming calling the meeting and knew the others would be along very soon.

Sol's mother waited a few minutes for more elders to gather before starting. Akiiki came and stood silently next to her mother as next in line for chieftess. "My people, we have had an incident. I have heard Layla's side of things, and I have Sol here, who witnessed the end of it. I will begin by saying there is a third person who is not here to tell us her side of things, and we cannot know it as we do not have the opportunity to ask. I ask you to remember to try to look at the facts we are presented with as objectively as you can," his mother stated before telling them Layla's story. The crowd gasped at the news and began talking to each other. "Now," she continued, quieting the crowd, "Sol will tell us what he saw of the fight." She motioned for him to stand and speak.

This wasn't his first time standing in the crowd of elders, speaking to what he had seen. The last time was when he stood to tell them about how his father, their chief, died. "I saw Layla on top of the other woman." *Luna*, his mind demanded. *Her name is Luna.* "Layla had her pinned to the ground and was choking her. The woman grabbed a rock and hit Layla on the head with it, knocking her out."

Once again, the crowd was filled with gasps. The tribe's elders began speaking to one another, some shouting.

"What happened to the woman?" asked one.

"Was she Barden?" asked another loud shout.

"One question at a time," his mother reminded them.

They would go around the group with the oldest elder representing each family of the tribe going in turn by age.

"Was she Barden?" the oldest woman in the crowd asked.

"Yes," Sol answered.

The woman nodded.

A man across the crowd asked, "What happened next?"

"The woman left and I brought Layla here," Sol responded, leaving the details out.

"Do you think we are in danger of an attack?" asked a third.

Sol's mother answered, "No one can know that for certain. The woman was also injured from the fight, and we cannot know how their chief will respond. We have already placed warriors in shifts at the border in case of any sign of attack."

"They have no right! She was on our side of the land. Layla did what she had to," someone yelled from the middle.

"That is only Layla's side of the story. We do not know the whole of it," Akiiki answered.

"She's a Barden," someone muttered in the crowd.

"I found them on Barden's side of the river," Sol chimed in. His statement brought a questioning look from the crowd.

A few more questions from the elders and then someone asked, "What do you think, Chieftess?"

"I think we should not get ahead of ourselves. I think we should watch and wait to see if the Barden decide to attack.

If the woman was on our side as Layla said, her actions were justified. I don't think this is cause to start a war."

"My granddaughter almost lost her life—that is cause enough for me," Layla's grandmother said, speaking loudly enough for everyone to hear.

A few others agreed. "Yeah! They can't attack one of our own and get away with it. We outnumber them two to one!"

"Yes, we outnumber them. Our numbers near four hundred, and at least three hundred would be able to fight. Their numbers are only around one hundred and fifty fighting, but don't forget they are close friends with the Dabney tribe. The Dabneys are on decent trading terms with us, but if we attack the Barden first, I have a strong belief that the Dabney tribe would join them, making our numbers even, perhaps even outnumbering us. Is it worth risking the lives of everyone in this tribe? She is alive. If she were dead, I would be more inclined to agree with you. The facts seem a bit muddled on this issue. I think we need to wait and see." Several nods of agreement came from the crowd. "Go make yourself ready in case there is an attack. If there is, one of the warriors at the border will warn us with the drums. Keep close to the village today, unless you decide to bring the children to the safe place."

The crowd dispersed at their chieftess's instructions.

Sol's mother turned to Akiiki. "Everyone must feel heard, but it is our responsibility to remain objective and think of what is better for the collective." Akiiki nodded at her mother's advice.

Sol's mother entered her longhouse and called his name. He went inside.

"You must go to the place where you meet her and find out if we are in danger of an attack," she explained. Sol looked at her with a surprised and confused look. "Sol, you have a duty to your people as well as your heart! Find out her side of things. Sol?" she asked, making sure she had his attention.

"Yes?"

"You have a choice to make that no one else can make for you." She looked in his eyes and nodded before leaving him alone.

Sol took a step back. He might have to choose between his family and the woman he loved. He ran out the door, back into the forest toward the waterfall. He ran the whole five miles and was breathless when he arrived. He searched the shore for Luna, but she wasn't there.

Sol waited all day, until the darkness came. Then he made his way back to his village, to his mother's house to tell her Luna had not shown up. She instructed him to go back the following day. The next morning, he set off to the waterfall on foot again, but this time he walked. He wasn't sure if she would be there, but he would wait.

Was she okay? Was she hurt? Was she angry at him for leaving her? Did it matter if she was angry since there was no way they could be together? He was the chieftess's son, and as such, he had responsibilities. He was loyal to his tribe, and he was the one who had broken the rules. It was his fault people were getting hurt now. He had to be the one to suffer the consequences; he just wished Luna wouldn't have to suffer, too. She would hate him after this, he was sure of it.

CHAPTER 12

Luna froze, staring into her father's reddening face. "Answer me girl! What happened to you?!" Gannon demanded, taking another step closer.

Luna instinctively backed up. "I-I was in a fight."

"That's obvious. Who laid a hand on you? Is this why you were at Alice's?" He stood towering over Luna with one hand by his side and the other motioning back to the village.

"Yes. I just needed some time to recover. I didn't want you to see me until I felt well enough—"

Gannon interrupted her, "WHO did this?!"

"It was my fault."

"Answer my damn question, girl!" He raised his hand in a fist and Luna shuddered.

"Gannon!" It was Alice coming from the gate. "Gannon, just wait a minute. Hear the girl out!"

Gannon turned to see his sister. "You knew about this and you kept it from me?"

Alice reached them, only a little out of breath. "Just listen to her. Calm yourself down and hear her explanation."

Gannon turned to face Luna once again. "Well, let's

have it."

Luna tried to find the right words. She took a deep breath before starting, "I went over to the other side of the river——"

"I knew it was a Net! Those people think they can touch the Barden chief's daughter and get away with it, but they have another thing coming!" Gannon's face scowled with disgust as he said the other tribe's name.

"Let her finish!" Alice interjected.

"I was on their side of the river. It was my fault. The woman found me there and thought I was a threat. I broke the law. I am at fault, not them."

The meaning of Luna's words seemed to stun Gannon momentarily, so Alice spoke.

"Brother, we have no grounds to retaliate. Luna was on their land, and they had the right to defend it."

Gannon crossed his arms over his large torso, and his face now turned a maroon red, much darker than Luna had ever seen. He said nothing at first. Luna held her breath. She was afraid of him and recoiled at his apparent disappointment in her. She didn't know what she would do if he acted on his deep-seated rage by deciding to attack the Nets.

Gannon finally broke his silence, and in that instant Luna wished it had lasted. "You stupid girl! How could you be so stupid as to cross the border? You are weak. You are forbidden to enter those north woods again!"

"She has already paid for her mistake, Gannon," Alice said firmly.

Luna opened her mouth to protest, but her father took a step closer and pointed his finger at her. "Do you hear me?!" he demanded.

"Yes," Luna said as she dropped her eyes to the ground, swallowing hard and holding back tears. Her stomach was still in knots and now her chest was beginning to ache.

"Those Nets will get what is coming to them soon enough. Go home!" he shouted.

Luna obeyed while Alice stayed with Gannon, speaking to him. Luna heard her aunt trying to convince him to calm down and to realize an attack would be suicide as the Nets' numbers far outnumbered the Bardens'.

Luna made her way through the village, catching the shocked glances of the guards and the tribe members she passed. She no longer cared about hiding her bruised face and body. The clouds in the sky were beginning to darken, and the air smelled like rain as Luna made her way into the dim and silent home. She placed the spear and her bow against the wall in her bedroom. How would she get to see Sol again? She couldn't risk going to his land, even though she was sure she would know the way to his lean-to by the ocean. She would have to wait for her opportunity and hope he was there when she could get away. Was he already there? What would he think after she hadn't shown up to meet him the previous day?

An hour passed in silence before Luna heard the door open and heavy footsteps walk into the common room. She held her breath and waited. She could hear pacing for a bit and then silence.

"Come here." Her father's voice boomed outside her bedroom door.

Luna stood up and obeyed, preparing herself for another verbal lashing. She opened the door and saw her father smoking his pipe by the roaring fireplace.

"I don't want you to worry about the woman who attacked you. She will get what is coming to her soon enough. We just have to wait until everything is aligned. I have spoken to the shaman and he has assured me that the time is upon us to make preparations—only preparations though." Gannon seemed disappointed by that aspect of the situation. "You have to stay out of the north woods and away from the river for now. When you go to the south woods, Alice will accompany you. As the chief's daughter, you are a target for those people." He puffed twice from his pipe.

Luna could see the absolute distaste in Gannon's eyes when he said *'those people'*. His mouth seemed to sour around the words. Alice had been right—there was no way Gannon would have agreed to let her join with Sol. How could she have been so naive?

"I am going to make preparations for the equinox feast with Bale. Stay here today. I don't want you leaving the house. Am I understood?" Gannon demanded as he paused his smoking.

Luna shook her head in agreement, afraid her voice would betray her if she spoke. Thunder boomed in the distance. It would storm, Luna guessed, distracting her mind from her reality.

"I'm going to go to Bale's now before the storm gets here. I'll see you for dinner. Alice will bring something over," Gannon said, standing up and taking another puff from his pipe.

Luna nodded and retreated back to her bedroom. She heard her father leave shortly after. Luna lay in the dim light on her bed with her heart and mind racing. Her body felt paralyzed in the blankets, but her heart urged her to move. Conflicting thoughts waged a war in her mind. He was her father and the chief of her tribe, of *her* people. She was supposed to listen to him, was supposed to obey him. She was his child, and that was the way things were. But…that wasn't how things were everywhere. Sol's tribe wasn't like that.

The very thought of Sol kindled a fire in her body. The fire was not one of lust, but of a devoted and passionate love. She felt like Sol was a part of her, and that part was missing. She *had* to see him! She *had* to leave this place. He deserved to know what she had set out to tell him that morning before Layla attacked. Her father would surely kill him if he knew—would maybe even kill her! After Gannon's reaction by the garden, Luna wasn't sure where she stood with her father. She had never been sure, but she had once felt some sort of connection. She still loved him despite all the pain he had caused her. Maybe Sol would agree to leave these lands and find another with her. Maybe they could travel far north and see where the lands went.

Luna jolted upright. The weight that had left her feeling paralyzed in the bed was still there, but the instinctual and intense draw of her intuition and her own survival urged her on. The rain was beginning to come down now, and the thunder boomed closer, almost right above her. Luna grabbed a large deer hide bag and placed a fur, a linen blanket, clothing, and the wooden bowl Sol had made for her inside it. She grabbed her bow and quiver and placed them on her back. Luna went into the common room and packed a loaf of bread, some boiled eggs, and a few of her most important salves and tinctures.

This is it, she thought—all of her life in one bag. Luna took one more look around the room she had grown up in. She could still remember her mother sitting by the fire, laughing while she sewed. A single tear escaped Luna's eye, and she wiped it away. She knew if she started, the floodgates would open and she would be a sobbing mess. She needed a clear head, and the adrenaline now coursing through her body helped with that. Fighting the fear that made her legs stiff and hesitant, she cracked opened the door, surveying the landscape. No one was out; the storm would provide her with good cover for sneaking out in the middle of the day. Luna took a deep breath, pulled the bag over her shoulder, and walked out the door.

Once Luna was outside, she walked to the edge of the wall closest to her house and looked around. She saw no one, and any trace of hesitation was gone as she scaled the barrier. Every movement seemed to burn and ache, but she was determined. She dropped the bag to the ground on the other side first, jumping down after it. Everything in her body protested the movement, but her heart urged her on. She walked as fast as she could, staying as low to the ground as possible. She reached the tree line and paused for a breath as thunder cracked, glancing back to see if anyone had seen or followed her. A flash of lighting revealed she was safe.

The rain was still falling lightly in the forest and it was cold enough for her to see her breath, but Luna barely noticed it. Her body was hot from the adrenaline, and from running. Luna pressed on, jogging up to the waterfall. She made her way through the forest on the path that had developed from her many trips, her heart beating anxiously. The lightening flashed in between claps of thunder, and the rain began to fall harder. The trees creaked and moaned from the strong gusts of wind. Luna heard an intense crack and looked over to see a large old pine tree fall to the ground and splinter into smaller pieces. She continued on, keeping a watchful eye on her surroundings.

Luna could hear the steady rush of the waterfall, and the air grew cooler as she approached the water. There was no sign of Sol. The rain fell harder, now coming down in buckets. Luna remembered the sweet memory of the last time they were there during a storm and made her way to the small cave. She saw a flicker of light and smiled a sigh of relief.

Luna entered the space and found the surprised and relieved face of Sol.

"Luna!" He watched her come through the dripping mouth of the cave. She was soaking wet, and her hair and clothing stuck to her. He quickly stood and embraced her.

"Sol!" was all Luna could get out. She collapsed into his warm strong arms. He pulled her farther in toward the fire he'd lit.

"Luna, you're freezing."

She started to shake, now realizing how cold she really felt. The wind blew into the cave, sending a shiver through her body. Sol pulled her tunic off and wrapped a linen cloth tightly around her naked freezing body.

"There are clothes in my bag," Luna said.

Sol noticed the hide bag for the first time and opened it. He pulled out a black tunic from under the array of other items, taking notice of the bowl he'd made her. Sol helped her get dressed in the dry clothes and then sat next to her in the small cave, pulling her body close for warmth.

"Luna, are you okay?" he asked, touching his fingertips gently to the healing wounds on her eye.

"Sol, there is just so much—" she choked, trying to hold

back the tears. She squeezed him tighter, laying her head on his chest.

"It's okay. Take your time," he said comfortingly.

"Is the woman alive?" Luna asked without looking up.

"Yes. She is going to be okay."

Luna breathed a sigh of relief.

"My people are worried about an attack from your father," Sol said.

"He said he wasn't planning on it right now. He is just making preparations, whatever that means. How did your mother and your tribe react?" Luna lifted her head and looked in his eyes with her question, her gaze full of trepidation.

Sol looked down at the fire. "My mother wants to hear your side of things. My people were angry, but they don't plan on retaliating at this point."

"Retaliating? She attacked *me*, Sol," Luna said defensively, feeling her anger rise.

"I know, I know. I avoided being straightforward with her. Maybe she thought there was a chance. I haven't gotten the opportunity to confirm with her yet."

"She told me she was going to tell you *I* attacked *her*. She said your name." Luna pulled a little farther away from Sol so she could fully face him. She wondered if she was good enough to keep a man like Sol faithful to herself, or if he was in fact seeing another woman, maybe even Layla.

Sol shook his head. "I believe you."

"My father has forbidden me to come here. I had to sneak out of the house today. I have everything I need with me. Can we just run away together?" Luna asked, leaning in for a kiss.

Sol's lips met hers, but he didn't kiss her back. Luna stopped, noticing his resistance, suddenly confused.

Sol turned to look at the fire before turning back to look at her. He saw the rejection in her eyes, and it felt as if his own heart had been stabbed. He entertained her idea for a moment, letting the thought gently flutter around in his mind. The prospect was tantalizing, and then the logical warnings assaulted his senses.

"Luna, if we ran away, your father would attack my people. Most likely, your people would be slaughtered by mine, and my people would lose many. My family could be killed. I can't leave them to that fate. I can't bring any more pain upon my mother than I already have. We can't start a war over our love."

Our love. The hopeful words echoed in Luna's mind. "Sol, I need you. You don't understand everything. I'm—"

Sol interrupted her and firmly said, "I understand enough. Luna, we can't be together."

"What do you mean?!" she demanded, her voice rising as she pulled away.

"I can't be with you." Sol stood in the cave, turning away from her. He didn't want to see her face as he knew the look of abandonment that would fill her beautiful features, and he didn't want to remember her that way. His voice was steady, but his heart was shattering into a million pieces inside him.

"Wait!" Luna cried.

Luna's own words came rushing back to Sol's memory: *Your father sacrificed everything so you could have a future. The best way to honor him is to live for him, to live a life your father would be proud of.*

Suddenly, Sol felt an urgency to run out of the cave, because he knew if he stayed much longer he would in fact run away with Luna. Sol also knew he would end up hating himself for being so selfish while his family suffered for his choices. His mother would most likely be stripped of her title of chieftess, another ruling family would be voted in, or Luna's father would wage a war against his people. Each scenario seemed likely.

Sol turned to face her with his fists clenched, suddenly enraged. "Luna! People are getting hurt because of our foolishness! We would destroy our families. Does loyalty mean nothing to you? You said I needed to live a life my father would be proud of, and that is what I am trying to do! We are from two different worlds and we *do not* belong together. Our love is not enough!" His words said the opposite of how he felt, but he didn't know what else he could do. He wanted Luna safe, and he knew she would have that as long as she wasn't with him.

Luna shuddered as his deep voice reverberated loudly in

the small cave. He had finally said it, had just admitted she was not enough for him. His words cut her deep, and she felt sharp shards of glass where her heart was supposed to be. Luna didn't know what to say, so she remained silent, remembering Alice's words: *You must never see that man again, for his own good, for the love you have for him. If it is real, you will be willing to do this to save his life.*

After a few moments, Luna nodded her head, and Sol shifted anxiously where he stood.

"You're right." She looked up at him, her eyes taking in his handsome face for the last time. "We both have a duty to our families."

Luna felt as if someone else was speaking for her. She could hear her voice, but she couldn't feel herself speaking. She couldn't feel much of anything in that moment except sheer unadulterated pain where her heart had once been. Somewhere, though, there was a strength that managed to speak clearly to her lover, her best friend, and her soul mate.

Sol couldn't stand the storm that was raging inside the small cave any longer. His heart begged to hold her in his arms one last time, to feel the warmth of her sweet kiss, but he knew that would just make things harder.

Luna stood to face him, her body craving the relief his closeness would bring her. She reached out her hand to him, and he took it.

Sol pulled her in for a kiss against his better judgment. Their lips met and he tasted her sweet breath.

Luna pulled his body closer to hers, kissing him back fiercely as tears streamed down her cheeks. She tried to memorize his taste and the feel of his lips as she melted into it.

Sol pulled away, ending their bittersweet goodbye kiss. He turned quickly and left Luna in the cave, alone. Sol began running back to his village as hard and as fast as he could. His hot tears mixed with the cold rainwater streaming down his face, and it felt as if someone had used a knife to cut out his heart.

Sol made his way to his mother's longhouse first. He burst in the door, garnering shocked glances from his younger brothers as well as his mother.

"Is there worry of an attack?" she asked.

"No, not right now, at least. She said they are making preparations but no moves," Sol answered before heading over to where he kept extra clothes and changing into a dry tunic and pants. He grabbed a fur blanket off of one of the beds and wrapped it tightly around his body before walking over to sit next to the fire in the middle of the longhouse.

His mother's reaction was of noticeable relief. "We should stay on the ready for some time then, just in case."

"How did you get this information, Sol?" Ata asked suspiciously.

Their mother answered for him. "Never mind that. That is Sol's business."

"How can we know to trust this information?" Atsu

chimed in.

"We can trust it," Sol said defensively in the most serious and firm voice he could muster.

"Boys, leave us to speak alone," Sol's mother commanded, and the boys left without protest.

"I see you have decided that your place is here with us," his mother started.

"It isn't really a choice, Mama. If I left, you would all be punished for my mistake," Sol answered in defeat.

"This was not your mistake. You took many risks and made choices I would not have necessarily made, but Layla made this mess," she said firmly.

Sol took in his mother's words. He was confused why she didn't think it was his fault, or even Luna's. He wanted to ask, but he was tired. He felt the storm that had raged within his body had been more than he could handle, and he just wanted to sleep.

His mother saw the exhaustion in his face. "Rest my son. You may see things clearer after some sleep."

Sol got up and walked over to his old bed in his mother's longhouse. He lay down, wrapped in the soft fur. Everything hurt, and he wanted it to stop. He stayed still, hoping for sleep to come. As he did, the words he'd spoken to Luna came back to him, and the memory stung worse than the jellyfish he had been stung by the summer before. He wished he could have her by his side, snuggled up against him in the fur. The memory of their last kiss was fresh in his mind.

He missed her already, and he knew the hole he felt would never be full without her. Finally, sleep came for Sol.

He slept until the early hours of the next morning. It was still dark out, but he made his way to his lean-to by the ocean. The sound of the waves and the fresh salty air brought him comfort, but not as much as usual. He sat on the edge of the shelter watching the fiery red of the sunrise break through the dark horizon. He watched the dark silhouettes of seabirds flock onto the sand, pulling out large clams and small crabs to eat for their morning meal.

The cool wind blew much more gently than it had the night before. Sol wondered what damage had been done to his possessions, and he looked around. He saw the house plans in a corner to his right, the house he had naively imagined Luna living in with him. He would still build it, he decided. It would give him something to do, something to distract him. The light shape of the wooden bear he had carved caught his eye in the brightening light. Sol picked it up and inspected it. He thought of the bear that had come to the waterfall, the reason he had dared to cross the river boundary in the first place. Sol also realized this was the first time a bear reminded him of anything else besides his father. Sol set the bear on the small wooden chest. It would serve as a reminder of the sweet stolen moments he and Luna had shared in secret over the last few months.

Sol stood up and decided he would walk along the coast while the sun rose. He needed the solitude.

* * *

Luna stayed in the cave, stunned for a few moments, trying to make sense of it all. Her heart was in pain as her mind replayed their conversation. She felt truly alone in the world in that moment. She felt like she couldn't breathe and started taking large gasps of air. She knew if she didn't slow her breathing down, she would black out again; she didn't care though. Nothing mattered anymore, nothing about her anyway. She hadn't been good enough for Sol, but she still had the opportunity to prove herself to her father.

Luna gathered her things, snuffed out the fire, and started the long walk home. The rain poured down, drenching the dry tunic she was wearing in minutes. The thunder and lightning had passed, but it still boomed and flashed in the distance. Suddenly, everything she had been holding inside came bursting out of her in an unnatural and primal scream. The screaming offered her some relief as an outlet. The tears came freely now. Luna collapsed on the ground, defeated. She had nothing left to live for. *Well, almost nothing*, she reminded herself. It probably wouldn't last anyway. Luna forced herself to stand up and walk toward her village.

By the time Luna had reached the forest's edge, the storm had passed and the rain was a light drizzle. Luna made her way to the wall, not crouching low this time. She stared at the ground until she reached the wall and climbed over. Luna passed a tribesman who looked at her, but he didn't say anything. She continued walking until she arrived at her house, opened the door, and went in.

Luna saw that the fire was still going strong and looked over to see a figure sitting in the chair, waiting for her return.

CHAPTER 13

"**L**una! You are going to catch a fever dripping wet in that cold. I can't believe you went out in that storm!" Alice said in a shocked voice as she got out of the chair and sped over to where Luna stood in a pooling puddle. Luna didn't respond, and Alice took in the sight of her disheveled niece. Her eyes were bloodshot, and purple rings had started to form under her dark eyes. Alice knew well that the wounds within Luna were far worse than the ones on her skin from the altercation. Alice wrapped an arm around Luna and led her into her bedroom, where she already had a fire going in the small fireplace.

Luna felt numb to most things except an overwhelming tiredness. She wanted to be alone and she wanted to sleep; maybe it would all end up being a bad dream. Alice undressed Luna and put a dry tunic shirt and pants on her with a pair of wool socks she found in the wooden chest. Luna was vaguely aware of her aunt's presence as she lay down in her bed and gave herself over to the beckoning darkness sleep offered.

Luna woke once in the middle of the night, shivering. Someone lifted a cup of bitter herbs to her, and she drank it, falling back to sleep soon after. When she awoke the second time, she could see a ray of sunlight coming through the cracks of the wooden section of her wall. Her body ached and her head pounded, but she didn't care. Luna heard muffled voices coming from outside the bedroom wall, and then the door to her house opened. Footsteps entered, and she heard a small knock on her door. Alice peeped her head into the room, not waiting for an answer.

"Good, you're up." She entered Luna's bedroom with a wooden tray that bore a cup of water and a bowl of steaming broth. She brought it over to her. "Drink this," she said, handing her the cup.

Luna sat up and drank the water, choking on the first sip but then drinking until the cup was empty.

Alice handed her the bowl of broth next. Luna didn't feel hungry, but the savory smell made her stomach gurgle. Luna drank the first sip, taking in the small comfort.

"You scared me last night, Luna. You had a high fever and I didn't know what I would tell your father if you had given in to it. He would have thought it was from the fight with the Net woman and all disaster would have broken loose. What were you thinking going out in the storm?" Alice asked incredulously.

Luna was silent.

"Did you say goodbye?"

Luna stopped sipping the broth and looked down at the bowl in her hands, the memory replaying itself word for word in her mind. "Yes."

"Good girl. It will take time, but you will get through this tough part. Life goes on," Alice said, failing at her attempt to comfort her niece.

Alice's words struck Luna and she felt an angry argument brewing inside her, but she remained silent. How could she get through this? Her heart was shattered, and she couldn't be with the man she loved. Any life worth living was now over. Now, she would do what she must so those she loved would be safe.

Alice stood up, taking the tray and the empty cup with her. "Rest today, but remember the equinox feast tonight." Alice walked out of the room, closing the door behind her.

Luna stared into the golden broth, taking her time to fully register her aunt's words. Luna's mind was in a haze. She didn't feel like seeing anyone, much less going to a celebration. She would, though— as the chief's daughter, she didn't have a choice. She set the soup on the ground next to her and fell back to sleep.

Hours passed with sleep coming in waves. When Luna woke, she would stare at the ceiling or the wall with no motivation to do anything else. The thought of even leaving her bed for more water was too overwhelming, so just she slept.

Hours later, her aunt's voice woke her. "Luna, wake up.

You have to get ready."

"I don't want to," she answered honestly.

"You have a duty to your people, to your father."

Luna opened her eyes and forced herself to sit up.

"I know you are tired. You will get to sleep again afterward. Luna, your father is making a very important announcement tonight, and you need to remember that it is in *everyone's* best interest if you seem enthusiastic about it. This will be a new chance for you, an opportunity that does not just come along every day, so make the most of it," Alice said, speaking more sternly than she usually did.

"What would he announce that anyone would care to hear my opinion on? I am a woman, and in our tribe, women are pretty much worthless," Luna said bitterly.

Alice took Luna's face in her hands. "Make sure you do not embarrass your father tonight, for your own good, child! And for the good of the man you loved. Women have their place in our tribe, and they are far from worthless," she snapped.

Luna was still stuck on the fact that Alice had used *'loved'* in the past tense, as if Luna had gotten over Sol after one night. She still loved him and knew she always would, even if they couldn't be together, even if he didn't want her.

Alice shook her niece momentarily as if trying to wake her from a dream. "Get dressed, put a smile on, and let's go."

Alice didn't realize that what she asked of Luna seemed momentous in that moment. Luna nodded her head. Alice stood and extended a hand to help her up. Luna took a deep breath, stuffed down her anger, and took her aunt's open hand. She already knew what would be expected of her. She would have to wear the white celebration dress and paint her face. This time she would paint a full horizontal black line across her face, covering her eyes. If she wanted to mask her true feelings for the night, she would need all the help she could get. Luna got dressed in the revealing white tunic dress and tied on her black sandals. She brushed her hair, but this time she tied it high on her head and then made three smaller braids that reached down past her shoulders. She pulled a silver triple forehead chain from the small chest in her room and placed it on her head. It had a teardrop moonstone that adorned the middle of her forehead, between her eyebrows. Above the stone was a small black half-moon. Luna finished accessorizing with a pair of hoop earrings that each had a hanging crystal pendant, one black onyx and the other a cloudy white quartz. Luna traced the shape of the purple shell Sol had given her; she would keep it on as it was the one piece of him she could carry with her always.

Luna walked out to the common room where her aunt was waiting for her. Alice's silver hair was hanging freely except for a small braid on either side of her face. Alice had woven grey feathers into the braids and added small black beads on the ends. She had painted a large, thin blue circle around her right eye with a vertical line on the outer edge of her left eye. Alice's tunic was black and flowing. Luna wished they could switch, knowing full well how exposed she would feel in the white tunic she now wore, especially in front of the Dabney chief and his son. She also knew this was what was expected of her. Feeling anger rise again, she pushed it down.

The latch lifted on the door and it opened. Gannon came into the house.

"Good, you're ready. Let's go, the tribes are waiting," Gannon said, motioning with his hand for them to exit.

Alice led the way and Luna followed. Their horses were outside waiting for them, and Luna mounted Willow. When all three of them were ready, Gannon led the way with his sister just behind him to his left side and Luna trailing slightly behind both of them to his right.

Luna could hear the music of the celebration drums from far off before she could see the lights of the large fire and several torches that created a large circle for the hundreds of people to join together within. The moon was full, and the stars were still visible away from the lights of the fires. Gannon led them to the center by the fire and dismounted his horse. Luna and Alice followed his lead. A boy was there to take the animals from them, and he walked the horses to the makeshift pasture nearby.

Gannon greeted Bale with a slap of their hands turning into a hug between the men. It was clear from the way Bale staggered backward that he had already been enjoying the fermented drinks. Next, Gannon shook Aidan's hand. "My boy! Welcome to this great feast!" Gannon said gleefully.

"Oh, you act like you are the only host of this celebration. You forget that we must be sharing much more now!" Bale hacked as he laughed.

Luna's eyes met Aidan's and she shifted uncomfortably. She didn't want conversation, didn't want to be around people. She wanted darkness and sleep.

"Shut up, you old fool. I have not announced anything yet!" Gannon bellowed.

Bale lifted his tall mug and drank the foamy liquid in large gulps, some dripping down the sides of his mouth onto his tunic, until the cup was empty. "Let's have it then! Let's get this feast started!" Bale wiped his mouth with his sleeve and motioned for a girl to refill his cup for him. She did so quickly as his free hand reached behind her. Luna saw the young girl, not more than fourteen, jump uncomfortably and spill some of the liquid out of the cup. Bale laughed before taking the full cup and drinking a few more gulps. Luna's stomach knotted in revulsion.

Gannon motioned to the drummers to stop with his open palm held out. "Barden tribe members and Dabney tribe members, we have gathered you all here to celebrate the fall equinox and the second harvest." Everyone cheered, striking anything they could to make more noise. "But!" Gannon said, quieting the noisy crowd. "We have something else to celebrate too." He looked over to Luna, motioning for her to come to him.

She hesitated but obeyed.

Gannon put his arm around her before continuing, "Tonight, we celebrate the joining of our tribes."

Luna felt a stab of panic.

"In three full moons' time, our tribes will be joined as one as my daughter Luna is hand-fasted to Chief Bale's son Aidan!" Gannon finished.

Cheers erupted from everyone in the large crowd. Luna felt like someone had just simultaneously punched her in the chest and in the stomach. Her father squeezed her body into the side of his own large frame before grabbing her hand and placing it in Aidan's.

Luna looked at Aidan's eager face. He was happy about this. This was what her aunt had meant. This was why her father had been so happy about the idea of joining tribes—he had thought she meant with the Dabney! The realization that he had never been considering letting her join with Sol took the breath from Luna's lungs. The full weight of the miscommunication landed heavily on her, and she wanted to run as fast as she could from that place. She hadn't thought the day could get any worse, but it just had.

"Are you happy with the match?" Aidan asked.

She was barely able to hear the question over the volume of the crowd. Her body screamed NO, but her words said the opposite. "Yes." Luna forced a smile with her reply.

She knew her duty and what was expected of her. Luna

knew she had lost her one chance at love and happiness in this world, and a small question whispered in her mind: *Could this marriage solve everyone's problems?*

"Let us feast!" Bale raised his drink, and the tribe members shouted their agreement.

The drums started again, and the rest of the musicians joined in. There were string and bag instruments, pan flutes, and various drums. The men and women took turns chanting as everyone danced. Several people had painted open eyes on their closed eyelids with charcoal, creating an always-watching, ever-wakeful effect.

As the music and songs got louder, Luna could feel the small force within her starting to grow as she tried to make sense of the disorganized thoughts all swirling in her head. Luna started to dance. She jumped and swayed, losing herself in the chants. She made her way closer to the band, drowning out her own thoughts until she felt completely alone with the moon and the fire. Luna sang at the top of her lungs, letting out everything she had been holding inside, making room for what, she wasn't sure yet. She danced in a trance-like state, making up her own chants as she went along, praying and pleading to her goddess. Luna felt outside of her body, reaching to be part of the skies. Suddenly, her mind felt clearer. If she wasn't going to have the life she wished, she would make the most of the life her mother had gifted her. She could protect Sol's people as the wife of the future chief of both tribes. It wasn't what she had wanted, but it was her duty to her people and to her father. Sol had said as children of chiefs, it was their duty to fulfill whatever they needed to for their tribes. He didn't think she was enough, and she was determined to prove him wrong. Finally, she felt a spark of something new growing within her. A new strength of determination started to intensify: resolve.

Luna felt a tap on her shoulder, immediately returning to her body and the crowd of tribe members. Aidan had found her and extended his hand. His lips moved, but Luna couldn't hear the words he spoke in the loud atmosphere. She took his hand, and he spun her around. They danced, spinning and kicking their footwork to the beat. Luna looked up and saw Aidan was smiling and having fun; then she realized she was smiling, too. She was good at wearing a mask, and that was what she would have to do to survive and make sure those she loved most would too.

After a while, Aidan led Luna away from the music toward the edge of the large group. Once they were far enough from the loudest parts and she could hear him again, he asked her, "Do you want to walk with me?"

Luna nodded in agreement.

"I am happy to see you tonight," Aidan said, his blue eyes meeting hers. Luna thought of the way Sol used to look at her, knowing no one else would be able to look at her the same way.

She gave him a small smile in response.

He took her hand in his. It felt awkward to Luna, but she didn't resist. His hand was slightly larger and softer than Sol's. Aidan was attractive. She looked at him, the moonlight spilling over his broad shoulders, highlighting his dark hair and muscular build. He was handsome, but he wasn't Sol. It hit her that Aidan was her future lover who she would never be able to fully give herself to. Her heart would always belong to Sol, but she would soon be joined to Aidan, and the sooner she got over the idea, the better it would be for her. She swallowed hard, ignoring the sick feeling in her stomach.

Aidan led her on, away from the fires and into the moonlit field that separated their lands.

"I want you to know that I was happy to hear your father accepted my request for your hand." Aidan stopped walking and faced her.

Luna was taken aback for a moment, realizing he had requested her hand. She had thought it was their fathers who'd arranged the whole thing.

"I didn't know you had asked," she answered honestly.

"I did. I know our tribes will be better for it, being united. We already have so much in common—our people, I mean. Once I saw you at the trade negotiations with your father, I knew I had to have you as my own," Aidan explained.

Luna felt a stab of defiance within her at the thought of someone thinking they had ownership over her. She knew she had to make things clear from the beginning with Aidan if she was to be content at all or maintain any sense of control over the undesirable situation. "I am not something to own. I am a woman, a person. I am a warrior. I am a chief's daughter." Luna's reply was gentle but firm.

A look of surprise crossed Aidan's handsome face. He swiped a stray black hair off his cheek and over his head before he clarified, "Of course. That isn't quite what I meant… You know what I mean, right?"

Luna watched him struggle to explain and felt a small tinge of satisfaction. "Yes," she said to put him at ease.

"Well, I would love to show you around our lands some time."

"As you wish," Luna agreed.

Aidan looked at the ground and then back to Luna. His gaze was uncomfortable, but she didn't have another option in that moment.

"I should get back. My father will be looking for me," Luna lied.

"Yes, of course. I'll walk you back."

She started walking and crossed her arms against her chest before he could reach for her hand again.

"Are you cold?" he asked.

"I'm okay. I just need to get back to the fires," Luna answered, picking up her pace.

When they reached her father, Aidan said his goodbye and Luna took her opportunity to sneak away from the crowd. She found Willow and mounted the horse before riding back to her village. Luna impulsively kicked her heels into the horse's side, urging her mare into a gallop. She rode to the southwestern most point of the river where she had met Sol that night he took her to the ocean. She patted the mare and signaled for her to stop. Luna's eyes scanned the woods, the moonlight shining down on her painted face. Nothing but darkness.

"Goodbye," she whispered into the night. Then she cried out, "Goodbye my love. For you, I do this, so that you and those you love most will be safe." Trails of tears came out of Luna's eyes. She closed them, lifting her hands up, open to the moon. "Mother, grant me the strength and the wisdom," she called out once again.

Luna grabbed the mare's mane and nudged her on. The horse walked along the river's edge until the wall surrounding Luna's village was in view. Luna led the horse back to her pasture before going home to the sweet relief of sleep.

* * *

Sol spent the day helping his mother and the tribe prepare for the equinox celebration. The drumming started the evening by calling the tribe members from everywhere on their land. When darkness came, the savory smell of spices from all types of delectable dishes filled the air. A large bonfire was erected in the center of the clearing by the tree line to the north mountain woods. Hundreds gathered together, and several different drummers beat their drums in unison. The children shook pebble-filled gourds that had been hollowed out. A few people played the wooden xylophones. Some of the voices made bird sounds, while others made popping and clicking noises with their mouths. Others played long slim didgeridoos that had been painted in bright colors. The rest of the voices sang in harmony in the ancient languages, expressing their thankfulness for the second harvest. Each family brought forth special meals and offered them to the other families. The community gathered together, dancing and sharing in their joy of the harvest.

Sol watched his family and his tribe members enjoy themselves. His face was serious, and his mind was not fully present. Luna was in his thoughts, and he wondered selfishly if that would ever change. He hoped not. As long as he thought of her, he could imagine her beautiful face, her contagious laugh. Sol saw Layla enter the festivities, and he approached her.

"Layla."

She turned to see him approach, her face still bruised, though the cuts were healing fast. "Yes?"

"Can we talk?"

"Lead the way," Layla said, and she followed him to another area that was quieter and empty of people. Layla crossed her hands and placed them on her chest. "Did you want to see how I am healing from that woman who attacked me?" she asked, more confident than she actually felt.

"I can see you are doing much better, and I am glad for it."

"No thanks to whoever she was," Layla said, watching Sol for his reaction, trying to read him.

"What happened up there, Layla?" Sol asked directly.

"Well, you saw it, didn't you? Isn't that what you told the council? I see she took a swing at you, too." Layla motioned toward the light bruise on Sol's face before uncrossing her hands and moving them to her hips. She sighed.

"I want to hear it from your mouth," he answered firmly.

"I went up there—"

"Why? Why did you go up there in the first place?"

She rolled her eyes before stepping closer to him. Layla placed her hand on his chest, tapping it. "I don't have to tell you my business, Sol. You don't own the forest, and you certainly do not own me."

"I just want to know what happened. Tell me your side."

Layla raised her eyebrows. "My side? What other side is there to tell?"

Sol looked away.

Layla brought her hand to his face and turned it back to look in her eyes. "I went up into the woods looking for you. I saw that…" She bared her teeth as she searched for the right words. "I saw that Barden girl on our land, Sol. The arrogant… She thought she could do whatever she wanted. I told her to leave and she didn't listen. She attacked me." Layla's eyes were alive with a jealous rage. "If you hadn't found me, I don't know what would have happened." Layla placed her hand back on Sol's chest. "How did you find me?"

"You don't remember?" Sol asked, moving her hand back to her side and taking a step back.

"No."

"You were in the river, bleeding from your head. It's a good thing I was nearby collecting lumber," Sol responded, omitting the details. The less she knew the better. Layla didn't seem completely satisfied with his answer, but before she could press him for more, he said, "I better get back."

"Sol," Layla called after him.

He turned back. "What?"

"Thank you." It was the first time Sol felt she was being genuine with him.

"You're welcome," he replied before returning to the celebration.

Sol sought out his mother and told her his plans for the evening before leaving the celebration early. He made his way to where one of the warriors kept watch for any sign of attack from the Barden. He relieved the warrior from his duty, taking his place. Sol was hidden in the darkness of the tree where he had waited for Luna the time he'd taken her to the ocean and shared so much of himself with her. The realization brought a stab of pain, and he welcomed it. He deserved the ache for all the agony he had caused her.

The moon rose higher, and then the sound of a horse galloping caught his attention from across the river. Sol stood in the shadow of the tree, straining to see who was coming, preparing himself for an attack. He saw her silhouette first, and then a jolt of electricity shocked his body. Were his eyes playing tricks on him? Luna. It was her, but her face was painted differently. The moon highlighted the chained metal jewelry that adorned her head. She was whispering something, and he strained to hear. The burble of the river was too loud.

"Goodbye my love. For you, I do this, so that you and those you love most will be safe."

She was speaking louder now and he could hear her. Did she know he was there? Sol wanted to walk out of the darkness and run to her side of the river. He wanted her in his arms. Was she crying? The tears glistened in the moonlight as he watched her lift her hands and glowing face toward the moon. She said something about her mother, but Sol was focused on the stunning sight of Luna. She had never looked more beautiful and strong as she did in that moment. He wished he could feel her body against his and he craved to be near her, but Sol stayed where he was. What was she doing so that he and his loved ones would be safe? They had both agreed this was what needed to happen since they could never be together. She nudged her horse and the animal led her north along the river, farther away from Sol. The only thing that kept him from announcing his presence was the thought of the pain another goodbye would bring her. If she had turned to look back, she would have seen him step out into the moonlight, watching her until she disappeared.

"Goodbye my love." His voice echoed softly in the darkness.

CHAPTER 14

Luna spent the next two months close to home. She sometimes foraged with Alice in the southern woods, but for the most part, she sought solitude. The air was brisk and cool in the mornings, the crows cawed from the tops of bare trees, and flocks of geese flew south, stopping for rest in their fields. The tribe members had harvested the corn and most of the vegetables from the giant gardens. There was still much to do, preserving the harvest. Luna dug up roots for medicine, knowing most of their healing powers were stored below the earth this time of the year. She kept her hands busy and did what she could to get through each day. Sol was always in her thoughts, and when she slept, he visited her dreams. It happened more often at first, less and less with each passing week. Luna still felt tired, and no matter how much sleep she got, a heavy fog seemed to follow her throughout the day.

One afternoon, Luna collected burdock root. She pushed up the long sleeves on her loose tunic and dug the shovel into the ground with her foot, pulling and twisting to loosen up the earth. She pulled the heavy weed, smelling the bitter green juices the plant leaked where it was wounded by the spade. Luna yanked the stalk of the plant, freeing the root system, and then shook the dirt loose. The large dirt clumps showered down, mimicking the sound of raindrops falling on a roof. She pulled out her knife and cut an inch up the stalk from the roots. Luna placed the foundation of the plant into a large linen bag she carried and tied it onto her horse, which was standing nearby. The southern woods were less thick than the north forest, and she called for Willow to follow her as she walked down the well-worn path.

Luna walked until she came to a clearing. There was a circular meadow within the forest of various younger trees. Luna walked into the center and felt the warm sun shining on her. She pulled her tunic sleeves back down her arms and then grabbed the fur wrap she had laid over the horse for safekeeping. The exhaustion overwhelmed her then. She felt as though she had hit an invisible wall. Luna lay down in the thick meadow grass and curled herself into a ball, pulling the fur wrap over her. She could smell the drying hay and what was left of the sleeping wildflowers around her. The gentle cool breeze blew over her, making the tall meadow grass dance and rustle in a quiet song. Luna placed one of her hands on the cold ground, digging up the grass until she felt the fresh earth, and she put the other under her head for a pillow.

"Mama," she whispered.

She felt closest to her mother's spirit when she was in

nature, but lately, even that was hard for her. Lately, all she felt was utter exhaustion and numbness to every sensation except the pain of heartbreak and the sting of not being enough for those she loved most. She heard crickets chirping and birds singing, momentarily distracting her, bringing her the sweet relief of the sleep she desired.

Luna woke hours later, cold. She opened her eyes before sitting up and saw the sun had moved from the blue sky to just under the tops of the trees. She sat up and looked around the meadow, relieved to see Willow still grazing nearby. Luna stood carefully, her body sore from sleeping on the cold hard ground.

She made her way over to the horse, wrapping the fur tight around her shoulders. "Come on, Willow. Let's go home."

Luna led the horse, deciding walking would be better for her stiff body than riding. She hummed as she walked until she reached the edge of the forest. Luna nodded to the tribesmen who passed her as they headed into the forest where she had just come from, hunting for game. Out of respect, they placed a fist to their chest as they passed, something more of the tribe members had begun to do since the announcement of her engagement.

Now that she was promised to another chief's son, her importance had grown. She knew very well that her position was going to be vital to the relationships of the tribes. The news of the engagement had been a shock. Finding out she only had three months—now only one—to prepare for her hand-fasting ceremony had changed her whole world. It was a lot for Luna to take in all at once, and it had happened so quickly. She was far from happy, but she pressed on with a deep-seated need to prove she was good enough. Piece by piece, she started to gather the fragments that were left of her. She began to rebuild herself into a new woman, a stronger version of herself. Pain can do many things to a person, and she decided it would make her stronger. Luna would be born from this fire she was now walking through. She was determined not to get lost in it.

Luna made her way to the horse pasture. She removed her bags from Willow, placing them over her own shoulders before heading home. When she arrived, she saw the smoke coming from the chimney and knew someone was already inside. She knew it would most likely be her father and Aidan, who had come many times in the past two months to spend time with her. He could carry on a conversation, and he was polite for the most part. They didn't have many common interests, but they both tried. Gannon always made sure they were never alone together, which Luna was grateful for. She saw the way Aidan looked at her, and she knew what he expected from her when they were hand-fasted together. The thought of being physically intimate with anyone other than Sol made her sick, so she pushed it out of her mind. She wouldn't worry about that today. Luna took a deep breath, putting on her invisible armor, and walked in.

Aidan was there, sitting at the table. He looked up from speaking with Gannon when she entered, and Luna masked her disappointment with a smile.

"Luna!" Gannon said, excited to see her.

"Hello, Father. Hello, Aidan."

"Can I help you with that?" Aidan stood up and walked over to relieve her of the leather strap the linen bags hung from. She let him take it, and he placed it on the table. He was quick to offer his help, and Luna was hopeful life with him would be better than it was there with her father.

"Luna, why don't you go clean yourself up," Gannon suggested upon taking in her disheveled appearance. "Alice collected the things you need to make a rabbit stew for dinner"—he motioned to the pile of vegetables—"and Aidan already cleaned the hare for you."

"Thank you," Luna said to Aidan before she turned and entered her room. She closed the door behind her and breathed a sigh of relief for the moment to herself. She lit the candles in the dim room before washing the dirt from her hands and under her fingernails from the work she had done that day. Luna washed her face and brushed her hair, finding a few stray pieces of grass from her nap in the meadow. She didn't bother reapplying the charcoal markings on her face, and she changed into a loose-fitting tunic dress with long dark purple sleeves. Luna blew out the candles in her room before going back out to cook dinner for her father and their guest.

She entered the common room, and Aidan's eyes were immediately focused on her. Gannon noticed this, and he seemed pleased with his future son-in-law's interest.

"Luna is a great cook. Just wait until you taste this rabbit stew."

"I can't wait. What did you do today, Luna?" Aidan asked.

Luna got to work preparing the food as she spoke. "I harvested burdock root."

"Oh," Aidan said, making an honest effort to sound interested.

Gannon changed the subject. "Luna, tomorrow you will go with Aidan and he will show you around his village. I'll meet you there in the afternoon. I have something else I want you to see."

"As you wish," Luna agreed. The men talked amongst themselves while Luna prepared dinner.

The fragrance of the dish made Aidan's mouth water. "How soon will it be ready?" he asked.

Gannon responded before Luna could. "Soon enough, boy. You are really getting the better end of the deal here as Luna is a great cook. I am going to miss her meals when she is joined to you. Maybe I'll have to move in with you." Gannon laughed at his own joke.

He was going to miss her *cooking*, but not *her*. Gannon's words stabbed Luna's already wounded heart.

"There would be plenty of room in the house," Aidan responded.

"Not for long, I hope." Gannon shot a glance at Luna.

"It's ready," Luna said, grabbing three wooden bowls from a small shelf. She scooped the stew into them and placed them on the table. Luna reached for the wooden spoons and placed one in each bowl. The men dug in without waiting for her to sit and join them.

They ate their dinner with agreeable conversation. Aidan asked for a second helping, offering to get it himself, but she got it for him. Gannon pulled out his pipe and filled it with dried herbs while she cleaned up. Luna got to work washing the burdock roots she had gathered that day, rinsing the dirt off in the bucket of water they kept in the house. When she was done, she tied some of the roots to strings she hung above the fireplace to dry out. She cut up other bits and placed them into jars filled with the strong alcohol Alice had gotten for her from Aidan's tribe. She kept busy, waiting for an acceptable time to excuse herself and go to bed.

When Luna announced that she was leaving to get fresh water, her father didn't stop the hunting story he was telling Aidan to respond to her; he just waved his hand in her direction. Aidan stood and nodded, his blue eyes meeting hers. She felt something different with him, thought maybe there was a chance she could find some happiness with this man.

Luna took her time collecting fresh water from the river. She sat there, looking at the stars but not making wishes. You need hope to make wishes, and she only had defeated acceptance now. Luna grabbed the bucket and stood before making her way home. When she arrived, the men were still smoking and talking.

"I am going to go to bed now," Luna announced.

Aidan looked up at her and stood again. "Good night Luna. I look forward to tomorrow."

"As do I," she lied. She had gotten good at it these past months.

Luna fell asleep listening to the men talk and laugh loudly into the night. Sleep came fast to her these days, and she was thankful for it. When she woke the next morning, she went through her normal routine, stopping to have tea with her father and preparing herself for the day ahead.

"Aidan will be here soon. Alice will be by before he gets here, though, so wait for her before you leave," Gannon ordered before setting off for the day.

"As you wish," Luna agreed.

Alice arrived shortly after, bringing an armful of her elderberry tincture. "Here, take these with you today. This is your portion from what you helped me with. Keep what you need and then bring the rest with you to trade. Gannon said you and Aidan would be going to the market today."

"Yes."

Luna took the tinctures from her aunt and brought them

inside. Separating the bunches, she put what she wanted to trade in the deer hide bag she grabbed from one of the wooden pegs in the common room.

"Luna, your father wanted me to speak to you," Alice started.

"About what?" she asked, sitting at the table to face her aunt.

"You will be alone with Aidan today, and he wants to make sure you remember certain things should only be shared once you are hand-fasted to him. I didn't think that would be hard for you, but I do hear the rumors about Aidan."

Luna didn't care about the rumors; she had heard them, too. What bothered her was that talk of them consummating their union was now anyone else's business. Luna didn't want to think of it herself, and now she had her own family focusing on the fact that her hand-fasting was only a month away. "I won't," she answered simply.

"Just try not to be alone with him if you can. You are not his yet, and if he was to have you, your standing in this agreement would not be as much as it is now," Alice said, choosing her words carefully. Luna knew Alice meant Luna's worth would be downgraded significantly if she were to share her bed with a man she was, for all intents and purposes, being traded to as a commodity in exchange for joining tribes, and therefore joining their forces.

"I won't," Luna promised.

Alice seemed satisfied. Just then there was a knock at the door, and Aidan walked in to collect Luna for their day together.

Luna greeted him. He offered his hand, and she took it. Aidan said goodbye to Alice and led Luna outside to his black stallion.

"No saddle?" Luna asked, surprised.

"No, I don't like it much," he said.

"Me either. My horse is just over there." Luna pointed toward where they pastured the horses beyond the walls.

"We can take mine together," he said, linking his hands upon his knee to give her a boost. She paused for a moment. The thought of their bodies so close while sharing his horse made her hesitate.

"Mine isn't far," she said.

"This will be fine," he urged her.

Luna placed her bare foot into his warm hands and took the boost to mount his stallion. Aidan was quick to join her with little difficulty and nudged the horse to start their journey out of the village walls and toward his tribe lands.

Luna had always felt larger than most women, and even some of the tribesmen. Aidan was much taller than her, and his broad frame made her feel small. He wrapped his arms around her and grabbed the horse's reins. Luna felt his hot breath on the back of her neck and heard him subtly inhale her scent. The warmth of his body was comforting on the cold morning, but every inch of her body rejected his closeness. She felt guilty for feeling that way toward him. She knew they would have to get much closer soon, as her aunt had just reminded her. Luna shivered as the horse trotted onward. She closed her eyes and imagined it was Sol behind her. The motion of the horse gently rocking their bodies up and down wasn't so bad when she envisioned the strong arms around her waist were Sol's. She remembered what their skin looked like naked against each other, her lighter olive tone contrasting with his dark brown.

"Well, this is it," Aidan said, interrupting her fantasy. "The start of my land, soon to be *our* land." He showed her into the village and to his home. They spent a couple hours walking around meeting the elders of his tribe, making sure to see his father, Bale.

"It's time to meet your father," Aidan said, reminding her of their appointment with Gannon.

"Yes."

He took her hand, leading her through the village. They walked west into the woods, further north than the path they had taken to come from her land. Luna started to get a bad feeling in her stomach the farther into the forest they went, away from other people. The thought hadn't crossed her mind before, but what if he was leading her out there so no one would see them? If he tried to do anything, would she scream? Would she fight? What could she do? Her father had given her to him, and yet the responsibility was solely hers to delay the consummation of their union until the hand-fasting celebration night. The hypocrisy of the double standard was glaringly obvious to her now, and yet everyone else seemed to have no problem overlooking it.

Luna decided she would start a conversation to distract Aidan as they made their way down a newly worn path. "What happened to your mother?"

"She died giving birth to me," he answered quickly.

"Oh, I am sorry to hear that."

"It was a long time ago. I didn't ever know her so it isn't like I can miss her," he said, trying to seem less affected than he was.

"I think you can miss someone you have never met. I only have a handful of memories of my mother, and I miss her every day, especially now," Luna said honestly.

Aidan hesitated before responding. "I suppose you are right." He glanced toward her, and her mouth curved into a genuine smile. She could relate to him in his pain of maternal loss.

"When we are joined, I have some ideas on how we can help our people to merge together," Aidan continued.

"Oh?" Luna asked, wondering if he wanted to tell her his plans because he wanted to know what she thought, or because he liked to talk about himself.

"I think if we combined our efforts, we could plant several more gardens and double the agriculture output. My father doesn't agree, but someday it will be you and me making the decisions," Aidan said, stopping to look into her eyes.

Luna realized he was waiting for her to answer. "It sounds possible."

Aidan smiled and grabbed her hand, leading her forward.

Luna wasn't sure what had just happened. He seemed to be different around her when it was just the two of them, and this Aidan, she had to admit, she liked.

A large wooden lodge came into sight. It was the biggest building she had ever seen. Wooden tree trunks were stacked horizontally, fitting into each other where they crossed at the ends, and there were two grand stone chimneys on either side of the house.

"Wow," Luna said, unable to hide her surprise.

"Come inside," Aidan invited. They walked onto the large wooden deck, up to the door. Luna expected Aidan to knock, but he entered right away. They entered a massive hallway with wooden pegs on either side. An antler chandelier hung with new candles set inside it, and Luna had never seen anything like it before. Aidan led her to where the hallway split into two directions. To the right was a large room with a vaulted ceiling and more large antler candle chandeliers hanging from ropes to light the room. The fireplace on the east wall was large and expertly crafted. Runes were carved into the wooden shelf that had been sculpted into the stone mantle above the fire. Aidan saw the awe on Luna's face and led her into the other room to see another large fireplace, this time on the west wall, with the same design. A long wooden table filled half of the room, the other half a large kitchen area that already had bowls and utensils organized on some of the shelves.

"What do you think?" Aidan asked, smiling.

"It's beautiful," Luna said honestly. "Who lives here?"

"We will," Aidan said, spinning Luna so he could face her.

"This is for us?" Luna asked incredulously.

"Yes. Your father had the idea. The plans were mine though. Men from both our tribes helped to build it exactly in the middle of both of our lands," he explained.

Luna realized her father had been planning this for months, before she even met Sol. All those nights away were for this. It was the most beautiful house she had ever seen, and certainly the largest. Luna thought of herself cooking in the large kitchen. She hoped there would never be enough people to fill the table, but she also knew she was to be a chief's wife and hosting the elders would be a part of it. She imagined that even with all the seats filled, she would still feel lonely inside the mansion.

"There's an upstairs too. Want to see?" he asked eagerly, and that hungry look appeared in his eyes again.

"My father should be here soon. Let's wait for him. I'm sure he will want to show me a part of the house," Luna said, wishing her father would arrive quickly.

Aidan took a step closer, taking her face in his strong hands. "Luna, this is our home. This is where we will build a life with each other. This is where we will come after the hand-fasting ceremony." He leaned his face closer to hers.

Luna anticipated this and turned her head as she spoke. "It is quite the surprise. What did you build? Show me," Luna said. Taking his hand, she walked over to the other large room and pointed to the antler chandelier, asking, "Whose idea was this?"

"That was mine," he answered, only slightly disappointed.

"Really? I love it," she said honestly.

"I hope one day you can love me, too," Aidan said, just above a whisper.

Luna froze. Her chest tightened, not sure what she should say, and she avoided eye contact. She thought of her love for Sol like a fire burning deep inside. Aidan wanted her to share that with him, and Luna knew it was impossible. She had already given that piece of her heart away, and she would never get it back. She didn't want it back. Luna knew there were several types of love, varying arrays of its realness and depth. She thought someday she could love Aidan in a way much different than how she loved Sol. Maybe someday their friendship would grow into something more than just a mutual respect, but she couldn't imagine feeling it now.

"Someday," she agreed, and he seemed satisfied.

Luna wasn't left waiting with Aidan by herself for long. Gannon came in and showed her around the downstairs again before showing her the four bedrooms upstairs. Four bedrooms—the insinuation that Luna would make children to fill those rooms was not lost on her, and she suddenly wanted to run from the great house of expectations. Gannon told her what they planned to put in each of the rooms before they moved in. Luna watched and listened to her life being planned out before her, wondering if he cared what she thought about any of it. Her father's lack of interest in her input gave her the answer.

They ate their midday meal together in the lodge before Aidan and Luna said their goodbyes and headed for the market. He showed her a few carts that were set up with his favorite foods. Luna traded a bottle of elderberry tincture she had brought in the deer hide bag for a batch of beautifully colored feathers from a tradeswoman.

A fishmonger waved a red fish out to them. Luna felt her stomach seize, and she covered her nose and mouth. She walked away quickly, dry-heaving and desperately trying not to vomit in front of everyone.

"Are you okay?" Aidan asked, concerned.

"Yes." She waved one of her hands and held her stomach with the other. "The smell of the fish was just…" Luna couldn't finish her sentence; she didn't want to even think of it out of fear she would throw up.

"I get it. You live in a village with a river as your only source of water, so you aren't used to the sea creatures."

"Right." It was a lie, but it was easier than the truth.

"Well, I am waiting on one of the other people I trade with to get here, and I have some other business I need to finish up. If you want to explore by yourself for a little while, go for it," he said. She noticed his eyes followed a tribeswoman as she passed, admiring her backside.

"All right."

"Go south. There is a nice route that way. I'll find you when he gets here," Aidan said, returning to look at Luna.

She nodded, turning to walk south.

Luna felt Aidan's eyes follow her for a few minutes. She walked along a path into a cedar and pine forest. The path led on, and the trees thinned as she approached a sandy hill. Luna reached the top and a salty blast of cold sea air enveloped her senses. All at once the memories of meeting Sol at the ocean came rushing in, like waves in a storm. She could smell him. She could feel the softness of his skin when his hard body was against hers. She could taste his kiss. The uninvited memories flooded in, knocking the breath from her lungs. She remembered the tears that night, and then she remembered the joy. Electricity buzzed throughout her body as she remembered the first time she gave herself to him, how easy it was. Luna remembered their conversations, and she missed him. She missed her best friend. She closed her eyes and thought of falling asleep wrapped in his arms. Her heart ached to be with him again.

Luna opened her eyes and walked down to the shoreline. Her feet touched the icy salt water, and she remembered how warm it had been that night she went swimming in the moonlight with Sol. She walked on for some time, enjoying the salty air and the bittersweet memories it brought with it. The sea was greenish grey, and Luna recognized the color of Sol's eyes in each ocean wave as the tide slowly started to recede. She looked out across the waves and followed the water as it swelled and crashed into itself before breaking off into smaller ones, finally leaving rippled wet sand in front of her feet. The tide brought in bits of small plant matter and larger seaweed along with broken shells of crustaceans seabirds had already devoured. A lonely unbroken grey circle caught her attention, and she picked it up gingerly, not sure what it was.

"It's a sand dollar," said a familiar voice.

Luna looked up, turning to see who was behind her. She held her breath and felt dizzy. Her heart beat faster at first then seized in her chest when she saw him. She thought she was imagining an apparition of the man who stood before her.

"Sol?"

CHAPTER 15

The past two months had passed slowly for Sol. He kept busy by building his house at the edge of the sea. The foundation was built high off the ground, and the framing of the actual house was done. Bomani helped when he could, and Akiiki came to visit almost every day. She was concerned for Sol, but he didn't want her to worry about him. She was eight moons along in her pregnancy and Sol didn't want to add stress to her life, so he assured her all was well and forced smiles when she was nearby.

Sol was working to finish the last of the four walls. He used piles of the twisted branches and clay to seal the pieces in place, making it airtight. Sol climbed down the ladder he had constructed to get inside the first floor of the house. He was walking over to refill his bucket with the clay mortar when a familiar voice spoke to him.

"It's come a long way since last week," Layla said, admiring his work.

She walked toward him from the path in the woods wearing a bright turquoise dress that accentuated her curves.

Silver bangles adorned her arms and wrists, a matching headband encircled her head, and colorful feathers were braided into strands of her hair. Layla had come by every week since the equinox celebration to see the progress and attempt to make conversation. She had good ideas about the structure, he had to admit. He had started to see a new side to her with each passing conversation. She was a friend, but that was all she could be to him; it was all any woman would ever be after Luna.

"It's coming along," he replied, pausing his work to sit and have a drink of water.

"I like it," Layla said honestly, putting her hand on her hip.

Sol nodded in response, taking another sip of water from a drinking gourd.

After a moment of silence, Layla asked, "I need to go to the Dabney market and sell the new jewelry I just finished. Is there any chance you would be willing to go with me? I could ask someone else, but I thought maybe you would want to."

Sol had been to the Dabney tribe lands only once in the recent months, and he was due for another visit to unload some of his wooden wares. After the ordeal with Layla and Luna, his mother had suggested that when anyone in the tribe traveled far from the village, they went in pairs for safety.

"Sure. I have a quite a few things to take myself. Let me gather them and I'll meet you at the horse pasture."

Layla nodded. "Okay. See you soon," she said before turning to leave the way she had come.

Sol took another long drink of water before finding a bucket to wash his hands off. He looked toward the ocean waves and wished it were warm enough for a swim. He took off his shirt and splashed water on his face, washing under his arms before heading back to his lean-to for a fresh white tunic. He gathered the wooden spoons he'd worked on by the fire at night and a couple bowls he'd managed to finish, placing them carefully in a large leather bag he wore across both shoulders on his back. Sol set off and met Layla by the horse pasture as agreed, and they set off together toward Dabney tribe lands.

When they arrived, the market was already starting to pick up from the midday break. Sol helped Layla lay out a fabric to arrange her wares upon, and she offered to share her space with Sol. He laid his wooden creations down next to the assortment of silver and crystal jewelry.

"Sol!"

Sol turned to see Aidan coming toward him. He extended his hand when he approached.

They shook hands and Aidan continued, "I was hoping you would be here today. I need to get more of the bowls if you have them." Aidan nodded a hello to Layla, who politely did the same.

Sol motioned toward the blanket of goods. "I brought what I have done. You seem to go through a lot." Sol laughed.

"Ahh, the lodge we are building for my new bride and I to move into is done. Just furnishing left mostly, and she is going to need a lot of this stuff," Aidan explained.

"Oh, I hadn't heard. Blessed be your union. I am honored you chose my woodwork," Sol said, giving him honest thanks.

"Yes, thank you. It was announced on the solstice feast. One more month until we are hand-fasted together," Aidan added.

"Oh," Sol replied.

Aidan looked toward the south, motioning with his hand. "Luna is just walking that way for a bit. I wanted her to come pick out what she wanted herself. Women know more about this sort of stuff than us men," Aidan joked.

Sol didn't laugh.

Luna. His bride-to-be was Luna. Sol felt the blood drain from his face. The solstice had been just after they'd decided going their separate ways was best for everyone. Had they decided it together, or had he? Sol had known this day might come, but not so soon, and certainly not to Aidan. Sol had known someone else would love Luna, but he hadn't thought it would happen so quickly. Maybe it was just that he had hoped she wouldn't have gotten over what they had together so soon. Sol knew instantly that it was a selfish thought. Maybe he was the fool and Luna had never loved him the way he did her.

"Are you okay Sol?" Aidan asked.

"Yes," he lied. His mind was still dealing with the blow of the news.

"I should go get her to find out what she wants, but I also want to pick her out one of these," Aidan said, pointing to Layla's jewelry.

"I can go find her for you. You get what you need and settle up with Layla," Sol said, heading south without waiting for Aidan to answer.

"Oh, okay," Aidan said to Sol's back. "She's wearing a purple dress and has black chief's tribal markings on her face!" Aidan shouted after Sol.

Sol continued on, his heartbeat increasing with each step he took. He walked quickly through the village until he was out of sight of the villagers then sprinted up the sandy hill. He stopped suddenly as Luna came into view a long way down to his right. He heard the beat of his heart in his ears, mixed with a ringing noise. His chest felt as if it was being squeezed by a strong fist. Sol took a deep breath and jogged to catch up to her, knowing they only had a few moments alone together.

When he was a few yards away, he slowed to a walk. She stopped to look at something in the sand before picking it up, looking at it quizzically.

"It's a sand dollar," he blurted out before realizing he'd spoken aloud.

She turned quickly, her eyes meeting his.

"Sol?" Luna said, finally finding her voice, not sure if she should trust the apparition.

"Luna."

They both stared at each other, paralyzed by an onslaught of emotions and a reawakened yearning for each other.

"What are you doing here?" Luna broke the silence first, looking nervously over his shoulder for any sign of Aidan.

"Trading," he answered.

Luna nodded, acknowledging his response.

"I heard the news," Sol said, more accusatory than he had intended, and he instantly regretted it. Luna looked as if his words were a sharp knife that had been thrust into her heart.

"I was informed of the arrangement at the equinox feast," Luna explained, trying to make an excuse. She wanted him to know it was not fully her choice.

Suddenly it clicked in Sol's mind. The last time he had seen Luna was the night of the equinox, the night she had spoken into the darkness of sacrificing all for her loved one's safety. Was it for him? The thought was too much to bear.

"Luna, is this what you want?" he asked.

She looked down at the sand, crossing her arms and avoiding the intense eyes of the only man she would ever love. "He wanted me, and no one else did."

The words hit him, and he stood there stunned. Why would she think no one else wanted her? Why would she think he didn't want her? Sol stepped closer to her and placed his hands on her shoulders, shaking them lightly so she would look at him.

"Luna," he said, wondering how she could think such a thing.

His touch was electric. Luna wanted nothing more than to be closer to him, wrapped in his arms. She wanted him to tell her everything would be all right, and she wanted his kiss. She needed him.

Sol felt the electricity buzz through his hands as he touched Luna's arms. He wanted her close to him, but he knew he had chosen this for her just as much as he had done it for his family.

"Nothing is about me. I have no choices anymore. Maybe I never did. I am a chief's daughter and my duty is to my people. My father wants us to join with the Dabney. I know if I do this I will have more of a say in the future of these tribes than if I didn't. I will have a better chance of keeping your tribe safe from an attack," Luna said, her voice quiet but strong. *A better chance of keeping you safe*, she thought to herself.

Sol looked at her. Something about her was different, but he didn't know what. "Luna, I am not your responsibility. Don't do this for me. My tribe is not your responsibility."

Luna took a deep breath at the rejection in his words. "It is now."

"What do you mean?" Sol asked, feeling anger rise. He would not let her be a martyr for him.

Luna took one of his hands from her shoulder and placed it on her abdomen. Sol looked confused at first. Then, a sudden look of realization and shock crossed his handsome face.

"Luna—"

Sol was interrupted by Aidan yelling from the sandy hill.

"Sol! Luna!" he called out for the second time.

Sol and Luna dropped their hands instinctively before turning and walking toward Aidan.

"Luna," Sol said quietly.

"Stop. Don't speak of this to anyone. I'll probably lose it like my mother did so many times. I only told you so you would understand. I'll figure it out." Luna hoped her words would silence him.

"You can't tell me this and then expect me to pretend I don't care, pretend it doesn't change things."

"Yes, I can. This is what you chose, and this doesn't change anything. This is why I didn't tell you. I wanted you to be free to choose for yourself, without having anything cloud your judgment. I wanted you to choose me because you wanted me, not because you had a duty. You made your choice and that is that."

"Luna!" Sol said, raising his voice.

"Quiet! He will hear you," she hissed, masking her distress with a smile.

"How long have you known?" Sol defied her but whispered this time.

She glanced quickly toward him. "Since you left me bloody at the waterfall."

The words struck Sol so much so that he staggered back a step. He felt the resentment in her voice, and it was the first time he had felt she was truly angry with him. Sol felt the collision of his conflicting emotions, and he struggled to breathe. All at once, he felt terrified and excited at the prospect of being a father. Sol wanted to talk with her about the enormous secret she had kept to herself this whole time but didn't want to risk her safety, so he kept still.

"I see you found my Luna," Aidan announced with his lips curling into a huge smile. He reached out for her hand and wrapped his arm around her, pulling her closer to his body, as if staking his claim on her. This was the side of him she didn't like.

Sol was still searching for his voice, so Luna spoke for him, asking Aidan, "Is this who you were waiting for?"

"Yes, this is Sol. He does the amazing woodworking on the bowls and other things in the kitchen from the lodge," Aidan explained.

"Oh, those were from him?" Luna asked, trying to hide the fact that her stomach was twisting into a knot.

"Yeah. He's got more for you to look at and pick out what you want, too. Your tribe doesn't trade with his people, but you are really missing out. Right, Sol?" Aidan asked.

"Right," Sol said, finally composing himself enough to speak. His face was solemn.

Aidan pulled out a large necklace from his pocket. It was too big and shiny for Luna's taste, but she took the gift with a smile. "Oh, wow. Thank you."

Aidan put it on her, moving her hair aside to fasten the clasp. Sol saw the simple purple shell he had tied to a string and given her was still around her neck, hiding beneath her tunic.

"Anything for my future wife." Aidan turned Luna to face him and leaned in to kiss her cheek. It was the first time he had been that bold, and Luna guessed she was being shown off. She winced from his kiss and hoped he wouldn't notice. He didn't see it, but Sol did. She wasn't ready for this type of physical contact with Aidan yet, especially in front of Sol.

Sol watched Aidan lean in, and it took all his strength to not tear him off her. He saw Luna was uncomfortable and begged her with his eyes to let him do something. She avoided his gaze and forced a smile. His jealous rage was animalistic, and it took all his might to remain where he stood.

"The beautiful woman Sol is with made the necklace. What's her name?" Aidan asked.

"Layla," Sol answered, watching for Luna's reaction.

Luna felt as though she had been struck in the face. *Layla?* The woman who had attacked her at the waterfall? *Layla,* the propelling force in this mess, had been the one to make the necklace that now hung around Luna's neck?

The woman Sol was *with*, as Aidan had described her! Luna shot Sol a look of betrayal as she felt her body heat from anger, her suspicions confirmed.

"Come on, let's do business!" Aidan said, grabbing Luna's hand and leading the way back to the village.

Luna took a deep breath as they headed back to where she would have to pick out dinnerware from the man who used to be her lover so she could put it in the house she would share with her arranged husband. She was on her way to see the woman who had tried to kill her, thank her for the gaudy jewelry, and pretend all was well about the fact that *Layla* was now with Sol. Sol joining with Layla after what the woman had done to her? *How could he?* In that moment, Luna's fears were confirmed: all men were the same, chasing the next beautiful woman who came their way when they were done taking all they could from the woman before. She hated herself for still loving him even though he had broken her to her core.

Sol followed behind Luna and Aidan. She was the love of his whole universe. He wouldn't call Aidan a friend, but they were on friendly terms. Aidan had seemed a decent man who genuinely cared for his people, but he liked women, and that fact had never been lost on Sol. Did Luna really know what she was doing?

Layla. Panic shot through his chest. He needed to prepare her before she saw Luna and put all their lives in jeopardy.

"I'll run ahead and see you when you get there," Sol

said, jogging past Aidan and Luna.

Sol ran to where Layla was just finishing bartering with a Dabney tribeswoman for a few jars of fermented drink in exchange for one of her necklaces.

"These people expect us to try to take them for everything they have." She shook her head.

"Layla, I need to tell you something. I need you to listen to me and not question me. I swear, I will explain what you need to know later, but I need you to trust me," Sol said in a panic, not registering what she had said to him.

Layla looked at him with confusion. "Is something wrong?" she asked worriedly.

"There will be if you don't help me. The woman who is on her way here with Aidan—I need you to pretend you have never seen her before," he hurriedly explained in a whisper.

"What do you mean? I don't know her," Layla said, bewildered.

"Yes, you do. Please, Layla, for the safety of us and our tribe, don't say a word," Sol clarified, turning to see Aidan and Luna almost upon them.

"Don't say a word about what? Oh!" Layla then saw Luna.

The women's eyes met.

Luna steeled her expression and forced a smile as Layla noticed the necklace she had traded to Aidan hanging around Luna's neck.

Sol spoke first. "Luna, this is Layla."

Luna followed his lead. "Layla." She nodded in greeting.

Layla's face turned into a soured expression as she nodded. "Luna." Layla said her name as if it was the key to a lock she had been trying to open for some time.

"Pick out what you want from Sol, and Layla too, if you want," Aidan urged Luna.

Luna felt she was in a never-ending nightmare, and she just wanted it all to end. "Oh…I don't know what you already have," Luna replied, trying to think of a way to escape this madness and find refuge in her bedroom far away from this mess.

"You can never have too much, not when you cook the way you do." Aidan turned to speak to Sol. "She makes the most delicious rabbit stew. I just can't bring fish around her, as I've learned today." Aidan laughed, remembering Luna almost losing her lunch just an hour earlier.

Luna blushed and hoped no one would see—impossible, since Sol wouldn't take his eyes off her.

"I'll take all of it then," Luna announced, trying to end the uncomfortable meeting.

She wanted to be home in her bed, alone with her thoughts so she could process everything. She hadn't meant to tell Sol, but she couldn't bear to keep the secret inside any longer. The fight at the waterfall two full moon cycles ago had brought the vision of her mother, who had told her she was fighting not only for her life but that of the unborn child growing within her womb: Sol's child. The changing of the season had brought about a missed moon time for her, and the blood from the goddess had been absent for three moons now.

"You heard the woman. We will take all of it!" Aidan said, laughing. "What would you like in return?"

"Nothing," Sol answered.

"What?" Aidan asked, incredulous.

"It's a gift for the soon-to-be-bride, and you, of course," Sol explained.

"That's too much," Luna argued.

"Wow. I have to agree with Luna on this Sol," Aidan said, offering his hand to shake Sol's.

Sol extended his hand. "It is my gift, and I won't take no for an answer. Take care of her." He motioned toward Luna.

Sol's gaze was more intense than Aidan had expected, and he laughed nervously. "Of course, and she'll take care of me."

Luna felt like she was going to be sick. All eyes were on her. Layla was staring at Luna, her eyes seething with unspoken rage. Luna felt Sol's wounded gaze, full of questions, or maybe accusations—she wasn't sure. Aidan looked at her now like she owed him something even though he had paid nothing for Sol's goods, and that was a debt she did not want to pay.

"Aidan, I am not feeling well. I don't mean to be rude,

but I would like to go home. It has been a long day," Luna said honestly.

"Oh, sure. I'll go get my horse." He left without hesitation.

"He seems to care about you," Sol said.

Luna didn't respond. She turned and looked at Layla's mouth curled in a snarl.

"Luna. So that's your name." Layla spoke as if her words were knives being thrown at Luna, who crossed her hands in front of her in defense of the invisible weapons.

"Layla, not now," Sol ordered firmly.

Luna saw Layla's disappointed grimace and then looked back to Sol. He was as handsome as ever, even with the serious look he had plastered on his face.

"I will go meet Aidan. Goodbye, Sol," Luna said, turning to leave and ignoring Layla.

Sol wanted to reach out and grab her arm. He wanted her to come with him. He wanted to get answers to the questions that now burned in his mind from the news that Luna was carrying a child—*his* child.

"I saw you that night, by the river, in the dark," he blurted out, following after her.

Luna froze mid-step then turned to face him.

He now saw the fresh tears that were escaping her eyes. He realized she had turned so quickly because she had been trying to hide them, and his heart broke again at the fact that he had caused her yet more pain. He hated himself for it.

"Then you know why this is my only option," she said before turning away, wiping the tears, and running to meet Aidan.

"Oh, you have some explaining to do, Sol." Layla said it like she was scolding a child.

"Wrap your stuff up and be silent until we are out of this village. Understood?" he snapped at her.

Layla recoiled from his reaction and knew he was serious. She thought it best to do as he said. She didn't want to start a scene in a village full of people who already thought so little of the Nets. She knew just because they were on trading terms, it didn't mean these people were safe.

Sol and Layla left in a hurry. Once they were safely on their tribal land again, Layla broke the silence.

"What was that? You knew her. Sol, you knew the woman who attacked me! *Luna*." Layla said her name like it tasted bitter in her mouth. "How?" Layla demanded an answer by stepping in front of him and stopping him in his tracks.

"We met at the waterfall."

Layla's eyes narrowed. "That is why you kept going up there day after day. I knew it! I knew I was right."

"Do you want to change your story now, about why you followed me up there? About *who* started the fight that day?" he asked, his anger at Layla surfacing at long last.

Layla looked as if she had been caught in the act of stealing something. "She is a Barden, Sol. She is not good enough for you."

"And you are, right, Layla? *You* are *selfish*! I will *never* be with you. How could you expect me to want to be with you after all you have done?" Sol yelled at her.

Layla genuinely looked hurt, and Sol realized she was not as tough or as uncaring as he had assumed. She did in fact actually love him in her own way, maybe more than he had realized.

"I have been selfish too, Layla. This is my fault. These are the consequences of my choices, and I should be the only one paying them. Now, the woman I love will pay for it with her happiness, and her safety." Sol spoke more to himself than Layla.

The look in Sol's eyes took away any enjoyment Layla felt at the thought of her rival enduring payback.

"Sol, I'm sorry. I really didn't know. I didn't think…" Layla searched for the right words.

"Neither did I."

CHAPTER 16

Luna made it through the horseback ride back to her house with Aidan. He jumped down first and extended his hand toward her. Luna took it gratefully and slid off the horse. She felt dizzy and grabbed his firm muscled shoulders to steady herself.

"Are you okay?" he asked, concerned.

"Yes. I just need a minute." He stood there with her, enjoying the moment much more than she did. "My head is spinning," Luna admitted.

Aidan picked up the deer hide backpack filled with elderberry tinctures she hadn't traded and slipped it over one of his shoulders. Next, he effortlessly picked her up in his arms and carried her into her house. Luna was relieved to see her father wasn't home yet.

"In there." Luna pointed toward her room. Aidan opened the door and gently set her on her bed. He placed the deerskin bag against the wall then knelt by her side.

"Do you need me to get someone for you?" he asked with a look of worry crossing his features.

"No, I will be fine. It was just a long day and a lot of

excitement. I just need sleep," Luna answered.

"If you are sure then I'll leave," Aidan said.

"I am sure." Luna pulled a blanket over herself.

Aidan leaned over her and Luna panicked. His lips gently kissed her forehead before he stood and headed to the bedroom door.

"Thank you," Luna called behind him. "For your help," she clarified.

"It was my pleasure." Aidan bowed low and then left the room, closing the door behind him. Luna listened for him to leave through the front door before she relaxed into her bed.

Her head was still dizzy, and all the hidden emotions she had repressed during the day came rushing upon her like a tall wave, drowning her in the intensity. Questions filled her mind, so many questions. Why was Sol there with Layla? Why had he spoken with her at all? Why did he still seem to care? Maybe he thought he had rights to her. *He isn't like that*, she reminded herself. He had been the one to choose this; he hadn't wanted to run away with her. Why did he expect her life could be anything but this now? Why had he said anything at all to her? Didn't he know his words were torture to her already shattered heart?

Luna remembered his hands on her shoulders and then the feeling when she placed his warm hand on her belly. For a moment, she had felt connected to him again. She had tried to tell him about the pregnancy in the cave, back before he told her he was choosing his tribe over running away with her. Luna realized the idea seemed childish now—running away from their problems instead of facing reality. She had just wanted their fantasy to live on as long as it could, but it had run its course. That was evident now that he was spending his time with Layla, the woman who had tried to kill her and her unborn child. Maybe now that Sol knew the truth, he would at least see Layla for who she really was. She was glad he knew now.

Aidan had been surprisingly quick to take care of her, and she recognized the difference in him depending on who he was around. Luna wondered who the real Aidan was. Was it the person he was when it was just the two of them? She had seen him look lustfully at the tribeswoman that had passed them, and even toward Layla once. Aidan was unpredictable, and she had so many questions about him. Luna decided to focus on what she knew. Aidan was forward and crass sometimes, but she had seen the vulnerability in him when he spoke about his mother and the plans he had for the merging of tribes. He seemed genuinely concerned for her and yet made his physical desires clear. Had he really asked her to fall in love with him? There was more to him; Luna was sure of it.

Luna's head was pounding now. She wished for sleep to wipe away the memories and stress of the day, even if only for a short while. She wanted to sleep without dreaming, and that was exactly what happened.

Luna awoke the next morning and went out to find Alice sitting by the fire in the common room.

"Alice?" Luna asked, surprised.

"How are you feeling?" her aunt asked, rubbing the sleep from her own eyes.

"I am well."

"Aidan told your father you were not feeling well last night, so your father stayed at the lodge and asked that I come here for you," Alice answered, responding to Luna's questioning face.

"Oh, I see. I am fine, it was just a long day yesterday. So much to take in. I didn't mean to worry anyone." Luna realized her aunt had spoken of the lodge, meaning she had known about it this whole time.

Alice stood and walked over to Luna with her arms crossed and a concerned expression on her features. "Luna, is everything really all right?" she prodded.

"Yes," Luna replied, lying again.

Alice hesitated, as if she wanted to ask Luna something. Alice must have decided she didn't want the answer and nodded her head. "Okay. I'll be headed to the market if you want to come back to Dabney tribe lands with me. You can start bringing some of your things to the lodge if you want," Alice offered as she headed toward the door.

"No." Luna answered too quickly, causing her aunt to stop abruptly and turn to face her. The thought of changing her surroundings a moment sooner than she absolutely had to caused great anxiety in Luna.

"Did Aidan try something with you?" Alice asked.

"No, Aidan was fine. I just need to forage for honey today, that is all," Luna said, trying to set her aunt at ease.

"All right. Enjoy your day." Alice left, closing the door behind her.

Luna breathed a sigh of relief and made her way to the tea Alice had prepared. After pouring herself a steaming cup of the herbal infusion from the pot, she sat down in the chair by the fire to enjoy it. Alice had known about the lodge and not said anything to her. It made Luna wonder what else her aunt knew about the situation and was keeping from her. Luna decided in that moment Alice shouldn't know about the baby, no matter what. Luna placed a hand protectively over her growing stomach. She was thankful for her larger frame for the first time as it was easier to hide the small curve that only seemed like extra weight at this point. The colder weather also helped as the long flowy dresses and fur wraps would keep her secret hidden for now. Luna guessed it wouldn't work for too much longer and Aidan would realize soon after the ceremony, if not that night. Luna swallowed hard and brought the fragrant tea to her lips, inhaling the aromatic herbs before taking a small sip.

What would Luna do about the child? She hadn't let herself think about it yet because she hadn't expected to carry it to term. At first, she thought she would miscarry as her mother had done several times. When the blood never came, Luna thought about the herbs she could take to end the pregnancy herself but decided that no matter the cost, she wanted this child. The union with Sol had been world changing for Luna, and her love for him would be eternal. They had not only connected their bodies but had woven their spirits together as well. Now, here was the physical manifestation of their union growing in her womb to prove it. Luna felt the goddess's presence as tiny spider-web-like strings of the portal between the spirit realm and the physical world began connecting for the child's spirit to make its final decent when it was ready to be birthed from within her. This child was special. This child was chosen. This child was hers.

Luna knew the child's differences would be obviously apparent, and that it would arrive several months too early for anyone to believe it was Aidan's. She would have to get him to help her, or maybe she would have to disappear for a few months after the ceremony was done. She could have the baby and then reach out to Sol to take it. The thought of separating herself from her baby ripped her heart in places she hadn't known were there, and Luna felt the tears stream down her face. Of one thing she was sure: she would do whatever was necessary to keep the child safe, even if it meant giving her own life.

Luna drank the hot tea and dried the tears from her eyes. She hoped the answer would come to her, but she wouldn't think of it any more that day. She drank a second cup of tea before gathering what she needed and then got Willow from the pasture.

Luna led the horse north toward the tree with the honeybees for the first time in months. She took her time, breathing in crisp autumn air. The fallen leaves crunched under Willow's hooves. The forest seemed naked now, with only the evergreens having leaves left. Luna remembered the last time she'd made this journey in the pouring rain, all of her worldly possessions in a single bag, ready to leave everything and everyone she knew behind to run into the unknown with the man she loved. *Loved*, she repeated to herself, the man she *loved*. Luna told herself the sooner she forgot about him, the easier this next chapter in her life would be. She would pretend she believed it, at least for the time being.

Luna came upon the tree with the beehive inside. She found a piece of bark and repeated the process she knew so well to retrieve the honey inside by coaxing the small insects to sleep with a billow of smoke. She would collect the golden sweetness from the combs intricately built inside the live tree and then return the way she had come. She didn't want to risk traveling to the waterfall. Reliving the tender moments of the magical summer afternoons she had spent there would be torturous.

* * *

Sol had come back angry after his trip to the Dabney market with Layla. He decided he would spend the rest of the day at his lean-to and forgo dinner with his family. His mother and sister were keenly aware when it came to reading his emotions, and he didn't have the energy to guard himself. Sol spent the night watching the tide come in and then recede. The sound of the waves brought him some relief from the thunderous thoughts and questions that filled his mind.

The image of Aidan pulling Luna into his body and kissing her cheek was seared into Sol's mind. He stood and started to walk down the beach. His body needed to move due to the angry energy coursing through his veins. Luna had allowed it, even though she was obviously uncomfortable, though maybe he had just hoped she was. Sol remembered the differences in their tribes that she had made clear, such as her being expected to do as the men wished because she was a woman. Luna had been the one to make her needs known to him when they were together. He knew she had strength in her, he just wished she would be empowered to assert herself in her own tribe, for her own safety.

Sol remembered the look in Luna's eyes when he grabbed her arms. She looked as if it hurt her to be so close to him. Sol reimagined the moment she'd placed his hand on her belly. He had been confused at first, and then he'd realized what she was trying to tell him silently, as if vocalizing the words would be enough to break the world in two. His child was growing inside of her. What was he supposed to do with that kind of news? How was he going to tell his mother? Should he tell her at all?

Why hadn't Luna told him she was carrying his child in the cave? Then he remembered that when she had said he didn't understand everything, he had cut her off. Sol chastised himself for being so arrogant. He should have listened and let her speak. It was his own weakness that had prevented him from hearing her out. He hadn't wanted to go with her out of fear, worried about the repercussions and what would happen to his family as a result, but also about being on his own, responsible for Luna's well-being, as well as his own. Sol hadn't admitted this to himself before, but now he could see that he was afraid he was too weak to protect her. He saw that the belief was deeply rooted within himself, and he remembered the first time he had felt that way as a little boy, watching his father be mauled to death by the giant grizzly. Sol accepted the realization and decided it was time to move on from what held him back. He would not live his life out of fear any longer, and if Luna gave him the chance, he would do everything he could to rescue her from the life that was being forced upon her. He promised himself he would do whatever he could to protect the child that now grew inside her body. He just wasn't sure how.

Luna had said she would figure it out, not that she

already had a plan. Sol wished he could find a way to meet her again. Somehow, he would find a way.

* * *

Luna was able to retrieve the honey without trouble this time. She placed the honeycomb inside a wooden container with a lid and as she approached Willow, she saw the animal was agitated. The horse started snorting and moving around.

"Sshhhh. What is it girl?" Luna asked, quickly placing the container and its contents into a linen bag on the horse.

Willow neighed and reared her head, standing on her hind legs before darting south, away from Luna, who was knocked to the ground. Luna rolled to her feet, quickly scanning the woods around her, looking for whatever or whoever had spooked the horse. Luna backed toward the tree with the honeycomb, where the bees were starting to wake and buzz, realizing someone had taken some of their golden life source. A dark figure moved across from Luna, getting closer to her. She saw it was a black bear, possibly the same one she had seen at the waterfall, only much fatter now from the summer foraging it had done. Luna realized standing next to the honey tree with her hands sticky from the sweetness was not the best thing in this scenario. She tried to back slowly toward where Willow had galloped away. *Thanks for leaving me, Willow*, Luna thought to herself as she tried to make a slow but deliberate getaway. Luna's heartbeat thudded in her chest. The bear nonchalantly walked closer, veering off the path in her direction, toward the tree with the hive.

Luna held her breath and tried to move the opposite way, walking backward, making sure to face the bear. She reached for her bow behind her then cursed herself for leaving it at home. The bear followed her and now stood between her and the path to safety. This was not how she wanted her life to end, nor that of the child within her who hadn't drawn breath yet. Luna pulled out the knife from the leather belt she wore across her dress, and it was still sticky from cutting the honeycomb. *Maybe I should shout*, she wondered to herself. Luna decided to change directions and walk west toward the river, hoping the bear would lose interest and go back to the honey. Luna walked fast, watching the bear for any sign of attack. The animal just watched her, calmly following. The black bear made a low growl when Luna tried to move left or right, almost like she was corralling Luna, leading her in one direction. Luna could hear the burble of the waters and saw the bear sit. She kept moving backward, glancing over her shoulder every few steps so she wouldn't trip on the roots. The bear had stopped following her, and now it just looked at her curiously. Luna took the opportunity and ran toward the river, putting as much distance between her and the bear as she could. Luna reached the water's edge and turned south, running as fast as she could, checking behind her every so often to see if the bear had followed her. Once Luna was satisfied that it had lost interest, she slowed to a walk.

"Little bear!"

Luna turned to hear a familiar voice calling her from across the river.

"Mama Dalila!" Luna stood shocked at the sight of the woman across the river from her and suddenly forgot about her encounter with the black bear. Luna remembered her mother's friend instantly even though her face had aged and her hair was greyed. Luna could never forget those kind eyes. Luna walked into the icy river without thinking. She would grasp at any chance for comfort and safety. The solution to her looming problems was in front of her and she wouldn't let it go, law or no law.

Dalila saw Luna walking toward her and walked carefully closer to the edge of the river, not stepping into the cold waters but reaching out a welcoming hand toward the young girl.

"Luna, come here," Dalila said, opening her arms as Luna approached.

She walked into the woman's welcoming arms and squeezed. Tears began streaming from Luna's face, and Dalila saw them as they loosened their embrace to look at each other.

"Luna, my sweet girl, you have grown into a beautiful woman. Something tells me those tears are not only from the joy of our reunion, but of a sadness," Dalila said, wiping them from Luna's cheeks.

"Mama Dalila, I need your help," Luna said directly, looking into the woman's wise dark eyes.

"Just before she died, I promised your mother I would watch out for you. Your father made that more difficult, but I have always kept you in my heart. I knew we would see each other again one day. What do you need?"

Luna started, "You did?"

"Yes. I know you were so young. Do you remember what she said to you?"

Luna answered, "Just pieces."

"She made me promise to watch out for you, but you were like a daughter to me already. She knew she was going to pass before I was certain. She turned to you and told you to trust yourself, no matter what anyone else told you. Then, she told you she loved you."

Dalila's words triggered the memory for Luna. Her mother's worried face turning calm as she used her last breaths to comfort her daughter, deciding the single most important words. Her mother wanted her to trust herself, contrary to how she had led most of her life until she met Sol. Luna knew she could trust Dalila, not only because her mother had, but because the small voice inside Luna told her she could. That voice had gotten louder in the past months as Luna started to listen to it.

Luna confessed, "I am with child, and the child is half Net."

Dalila's expression was one of surprise, but not total shock.

Luna continued, "I will need to disappear for a few months, until I can give birth. I will have to leave shortly after I am hand-fasted to Aidan, the Dabney chief's son. I will work that out later, but I just need to know you can help me and hide me somewhere away from all the tribes. After the child is born…" Luna hesitated, gathering her strength. "I must ask that you bring the child to the father. His name is Sol. Can you do that without telling anyone? Can you keep my secret and save the life of my child? Will you look after the child as if it is your own blood?" Luna begged, tears streaming down her face.

Dalila pulled Luna into a tight hug of protection so the girl would not see the tears streaming down her own face.

"Yes," she promised without hesitation.

Luna let herself sob into Dalila's shoulder until she felt she could compose herself. Dalila released her when she was ready, and Luna saw the tear stains on the older woman's face as well.

"I wish our meeting was a happier one," Dalila said gently.

"Me too," Luna agreed. "Please don't say anything to the father until it is done. I don't want him worrying about any of this, and I told him I would figure it out. Can you keep an eye on him, in case he tries anything? He is the chieftess's son. If my father, any of my tribe, or any of the Dabney tribe members found out, I am sure they would kill her." *Her.* Luna realized she had referred to the growing fetus in her womb as *her.*

"Little bear, your mother would be proud of the woman you have become."

Luna looked down in shame. "I don't think so. I have made so many choices I don't think she would be proud of, and now I must deal with the consequences."

"You love this man, don't you?" Dalila asked.

"Yes, I do."

"Now, you are doing the hardest thing in the world so your child can be free. That is noble, and your mother sees it. She is still with you, Luna. I can feel her presence. Little bear is what she used to call you because she knew you would grow into a strong and resilient mother bear one day."

Little bear. The name sent shockwaves through Luna as she remembered the black bear that had led her to where Dalila was waiting for her. Could the bear have been her mother's spirit guiding her along this tumultuous journey? It had been warnings of bear sightings in the south woods that had propelled her journey to the north forest that fateful day, and it had been fresh bear tracks that had led her to the waterfall where she met Sol. It had been a bear that had caused her and Sol to cross those first boundaries together, thrusting them together behind a tree to hide from possibly the same bear that had led her to the river today. The revelation came down on Luna's shoulders like rocks falling from a great mountain.

"My mother," Luna responded, still reeling from the discovery.

All at once she felt at peace, knowing her mother's spirit had guided her this far, and now to Dalila. Luna was sure she was making the right choice in that moment, even though it was tearing her apart inside.

"When and where should I meet you?" Dalila asked.

CHAPTER 17

Luna made her way home walking between the forest's edge and the river. Her steps seemed lighter than when she had begun her day. She knew her child would be safe and have loving and diligent guardians. Mama Dalila agreed to meet her three days after she was hand-fasted to Aidan on the solstice, long enough for Luna to prepare, long enough for her to come up with a story to tell Aidan and her father so they would not go to Net lands searching for her. Luna wasn't sure what she would tell them, but the hardest part of her dilemma was solved, and she had faith that things would work out now because she knew her mother was watching over her.

There was still no sign of the horse, and Luna hoped Willow would be waiting for her by the raspberry bushes when she arrived. When Luna was almost there, she called out the horse's name as she had several times on the trek down to her village.

"Willow?"

"Luna? Luna!" came Aidan's voice through the trees.

"Aidan?" Luna asked, surprised.

He came out of the forest, sweeping a tree branch out of his way before stepping into the sun where she could see the relieved look on his face.

"We have been looking for you. Your horse came back without you, spooked. Are you all right?!" He cupped his hands over his mouth, magnifying the whistling noise he sent into the forest.

"Yes, there was a bear, and the horse took off. I took this way back to avoid the bear's path," Luna answered, feeling no need to lie. She heard another whistle in the distance in answer to Aidan's.

"A bear?! How did you get away?" he asked, intrigued.

"It just wanted the honey. It let me go my own way."

"I will gather some men and hunt it—with your father's permission, of course," Aidan offered.

"No, please don't. It meant me no harm, and those woods are more the bear's than mine," Luna said. She thought explaining that the bear was really the spiritual guide of her dead mother would be too much information to share with him. "Can we keep this between us?" Luna asked, testing his trustworthiness.

Aidan looked baffled. "Why don't you want your father to know?"

"My father doesn't like me going into the woods alone as it is. Foraging is my one joy, and I would hate to have that taken from me," she explained truthfully.

He hesitated momentarily, thinking it over. "Okay. It's

our secret."

Luna smiled with a glint of genuine happiness. "Thank you." In another world, in another life where she hadn't met Sol, Luna thought she just might be able to fall for Aidan.

He took her hand. "Your father is worried. We should let him know his only daughter is safe."

He led her into the forest and they walked the rest of the way until they reached the clearing where her village's wall came into sight. A few other Dabney and Barden tribesmen came out of the woods shortly after them, nodding to her as they headed back to their duties.

"I guess he was worried if he had all these men out looking for me."

"It was my idea," Aidan said simply.

Luna realized Aidan might care for her more than she realized. "I have to ask you a question, Aidan, and I just want an honest answer. It doesn't matter to me either way." She felt a pang of hypocrisy asking him for honesty when she was hiding so much.

"What is it?"

"I have heard a lot of rumors about you when it comes to other women," Luna said bluntly, testing the waters.

Aidan shrugged his shoulders before stopping to face her. "I am a man. I have needs. Is that a problem?" he asked, stunned.

"I see. Thank you for your frankness," Luna said, partly surprised at his directness but mostly by the fact that he felt entitled to having his needs met. That small voice inside her wondered if these women he had been with had gotten their needs met too, or if they were solely objects to meet his voracious lust.

Aidan started walking again and pulled Luna closer, putting his arm over her shoulders. "That is something you need to know about me. I am direct, so don't ask me a question you don't want to know the answer to." It was a warning. "Luna, you will be my wife, and we will build a home together. You will have several children and take care of the home, and I will deal with the more important things. I didn't like the idea of settling down yet as I feel I am so young, but your father helped me see the value of having a wife at home," Aidan explained.

Aidan was painting a picture for Luna about what their life would look like together. It was the life she had been raised to live, the life her father expected of her. Self-conscious as she was, she didn't feel she would adequately keep a man like Aidan's interest for very long. Luna guessed he would not be content with just her in his bed after they were married. He'd made his expectations clear: he would be the one making the decisions, and she knew she shouldn't expect anything less.

Luna shuddered as they approached the wall to her village, and she didn't bother nodding to the men at the opening, keeping quiet until they reached her home. Aidan said goodbye outside her door, leaning down expectantly for a kiss. Luna turned her head so he only grazed her cheek.

"Aw, come on now. I risked my life to save you from a bear in the forest and promised to keep your secret—haven't I earned a kiss yet?" He spoke in a threatening whisper, towering over her. Luna wasn't sure if he would tell her father about the bear and the fact that she tried to keep it from him, but she was sure about one thing: Aidan felt entitled to not only a kiss from her but to her body, and that was something she had to get used to in order to play along and keep her child alive. Luna realized Aidan was a man who had never been told no, and she instinctively knew that made him dangerous.

Okay, I'll be whatever you want me to be. I'll give up whatever pieces of myself are necessary so my child can live, Luna decided in her thoughts. She closed her eyes and stood on her toes to meet his lips with hers. Aidan's lips were warm and wet. Luna tried to keep the kiss as only a peck, but he wrapped his arms around her, pulling her closer, and locked his mouth to hers. His kiss was salty and aggressive. She wanted to get away and prayed to the gods for aid as the sickening knot in her stomach grew stronger.

As soon as Aidan released her, Luna opened the front door, closing it quickly behind her. She panted in the dim house, feeling violated and unfaithful all at once. Luna ran to her bedroom and closed the door behind her. She cried into her pillow silently. She would do what she had to for this baby, and the reality of what that would entail hit her hard with the taste of Aidan's kiss still on her mouth.

Luna fell asleep and woke to the sound of knocking at her door.

She jolted upright, worrying it might be Aidan, but the sound of her father's voice brought her relief.

"Luna? Luna?"

Luna rubbed the sleep from her eyes as she stood to answer her door. "Yes Father?"

"Just making sure you were home. Aidan said you were. I'm ready for my meal."

Luna felt a surge of panic—she had lost track of time and not prepared anything. "Oh, I am sorry. I fell asleep." She followed him into the common room, seeing the wooden container she'd collected the honey with on the table.

"Eggs and bread is fine," he said, agitated.

"As you wish." Luna got to work making him fried eggs on a flat stone over the fire. She warmed up a hunk of bread she had made the day before, taking a piece for herself as well.

"Aidan told me you two spoke today," Gannon said with his mouth full after taking a bite of the bread.

"Oh?" Luna asked, not sure what it was exactly Aidan had spoken to her father about.

"Aidan is young and ambitious. Once you two settle down and start having some children, he will be content. There are certain wifely duties we all expect from you, Luna—me more than anyone," Gannon continued.

Luna felt extremely uncomfortable. She was not sure where her father was going with what was possibly the most in-depth conversation she had ever shared with him. She was sure, however, that her father believed she would be solely responsible for making Aidan happy and settled when they shared a home. *Why isn't Aidan charged with finding his own contentment?* Luna wondered defiantly.

"I need you to have an heir as soon as possible. I never told you this, but after your mother died, the shaman had a divination that you would have a child to help me…to join the two tribes." Gannon paused, searching for the right words.

Luna got the idea that he was hiding something from her. She remembered that day, and she remembered the shaman's words. Luna also remembered her father's bloodlust for the Nets that night; even now she could sense it bubbling under the surface. The fight with Layla had reignited his hatred, making him more emboldened when he talked about the Nets to Bale and Aidan. Both men had laughed with Gannon, making Luna wonder if the Nets knew how the Dabney acted one way in the trading spaces and another behind closed doors.

Gannon finished the rest of his meal in silence and Luna went through the motions she knew so well until he gave her permission to go to her room. Luna sat on her bed, watching the fire burn in the small stone fireplace with her face in her hands, a wildfire of righteous indignation blazing inside of her.

The anger grew within Luna at the many injustices she was just now recognizing. She had been angry about being born a woman for so much of her life, but in this moment she was angry at the people who made her feel less than because she was born female, as if that was a weakness. She was angry at the people who made her ashamed of her femininity, talking about her womanhood like it was something dark and sinister. She was angry about the fact that she felt she needed permission to even go to her own bedroom when she wanted, or to leave her home and go where she wished. She was angry that she second-guessed herself and didn't feel she could trust her own intuition because of this conditioning. Luna felt enraged at her society, at those who perpetrated the mistreatment of women and those who thought women inferior. She knew she didn't want any child of hers to live in a place like this. This place was not safe if you were born female, nor if you had other differences such as skin color, like the Nets. Her child would have both strikes against it if her inclinations of the baby being a girl were correct.

She watched the fire burn until her eyelids were heavy with sleep. Luna lay on her bed and drifted off, dreaming of a world where she got to keep her baby and live with the man she loved.

* * *

Sol kept to himself for a few days, prolonging the inevitable. He knew the longer he stayed away, the more questions his family would have for him—that is if Layla didn't say anything to them first. Akiiki had come by once, but he'd told her he was just busy with getting a roof on the house before the first snows came. She accepted his answer reluctantly and left him alone.

Sol washed his body and changed into clean clothing before heading to his mother's home for a hot meal. When he arrived, he saw his family already sitting comfortably, laughing and enjoying conversation with each other. When Sol approached them, they grew silent. He scooped himself some of the stew into a bowl and sat on an empty stump to have his dinner. *Did Layla tell them what happened?* Sol wondered.

"Don't let my presence keep you from enjoying your meal," he said.

"I don't think anything could spoil my wife's cooking, not even your sour face," Bomani joked, making everyone laugh. Akiiki sat near her husband with her bowl of stew balanced on her large belly.

"Only one more moon or so until we meet your first grandchild, Mama," Sol said, keeping the focus of the conversation off of him.

Sol's mother looked like something was on her mind, and he could tell her smile was distracted. He guessed Layla had spoken to her and she was worried about an impending attack.

"Yes," she responded, reaching over to rub Akiiki's stomach in a circular motion.

"Sol, how is the house on stilts coming?" Ata asked, sincerely interested.

"Good. I could use some extra hands for the roof though."

"Ahhhh, you only come to dinner when you need something from us, aye?" Atsu joked.

"I can help you tomorrow, Sol, as long as you promise to come to dinner again," Bomani offered.

"It's a deal. You really missed me that much, brother?" he asked jokingly.

"Aye, I missed you being the one who is chastised for eating so much. When you are here, everyone knows it is you who eats the most!" Bomani laughed.

They ate the rest of their dinner and enjoyed conversation with each other. They retired to bed one at a time until it was just Sol and his mother left.

"What's on your mind, Mama?" he finally asked.

"I'd much rather know what is going on in your mind," she replied, looking at him intently.

"Layla spoke to you?"

His mother looked momentarily confused. "Tell me," she directed.

Sol looked at the dying fire and added another log,

creating red sparks before he started.

"Layla and I saw the woman I had been meeting in the north woods while we were at the trade in Dabney tribe lands. I only told Layla what she needed to know about Luna to keep her quiet. I don't think there is anything to worry about, Mama," Sol finished, his eyes meeting hers.

"That's it?" his mother pressed.

Sol looked back toward the fire as he answered, avoiding her eyes. "No," he told her honestly.

"Tell me."

"Luna is with child." He paused, looking back up toward his mother. "It's mine."

"I know," she said matter-of-factly.

Sol looked at her, his mouth agape from shock. "How?"

"That is not what matters. What matters is that you should have been the one to tell me, Sol."

"Mama, I didn't know how to tell you. I didn't know what I was going to do—I still don't," he admitted.

"You will do nothing. Do you hear me? It will be taken care of," his mother ordered firmly. "She is a very strong woman—I can see why you fell in love with her."

"Mama, I can't sit here and do nothing. I need to know that she and the child will be all right," Sol challenged. "She asked me to run away with her. Had I known she had my child in her womb, I could have prevented this."

Sol's mother stood, walked over to him, and took his face in her hands.

"Running was not the answer either, my son. They will be safe with the goddess Isis's protection. You must do nothing, or you will jeopardize their safety. Do you understand?"

"How will they be safe? Tell me what you know so I do not go mad with this anxiety," Sol begged.

"She asked that we find a shelter for her to go to for the remainder of her pregnancy after she is hand-fasted to the Dabney chief's son on the winter solstice. After she has the child, she will give it up to you to raise. Then, she will go back," Sol's mother explained solemnly.

"She will hide for months in a shelter to secretly give birth to a child she knows she cannot keep then give the baby up to me? And she plans on returning to those people and hopes they will take her back after months of absence?" Sol repeated, making sure he'd heard her correctly.

The thought of Luna being with another man and then having to give up her child—their child, his child—made his heart shatter all over again. Sol was livid at the thought of Luna losing so much, and the fact that he felt powerless to stop it.

"It is her choice, my son," his mother reminded him.

"She doesn't understand that, Mama. She lives in a world without choices, and I put her back in that position to be exploited." Sol put his head down, feeling utterly powerless.

"When she arrives, you can go to her. Spend your months together. You will have a choice to make then, too." Sol's mother's words gave cautious hope. She knew it would be enough to help him wait for Luna's plan to be put into motion.

Sol sighed and nodded his head, agreeing. Although the thought of doing nothing seemed like absolute torture to him, he saw a new prospect beginning to form from his mother's words. For now, Sol would wait as Luna wished him to.

* * *

The weeks went by too quickly for Luna and not slowly enough all at once. The solstice and hand-fasting ceremony was only a week away now. It was getting much harder to hide her growing bump. Going out into the late autumn weather wearing multiple layers of clothing was the only time she felt confident no one could tell, so she stayed outside as much as she could. Luna had kept busy preparing small items for the baby, bags of herbs and dried foods she then buried near marked trees. That way she could collect them on her journey to hiding, or when it was safe to do so.

Luna had brought up the subject of childbirth with her aunt, saying she wanted to start to prepare herself for after the marriage. Alice thought her niece was getting ahead of herself, but she shared her knowledge of useful plants and the basic process. Even though Alice had not had any children of her own, she had assisted as a healer several times when needed for other tribeswomen. Alice seemed suspicious of Luna's questions, so Luna didn't risk asking for more information. Although limited, Luna was grateful for the knowledge.

Luna spent time sewing a wrap to carry the baby in. She had seen other tribeswomen carrying their babes in them and thought it would prove useful, even if she would not be the one to wear it. Luna decided that even if she would not get to raise her child, she would provide as much as she could within the limits that were thrust on her. Luna hummed as she worked by the crackling fire in her bedroom, singing a song she'd made up for the unborn child when she was alone in the house.

Hush now, my baby bear.
Hardest is the choice I make.
Hush now, my love, my world.
I let you go for freedom's sake.
In my heart, I'll carry thee.
You'll never be alone.

Luna was going to bring some of her items to the great lodge, which was now finished. She had put it off as long as she could, but Gannon was now insistent. Luna packed the last of the items she wouldn't need in the week she had left at home with her father. All that was left in her room was the bed and the small wooden shelf with her charcoal paint, oils, and the few pieces of jewelry she owned, save for the purple shell necklace from Sol that she always wore tucked under her tunic. Luna picked up the wooden crate filled with various items and headed out to where her father was waiting. She saw he was atop his horse, so she placed her things in the back of the wooden cart.

"Is that everything?" he asked.

"I believe so, for now at least," Luna answered.

"I'll bring it over to the lodge, and you can put it where you want when you come this week. Some of the tribeswomen have already started to set things up," Gannon said before signaling the end of the conversation and nudging his heels into the horse, urging it forward.

Luna watched her father disappear behind other houses on his way out of the village before going back inside. She still hadn't worked out what she would tell Aidan about why she needed to disappear for a few months without having him worry about his new bride. Luna realized the insanity of the thought. She would simply have to run away and deal with the consequences when she got back. Would anyone believe she of all people got lost in the woods and waited out the winter? Her escape would only work if there was no snow to illuminate the tracks she would leave behind, or if she left during a heavy snowstorm. A storm would be wishful thinking this early in the cold season, but they were not unheard of.

Luna painted her face with her tribal markings and gathered her things before heading out the door to help

Alice make syrups for the day. Luna stepped out into the brisk midmorning air and noticed that even in the village, the world had already begun to get quieter with sleep. Crows cawed as Luna took a deep breath of air that smelled of snow. She made her way to Alice's home and saw the first snowflakes of the season falling gently from the sky. Luna instinctively opened her mouth to catch a few snow crystals on her tongue and took them as a sign of hope.

CHAPTER 18

Luna awoke the next morning and heard what sounded like rain pelting the roof. The noise was comforting to her. She took her time sitting up in bed. The muscles around her abdomen had started to get tight and sore. Luna massaged her lower back with one hand and placed the other on her growing stomach as if to silently say *Good morning* to the tiny fetus developing inside. The private space of her room was the only place Luna felt safe enough to do so. Luna could see her breath in the frozen room, and she shivered as she carefully rolled out of bed. She grabbed some small pieces of kindling wood and placed them in the fireplace, willing the dying flame to spark to life. She got the fire going better and grabbed a warm fur to wrap around herself, as well as putting on some wool-lined moccasin boots her father had traded for recently.

A clatter of noise from the common room let Luna know her father was awake and would be expecting her company. She reluctantly made her way away from the warm fire and opened her door to see her father restarting the fire in the shared space. He worked quietly until the blaze was steady. The smell from his pipe filled the small home quickly after it was lit. Luna normally didn't care for the stench and would only breathe through her mouth so the smell would not be as terrible for her senses. Since carrying the baby, though, her nose was fickle, and she now enjoyed the earthy notes from the scent of the burning herbs. Luna sat closer to her father than she usually would when he smoked so she could fully immerse herself in the aromatics.

"I'll be going to do some business today. I assume you will be staying home with the weather?" Gannon asked, breaking the silence.

Luna placed some dried peppermint and nettle into the pot where they heated their morning tea. "Yes, I have some things I can get done here today."

"Good. Tomorrow you can go to the lodge to get your things in order and prepare the house," he ordered.

Luna sliced some ginger root she had on a shelf and added it to the pot before handing it to her father to place on the fire. They waited for the tea to be ready in silence. After Gannon finished his tea, he set off about his business. Luna sat by the fire, taking her time to enjoy another steaming cup of the comforting herbal infusion. She saw no reason to change her clothes, so she didn't, nor did she paint her face. Luna's plan for the day was organizing the dried herbs she had left into bags, further preparing what she needed for the months she would be in hiding.

The morning passed slowly. The rain and snow mixture drizzled outside while the fire kept Luna warm inside. She ate her midday meal then lay down to take a nap after feeding both fires. She had already made fresh bread and a stew from the hunk of venison a tribesman had delivered to her door. She assumed her father had sent him because he wanted a hot meal after being in the wet weather all day rather than fried eggs and bread.

Luna woke to shouting. She jolted out of bed, her ears craning to hear what the uproar was about as her heart thudded in her chest.

"That's it!" It was her father's voice, and he was drunk.

Luna cracked open her door to see Aidan and another man helping her father stumble inside, soaking wet from the slush.

"I know. You've said many times." Aidan tried to calm Gannon as he nodded for the other man to leave.

"Your father doessssn't know wha' he'ssssss doin' letting that—" He hiccupped before continuing, his voice rising in anger. "Go. That imbecile…" Gannon paused, forgetting his thought for a moment.

"I hope you mean that Net man who wouldn't let you pass into their lands is the imbecile and not my father," Aidan said, crossing his arms.

Gannon burped. "Nahhhh, Bale is a"—another hiccup—"good man. He is the best chief, essssept for me self of course," Gannon slurred, his face red from the ale.

"Well, it was his land, and he had every right to refuse you entry. You refuse the Nets entry onto your land on pain of death. Now, it seems you have enraged the Net tribe so that it goes both ways. I just don't see why we can't find a way to peacefully live together," Aidan explained, but Gannon cut him off, standing unsteadily to challenge him.

"You don't know those people! They took everything from me. They tried to kill Luna, and you know our agreement!" Gannon boomed, pointing a swaying finger in Aidan's face.

Aidan was eye level with Gannon. "I know what my father agreed to, but that doesn't mean I have to like it. I never would have made such an agreement if I were chief," he said firmly, remaining calm.

Luna saw Gannon's face turn a darker shade of red, and his hands clenched into fists.

Luna burst out from her bedroom door. "Father! I have made you dinner. Sit down by the fire and warm up. I will bring you a bowl of venison stew right away."

Luna darted between the men, gently putting her hands up to Gannon's shoulders and encouraging him to move toward the fire, away from Aidan. He stumbled to the chair, and Luna heard Aidan let out a deep breath before she turned back to retrieve a bowl for her father, thankful she had prepared it ahead of time.

Gannon grunted as he clumsily took the bowl from her and it dropped to the ground.

"You stupid girl!" he yelled, swinging his arm. His hand met Luna's cheek with a slap, and she crumpled to the ground with a loud thud.

"Woah!" Aidan said, holding up a hand and walking over to Luna. She held her hand up in protest.

"It's okay. I'll get you another, Father." She scrambled to her feet and grabbed another bowl, filling it quickly with shaking hands. Luna handed the bowl to Gannon with both hands this time, making sure he had a good grip before she let go. Gannon took the bowl, gobbling up the stew immediately, the messy gravy dribbling down the sides of his face. He didn't even bother wiping his mouth with his sleeve.

Luna walked over to Aidan and pulled him toward the door by his hand.

"I think it is best you leave now," she directed.

"Are you okay? Will you be all right if I leave?" he asked, concerned about the red hand-shaped welt on Luna's left cheek.

"Yes, I will be fine. Your presence will just make him angrier while he is drunk. Let him eat and sleep, and give him time to calm down," Luna said, rushing him through the door into the sleet.

"As you wish," Aidan said, glancing back to Gannon, who was now passed out in the chair where he sat, the empty bowl resting upside down on his large belly. "I could stay in your room," Aidan said, exploiting the opportunity.

Luna shut the door in his face and walked over to collect the bowl from her father's belly, as well as the one from the floor. She cleaned up the mess but left him to sleep in the chair, passed out and snoring loudly.

Luna went to the refuge of her bedroom, shaking. Her father had yelled at her several times, but he had only ever insinuated that he would be physically violent toward her, and Luna had imagined it was only to strike fear into her to get her to obey him. He had never laid a hand on her before. She pressed her hand to the welt, wincing from the burning pain. Now, Luna wondered if the lack of physical violence toward her was only because she usually avoided him when he was this drunk.

Tonight had been different; she had seen what her father would do to a man when challenged or drunk. Luna knew he had been both when Aidan made it clear he didn't agree completely with whatever they were arguing about, and that had made her father feel threatened. What was it though? What was the agreement they had made? Why was her father trying to enter Net lands? Was Sol the one who'd stopped him? Had Aidan said the Nets would now also kill any Barden who tried to enter their lands? Luna's head swirled with questions, and her nerves were still on edge from the assault. Luna hoped she would get answers but knew it wouldn't happen that night.

She kept to herself for the rest of the evening. Once she had calmed down enough to feel hungry, she retrieved a bowl of stew from the room where her father snored loudly, bringing it back to her room to enjoy by the small fire. Gannon's loud snoring assured her she would be left alone for the remainder of the evening. Luna worked on sewing a soft piece of linen to a small fur, making a blanket; the baby would need something to keep it warm in the winters.

The next morning Luna awoke before her father, staying quiet in her room, getting dressed and painting her face, preparing for the work she had to do at the lodge as she was expected to that day. She readied herself to act like nothing had happened with her father while at the same time cultivating unthreatening questions for Aidan about the previous night's events. What agreement had these men struck that concerned the Nets? Luna needed to find out, for the safety of those she loved in the Net tribe, and for her own child.

Luna set out into the shared room and made the tea so it would be ready for her father. She knew he would be even more impatient and short-tempered with her after a drinking episode such as the one the night before. He came out of his room and walked over to the fire as he usually did, squinting from the brightness of the flames. Gannon lit his pipe while Luna poured him some chicory root tea. He took the cup without looking at her and drank in silence. Luna waited patiently until he was ready to leave.

"I'll go get the horses," she offered, careful to keep her voice quiet. Gannon only nodded in response.

Luna tied a white and grey fur wrap over her shoulders and headed outside the small house with a deep breath. The day was brisk with the promise of snow in the air, the ground still wet from the slush that had fallen the previous day and evening. Luna was careful not to slip as she made her way to the pasture, retrieving both horses. She led Willow near a wooden stool, using it to help her as mounting the horse had proven more difficult with her growing belly.

Gannon came out of the house, wincing in the sunlight, which was bright though limited by the clouds in the sky. Gannon looked at Luna then, seeing the reddish-purple bruise across her face for the first time. His eyes darted to the ground momentarily before going back to his horse, which he mounted quickly.

"Come on then," he said, leading Luna toward the great house of expectations, as Luna thought of it now.

They walked the horses in the slick slushy leftovers that covered the ground until the lodge came into sight. Luna awkwardly dismounted her horse and went inside. The house was empty, but the fires were going in every room. Luna scanned the vast rooms, admiring the work the tribes-women had done in decorating the walls with embroidered linens. Furs adorned the wooden benches, and a bear skin rug lay in front of the roaring fire in the colossal sitting room. Luna turned to enter the kitchen and dining room. She saw the pile of wooden bowls and utensils she knew were from Sol and swallowed hard. There were candles across the table and counters, and garlands of greenery weaved among them, reminding her of the impending celebration.

The winter solstice had always been one of her favorite celebrations of the turning of the wheel. Her people would light fires to guide them through the longest dark night of the year while they performed ritualistic dancing and storytelling about the ancestors who had proceeded them, stories of the mother goddess and the man of green from the wildwood. The green man brought them holly and evergreen to remind them that the green that gives her people life would spring forth again and the light would return. Luna wondered briefly if the light would actually shine upon her again, and the story brought her comfort that the darkness wouldn't last.

Luna made her way upstairs, noticing the smaller rooms had items moved in; she assumed they were Aidan's. The smallest of the four rooms contained a small crude wooden cradle that rocked. Luna had seen them before and wondered to herself why anyone would think she would separate herself from her child to sleep alone. Luna remembered the comfort being close to her mother had given her, and she remembered what it was like to sleep alone. It had been scary as a child, and even more so after she knew her mother was not in the next room anymore. Luna wondered how her child would feel with her mother so far away. She hoped Sol would take care of the child as she would if she had the chance.

Luna turned to enter the large master bedroom across from the smallest. There was a large bed with four sturdy wooden posts that reached high into the vaulted ceilings. Heavy wooden beams crossed overhead with more greenery woven around. The fire roared, lighting the room enough to see the wooden chest and the rest of her belongings in a small pile on the opposite side of the room. Luna walked over to her things, taking them out and arranging them as if she was setting up a house for a doll to live in. That was how she felt: like a child's toy being played with. Luna glanced back to the bed covered in soft furs and linen. She walked over and placed a hand on it as a knot formed in her stomach. Luna heard voices downstairs and quickly removed her hand from the bed, focusing her attention on organizing again.

Hours passed. Though no one had come upstairs, she knew they would be expecting her to make the midday meal, so she gathered her strength before going down to greet them. Luna saw Gannon sitting on one end of the wooden bench by the fire in the great room and Bale sitting at the opposite end talking about nothing important. She saw Aidan glance up from where he stood, leaning against the wall near them. He looked back to Gannon and then walked over to meet her. Luna moved from the bottom of the stairs into the kitchen to search the cupboards for something to cook as Aidan followed.

"My father arranged for a tribeswoman to bring something for us all to eat. She should arrive soon," he said.

"Oh." Luna closed the small wooden door and stood in the large kitchen, wishing she had something to do with her hands.

Aidan took a few steps closer to Luna. She backed away instinctively, afraid he might discover her secret if he pressed his body close to hers. Thankfully, he had been none the wiser about the pregnancy up to this point. She figured they would spend their wedding night in the darkness of the room and thought he would be more concerned with the reward than her body. Maybe he would still think she had extra weight; it was possible seeing as her belly was where she carried most of her extra weight anyway.

"It looks like it hurts," he said with a squint of his eye.

"I'm all right," she answered.

Aidan looked genuinely displeased when he asked, "Does he do that often?"

Luna had an idea. "No, I usually stay out of his way. Last night he wanted an outlet from the argument you were having, and I knew he was going to take his anger out on you if I didn't do something. It could have been much worse."

Aidan hesitated. "You came out so I wouldn't get the brunt of it?"

"Yes." She hoped he would feel indebted to her in some small way. "I have to ask," she said, now whispering. "What were you arguing about?"

Aidan looked back toward their fathers laughing in the other room before answering, "It doesn't concern you."

"It's my face that paid for it," Luna dared in a husky voice as she took a step closer to him.

Aidan seemed to think it over before responding. "On second thought, I think you should know what price I and my people are paying to have you in my bed."

Luna eyes flashed with intrigue, and she reactively took another small step forward. "What is it?"

"Soon enough, you will hear it from their own mouths," Aidan said before leaning down to kiss her lips, collecting what felt like a payment he believed he was entitled to for a debt she didn't really owe.

A knock at the door gave Luna the opportunity she needed to unlock her lips from Aidan's. She darted away from him to see who the guest was—the tribeswoman with a basket of food for their lunch. Luna gladly took the gift, giving the woman a warm smile and mentally thanking her for rescuing her. Luna retreated to the dining room, laid out the feast, and then went into the room where Aidan had rejoined their fathers. The men followed soon after her announcement that the meal was prepared and joined her at the table. As they filled their mouths with the boiled meat and roasted squash, Luna wondered what Aidan had meant and when she would get her answers. They finished their meal, and she cleaned up after them.

"I need some fresh air. I'll be outside," she said, tying the white and grey fur around her shoulders. Luna stepped onto the large porch and watched the snow fall, fully covering the now partly frozen ground. Luna enjoyed watching the snow come down for hours until the sun was low and she could barely feel her nose and the tips of her fingers. Just as she stood to head into the house, she saw the familiar man in red and white approaching the lodge. She recognized the shaman with his long white beard immediately.

"Luna," he said, nodding as he waited for her to open the door.

Luna waited for him to enter before her. He did so, and she followed, curious why he had come.

"Father, the shaman is here," Luna announced before hanging the fur wrap on one of the wooden pegs lining the entrance hallway.

Luna took the man's hat when he handed it to her, revealing the few strands of wiry silver hair he had on his head. Gannon immediately stood out of respect for the holy man and offered him a warm seat by the fire. When the shaman was settled, Luna brought both him and herself a cup of tea before sitting down by the fire on the floor. As the flames began to warm her frozen body, Gannon started speaking first.

"Thank you, shaman, for coming to give us direction," Gannon said with an honest reverence.

There were few people Gannon listened to, and the

shaman was at the top of the short list. Gannon truly believed what the holy man read from the runes was absolute truth, even when he didn't agree with it.

The shaman nodded before scanning the faces in the room one at a time. He stopped to pause on Luna, arching one of his eyebrows, his wrinkled face studying her. Gannon turned his gaze to her, wondering what the shaman saw. She felt a surge of uneasiness and shifted closer to the fire.

"The prophecy I gave you the night your wife died is upon us."

An audible gasp was heard from Gannon, who looked back to the shaman, and Luna wondered if the wise man would reveal her secret.

He continued, now looking toward Gannon, offering Luna a small respite from his intense stare. "Before I read the runes, I will remind you of the divination I gave you that day."

Gannon nodded for the holy man to continue.

"I told you of a new life, a child that represented both darkness and light. I told you of two great forces, two tribes joining together as one." The shaman spoke slowly and emphatically.

"Yes," Gannon agreed, nodding his head at every syllable the shaman uttered. Bale and Aidan stayed silent, their attention fixed on him as well.

The words the shaman spoke brought a realization to Luna. She finally understood the prophecy, and an excited anxiousness filled her body.

"Now…" The shaman paused, pulling a leather pouch from his waistband and holding it up. "We will read the runes."

Gannon pulled a small table over to him, and the holy man dumped the pieces out, scattering them across the surface.

Everyone held his or her breath expectantly.

Luna didn't know if she should run before she was found out or stay where she was to find the answers she desired. She stayed put.

"Hmmm…" The shaman looked at the runes and then to Luna before looking back to the assorted pieces. "The time is surely upon us. This prophecy will come to fruition. It has already begun."

Gannon let out a burst of excited agreement as Bale patted his shoulder.

"The darkness and the light will make themselves known to you, Gannon, and you must protect this twilight creation at all costs. The moon—you must heed the moon."

The meaning of the shaman's cryptic message was lost on the three other men in the room, but Luna saw it in his intense stare with her own eyes. She understood enough to know the holy man was speaking of the twilight child in her womb, and she took to heart his warning of protection.

"Thank you, shaman," Gannon said as the shaman picked up his belongings and readied himself to leave. He glanced back at everyone, making eye contact with Luna once again before heading back out the front door.

"What did he mean about twilight creation and the moon? Do you talk with the moon too?" Bale asked, laughing at his old friend.

"I don't know the details. All I know is he just told me the time is upon us. It is time we make plans for your end of the agreement, Bale," Gannon commanded as he walked toward the kitchen. Gannon sat at one end of the long wooden table, and Bale sat at the other. Aidan sat nearest his father on one of the side seats. Luna wasn't sure if she should stay nearby to listen or risk joining the men at the table.

"Luna," Aidan called, making the choice for her.

"No, she doesn't need to be here for this," Gannon barked.

"She is almost my wife, and as such, she needs to know what my tribe is giving up in order to join with yours," Aidan said firmly. Gannon looked toward Bale, who nodded his head in agreement with his son's words.

Gannon gave in. "Fine. The shaman seemed very interested in her role tonight anyway."

Luna found a seat closer to her father, though still leaving a seat separating the two of them, her bruised cheek facing him.

Bale started, "We agree to give our warriors to join with yours, but not until after the hand-fasting ceremony is complete. You must give my son the joys he is entitled to, having a wife for at least a week before we agree to follow you into this revenge-fueled battle."

Luna panicked, her heart beating faster. *What battle?*

"Aye, that sounds fair. We will go exactly one week after the ceremony. I want Dalila and her family for myself. Is that clear?" Gannon demanded, raising his voice.

Aidan looked at Luna before speaking. "A battle to exact revenge for a natural death, risking the lives of our tribe… this fight with a tribe we have been on trading terms with and who offers so many resources to us," Aidan clarified.

Luna felt her body start to shake from fear and protective rage all at once.

"We are also getting the power that comes from joining forces, my son. We must make certain sacrifices to assure our own safety in case the Nets decide to attack us someday," Bale replied, trying to convince his son.

Luna was hit with the reality that her marriage to Aidan was a grab for power by her father and Bale. In that moment, Luna realized she had been a piece in this puzzle that had been moved around since her mother's death and placed exactly where they wanted her to be. The grave reality of the situation hit her with full force. Her father was marrying her off to join with the Dabney so he would have more warriors when he attacked the Nets, Mama Dalila's family, and Sol. Any hope she had of rescuing the child that grew within her womb seemed to disappear.

"No," Luna said, though only as loud as a whisper at first. Her voice was so quiet she didn't know if she had actually spoken out loud. She stood to face her father with her hands clenched, the mother bear instinct rising to the forefront, winning out over her fear. Surprised and confused looks crossed all three of the men's faces. "No!" Luna said again, her tone more commanding than she felt.

CHAPTER 19

The three men stared at Luna, trying to make sense of her proclamation.

"Luna," Gannon warned.

She took a step backward from the table, making sure she was out of reach of her father's hand. "Starting a war between our three tribes is not how you get power. You will lose so many people. Why not a peace treaty, and we can begin trading with the Nets? We have so much we could learn from them." Luna thought reasoning with her father would be the best option, helping him to see what he would gain from befriending the rival tribe.

"They have NOTHING to teach us!" Gannon said, slamming his fist on the table in anger.

"I have spoken to one of the Nets," she started.

Gannon's body shook with anger. "When?" he demanded.

"At the market, there were Net tribe members," Luna said, getting creative with the truth again. She hated how easy it had become for her now.

Gannon seemed only a bit calmer after her response, so

she turned to speak to Aidan instead.

Avoiding her father's disapproving glare, she continued, "They have an ability for taking craftsmanship to another level that our people have not managed. They have an understanding of herbal medicine that goes far beyond our knowledge, and with that comes a better maternal outcome, which is why their numbers are greater than ours. We have so much we could learn from them."

"That is stupidity! Luna, those people killed your mother!" Gannon boomed, standing abruptly.

Luna turned back to meet her father's eyes as she finally confessed, "No, Father. It is I who killed my mother." Luna's body trembled as she spoke the revealing words with both fear and a deep relief from letting go of the secret she had internalized for so long.

Gannon's face went white, and he staggered back a step from the blow of Luna's confession. The vein in his neck bulged, and he clenched his fist. When the color returned to his face, it was a rapidly deepening shade of red. "What do you mean?!" he demanded furiously.

Luna kept eye contact with her father as she told him the details, tears streaming down her cheeks. "I was stuck in a tree, and she climbed up after me. When she jumped down, she was in pain. That's when we started to make our way home, and Mama Dalila found us."

"That woman does not deserve to have her name spoken aloud!" Gannon snapped.

"It was too late for my mother, because of ME, not because of Dalila. Dalila did everything she could, Father. I remember—I was there," she explained, her voice wavering.

Luna's last words struck Gannon as an accusation, and he winced. A man had no business being in the room while his woman gave birth. He refused to be blamed for abandoning his wife when she needed him most. His anger had risen when Luna had spoken out of turn and then challenged him in front of Chief Bale. Now, he seethed with anger from this revelation that his anger might have been misplaced this whole time.

No, he wouldn't think of it. Those people deserved every ounce of the hatred he'd harbored for them ever since he was a child. His father before him had told him not to trust the Nets. Gannon's father had told him what inferior people they were, *only good as slaves!* Gannon wanted the power and control over the Nets, fearing what their rising numbers would do to him and his people. He feared their differences and their talent in so many areas. He feared the ideas he had been raised to believe about them. Gannon hadn't admitted it before, but he feared what they would do to his preciously pure bloodline. He would never admit this fear, not even to himself, because his father also had taught him that men were not afraid, or sad, or emotional. Anger was the only exception to this rule.

Gannon took a step toward Luna with his arm stretched out to grab her.

The image of the imprint Gannon's hand had left on Luna's soft cheek still burned into Aidan's mind, and he stood and yelled, "Gannon, wait!"

Gannon hesitated only momentarily before roughly taking Luna by the arm and pulling her toward the door.

Bale put his hand up to halt Aidan, and he stood conflicted for a moment before sitting back down, staring at the table.

"Go home, brother, and get your house in order," Bale said.

Gannon pulled Luna past the fur that hung on the wooden peg in the hallway and opened the large wooden door as a gust of cold wind and snow rushed upon them.

Luna shook from the cold. She was scared for the tiny life that grew inside her. She had seen what her father could do when he was angry, and here she was again, the target of that fury.

She wanted to be the one person in the world who pleased him. Ever since Luna was a little girl, she remembered seeking out his approval, wondering if she was enough. The rare times he noticed, the simple praise of *Good girl* caused a short-lived rush of happy feelings of being enough. The excitement didn't last very long, though, and so she had lived addicted to the fleeting rush, seeking out that love and approval of herself, and all that was interconnected. Luna realized in that moment that she would never meet his expectations, and she knew she would be okay with that. Luna had found the love of her existence in Sol, and his respect and compassion had taught her that she was worthy of it. Even if she hadn't been enough for Sol in the end, she was learning she was enough for herself. Luna was worthy of respect and worthy of love. The only concern she had in that moment was for the baby in her womb.

"Father, do to me as you wish, but know this: I will not be hand-fasted to Aidan so that you can destroy our tribe as well as theirs. You can do whatever you wish, but I will not join with him if these are the terms."

"You insolent girl!" Gannon boomed as he shook her violently, his hand squeezing her arm hard. Luna cried out from the pain on the soft skin of her underarm.

Bale held up his hand before speaking. "Luna, is this your final word? Will you still be hand-fasted to my son on the solstice?"

Luna glanced at her father, who squeezed her arm tighter. She winced from the pain and looked back to Aidan, preparing herself for the repercussions.

"No."

"Gannon, our agreement is terminated," Bale said simply.

Gannon yanked Luna, seething with rage. He grabbed her other arm and dragged her down the steps to the horses. Gannon picked her up as if she weighed nothing and plopped her onto Willow. He got on his own horse and put a rope around her horse's neck to lead them home. They rode briskly through the land until the walls of their village came into view. Luna was shivering from the cold and the snow with only her long-sleeved tunic covering her body. She wished for the warm fur she hadn't had the chance to grab as she was violently dragged from the dining room to the door of the lodge. Her arms burned where Gannon had squeezed them, and she knew the redness would give way to purple soon enough.

As they entered the gates, Gannon broke the silence abruptly. "Get the elders! Get Alice, and tell them to meet me at my house!" he barked at one of the men standing guard at the entrance.

Luna jumped at his booming command. She knew she was in trouble. She began preparing herself for the verbal—and possibly physical—lashing she would receive. She readied herself to be shamed, questioned, and accused as her father led Willow to the front door of their home. Luna got down from her horse and proceeded into the house, her father right at her heels.

"Sit!" he commanded as he walked over to the dying fire.

The room was cold, and Luna trembled, making her way as close to the fireplace as she dared. The flames were soon roaring, and the light filled the dim room just in time to illuminate the first face that burst through the door.

"What is it, brother? What is the alarm?" Alice glanced at Luna, who held her head high, unwavering, and then looked to her brother, who was still red with anger.

"The girl refuses to be married to Aidan!" Gannon

growled through clenched teeth.

Realization crossed Alice's features, but she had questions. Luna pleaded for Alice's silence with her eyes. Only Alice would know about Sol. If her aunt told Gannon, all would be lost. Luna held her breath.

"Why not?" Alice asked.

Luna exhaled in relief.

"The girl is defiant! I have given her too much freedom. She is too much like her mother!" Gannon yelled, turning to face Luna with his fist in the air.

Alice looked to Luna without saying a word.

"I only refused because he was trading me for warriors to attack the Nets," Luna explained, looking at her aunt to see any sign that Alice had known about her father's plans all along.

"You have ruined everything, Luna, everything I fought so hard to give you," Gannon snapped. "My agreement with the Dabney is null! Now the Nets will pay, with or without the Dabney's warriors. I will conquer those people!" Gannon slammed his fists down on the table in front of his daughter, making both her and Alice jump.

"Father, it is I who has caused you grief—why would you still attack the Nets?" Luna demanded, standing to look him in the eye. "I will still join with Aidan if you make a new agreement that doesn't involve inciting a war!" Luna pleaded.

"The shaman said the time is finally upon us. He must

have known this would happen, and it must be part of the gods' plans somehow. I will get the revenge I deserve for so many atrocities toward our tribe from the Nets. I have waited sixteen long years for this chance—not that I need to explain myself to a girl!" Gannon yelled.

"If the Nets had skin like us, like the Dabney, would you still be taking your misdirected anger out on them? If the Nets treated their women as inferior like our tribe does, like the Dabney do, would you still hate them? If it wasn't a woman who leads them, would you still challenge them?" Luna dared, her courage rising to meet her father's rage.

"You insolent—"

Gannon charged toward Luna, but she held her ground, instinctively wrapping her arms around her belly for protection. Suddenly, a scream erupted, and Luna was shoved aside. She saw it was Alice who had cried out and not herself. Alice stood, pressing herself between Gannon and Luna, attempting to hold him back. A ringing filled Luna's head. She was shaking from the adrenaline and the increasing threat of physical violence.

"Luna, go to your room!" Alice commanded, and Luna quickly obeyed.

She heard her aunt shouting and arguing with Gannon and objects crashing from being thrown. The door opened a few times as the elders filed inside the shared room outside her bedroom door. Luna heard her father bark orders about a predawn attack on the Nets.

"What do you mean without the Dabney?" a male elder asked loudly.

"There will be no agreement and no joining!" Gannon yelled impatiently, not wishing to divulge the specifics and lose respect from the men gathered in the small room.

"Surely we should wait until a new agreement can be made. The Nets' numbers far exceed ours—"

The second elder was cut off by Gannon's bloodthirsty yell. "We have been training for this for months! It will be a surprise attack, and the shaman predicted the time was already upon us! Do you question the holy man?" Gannon challenged.

The silence told Luna no one disagreed with her father. Gannon was unraveling, and Luna knew there was no reasoning with him. She saw the clear choices in front of her. First, she could choose to stay there, enduring what would come until the child was born and hope her father stood true to his belief that it should be protected. She wondered if his faith was deep enough to outweigh his hatred for a half-Net child. Her second option was to run away, leaving this mess and all she had ever known behind. The third option was the most dangerous for her, but it gave her the most hope for the protection of her child and the man she loved.

Luna felt the familiar fears of defying her father and abandoning all she had known. She knew if she stayed there or ran away, many of Sol's family would be slaughtered while they slept, if not Sol himself. Luna thought of Mama Dalila and all the kindness she had shown her. She remembered that Aidan and Gannon had said Barden were now forbidden on Net land on pain of death and wondered if she would even be able to make it to Mama Dalila or Sol before other Nets tried to kill her. So many risks for a man who chose not to be with her, and instead was with the woman who had tried to kill her. Luna loved Sol with everything in her, and she knew she had to warn the Nets, no matter the cost to her. If that choice meant the death of her then so be it.

Luna wrapped her hand around her pregnant belly. "If I don't try to warn him, you would have no future anyway," Luna whispered to the developing bump. "Trust me," she said as she promised to do the same.

Luna stood and changed out of her clothes. She wrapped a thin white strip around her chest to cover her breasts then donned a fresh white tunic. She tied black fur pelts around her arms for warmth and in case of combat. She fastened the leather belt securely under her growing belly at her hips before tying another knife to her hip with a sheath. Luna washed her purple-splotched, bruised face before gingerly drying the skin. Next, she painted the black lines above and below her eyes, her curly hair flowing wildly with black and grey feathers braided into it on each side of her head.

"If it is a war he wants, I will give it to him," Luna said under her breath, making her decision before tossing her bow and quiver over to the bed.

She listened with her ear to the door. Her father was barking orders and having men gather supplies to prepare for war. Luna glanced around the room where the moonlight was beginning to shine through the small crack in the wooden section of the wall. She tied a rope around the latch of her door, hoping to deter anyone from entering, even if it only bought her seconds.

She waited until the roomful of elders and warriors grew loud with shouts, timing each thrust against the wooden boards. She paused to use her knife, loosening the wooden pegs that held the structure in place. It fell to the ground outside their house, but Luna struggled with the second board. She lay on her back with her feet against it. A loud cheer from inside the common room gave her the opportunity she needed. She pulled her center of gravity and pushed with all her might. The board went flying into the white snow and darkness outside the bedroom wall. Luna paused to listen to see if anyone had heard the noise before grabbing the bow and quiver. She put them over her shoulder. There was no time to look around her almost empty bedroom to say goodbye this time, and she was surprised that she didn't feel the need.

Luna carefully crawled out through the small space in the wall. Although her body was warm with adrenaline, she reached back in for a white fur blanket to wrap around herself, just in case. The white would help her hide from view in the snow that was still steadily falling in the now complete darkness. The half-moon behind the thick clouds cast an ominous misty white pall, making it hard to see very far ahead in the heavy snow. Luna heard a noise and froze against the side of the dark wall opposite her house. She held her breath and saw that the noise had come from Willow as she tried to find bits of green to graze on amidst the snow. Luna thanked the goddess and made her way to the horse as quickly and quietly as she could. She mounted Willow, using the stone wall for a step up, and weaved around the houses in her village, using the blanket to hide her face from the scrambling villagers. Luna approached the gate and saw that no one was guarding it; she guessed they were too busy preparing for the cowardly attack.

Luna kicked her heels into Willow and the horse ran through the gates, toward the river. Luna clutched her mane as the horse galloped across the snow-covered ground. The sight of the river boundary came into view, and Luna steered the horse south where she had crossed the river with Sol. He had said he'd seen her that night, and she hoped with everything in her that he would be there again.

* * *

"Mama, let me stand guard tonight. Let me help," Sol begged.

"No. I don't want to take any chances now that the

chief of the Barden was bold enough to try to enter our lands and threaten Bomani," Sol's mother replied firmly. "Layla, Ata, Atsu, Bomani, and the other warriors will be standing guard at the posts tonight. You need to give yourself a night to rest. You need to be at your best, just in case. Two nights of looking out will only hinder your ability to be of any use to us."

Since the argument between Gannon and Bomani, the Nets had set lookouts just in case Gannon was bold enough to try something again. Sol had taken the first post that night and wanted to stand guard again, but his mother was right. Sol did need rest so he could perform at his best if needed. He knew staying close to home was a good idea and decided he would sleep in his mother's longhouse. Sol wondered if Luna was safe. He had even been to the waterfall a few times since seeing her in the Dabney lands, hoping to get a glimpse of her at the very least so he would know she was well.

Sol gave in. "All right. Tomorrow, I will take my turn. Who will be at the south river post?"

"Layla," his mother replied.

CHAPTER 20

Luna slowed the horse as she neared the large tree across the river where she had crossed four months before to meet Sol. She felt so much older than she had then. It felt as though years had passed instead of just four moon cycles.

Luna called out into the night, "Sol? Is anyone there?" No answer.

She took a deep breath, looking back the way she'd come from, her thoughts conflicted again. She would truly be giving up everything if she crossed this line, risking her life for a man who didn't think she was enough for him. She knew the reason she was there was so much bigger than herself, and even than the man she loved. It was for Mama Dalila, Sol's family, and all the innocent Net tribe members who deserved a fair chance to defend themselves against the invaders who would take all they could from their tribe, their culture, and their persons. Luna could not let that happen without trying to help. Her body heated with an electric energy as it vibrated, her arms and legs prickled with gooseflesh. She placed a hand over her swollen belly and nudged Willow to cross the river, her decision made. As soon as Willow trotted over the embankment onto Net tribe lands, an unnerving yet familiar voice called to her.

"Luna."

She turned her horse to see Layla step out from the darkness of a tree, standing between the river and her. Snow fell softly, and the moon moved out from under one of the thick clouds, illuminating the bow and arrow in Layla's hands. It was aimed right at Luna.

"Layla," Luna answered. The women stared at each other in a moment of silent decision-making.

Luna spoke first. "Layla, I have a message for your chieftess, and it is of the utmost importance that she hears it for the safety of your tribe."

"How do I know your tribe is not waiting to attack?" Layla demanded.

"They are going to attack! That is why I'm here!" Luna exclaimed.

A look of confusion crossed Layla's determined features for a moment. "Why would a Barden woman like yourself warn my people?" she asked suspiciously.

Luna slowly held up her hands. "Because you do not deserve to be killed in your sleep. Because your tribe has shown me kindness when I most needed it. Because, even if Sol doesn't love me, I will always love him." Luna felt no need for lies, choosing complete honesty from one woman to another. Strong women had an ability to smell lies a mile away, and Luna wouldn't risk it. Her life had been full of secrets and lies, and she was done with them.

Luna's honest words struck Layla. She wasn't expecting the directness, especially from a Barden woman. Layla had cared for Sol, and she'd fought hard for him—literally—but she'd also realized the day she and Sol argued coming home from the market that she would never be with him because his heart was taken by another.

"Do you know that I have been given permission to kill any Barden who cross the river onto our land?" Layla asked, stepping closer to Luna.

Luna felt a panicked knot form in her stomach. "Yes." Her voice trembled with the answer.

Layla lowered the bow in her arms just enough so she could reach for a small ram's horn behind her back. She blew it three times in succession.

Luna started from the noise that burst from the instrument. She was not sure what Layla was up to. Luna heard more horns farther away, repeating the same blasts. Layla had sent a rhythmic message, and Luna was unsure what that meant for her.

"My father will discover my absence soon, if he hasn't already. Please take me to your chieftess," Luna begged.

"You're wrong you know—about Sol," Layla said, giving a loud whistle.

A black horse came galloping toward them from the forest's edge with a young Net warrior atop it. Luna watched the rider and his animal run straight to Layla. The warrior dismounted and took Layla's place at the tree. She mounted the horse, staying behind and to the right of Luna.

"What do you mean?" Luna asked.

"Go on. Straight ahead. Keep your hands where I can see them," Layla directed.

Luna nudged her horse, careful to keep her hands up even as they grew heavy. What had Layla meant about Sol? He had made it clear he was with Layla…hadn't he?

Luna followed Layla's directions into the forest where a small army of Nets, already prepared for battle, waited in the darkness with their weapons and white war paint. Layla urged her on, and Luna continued through the snowy forest until torches came into sight. The lights grew brighter as she approached, as did the audience forming in response to the alert of the horns. Drums began beating and continued in a rhythmic succession as Luna rode Willow into the center of a much larger group of Net people who had gathered, many of them with white paint on their skin and weapons in hand. Luna swallowed hard, searching the faces for Sol.

They reached a large fire burning near a longhouse. Layla dismounted her horse and directed Luna to do the same. Then, Luna saw a familiar face as Mama Dalila walked through the crowd toward her with arms wide open. Luna dropped her heavy arms and dismounted her horse, running into Dalila's arms. Luna sighed with relief upon being embraced by the familiar comforting arms.

The crowd gasped and starting buzzing with questions.

"Luna! Why have you come?" Dalila asked.

"My father is planning to attack you all before dawn!" Luna explained quickly.

The crowd was humming curiously, reminding Luna of the bees in the honey tree.

Dalila looked at Luna. "Is Gannon coming with the Dabney?"

"No. There will be no agreement, no joining with them," Luna answered.

"You have risked much to bring us this news." Dalila gave Luna her thanks and issued orders to her warriors to join the others waiting at the tree line for an attack. Dalila told the crowd if any of the children and elders had not already gone to the safe place they had prepared deep in the woods as a precaution, they should do so now.

"Mama Dalila—" Luna started, but she stopped abruptly when she heard another familiar deep voice.

"Mama, what is happening? Luna? What are you doing here?" Sol asked. He'd heard the drums and had run to check on the border, just missing Luna. When he heard the news that a Barden woman had crossed into their lands, he ran back as fast as he could. Seeing Luna in front of him reignited the fire that burned inside him. He wanted to wrap her in his own arms and pull her close to him where he needed her, but he stayed where he was, waiting for answers.

Luna looked at Sol, seeing his green eyes lit from the fire. Her heart seized and her body sparked alive with yearning. Luna forced the feelings aside when she realized he was speaking to Dalila.

"Mama Dalila? *You* are Sol's mother? You are chieftess?" Luna asked, stunned as her brain made the connections.

Sol stood, mouth agape momentarily before asking his own question. "You know Luna?" Suddenly his mother's knowledge of Luna's pregnancy made sense.

Dalila looked between her son and Luna before answering. "Seeing you bring home the leather satchel your father made confirmed my suspicions. I gave it to Luna's mother, Terra, as a gift. She was my friend. My children, I know you have many questions, but right now we have a much bigger problem. I must head to the border. Luna, you should go with the children to the safe place. This is not your fight." She leaned in closer and whispered, "And you are carrying *my* grandchild."

Luna stood in stunned silence, watching Mama Dalila leave to prepare herself and her people for war. Several Nets moved around them, their stares questioning but not accusatory. The crowd slowly dispersed in the fresh snow to wait for the invasion.

"How are your people ready? Did they already know?" Luna asked.

"My sister had a dream that there would be an attack. The last time she had such a vision, she predicted my father's death," Sol explained.

Luna hesitated, stunned by the revelation. "So, I didn't need to come?"

"I am glad you came." Sol approached Luna, his touch fiery as he took her hand, shocking her back to the present. He noticed the bruises across her face, gently running his finger across her cheek. "Who did this to you?"

Luna looked toward the fire without answering.

Sol's hands clenched in anger.

After a moment, Luna spoke. "He is so angry. He was planning to attack your people when I was joined to Aidan. I was being traded for warriors." She looked back to Sol. "I tried to reason with him. He wouldn't listen, and he was furious." She hesitated. "I told Bale no, so the agreement is null. My father was furious at me, and he is directing his rage at your people. I had to stand and say something. The thought of you and your family being murdered in your sleep—" Luna's voice caught with emotion.

"I should have taken you with me that day at the waterfall, no matter the cost," Sol admitted.

Luna turned to meet his eyes with hers, his face close.

"Well, now you have Layla," she said, more hurt than accusatory.

His face scrunched from the insinuation. "What? Why would you think that?"

"Because when Aidan said you were with her, you didn't correct him, and because I could see you cared for her at the waterfall. How could you be with someone who tried to kill me? What else am I supposed to think? You left me that day at the waterfall for her, leaving me bloodied and barely able to breathe, not to mention the fact that she is beautiful and you're a man," Luna explained bitterly.

Sol seemed deep in thought, processing what Luna had said, and then his serious face broke into a smile.

"I don't see what there is to smile about," she snapped.

"I'm sorry. It's just, I see why you would think that way, I guess, but Layla and I have only ever been friends, and that's all we will ever be. I am so sorry you thought I had abandoned you, sorry you thought for one second you were not enough for me. I am the one who was not enough for you when you needed me most. That will never happen again, Luna. It is not fair to project what you have understood a man to be like from your limited experience onto other good men. I am not your father. I am not Aidan. I am me. I am sorry I have ever given you a reason to doubt my love. You told me you were okay at the waterfall, but Layla needed the healers or she might have died, creating a much larger problem for the both of us. It was for your safety that I left you, both times, but I now see I was wrong. I especially should have listened to you in the cave and given you the chance to tell me about our child. I should have worked with you to come up with a better solution together after having all the information. I can only do my best from here on out. Do you forgive me?"

Luna felt overcome with the revelation of Sol's insight. If she had known this was his intention, maybe things would have been different. What mattered most was the knowledge that he'd never stopped caring for her, and everything he'd done was what he thought was best for her.

"I don't want you to save me, Sol. I don't want you to make choices for me. I want you to stand by me as I make *my* choices. I want you to be there with me when I save myself," Luna said.

"I will, I promise," Sol agreed.

Luna realized this whole thing had been one large miscommunication and her own insecurities had only fed into her belief in it. She was enough, and she shouldn't have needed him to tell her so. Luna felt the pull of Sol's strong gaze, and when he opened his arms to her, she didn't hesitate.

Sol and Luna embraced, both of them aware of the small bump between them that hadn't been there the last time they were that close.

Sol released Luna so he could kneel in front of her, placing both of his hands onto her belly before he kissed her stomach.

Luna felt like she was joined to him again, a warm wave washing over her body. She loved this man with every fiber of her being, and now she knew he loved her too. He stood, his eyes meeting hers. Sol placed his hands on Luna's face, softly kissing her bruised cheek before bringing his warm lips to hers.

She seemed to melt as the sensations coursed through her body from his touch. The passionate kiss enveloped all her senses, and for a few moments Luna forgot where she was, forgot the impending trouble surrounding the night.

The kiss ended, both of them wishing it could last. The change in the rhythm of the drumbeats alerted them that their time alone together was over.

With the taste of Luna's sweet mouth still lingering on his lips, Sol said, "We have to get you to the safe place."

"No. I want to stay here and face my father," she said adamantly.

"Luna—"

"I know you want me to be safe, but my place is here with you. My people need to know they have no rights to this fight. Our tribes are now bound with blood. The shaman predicted this child, and my father's belief in the wise man might be enough to stop this madness. The shaman told him he had to protect the twilight creation at all costs. I believe this child in my womb is what he spoke of. I am the moon, the darkness, and you are the light of the sun, Sol."

Sol considered this information and saw the resolve in Luna's eyes. He knew she would be better off with the others in the safe place, but he also knew he could not make her choices for her. "As you wish."

He took her hand and helped her back onto Willow before mounting the horse behind her. Feeling his warm body pressed against her as they rode to meet Dalila made Luna feel at peace. She finally felt like she was home, next to Sol, exactly where she was supposed to be.

When they arrived at the encampment, small torches appeared across the river: the Barden quietly making their way toward them. The Nets stayed silent and concealed in the cover of the trees. Sol took Luna by the hand and led her to where his mother stood, ever watchful.

"What is she doing here, Sol?" Dalila demanded.

"This is my place," Luna answered for him.

"Both of you stay safe," Dalila said after a moment, giving in.

"Yes, Mama," they agreed with a small bow of their heads.

Luna waited in silence with Sol's arm around her. She watched the torches in the distance loom larger as they got closer. The Barden crossed the river onto Net tribe lands, and Luna could feel both Sol's and her own heartbeat grow faster in watchful anticipation.

As the Barden approached the tree line, Dalila and a small group of warriors exited the woods to greet them. The snow ceased and moonlight moved out from behind a cloud just in time to illuminate the white paint on their faces. Sol held Luna in place, and she waited.

Gannon and his warriors were surprised by the Net's sudden appearance. He shouted at his men to get into their battle stances.

"Gannon, why have you come to our lands?" Dalila demanded.

"I don't have to answer to a woman!" Cheers from his warriors erupted, and Gannon hesitated. "How did you know we were coming?" He searched the small crowd suspiciously.

"The goddess alerted my daughter, and my people prepared because they know what a woman's knowledge is worth," Dalila answered.

Gannon didn't seem satisfied with the answer. "Surrender now, and we will only slaughter those who resist us." The Barden banged their weapons on their wooden shields, unafraid of making noise now.

"We could live in peace with you as we have with the Dabney. Retreat now, back to your lands. We will spare all of your lives," Dalila promised.

Gannon scoffed. "My army outnumbers those you have here. Why would I do a thing like that?"

Dalila nodded her head, and Atsu blew on a pan flute that hung from his neck. The confidence faded in Gannon's face as he saw the giant army of warriors exit the tree line, all of them ready for battle. A small figure in white caught his eye.

"Luna?"

She heard her father's voice and made her way through the Net warriors in front of her to join Dalila. Sol followed her lead, staying close to her side.

Gasps from the Barden could be heard, and Gannon looked as though his suspicions had been confirmed as the sight of Luna with the Nets became clear.

"Traitor!" shouted a voice from the Barden clan, and it was quickly echoed among the rest.

Alice stepped forward to make herself seen near Gannon, placing her hand on his arm. "Hear her out," she encouraged.

Gannon stepped forward. "What have you done now, you stupid girl?!"

"I have done what I felt was right," Luna answered, her voice catching from the emotions swirling through her body, sending chills and vibrations throughout her being.

"You warned them?!" Gannon demanded.

"No, the goddess warned us, Gannon," Dalila answered for Luna.

"Why would you betray your family and your people for *them*?" Gannon shouted, pointing toward the Nets. "I have been too lax with you. You have not learned your place!"

"The gods set this in motion long ago. The day my mother died, the shaman told you there would be a child to unite the tribes. Just yesterday he told you this was a twilight child, made from the moon and the sun, and you must protect it at all costs." Luna spoke with growing confidence.

"Why would you do this to me? After all the freedom I have given you, after all I have done for you to set up a good marriage with a man who would take care of you!"

Gannon yelled, daring to take another step closer.

Luna noticed the hurt in her father's eyes, and she was overcome with guilt. Although she knew she had made the right choice, it didn't make this moment any easier.

"Gannon, take your warriors and leave," Dalila commanded.

"The gods proclaimed this day. The gods must have a plan." Gannon looked toward the red splitting the dark horizon, the moon still glowing and the predawn sky now clear of any clouds. "It is twilight now."

Luna knew what her father meant with the phrase and felt the impending battle cry.

"Wait!" she cried, quickly untying the fur from her shoulders and letting it drop down in the fresh snow. She untied the leather belt from her waist and lifted the tunic off so she was naked from the waist up except for the thin linen binding her breasts and her dark tribal tattoos. The cold air chilled her to her core, and her warm breath was visible. "This is the twilight creation."

It was as if both tribes were one as they took a large communal inhale of shock. Sol gasped with the crowd as he saw the darkening purple around Luna's arms to match her face, and he clenched his fists with rage.

"I am with child!" Luna exclaimed in a confident and firm voice.

Gannon stood, frozen in his tracks except for the trembling of anger. He gaped as he looked to Luna with disbelief, zeroing in on her swollen belly.

"You have always wanted me to have an heir," Luna exclaimed.

"*Not like this!*" Gannon seemed ready to snap in two. "You have ruined *everything*, Luna, *everything I fought so hard to give you!* Aidan has already shared his bed with you and you are ruined. He has no need to have a marriage with you now! My agreement with the Dabney is null!" Gannon screamed out in hostile frustration.

"I have not shared my bed with Aidan!" Luna shot back, knowing he would find out soon enough anyway.

Gannon's face turned from anger to shock then back to a seething fury.

"The child is a twilight creation, made from the darkness of the moon—myself—and the light of another. The shaman told you this child would join two tribes, creating a better power than any one could ever hope to possess. The wise man told you to protect this child. This means the child within me has connected our tribes through blood now. The gods have—"

"*Who* is the father then?" Gannon demanded as he moved toward his daughter. He completed two long strides before he saw Sol place a hand in front of Luna as a gesture of protection.

Luna watched the mixed disapproval and anger on her father's face disappear. It was replaced with an accusatory and shaming glare.

"I am," Sol said, stepping in front of Luna. Gannon was now only a few feet away from them.

Gannon looked to Sol and then Luna as understanding finally dawned. His hands clenched into fists, and he shook with rage. "The child in your womb is from *him*?!" Gannon screamed, pointing to Sol. "The child is a *half-breed*?! Answer me, *whore*!" He screamed out as he lunged forward, his body crashing into Sol's.

The force of the men's bodies shoved Luna to the ground. She yelped in pain as she landed on her belly atop a snow-covered stone. The men were wrestling on the ground next to her. Gannon was on top of Sol and swung his fists, hitting Sol's jaw. Sol wrapped his legs around Gannon to reverse directions so he could get out from under the older man.

Luna screamed at the men to stop as she clutched her stomach in pain. Dalila rushed over to help Luna to her feet but ordered her warriors and other sons to stay back.

The Barden gasped at the revelation, standing stunned as they watched their chief attack the Net man next to Luna. They knew well that this child meant they were now bound together with the Nets. The Barden tribesmen were confused about what they should do since the Nets were not attacking. It was only their chief and the one warrior fighting him, the very man who'd impregnated the chief's daughter. Alice held up both hands to protest their involvement, and they obeyed. The Barden knew they didn't stand a chance fighting against the Net warriors, whose numbers far exceeded their own.

Gannon and Sol tumbled with fists swinging. Sol struck Gannon's side, making him cry out in pain. Gannon was much larger than Sol, but Sol was fast and strong. Gannon swung his fist, barely missing Sol's head but catching Sol's eye with his left hook. Sol staggered backward from the force, trying to regain his balance before Gannon got too close. Gannon started to pull a knife from his belt, the blade shining in the moonlight. Sol ran into Gannon with his shoulder low, meeting with his stomach and temporarily knocking the air out of his body. Sol stripped the knife from Gannon's hand and held it to his neck. He was ready to end the life of the man who had caused Luna so much pain. The purple and red splotches on her face and naked arms were vivid proof.

"*Stop!*" Luna commanded, looking to Dalila to end this. Luna was scared for Sol, but she didn't want her father killed either.

Sol kept the knife close to Gannon's throat, both men breathing heavily, waiting.

Dalila began, "You want power—that's what this is all about, yet you would have more power if our tribes were united. We would all be a stronger people if you would learn to accept us and see our worth as equals, every man, woman, and child. Your anger is not at us, Gannon. You are angry at yourself for not being able to save Terra. You are angry at so many things and use our people as your excuse to remain that way because you are not strong enough to face your own fears. Don't mistake my patience for weakness. We will kill every last one of your warriors if you decide to attack us."

Gannon blinked a few times but stayed silent as a will to survive cleared the fog of the blind hatred in him, at least for the moment. Dalila motioned for Sol to get off Gannon and let him go. Sol obeyed his mother and stood by Luna, keeping the knife in his hand.

Gannon stood up quickly, walking back to his own clan of warriors.

"Brother, there is wisdom in her words," Alice said, loudly enough for all to hear.

"Silence!" he ordered.

"If your daughter is with child and that child's father is a Net, our bloodlines are joined. The shaman told you this would happen, and now it has. You must heed his warning," Alice continued.

"I know what he said!" Gannon snapped, irritated and recognizing his defeat. He angrily glanced at the moon and then to Luna.

"Chief, we stand no chance of victory with so few numbers," came another voice from the tribe, and several more voiced their agreement.

Gannon stood humiliated and defeated before both tribes, his unfounded hatred telling him to do one thing, his reverence for the wise man another.

"Go back to the village!" he commanded his men, and they obeyed without hesitation, except Alice, who stayed by her brother's side.

Gannon looked at Luna. "You are coming with me."

CHAPTER 21

Luna felt Sol's hand on her shoulder. "No, she will stay here with me," he said, still wielding Gannon's knife.

Luna hesitated, not sure what she should do. She wanted to stay with Sol, but she also clearly understood if she didn't obey her father, it would be the final act of rebellion and he would disown her. It was her decision to make. She had a choice, although one fraught with contradiction and pain. Before Luna could voice her decision, a sharp pain cut across her abdomen.

She lurched forward, grabbing her belly. Strong cramping began in her stomach, reaching around to her lower back, and she felt a warm trickle down her leg. Luna placed her hand on her inner thigh and saw the crimson stain. Panic and horror paralyzed her. She could hear distant voices arguing, but none of them made any sense to her. She stood frozen in time from shock and disbelief.

While Luna stood stunned, Sol was the first to see the blood between her thighs. He turned immediately to Gannon and screamed, "Look at what your ignorance has done!”

Gannon looked at Luna. She was staring at her blood-stained fingers as if she had discovered the secret to immortality written across them. His anger turned from Sol to himself in that moment. It wasn't his fault—was it? Gannon noticed the large grey stone that had been covered with snow before he lunged toward the Net man who dared to touch his daughter, and he suddenly realized he had knocked her over.

Dalila walked over to Gannon, three of her warriors and her two sons following close by.

“Gannon, let me take her to our healing tent,” Dalila said gently.

“Leave her with you? You killed her mother, and now you wish me to give my only daughter over to you?!” Gannon said, his voice catching.

“Gannon, your anger at me and my people is unfounded. It was not *your* fault Terra died, and it was also not mine. It was no one's fault. You believe your gods manipulate the outcomes in our world, and I know you do not wish to blame them. You know I speak the truth when I tell you I am Luna and the baby's best chance for survival. Your daughter is a fighter. She is a strong woman like her mother. Let me and the healing women from my tribe try to help her.” Dalila's voice was firm but gentle.

Gannon seemed to mull over the idea.

Luna's eyes fluttered as she came back to the present,

Dalila's voice breaking through the fog of throbbing pain and numbing shock.

"Father, I love you, and I am sure a part of me always will. I must choose what is best for me and for the child in my womb. I trust Mama Dalila." Luna looked in Gannon's eyes as she spoke, and a single tear fell down her bruised cheek.

Gannon started, his voice sounding softer than it had in so many years, "Luna—"

He was interrupted by Luna crying out in pain. She grabbed Sol's hand as she bent over from the intense cramping.

Sol picked her up in his arms. "I am doing what is best for my child and the woman I love. I am doing what Luna wishes." Sol didn't wait for Gannon to answer. He turned to carry Luna back to their village to seek refuge at the healer's tent.

Dalila said, "I will take good care of her, Gannon, as if she was my own daughter. That is my blood coursing through the child in her womb, too. You are welcome to come and wait for her, but not your warriors." Dalila turned and followed after Sol and Luna.

Gannon stood still, not sure what to say, his hatred for the Nets and his love for his daughter at war within him. He never told her he loved her, he realized—never. He admitted to himself that what he felt for her wasn't the sort of love he should have had for his daughter, but it was more than just an obligatory feeling of connection because she was his offspring. He had loved her as best as he could, the most he was capable of. Gannon felt attached to Luna, even if it was only their blood that kept them that way. Luna was more like Terra than him, and sometimes he resented her for it. Gannon didn't want his daughter to die, nor the twilight child in her womb the shaman had told him he was supposed to protect at all costs. Gannon was disgusted at himself for making such a mess of the whole thing, and now the child, his heir, might suffer the consequences. It still made him sick to think of a Net being with his daughter, but he couldn't deny the truth of Dalila's words.

Alice broke her silence. "Gannon, I can go to be with her if you wish."

He nodded his head and Alice followed Dalila through the trees toward the Net village. Some of the warriors followed Alice while most remained at the border, waiting and watching. Gannon turned to go back the way he had come, his head hanging low. The deep fiery red that burned the twilight of the horizon mixed with yellow and purple hues. He walked home with only the sound of the crows and his feet crunching through the fresh snow.

* * *

Luna held on tight to Sol, wincing from the pain that radiated from her abdomen. She watched over his shoulder as her only family and most of what she had known in her life grew smaller as she was carried away. Luna had been worried she would miscarry the child in her womb as her mother had so many times before, but with each passing month, she had gotten a little more hope. Now, it seemed the crushing reality of the inevitable miscarriage would happen, just as she had feared for so long. There were several times when Luna had wished her mother was there, but in this moment, she wished more than ever that Terra could hold her hand and assure her everything would be okay.

Sol carried Luna past the longhouse where she had been before to a red, round building. A woman was there waiting, holding the cloth door open for them. Sol carefully made his way into the dimly lit room. There were candles everywhere and a fire in the center. Beautiful tapestries hung along the walls with goddesses and their symbols. One healer woman used a small metal bowl and a wooden instrument to make a low vibrating noise, and the smell of various herbs filled the air. Luna felt panicked as memories came back in flashes, reminding her that it was the very room her mother had died in.

Sol saw Luna's distress and laid her gently on the soft cushions. He took her face in both hands and spoke in a hushed but firm voice. "Luna, you are safe. I am here, and I will not let anything else happen to you." He said the words, but even he knew he had no power to stop a miscarriage.

Luna felt her body relax in his strong grip. Silent tears escaped her eyes, falling down her cheeks in trails.

Dalila came into the room and gave orders to the other three healers before turning to Sol. "We need to undress her. Sol, why don't you wait outside."

Luna grabbed Sol's arm, begging him to stay.

"No, my place is here with Luna," he said.

Dalila nodded her head.

The women healers got to work, carefully stripping the stained clothing off Luna and cleaning her up. She felt terrified and self-conscious at the same time. They placed a warm blanket over her hips, covering down to her feet. She took a deep cleansing breath and let it out. Sol held her hand and kissed her forehead.

Mama Dalila hummed as she worked to prepare a tea for Luna. When it was ready, she had Sol lift Luna's head enough to meet the cup with her lips. The tea was sweeter than Luna expected.

"You look so much like your mama, child. You are strong like her, too." Dalila tried to offer her comfort. "Your aunt is here, and she wants to know if she can come inside to be with you."

Luna perked up. "Alice is here?"

Dalila nodded.

"Yes, I would like her to come in," Luna answered.

Dalila got up and disappeared through the flap, returning a moment later with Alice. She came and sat next to Luna's hip, opposite Sol.

"Your father sent me, Luna, to make sure you are well," Alice explained.

"Thank you. Thank you for everything," Luna said, referring to far more than just her aunt's presence there in the healer's tent.

"Ssshhh now. You rest," Alice told her gently.

Dalila brought over two different herb-infused oils and handed one to Alice before opening the other jar herself. Dalila poured the oil over Luna's belly then rubbed gently over her lower abdomen, motioning for Alice to do the same with the contents of the jar she held.

Sol kept offering Luna sips of tea as his mother instructed him. They kept her warm and supported. One of the women began chanting in a low voice while the other played the sound bowl. Luna felt relaxed, and the throbbing in her abdomen dulled. Luna felt so many things, but Sol's touch helped her to feel grounded. She didn't know what would happen, but she felt at peace.

Sol watched as Luna drifted off into a peaceful sleep. He was terrified for her, but he knew his mother's knowledge of healing was from the wise woman tradition, which was matched by none. He trusted in her abilities and wisdom.

When Luna awoke, she felt Sol's head resting near her arm. He was gently snoring, and the sound made her smile, remembering the night they'd spent together in the small cave so long ago. She opened her eyes and saw the smoke rising out of the hole in the top of the red tent. Luna glanced around the almost silent room and saw Dalila stirring an herbal infusion in a pot over the fire. The woman looked up and greeted Luna with a warm smile.

"Good morning, baby bear." Dalila's words woke Sol and he sat up abruptly, gingerly rubbing the sleepiness from his swollen eyes.

Luna noticed the wounds on his bruised face for the first time, and the sight brought her sadness.

"Luna, you have stopped bleeding. How is your pain?" she asked.

"It's not that bad," Luna answered, turning her face to look at Dalila. Her womb felt sore with a dull ache, like she had overworked her groin muscles.

"Good. That is good news. I think you are in the clear of a miscarriage, but you will have to remain in bed for the time being. Continue taking the herbs, and get some healing foods into your belly. You are eating for two people now," Dalila said, smiling.

Luna breathed a sigh of relief as she softly touched her stomach. Sol's hand rested gently next to hers, and a subtle succession of taps made their eyes meet.

"Was that…" Sol didn't complete the sentence because Luna was already nodding her head.

"I think so," Luna said, feeling such awe as the little twilight baby in her womb made its presence known to them.

Sol looked at Luna, the woman he loved so fervently. She was so beautiful. Something had changed in her since he met her at the waterfall so many months before. Sol craved her, wanted to join his life to hers. Sol wanted to live his life in partnership with the woman who squeezed his hand and looked up at him in that moment. Emotion overcame him and he leaned down to kiss Luna. Her lips were soft and warm, and he didn't want to stop.

Luna wished the kiss could last longer, but she was also conscious of the fact that Mama Dalila was in the room, the woman who also happened to be Sol's mother.

"Where is Alice?" Luna asked.

"She went to tell your father you are doing better. She said she would be back today," Dalila answered.

The next week was spent mostly inside the red tent with the healing women. Sol stayed by her side for most of the time, usually coming back to greet her with flavorful and delectable dishes that made Luna's taste buds explode with sensations, including many flavors she had never tasted before. The food warmed and healed her, as did the conversations and laughter she shared with the Net tribe members who came to meet her.

She especially liked Akiiki, Sol's sister. She had barely taken one look at Luna before she brought her into a warm hug with their pregnant bellies between them. Luna saw how Bomani looked at Akiiki and saw the true love and respect in his eyes. He made Luna laugh harder than she ever remembered laughing before, especially when he and Sol would joke about each other. Ata and Atsu also came to say hello, and she thought they looked a lot like Mama Dalila.

Layla came to visit Luna when Sol was not there and told her she wished her well with healing. Luna wasn't sure what to say other than thanking her. Luna saw another side to the guarded woman, and she recognized the strength within her. Luna found that even though she didn't fully trust Layla, she respected her.

Alice came every day to see Luna's progress and report back to Gannon. She promised to speak with her brother and try to get him to see the value of a peace treaty. Alice wished Luna had told her about the pregnancy, but she also understood why she'd kept it to herself.

It was the winter solstice, and Luna was going to finally get out of the tent and walk around with Sol. She was itching to move her body after being kept in the confines of the beautiful red healing tent. Luna could hear the music already playing before they stepped outside. Voices began singing in an ancient language, and horns blew. Sol placed a warm fur coat around her that almost reached to the ground, and when he smiled at her, she felt an immense gratitude. Butterflies of excitement stirred within her as he took her hand and led her out of the tent, and the first blast of aromatic spices from the savory foods the whole village had prepared pleasantly teased her senses. Luna saw the bright torches lining the way for all of them to make their way to a much brighter light in the distance.

Sol dropped her hand and put his warm arm around her, leading her down the torch-lit path toward a clearing before the tree line of the north woods. As they walked, the music got louder, and Luna could see a large bonfire had been lit. She knew the fire would be kept burning strong throughout the night as they all prayed and chanted to the gods and goddesses to bring the great light back the following day. The fire would keep their hope alive through the longest, darkest night of the ever-turning wheel of the year. Around the fire there were hundreds of people forming a circle, and some had already begun dancing. Luna saw the tables were full of delectable dishes, their enticing scents making her mouth water.

Sol brought Luna over to greet his mother, who was dressed in a white fur vest with a matching tunic dress and pants. Dalila had gold cuffs on her wrists and a matching necklace. Luna saw that most of the people who gathered wore an array of colors but had chosen gold jewelry as it represented the light of the sun.

"How are you feeling tonight, Luna?" Dalila asked, moving her body to the beat of the drums.

"Very well, thank you." Luna bowed her head in respect.

"I am happy to hear that. You must eat, child." Dalila turned to Sol and spoke in their ancient language. Luna liked the way their language sounded. She had never heard

Sol—or any Net tribe member—speak it before.

"Yes, Mama," he agreed with a laugh.

When they were out of earshot, Luna asked, "What did she say?"

Sol smiled. "She told me to feed you because you are too thin."

Luna was surprised. She had been called many things in her life, but never thin. She felt the acceptance and let it wash over her as she laughed with Sol and ate the various fragrant, delectable foods. As she enjoyed the rich, spicy, and savory dishes, not only was her body fed, but also her soul.

"This is the most amazing food I have ever eaten," Luna admitted.

Sol laughed. She loved that laugh, and she hadn't realized how much she had missed it because she had tried not to feel anything while they were apart. Now, though, they were together again, and she relished the sensations.

Bomani spoke and they turned to look at him. "It is a wonder your people have survived this long without proper food, Luna. You better be careful, Sol—you fed her your mama's food, so now she will never leave you. I see you have already made a mark on her." Bomani laughed and then walked away.

Sol and Luna laughed with him.

She turned back to Sol. "What did he mean about a mark?"

He burst into hysterical laughter.

"What is so funny?" Luna asked honestly.

"You have some stew on your face," he said, wiping the space above the corner of her lip.

She blushed. "Oh, thank you." She felt embarrassed but then laughed along with him.

They stayed and enjoyed the company of the tribe. The children ran free and played throughout the gathering. Luna smiled at a little boy who was secured to his mother's back, reminding her of the wrap she had made and buried for her own child, reminding her how close she had come to losing her baby. As the hours flew by, they were warmed by the fire, the food, the community, and a warm, sweet, spiced cider. Luna was surprised there were not many people drinking anything fermented. Her tribe and the Dabneys' feasts had always been full of ales and strong distillations. Luna preferred the Net's celebration over her own. The thought quickly reminded her this was the night they had planned for her to be hand-fasted to Aidan. Luna swallowed hard, deciding she would speak to Alice and make arrangements to speak to her father.

"Luna? Do you feel okay?" Sol asked. He was sitting next to her as they watched the dancers around the fire. His eyes reflecting the flames, and he squeezed her hand. He was still concerned about her health and the chance of a miscarriage. He didn't want Luna to overdo it.

"Yes. I feel wonderful. Your culture is truly magical," Luna replied, her eyes alive with a newfound zest. She would worry about tomorrow when the morning came.

"I have something I want to show you, if you are up for it," Sol said.

Luna was intrigued. "Yes, of course!"

He smiled and stood before extending his other hand, helping her to her feet. They walked through the gathering, drawing many stares, most of them followed by waves and smiles. He walked, leading her farther away from the lights and the music. The sounds slowly drifted away as the night grew darker. Sol led her to the horse pasture and helped her up. He directed the horse through their quiet village south until the snow turned to sand. The salty breeze and the sounds of the waves crashing occupied her senses. Luna smiled and took a deep breath of the brisk wind. Eventually Sol helped her down off the horse and pulled the fur coat tighter around her.

"I'm warm enough," she assured him.

"I have a surprise for you," he said, taking her hand in his. Luna's surprised glance made his heart beat faster with anticipation. Sol led her down the snowy shoreline, watching the white caps of the dark ocean waves crashing as the tide made its way back in from the sea. Soon enough torches appeared in a line, leading the way to where twisted branches came into view, high on sturdy tree trunks that were buried deep within the earth. Luna glanced up to see the creation Sol was looking at. She glanced back at him and then gazed at the house he had built.

Her mouth opened in awe at the sight of the artistic dwelling. She wasn't quite sure it was a house at first, as it was unlike anything she had ever seen. The way the branches twisted into each other making circular windows with bright light shining out made it look like it had been crafted by an unearthly magic. Sol tugged Luna's hand gently, and she followed curiously. He led her under the home where steps led to a circular opening directly above them. Sol led the way, opening the latch, and she followed. He helped her up, and she stood gasping at the brilliance of the brightly lit wooden home.

Sol was thoroughly satisfied with Luna's awe. "Do you like it?" he asked with only a small fear that she wouldn't.

"Yes! It is the most beautiful thing I have ever seen. You built this?" Luna asked as she walked around, inspecting the handiwork. She could see the ocean through one of the small open windows. Lanterns hung on the walls, and a small bed had been made with the items she recognized from Sol's lean-to.

"With Bomani's help," he said humbly.

"Sol, this is…" Luna hesitated, trying to find the right word. She couldn't choose one, so she said, "Amazing, beautiful, and magical! It is perfect!" She touched her hand to one of the branches that formed part of a wall.

"I built it with you in mind. I built it for us."

Luna turned around to look at him, feeling like it was getting harder to breathe.

Sol walked up to her, pulling her close in his arms, the fire of their closeness igniting both their bodies.

"Marry me?" he asked. "Marry me and spend the rest of your life with me. Give me your hand so it can be fasted to mine. Let me be your partner in life and help you achieve all you wish to in this world," Sol pleaded.

Luna didn't answer. His words were filled with passion and promise, and she was reeling with awe from the possibility of everything she had wanted for so long coming true. She wondered if this was a dream and she would wake at home in Barden tribe lands waiting for the sun to rise and then make tea for her father. It didn't feel like a dream, though. The fiery touch of Sol's body reminded her that this was real, and the man she loved was waiting for her answer.

Luna parted her lips to speak, but rather than using words, she met his mouth with hers. She pulled him tight against her body, enjoying the buzzing electricity that mixed with the heat that washed over her. She released him long enough to reply, almost speaking in a whisper. "Yes!" she gasped.

CHAPTER 22

After Luna agreed to join her life to Sol's, they enjoyed kisses filled with passion and delighted in each other's warm embrace. Luna yearned to join her body with Sol's but she hesitated.

Instead, Sol took her back to the solstice celebration to wait out the morning light, not trusting his own restraint if they stayed alone together. Luna watched the flames and the people of the tribe dancing to the music playing throughout the night hours. They eventually ate again, filling their stomachs while listening to the elders pass on the knowledge of their ancient ancestors to the younger generations.

Eventually, the crowd began to disperse, most of them leaving with younger children sleeping over their shoulders. Luna and Sol lay together on a communal bed made from furs and tanned hides for those who wished to stay. She put her head on Sol's chest, feeling his breath and hearing his heartbeat. Luna knew in that moment that she was home, and she fell asleep in the arms of her lover, waiting for the sun to rise.

When Luna woke, she could smell the smoke from the dying fire mixed with the incense the women of the tribe had added to the flames in thanks to the goddess for the sunrise. The pink sky was a promise that the longer days of light would come again. Sol sat up once he realized Luna was awake, and they both rubbed the remnants of sleep from their eyes. Surrounding them were several other tribe members huddled together with their loved ones, still sleeping peacefully.

Sol kissed Luna's cheek and whispered, "I love you," in her ear.

Luna smiled. "I love you, too."

Sol stood up and stretched before extending his hand to her. She took it gratefully and stood then immediately felt dizzy, grabbing Sol's arms to steady herself.

"Are you okay?" he asked, concerned.

"Just dizzy. I got up too fast," Luna assured him, giving Sol a smile to let him know the feeling had passed.

"Let's go get you something to eat," he said, taking her hand.

They wove through the sleeping figures and walked back to the tables where several more Net men and women were preparing heated foods and herbal infusions. Sol took a wooden bowl and filled it with steaming rice. He added a scoop of a spiced vegetable sauce and two boiled eggs to share with Luna. He handed her the bowl so he could fill two wooden mugs with tea. They set the dishes down and washed their hands in the pan of hot water before bringing their breakfast to an empty table.

"We forgot spoons," Luna said, standing to get them.

Sol put his arm up to stop her. "Sit. We don't need spoons. This meal is better when you use your hands."

She sat back down, hesitant but curious.

He used his right hand to pick up some of the bits of rice, dipping it in the red and green vegetable sauce before placing it in his mouth. "Go ahead," he encouraged.

Luna dug her fingers in, managing to get some of the rice and the savory sauce into her mouth. Her hands were not as clean as Sol's after the attempt, but it was different, and she enjoyed experiencing her food with the added sensory element. They smiled at each other and continued their meal.

After they had finished eating and enjoyed their tea together, Luna told Sol of her intentions to reach out to Alice for a meeting with her father.

"But, I can't go with you. How do I know you will be safe?" Sol asked, knowing if a Net crossed onto Barden land, there would be no mercy, especially not for him in particular.

"My father will not hurt me while this child is in my womb. He fears the gods, and they have told him to protect the child," Luna encouraged.

"What if he keeps you there?" Sol asked with worry in his voice.

"Then I will escape. I have to speak with him, and I know he will not come here to meet me. Alice will be with me. When she comes today, I will ask her to arrange the meeting," Luna explained in resignation.

Worry filled every bone in Sol's body, and he pulled Luna closer to himself. He knew she had to make her own choices. He knew this meeting was a necessity, but he wished he could be there to protect her. He had just gotten her back, and now he would have to let her go. He let his hug linger.

Later that afternoon, Alice came and spoke to Luna, happy to see her niece was healthy. Luna told Alice about her choice to be hand-fasted to Sol. Her aunt didn't seem surprised, but she wasn't entirely happy about the news either. Luna asked her about a meeting with Gannon, and Alice agreed it would be a good time to do it. Alice promised she would be back the following day to meet Luna at the river in the morning. They parted ways and Luna went to find Sol at Mama Dalila's longhouse.

He was carving a bowl and looked up when he heard her approach. "What did she say?"

"Tomorrow morning," Luna said.

Sol focused back on the carving in his hands. "Mama?" he called.

Dalila came out of the longhouse with three steaming cups of hot tea. "Yes?"

She handed one of the cups to Luna first.

"Thank you," Luna said, accepting the cup and smelling

the familiar herbal infusion.

Dalila set one of the cups near Sol so he could take it when he was ready before sitting down by the small fire to enjoy her own.

Sol started, "Luna is going to meet her father tomorrow, alone." The women could hear the fear and disapproval in his voice.

"As she must," Dalila answered simply.

Luna looked toward Dalila. "I will see where things stand and inform him of my decision." She looked back at Sol, hoping he could see why she must do this.

Sol paused his work to meet her eyes. "Is this what you feel you must do for yourself, or for my people? We don't need you to save us," Sol told her.

"I understand you don't need a Barden to save you. I do this for myself so I can face him with honesty as a grown woman making my own choices. I will try to reason with him, because I do not know what else I can do. I must try for peace at the very least. I cannot be joined to you knowing my father will retaliate against your tribe," Luna said, her voice soft but firm, hoping Sol would understand and give her his blessing.

Dalila walked over to Luna and gave her a hug. "You have to choose what is best for you, my child. I agree that this seems like the best course of action for you. If you father chooses to attack us, I know we will prevail."

"Unless the Dabney join him," Sol said.

The women released each other to look at him.

Luna said, "Aidan does not want a war. He sees the potential in what a peace treaty and open trading would do to benefit all our tribes." Luna saw the look of jealousy on Sol's face when she mentioned Aidan.

"Well if Aidan sees our value then all is saved," Sol snapped.

"Let me deal with the Dabney," Dalila responded in a serious tone, and Sol got her message. "There is promise then. Do not worry about this, my children. That is my job as chieftess. Luna, your job is to clear your conscience with your father and decide what will make you happy."

Luna had never heard Dalila direct her commanding voice toward her, and she knew immediately why so many respected the woman.

"As you wish," Luna replied. Sol looked to Luna, his eyes pleading with her not to go.

"Now, I must go. I am about to watch the birth of my first grandchild!" Dalila said exuberantly with a large smile crossing her features.

"What?" Luna asked in surprise as Dalila left.

"Akiiki's labor pains started last night, and she has been laboring all day. The portal is opening, and the time is close," Sol explained, still upset that Luna wanted to leave him and go back to her father without his protection.

"Oh, that is exciting," Luna said, trying to break the tension they could both feel in the air. Sol turned his attention back to the carving in his hands. Luna sat and enjoyed her tea, watching the steam rise in the frozen air. They sat in silence for over an hour, although both their minds were active wondering about the other. Sol was worried for her safety and the fact that she would choose to put herself and their child in danger. Hadn't she just risked everything to come to him, and now she was going to leave?

Luna was unsure why Sol was being so cold toward her. She knew she would never forgive herself if she didn't face her father and try to make peace or say goodbye forever, if that was the case. This was something she needed to do for herself. Why wouldn't Sol support that? Why was he being so distant? Before Luna could form the words to ask him, Ata came running up to them.

"The baby is here!" he said in excitement, out of breath from the sprint.

Luna sat up straighter and smiled. Sol set aside his woodwork and stood to give his younger brother a hug.

"Yeah! Is Akiiki doing well?" Sol asked him, releasing Ata.

"Yes. Bomani looks a bit overwhelmed though." Ata laughed, and Sol echoed his joy. "Mama says for you to come," Ata said, waving for them to follow.

Sol looked to Luna.

"I will wait here," she offered.

"No, Akiiki asked for you to come also," Ata assured her.

Sol extended his hand with a smile, deciding he would

speak to her about his worries later.

Sol and Luna followed Ata to Bomani and Akiiki's home, where a large group had gathered. Sol motioned to the people before explaining, "Most of them are blood family, but some are here to wish their future chieftess well with gifts of herbs and meals."

Luna nodded her understanding and followed the brothers into a wooden cabin. The home was warm and well lit, bringing some relief to Luna's face, which was bright pink from the cold. Ata and Atsu left with a greeting to Luna, making room for them. Mama Dalila sat next to Bomani's mother near the large bed that was raised off the ground. Akiiki lay in the bed with her husband, Bomani, who had a large smile of amazement plastered across his face. They were both looking at the fresh newborn with curly black swirls covering its head. As Luna got closer, she could see the milky yellow substance that covered the baby, and it was wrapped in a bright blue blanket. The umbilical cord led from the baby's belly over its mother's arm to a bowl where the purple-red placenta was placed, still attached. Luna felt unsure if she should be present at such an intimate gathering. Akiiki looked up from the newborn's face and saw Luna.

"Come, sister. Meet my son," Akiiki invited. Luna looked at Sol quickly before stepping closer.

"That is a beautiful baby," Luna said with a smile.

Akiiki smiled. "Soon, you will have your own."

"I hope so," Luna said honestly.

"I've seen it."

The information surprised Luna, and she couldn't respond.

"You dreamed about our child?" Sol asked.

"Yes," Akiiki said.

"Leave the new mother alone with your questions, Sol. She has just given birth to life itself. If you are to be here, you must give to her now," Dalila said.

Sol nodded.

They stayed and spoke about the birth. Hot spiced cider was served, and they enjoyed the additional warmth. It was time to cut the umbilical cord when it stopped pulsating and turned white. Luna watched as Dalila offered the knife to Bomani and directed him to cut above the tied thread by the baby's navel.

He hesitated. "Will it hurt him?"

"No," Bomani's mother promised.

He cut the cord and smiled with relief. Dalila took the bowl with the placenta and placed it in another pan to boil over the fire.

"Why is she doing that?" Luna whispered her question to Sol.

"She will cook it so Akiiki can consume it as needed these next few weeks to help her body recover from the shock of not having to grow a child. It helps with her milk too," Sol answered informatively.

Luna was amazed by this birth event and all that came with being a woman in the birthing process. It was so open in this tribe. The men being in the room surprised Luna, but now she knew Bomani had been there the whole time with Akiiki. The way the Net culture dealt with the facts of childbirth and women's bodies was a stark contrast to the way Luna had been taught growing up. Her tribe kept such things silent for the most part, unless it was used for shaming or to claim a woman was unclean.

Sol approached Akiiki and kissed her forehead before patting Bomani on the shoulder. He was usually full of jokes, always having something to say, but now he sat in silent awe of the queen who had birthed his child from the world of the gods to theirs. Akiiki had been a human portal for the soul of their child, and he had watched every moment of it. Luna saw Sol with Akiiki and wondered how their birthing experience would be. She wondered if Sol's reaction would be one of awe, like Bomani.

"We will let you rest now," Sol said.

"Good night," Luna said before taking Sol's hand and leaving the cabin. They left the warm dwelling and were greeted with a dark sky and a full moon. Luna took a deep, tired breath of the frigid air.

"Let's go home," Sol offered.

Luna's eyes looked up at him questioningly.

"Our home," he clarified.

Luna nodded with a smile, and they silently made their

way on horseback to the home Sol had built near the sea.

When they arrived, Sol helped Luna up the stairs in the dark and led her to the bed then started the fire. Within a few minutes, it was roaring and the lanterns were lit in the cozy home. Sol heated soup broth for them both to eat, and they enjoyed it together.

"Sol," Luna said, breaking the comfortable silence. "I don't want to go unless you give me your blessing. I don't want to leave you knowing you are angry with me. I am not asking for permission. I just need to know you trust me and support me no matter what I need."

Sol appeared to be deep in thought. He took her empty bowl, placing it on top of his on the small table in the room before he turned to face her on the bed of furs. "Luna, I was wrong, I see that now. I am worried for your safety, but of course I will support you no matter what you choose. I am here for you."

Sol's gaze was intense. He placed his hand to Luna's cheek and kissed it before moving to her other side. The fire glowed on Sol's face, igniting the desire Luna felt. He kissed her forehead, and she closed her eyes, enjoying the feeling of his warm lips as they met with her skin. She felt electric prickles dance down her arms and legs, creating gooseflesh. Luna's body ached for him, but she wasn't sure if he would continue. In the red flames of the dim room, Luna felt Sol's hands pull at the fabric of her tunic.

He watched as she opened her desire-filled eyes and

recognized the same hunger within his own body. He pulled the tunic over her head then removed the pants she was wearing, exposing her naked flesh in the firelight. She was more beautiful than he had remembered. He could see all five lines of her tribal tattoo fully, the lowest stopping just before each of her naked breasts.

She sat, bare and waiting for him to lead. Luna watched as Sol stripped and a flurry of clothing fell to the floor.

He took her face in both of his hands and kissed her. His kiss was hot with passion, his lips soft with desire. She felt herself melt into him.

The air was thick with anticipation, and Luna felt herself gasp as he pushed his naked chest against hers. She pulled him closer and they twisted in and out of a sensual knot of love and rapture.

His hot kisses tasted of ecstasy and left no area untouched. Her legs tingled with excitement and her toes curled as a sensual shockwave of orgasmic pleasure rocked her body, causing her to tighten her grip on Sol's back.

Luna's pale, soft flesh against his warmed Sol's body and fed the ravenous need within him to experience the entirety of her. He wanted her. He wanted all of her. When Luna struggled against him from the overabundance of pleasure, he hesitated. "Do you want me to keep going?"

"Yes," she said breathlessly.

Sol put his hand on the back of her neck and grabbed her hair firmly.

Luna and Sol joined together, reawakening their physical fervor for each other, their feelings complete. Their souls left their bodies, intertwining somewhere above them in a spiritual plane. Luna felt completely desired and alive throughout the hour they spent tangled in each other's arms. They locked eyes and watched each other hypnotically, the intensely visceral pent-up need for each other finally being released after all the months of waiting.

They stayed stuck together, breathing heavily, their bodies fully relaxed. Sol lay next to Luna, and she placed her head on his chest, listening to his rapid heartbeat. Luna felt warm and tingly everywhere, fully and completely satisfied in every way. Sol ran his fingers up and down her arm. They fell asleep snuggled in each other's embrace, listening to the sounds of the fire crackling, the wind blowing outside, and the waves crashing on the sand.

CHAPTER 23

Luna felt Sol's arms wrapped around her naked body when she awoke. The crashing ocean waves sounded farther away, but she could hear a chorus of seabirds feasting on what the tide had left behind. The room smelled of smoke from the fire that was only barely going now. She guessed Sol must have added wood at some point in the night for it to still be burning at all. She could see her hot breath in the room, but she wasn't cold with the warmth of Sol behind her. His arms were wrapped around her under the layer of linen and fur blankets, one of them resting on her growing belly. Luna smiled. She was truly the happiest she had ever been.

She felt Sol's callused hand run down to her thigh as he leaned over and kissed her cheek.

"Good morning," he said.

"Good morning," she echoed.

They stayed wrapped up together for a few moments before Sol sat up, freeing his arm from under her head. He put one of the blankets around his shoulders, leaving the bottom half of him exposed. Luna laughed at the sight, enjoying the view. She couldn't help but smile as a wave of absolute gratitude came over her that she was able to have such a man love her. A question popped into her mind as he got the fire roaring again.

"Why do you love me?" she asked.

Sol turned back to her in surprise before he hung a pot of partially frozen soup over the fire and rejoined her.

"You are so easy to love, Luna. It's who you are that makes me love you," he replied after some thought.

His answer was not what she had been expecting to hear, so Luna responded with another smile and a kiss.

They ate their breakfast, both of them not wanting to think of it possibly being their last time together for a while. Neither wanted to say goodbye. Sol knew Luna was an individual who needed to make her own decisions and do what she needed to for herself. He had wished so many times that he could have had the chance to speak to his father after defying him. For so many years, Sol had told himself it would be to explain to him why he hadn't listened. Now, Sol knew what he really wanted was to hear his father tell him it was okay, he forgave him, and he loved him. Sol knew there were things a child needed to say to a parent and other things a child needed to hear from their parent, no matter how old they were. Sol decided he would not take that away from Luna, even though the risks were many.

Luna was thankful for Sol's silence on the subject. She would face her father without anyone else around, except for Alice, and she would speak her truth. The thought in itself was cleansing, and she knew it was the right decision for her. She tied her leather belt around her waist and gathered the fur coat Dalila had given her. She liked the garment because it covered her arms and tied together nicely in the front, keeping her warm in the frigid weather. Sol put on his own coat and opened the latched door in the floor. Luna glanced around the small round home that had been so artfully crafted. She imagined the hours of work he'd spent creating each section of the branched master-piece. A small wooden figure caught her eye, one she didn't remember seeing before. Luna picked up the little bear carved from wood and examined it closer.

"I made it to remember you," Sol said, answering her silent questions.

"It is so intricately done. It will be perfect for the baby." Luna placed a hand on her womb.

Sol smiled as he nodded, a hopeful prayer in his eyes. Luna went down the stairs first, and Sol followed behind to latch the door. They made their way to the horses and rode together, side by side, to the river to meet Alice.

When they reached their destination, they could see her already waiting. Sol dismounted his horse and walked over to Luna, helping her down. He pulled her close, kissing her lips softly. They both hoped it wasn't goodbye for long, and they let their farewell kiss say what words could not.

Sol released Luna from his embrace, and she looked

up at him, breathless. "I love you, Sol. I will be back," she promised.

He believed her, and he promised himself he would stay hopeful. "I'll wait here, all day and all night if I have to." He kissed her forehead.

He helped her mount Willow again, and she walked the horse across the river to where Alice waited on her own horse. The women nodded to each other silently and rode toward the Barden village. Luna glanced back to see Sol waiting where she had left him, and he waved to her.

"Is he in a better mood today?" Luna enquired, referring to her father.

"He has a lot on his mind," Alice answered as the wall came into sight.

Luna noticed the door was closed. Alice waved to the usual two warriors at the doors, but when they opened it, Luna could see that they had tripled their guard to six. A knot formed in her stomach, and she began to second-guess her decision. Luna followed behind Alice, feeling the stares of the warriors and every Barden tribe member they passed. They either stood stunned with their mouths gaping, or they whispered stolen secrets amongst themselves.

The home she'd grown up in came into view as they rounded the corner near the wall, though Luna noticed it didn't feel like home anymore. Her stomach fluttered in knots of anxiety as she dismounted her horse. Alice opened the front door, and Luna followed her into the dark room, preparing herself to assess the situation. She would use the gifts she was given by the goddess and feel what she should say this time.

As Luna entered, everything was where it had been before she left, like it was any other day. Her father sat by the fire in his chair, smoking his pipe of dried herbs, his long grey beard twisted in the familiar braids. Luna was still scared of him, but her fear was less now. He didn't look as big as she remembered. She saw the lost look on his hard face and pitied him. As distasteful as the thought was, Luna wanted to try to see why he believed the way he did, why he felt the way he did about the Nets.

"Father, I hope you have been healing well," she said, breaking the silence and offering a peaceful beginning. She could see the anger and disappointment in his eyes when she spoke.

Alice silently took a seat at the table.

"How is…" His voice trailed off, not able to finish his sentence.

"I am healed. All should be well, all things considered," Luna answered as she stepped closer to him. She took a stool and sat close to the fire. "Father, I wish to understand why you feel the way you do about the Nets."

Gannon looked at Luna confusedly and then back to the fire, taking a puff from his pipe and releasing it into the quiet room.

"For so many generations, those people have taken

advantage of our people," Gannon started.

"How?" Luna asked, wanting specifics.

"My father told me they cheated him when trading. They were more violent, and they didn't even take care of their own children," he said indignantly.

"Have you seen this with your own eyes?"

Gannon stood and angrily replied, "I don't need to see it. I have had my own dealings with them."

Luna interrupted before Gannon could say more. "I have seen the opposite with their tribe. Father, in all these years, why have they never attacked us? If they are such blood-thirsty criminals, why have they not provoked or attacked us in these past sixteen years? Not even after they have had the right to retaliate?"

"I don't know," Gannon admitted, flustered.

"I ask that you try to forget all you have believed about them and get to know them firsthand. That is the only way to make a fair judgment, not from a few examples or gossip, but from an actual personal relationship." Luna could see the distaste across her father's face, but he held his tongue, and she took it as a sign to continue. "Would you be willing to join a peace agreement with them?"

"No. I am still dealing with the repercussions of you breaking my agreement with the Dabneys. Just because Bale and I are friends does not mean this has been taken lightly. We both have our tribes to answer to. You betrayed your own people, Luna. Now the elders are deciding whether or not to choose a new chief to lead them."

Luna felt the weight of her father's words. He had never been one to communicate much to her, but she felt the importance of what he said. "I am sorry you are having to deal with this, Father. I truly am. I wish it hadn't happened this way. I tried—I really did. I tried to do things your way, but I was losing myself piece by piece. I couldn't live like that, with or without a child in my womb that was half Net," Luna explained gently.

Gannon's anger rose at the thought of Sol and Luna together. "He took advantage of you, Luna! They prey on the weak! You are just a prize for him to show off!"

Luna felt a protective urge to stand up for Sol and took a deep breath to calm her reaction. "The one time I felt like I was a prize, like I was being shown off, was with Aidan and you, Father. I feel like I have been a pawn in some game of strategy. I know Sol didn't take advantage of me because I am the one who asked to meet again. I crossed the river when he saved my life from a bear. I kissed him first. I asked to share his bed. It was me, not him."

Luna saw the disdain in her father's features as he slammed his fist onto the table. "As a chief's daughter, you have responsibilities to me and our people."

Luna remained calm. "I understand that. I believe it is in everyone's best interest for us to make peace with the Nets. Your grandchild will be half Net, the child the shaman predicted, the twilight creation the gods entrusted you to protect at all costs."

Gannon turned to face Luna. "It seems the gods might not let that happen after all."

His words stunned her. "What do you mean?" she asked, looking to Alice and then her father.

Alice explained, "The shaman came here with a reading for your father. Death will come to someone close to Gannon."

Luna was struck with shock and wondered if she would die in childbirth after all. She felt her body shake with an overwhelming mixture of emotions. "Even if I am to die, my child will live—Sol's sister has seen it." Luna's voice wavered as she blinked the tears away.

"What does a woman know about the future!" Gannon shouted.

Luna's eyes cut to him. "She knew you were coming to attack."

"Before or after you crossed into their land?" he demanded.

"Before. They were ready when I got there."

Gannon was silent, deep in thought. He wouldn't admit it, but the news brought him some relief.

"Your own gods have told you this child will join two tribes and make them into a great nation. Why are you resisting it?" Luna asked in disbelief.

"Gannon, her words are worth considering," Alice encouraged.

"Enough!" Gannon slammed his fist on the table again.

"I love you, Father. I don't know if you ever felt the same about me, but know that I forgive you." Luna felt relief upon speaking the words, though she had no expectation of a response. She turned to leave but hesitated when she heard her father's voice.

"Where do you think you are going? Your things from the lodge I spent so much time building with the tribesmen have been moved back here to your room."

"I am going home to the man I have decided to join my life to," Luna stated with resolve.

Gannon stood, waving his hand in the air. "What? Luna, think of what this means to your people. You would choose a Net man over them? Over your duty? Are you really that selfish?! I guess I should not have expected so much from you. I thought you said you forgave me… You are not going anywhere!"

"Forgiveness is for myself. It doesn't mean what you have done or what you continue to do is right. It doesn't mean I will forget or tolerate your offending actions again. I know I was never good enough for you, nor will I ever be, and that is something I will learn to accept. The only opinion of me that matters now is my own. My duty is to myself first, and my people will benefit from this union whether or not you are their chief. I believe this is right, no matter the consequences to myself," Luna said, her voice firm. She turned and opened the front door defiantly.

"If you walk out that door, you will no longer be my daughter," Gannon threatened.

Luna felt there was nothing left to say. She took the first steps of her independence, leaving through the open door. It hurt, leaving her father behind like that, knowing she had just shut more than the door to her old home behind her. Luna was surprised the pain of separating herself from her father didn't affect her as much as she had expected. Through the sadness, she knew she was making the right choice for herself and her unborn child.

CHAPTER 24

As soon as Luna exited her father's house, she could see a large crowd had gathered, waiting. Luna climbed onto her horse, the whispers of accusations growing louder. She nudged Willow to walk through the crowd, and they separated enough to let her through. The tribe members followed her back to the closed gates, where four armed guards stood waiting.

"Open the gate," Luna commanded, but the men only glanced at each other with questions on their faces.

"Dirty whore!" shouted someone from the crowd, which was beginning to turn into an angry mob.

"Open the gate. Now!" Luna shouted. The guards shifted uncomfortably where they stood but didn't attempt to open the doors.

Luna felt herself beginning to panic. The crowd was getting restless, and she was now being called a traitor, among other things.

"I have done what I think is best for our tribe, for all of you. There is so much the Net tribe could bring to our people," Luna attempted.

The mob only got more defensive, hurling slurs about her and the Net.

"Let her go," came a firm voice from behind her. Luna turned to see Alice watching the events unfold with her arms crossed.

The guards jumped into action, opening the locked doors. Luna nodded to Alice then left quickly for fear they would shut her in again. She nudged Willow into a trot until they reached the river's edge, where she was happy to see Sol waiting for her. She saw him smile and stand up when she came into sight. Luna crossed the river, Willow's hooves splashing in the icy water then walking over to where Sol had been waiting in the snow by his horse.

"I was worried I wouldn't see you again today," Sol admitted.

"Me too."

He kissed her hand and mounted his own horse before asking, "How did it go?"

Luna nudged Willow back toward the Net's village before she spoke. "Not well. He chose to hold on to his pride and his hatred. I am no longer his daughter."

"I am sorry, Luna. I know you were hoping for a better outcome. The important thing is that you were able to come back to me," Sol said as he reached his hand out to hers. They rode along side by side.

Luna continued, "I said what I needed to say, and for that I am grateful. I am not sure he heard me, but I said it for myself anyway."

"Is that everything?" he enquired.

Luna looked away to the tree line in front of them. "No. He said the shaman came to him with a message that someone close to him would die."

"Luna. Look at me, Luna," Sol said, catching the distress in her voice.

She turned to look at him, feeling the tears well up in her eyes.

"It doesn't mean it will be you. Akiiki has seen our child."

"Has she seen *me*, though? Sol, I could die like my mother did. The thought of my child living no matter what brings me joy, but a life without a mother is not one I would wish on anyone." Luna could not hold the tears back anymore, and she let them fall, streaming down her cheeks.

Sol rode around the front of her horse, causing Willow to stop. He went over to her other side and faced her then reached his hand out to her cheek, wiping away the tears. "Let's not get ahead of ourselves and worry for worrying's sake. Let us talk to Akiiki."

Luna nodded her head and kissed his warm hand, which was wet from her tears.

They rode the horses back to the pasture then headed to Akiiki's home together. When they arrived, Sol knocked on the door, and Bomani answered.

"Can't get enough of the baby, eh?" he joked, moving aside and waving his arm for them to enter.

Sol and Luna laughed, happy for the break in the seriousness of their day. When they entered the dim room, they could see Akiiki in the same place she had been the night before with a yellow linen blanket covering the sleeping baby, lying skin to skin on her chest.

Akiiki smiled at them and said, "Welcome brother, and my sister."

Bomani quietly brought two chairs into the room for them to sit by Akiiki, and they thanked him before sitting down.

"He is so lovely," Luna said genuinely.

"He is full of milk. He was up all night and most of today suckling," Akiiki said.

"Which means Akiiki didn't get much sleep. This is what you have to look forward to. Enjoy your sleep now." Bomani laughed, although he was completely serious.

"Akiiki, he is truly a blessing from the goddess," Sol said. "I must ask you something though, and then we will leave you to your rest."

"You want to ask me about my vision."

Luna and Sol both nodded with pleading eyes.

"I saw the child, alive and healthy," Akiiki said.

"Did you see Luna as well?" Sol asked.

Akiiki was silent for a few moments before answering, "No, only the child, but that doesn't mean something will happen to Luna."

Sol could see the disappointment and fear on Luna's

face, even though she tried to mask it with a smile.

"Thank you Akiiki," Luna said.

Sol thanked her as well, and they took their leave to let the new mother sleep while she could. Bomani walked them to the door.

"Do you need anything?" Sol asked him as they turned to say goodbye.

"The tribeswomen have been bringing us meals, and the healers have been by to massage and help Akiiki relax and heal. Our mothers have been taking turns checking in, so we have all we need," Bomani answered.

Sol nodded his goodbye before Bomani shut the door. Luna could see snowflakes starting to fall, and she felt the cold all the way down to her bones. She was tired and weary from the emotionally draining day.

"Can we go home?" Luna asked.

Sol put his arm around her as they started walking back. "Yes. Let's stop by my mother's home for some dinner to bring back—I have not stocked the house with what we need yet."

Sol and Luna made their way home. They spent the night distracting themselves from worries about things they could not control with warm savory food. When conversation seemed too much for their anxiety and weariness, they spent time rediscovering each other's bodies until they drifted off into a sound sleep.

Days passed until they were brought news that Dalila had

called a meeting with the Dabney tribe. She had managed to make a new peace agreement with them, making as sure as she could that they would never be able to join with the Barden to attack them unless the Nets themselves broke the treaty. Dalila knew betrayal was always a possibility, but she was thankful that things seem to be set at ease for the time being. She came back and spoke with the whole tribe, letting them know what had occurred and what had been agreed on. The tribe echoed their gratefulness for her wisdom in discerning the issues that had come up in the past month. There were still worries about retaliation from the Barden, but at least they knew the Dabney would not join either tribe in a war.

"I have other news, which is why I believe all of this was able to come about," Dalila explained. She saw the curious faces of her tribe watching her intently. "Chief Bale has died, and his son Aidan is now chief."

Luna gasped at the shock of this news, and looking around, she could see the Net tribe shared her surprise.

"Chief Aidan seems more open to sharing ideas and learning from each other's tribes with more community. I am sorry Chief Bale left this world under the circumstances that he did, but the goddess has given us a blessing in this. Now, go be with your families and enjoy their company. We never know when each of us will be done in this world." Dalila finished speaking and went inside her longhouse while the people dispersed.

Luna looked to Sol. "I have to speak to Mama Dalila, but I will meet you at home."

Sol nodded his head in understanding and kissed her forehead before leaving. Luna watched him until he was out of sight then entered the longhouse.

"Mama Dalila?"

"Yes, Luna?"

"I am happy to hear of the new agreement you and Chief Aidan have made. I just wondered if he knew I have come to live with your people…with Sol?" Luna asked, searching for the right words.

"He knows. He didn't let his personal issues with the situation cloud his judgment when it came to choosing what was best for his people. That is a good quality for a chief to have," Dalila answered.

"You're right. He does have good qualities. I am just glad everything worked out."

"Is there something else?" Dalila asked, seeing the anxiety on Luna's face.

"Bale was my father's closest friend. He will be going through a hard time right now. He will be very angry," Luna said worriedly.

"I know. I already have guards posted at the tree line, just in case."

Luna nodded, feeling as if she'd underestimated the wise woman. She left the tent and made her way home, where Sol had just finished cooking their dinner. She could smell the familiar scent as soon as she entered the home.

"I made your favorite," he said.

"It smells delicious," Luna responded, licking her lips.

Sol set a bowl of yellow rice on the table in front of her, and then another with steaming red crabs.

"I have to cook for you one of these nights," Luna said, feeling guilty she had not contributed much since she had been there.

"When you feel up to it. I enjoy cooking for you," he told her with a smile, cracking open one of the crabs.

"Are you scared of my cooking?" Luna asked jokingly.

"I have never had good food cooked by the Dabney, and I am assuming your people do not have many good recipes either. I am only looking out for the baby's safety." Sol smirked, and then they both burst into laughter.

"I will show you, tomorrow night. I just need a rabbit," Luna said determinedly.

They ate their dinner, enjoying every morsel of the sweet crab meat and savory spiced rice.

Later, they lay on the bed, snuggled in each other's arms, listening to the sound of the crashing waves of high tide when Sol broke the silence. "It was Bale that was going to die."

Luna could feel the steady inhale and exhale of his chest as she snuggled in closer to his arm. "I hope you're right. We won't know for sure until the day comes, though."

Sol turned his body to face her. Looking into her eyes, he placed his hand on her belly. The irregular pulsing started up at the warmth of his hand. They both smiled, knowing their child was kicking and letting them know all would be well. Luna would continue to hope.

The next evening, Luna and Sol set off to meet Aidan as Sol had arranged that morning. They both felt the need to face him. When they arrived at the river border, they could see him already waiting on horseback. Luna and Sol rode to the water and crossed over to his land. All three of them dismounted their horses, Sol reaching his hand out to shake Aidan's first. Aidan shook Sol's hand and nodded to Luna.

"Aidan, I wanted to say thank you for not holding what happened between us against the Net tribe. I didn't mean to cause you or your family any pain. I had met Sol months before I agreed to our fathers' arrangement at the autumn solstice. I did what I thought I was supposed to do," Luna explained.

"I know it was for the best. I wish you had told me, but I also understand why you didn't. When I am ready to commit to a woman, I don't want to have to convince her to be with me, especially as part of a trade agreement," Aidan replied, his words heartfelt.

"I didn't know until that day at the market where you had me meet Luna that you were supposed to be hand-fasted together. I didn't know about the pregnancy until then either. I genuinely meant it that day when I wished you well and told you to take care of her," Sol told him.

"There is no bad blood between us. You are a good man,

Sol, and I know you will take care of her, probably better than I would," Aidan said.

Luna noticed that he seemed more open and kind. She assumed his demeanor was a result of his father's sudden death. When the realization of just how fleeting time truly was in this life was brought to the forefront of one's mind, it put things in a different light. She knew he would make a great leader to his people if he remained this way.

"I am sorry to hear about your father, Aidan," she said softly.

"He left this world with a pint of ale in one hand and a woman in the other—two things he truly loved in this world. He had a smile on his face when he died." Aidan tried to sound positive, but his eyes glazed over.

"He loved you, too," she told him, placing her hand on his arm.

Aidan smiled, Luna's touch shaking him enough to bring him back to the present with them.

Luna and Sol said their goodbyes and headed back to their home, where Sol had a rabbit strung up waiting to be cooked for dinner. Luna didn't feel alone; she had Sol by her side, Mama Dalila, and the mostly welcoming Net tribe. She knew she and Sol still had so much to figure out, but their conversation with Aidan was no small victory. Luna made Sol her rabbit stew, which put his jokes about her cooking to rest. They spent that night and every night after that together in their home on stilts by the sea. They enjoyed each other and their conversations throughout the five months that followed. The stretch marks on Luna's skin let her know her pregnant belly had grown to its limits. Everything was harder to do, and her hips ached. Akiiki showed her how to use a linen wrap around her belly to help with the discomfort and give her extra support. Akiiki and Bomani had held a naming ceremony just one month after their son was born, and they'd named him Asim.

The Nets had begun trips in groups to meet the Dabney for trading and teaching each other skills. Luna went to listen and learn about herbal medicine. She saw Aidan there several times, and he greeted her and Sol kindly. Luna had not heard anything from her father, but Alice came to meet her at the Dabney border once every half-moon to check in on her.

Spring had come, and with it the lushness of green forests. The birds returned, singing their sweet songs. Sol had already been searching for more twisted branches with the hope of adding on to the home they shared. He created a new door on the side of the house with wooden stairs leading up to it for easier access for Luna. He grew his beard out over the winter, and Luna liked the mature look on him.

Luna left the house that May morning needing to move her stiff body. She enjoyed the fragrance the warm sea air and blooming spring flowers made together.

"I'll be back in a while," she promised, heading down the sandy beach to the west.

"Why don't I come with you?" Sol offered.

"As you wish."

He joined Luna as they walked on the sand hand in hand. They watched the green waves grow and crash over each other, creating sea foam before finally spreading out onto the beach. As they walked, the icy spring sea water washed over their naked feet. Luna had to stop every few minutes, wincing from the pressure around her pregnant belly.

"Are you in pain?" Sol asked, concerned.

"It is these practice surges. Mama Dalila said they were just preparing my body for the birth. I will be well. It will pass," Luna assured him.

They walked a little farther and were about a mile from their home where the sandy coast turned into a rocky shoreline with tide pools. The tide was coming in and crashing along the large boulders, washing all types of green sea plants up onto the shore. The sight and sounds were beautiful and relaxing. However, the waves of pressure in Luna's abdomen were getting more powerful and more frequent, mirroring the incoming tide.

"I think I need to go back," she said through gritted teeth.

"All right, take your time," Sol told her, following her lead.

They turned and made it halfway, the need to stop and breathe through each surge becoming more intense.

Luna panted through the contractions with her arms around Sol's neck. She slowly shifted her hips side to side instinctually, which brought her some relief.

"How about you try to rest here?" Sol said with more concern in his voice. "I can go get—"

Luna interrupted him as she knelt down, feeling the need to roll onto her hands and knees, still rocking. "No. You can't leave me here alone!" she cried out just before a large wave of pressure came crashing over her.

Sol wasn't sure what he should do, but he knew these were not the practice contractions Luna had thought they were. Panic filled his belly, along with excitement. He knew life as they knew it was about to change forever. They were becoming a family of three. The anticipation of this day had been building within him over the months, and the time had finally arrived.

The surge passed and Luna breathed a sigh of relief. "Go! Get Dalila. Tell her the baby is coming. Quick! I don't want to give birth alone on this beach!" Luna said hurriedly, preparing herself for the next wave of pressure.

Sol smiled from ear to ear and kissed her cheek. "I will be right back," he promised, lingering for one more kiss on her cheek, which only served to irritate her.

"Hurry!" Luna yelled through clenched teeth. She closed her eyes and started the journey deep inside herself, summoning the strength that had been passed down to her from each of her goddess ancestors who'd birthed lives before her.

Fear and excitement coursed through her veins. Her child was coming! Worry that she would not survive the birth still weighed heavily on her mind, but when the waves crashed in her womb, all she could do was focus on her breathing. Luna searched out that dark and tranquil place within herself, drawing strength. "You were made to do this," she said aloud, encouraging herself and drowning out the fearful voices in her head.

CHAPTER 25

Luna made her way closer to the home she shared with Sol between the frequent contractions, feeling sharp pains with each step. She stood, panting through each surge, rocking her hips until the wave of birthing receded. Suddenly, Luna felt a warm fluid flow down her legs. She looked down to see the murky liquid Mama Dalila had told her would come. With the burst of her waters came a temporary relief from the surges, and Luna smiled, facing the warm spring sun. The smell of the lilacs mixing with the sea water was much more pungent than it had been when she left the house that morning. The sun seemed brighter, and the pounding of the crashing waves sounded louder.

"It is a beautiful day to die," Luna said aloud to herself, but then she was cut off by a surge so much stronger than any of the ones that had come before. She knelt down on all fours on the wet sand just as a splash of sea water overcame her, soaking half of her body. The icy sea brought her relief from the hot storm raging inside her womb.

Luna looked up to where Sol had run to fetch his mother

and the other healers, wondering what was taking him so long. She didn't think she could walk any farther, but she knew she had to try. Before the next cool wave could splash her, Luna carefully stood and took a few more steps. Her white tunic dress clung to her as the warm spring wind blew. Luna's dark curly hair blew wildly as she opened her mouth and began chanting to the mother goddess for strength.

Luna staggered a few more steps. Another surge came. She rocked her hips, but no relief came this time. Luna found herself on all fours in the sand yet again, letting out primal sounds as she panted through the surges. Luna heard a roar and thought it was her own mouth making the noise.

All of a sudden, her head snapped up. A large black bear shifted from the shadows of the forest and peeked through the sea grass, calling out loudly. Luna stayed where she was, frozen in fear. The bear looked at her. It seemed to be just watching her and waiting.

"This is how I am to die? Mother! Where are you?!" Luna cried out, feeling her need for survival with another surge.

The bear stood on its two hind feet, roaring in challenge. Luna thought this was it. It was truly the end. This was how she would die, and Sol and Mama Dalila would get there to find her body and save the baby. Luna took a deep breath of resolve and stood. The next surge came and she didn't hold back. She let out a long, loud, primal roar, half afraid of her own voice. Luna had always been afraid of motherhood and birthing, even though it was her birthright. Something changed inside of her, and she felt her own mother bear instincts well up. The bear went back down on four paws and seemed to nod its head to her before disappearing back into the woods from which it had come. Luna breathed a shaky sigh of relief.

A distant voice called her name. She turned in time to see Sol on his horse, galloping toward her. He halted the animal abruptly and jumped off before running over to Luna.

"You are soaking wet. Are you all right?"

"I am going to have this baby right here if you don't get me home," she snapped impatiently.

"Of course. Mama will have everything ready at the house when we get there." He helped her on top of the horse in between contractions. Luna screamed through the pain of the horseback ride the quarter of mile to their home. There was nowhere for her to go, no way to move her body through each painful surge. The intense pressure she had been able to breathe through before with her eyes closed seemed excruciating while on the horse. Each bump and jostle caused her to cry out from sharp stabbing agony in her lower abdomen.

When they got to their home, Sol jumped off the horse and reached up to grab Luna, pulling her down in front of him halfway through one of the crashing waves of labor. Luna was elated to be off the horse, and leaning against Sol for support brought her some relief. She saw the stairs and wanted to cry. Sol took her hand and wrapped her arm over his shoulders while curving his around her back to help carry her up the agonizing steps.

"You can do this, Luna. I am right here to help you," he reassured her.

Mama Dalila heard them and opened the door. "My child, from the sounds of it, you must be close."

The words brought comfort to Luna as she gritted her teeth and took the steps one at a time, pausing for a contraction and then making it onto the bed Mama Dalila and Akiiki had prepared for her.

"Change her out of these wet clothes," Dalila told Akiiki.

"I can do it," Sol offered.

With a nod of approval from his mother, Sol pulled the wet tunic over Luna's head while she sat on the bed. Sol was worried about Luna's obvious discomfort, but he knew she was in good hands. He trusted his mother's wisdom, especially when it came to birthing and women's health. Sol noticed the naked shape of Luna, her darkened nipples and the hint of a line running down from her navel. He watched as the surge came and her belly changed shape, squeezing his child lower to the birth canal.

"Get in whatever position makes you feel most comfortable Luna. Listen to your body and trust it." Akiiki's kind voice encouraged her.

Sol picked up another tunic for Luna to put on, but she shook her head.

"She is probably feeling hot," Dalila explained.

Sol briefly wondered how Luna could be so comfortable completely naked in front of his mother and sister before his thoughts turned back to wondering how he could help her though this once-in-a-lifetime experience.

Luna closed her eyes and listened for the waves outside their house, imagining each surge inside her body as a wave building, crashing, and then receding, building, crashing, and receding, over and over again in one of the body's most rhythmic experiences.

"Did your water break yet?" Dalila asked.

Luna nodded her head.

"That's good. You are doing a great job. Soon you will be holding your baby, making all of this worth the struggle," Dalila said as she rubbed a cool cloth over Luna's forehead.

Luna lost all sense of time as she swiveled and rocked, trying different positions. Her body did best when she was on all fours, and Sol sat close to her, rubbing her lower back and offering her encouragement. Luna was glad to have all of them in the room with her. She felt safe. Whenever Luna would get distracted with fear, the pains would become more intense. As long as she could close her eyes and go to the quiet place within her mind, the crashing waves in her body were manageable. Luna felt connected to a source of strength, the very child she was birthing, and whispered to the baby in her thoughts. She told the baby's spirit that she loved her and thanked her for choosing her to be her mother.

The pressure became immense, and Luna yelped.

"Breathe out. Remember to breathe. Blow your lips together when it gets to be too much," Dalila directed, showing Luna what she meant.

Luna tried it, and it did bring her some relief.

"I need to…push!" Luna exclaimed.

A flutter of excitement filled Sol as he watched intently.

"Akiiki, grab the stool," Dalila said.

Akiiki handed her mother the low wooden stool, and they helped Luna onto it.

"This can be more effective sometimes," Dalila explained.

Sol held one of Luna's hands and Akiiki held the other while Dalila went around to rub her lower back. Luna squatted low on the stool, feeling the immense pressure and need to push that not even her own fear could make her stop.

Luna roared through the next contraction, pushing as hard as she could. She felt no relief and took a breath before the next contraction.

"That's it, Luna. You are doing great. Is it okay if I check you?" Dalila asked, coming back to Luna's front. Akiiki took over rubbing Luna's back.

"Yes," she replied quickly.

Dalila inserted her hand and brought it back immediately. "Luna, you are so close. Reach down and feel your baby." Excitement shot through Luna as she reached her hand inside the opening portal of souls and felt the bump of her baby's head. She smiled, a tear escaping her eye. The next surge came and Luna instinctively pushed, feeling the baby moving closer to the door into their world.

A knock sounded at the door to the house, and Akiiki left Luna to open it. A tribeswoman spoke to Akiiki, and she turned to Luna. "Would you like Alice to be here?"

Alice? Luna was momentarily stunned by the question.

"Yes," she gritted out, clenching her teeth and pushing with the surge.

Alice's white hair and blue eyes appeared through the door before she fully entered it. Luna cried out as she pushed with all her might.

"Luna, the head is born!" Sol exclaimed.

Alice found her place at Luna's side, holding her hand opposite Sol.

Luna breathed with excitement and released Alice's hand so she could feel it for herself. The slimy bump brought her the encouragement she needed, letting her know she was almost there. Luna closed her eyes and pushed again with the next wave, catching her baby in her hands. She looked down at the crying baby with tiny squished features, her black curls matted with slime, instantly falling in love. Sol's warm hand wrapped around Luna's, drawing the baby to her naked chest, and the newborn stopped crying immediately.

"Sssshhh, it's okay my daughter. We have you, you're

safe." Sol soothed the newborn and rubbed her little back.

Hearing that the baby was a girl brought Luna joy in knowing her intuition had been right all along. Luna panted, crying from the overwhelming love she was experiencing, as if the goddess herself was pouring the emotions into her body from the spirit realm. She had helped this tiny person cross realms, and the realization left her in absolute awe. Luna looked over to see an entirely new emotion filling Sol's face. He was in awe himself. He was smiling the largest, most joyful smile she had ever seen on him, and there was a new light in his eye.

"I am so proud of you," he said, kissing her cheek and then her forehead as tears escaped his own eyes.

"Me too," said Alice.

The newborn lay on Luna's chest, bobbing its head, rooting for her milk. Luna brought the baby to her breast, and Mama Dalila showed her how to latch the baby after wiping the slime from its eyes. Luna watched as the tiny fingers squeezed the soft flesh of her breasts, knowing instinctively what to do as it suckled. In that moment, Luna realized her child already had everything she needed inside herself. Her child knew instinctively what she needed. Luna wondered if all babies had this knowledge, and it was only time and the environment that taught children not to trust themselves. Luna realized she, too, had everything she needed as long as she trusted in herself. She promised her daughter she would do everything she could to heal herself and to love herself so her daughter would learn to do the same in turn.

Luna enjoyed the euphoria of her new little family for over an hour, and the concerned expression on Dalila's face went unnoticed.

She brought tea for Luna. "Drink this."

Luna drank the strong herbal infusion then handed the cup back to Dalila, finally noticing the worry in her features.

"What is it?" Luna asked.

"Akiiki, get the oils." Akiiki moved swiftly, not waiting for her mother's instructions before pouring them onto Luna's stomach and massaging, gently at first.

Luna began to panic, looking to the sleeping newborn and to Sol. "What is it?" she demanded.

"The placenta has not come out yet. It seems to be taking its time, but do not worry. We have some things we can try," Dalila explained calmly.

"I am going to need to massage you harder, and it will be uncomfortable," Akiiki said.

Luna nodded her head, seeing her mother's death replaying in her mind.

Sol put his arms around Luna. "You are safe. I am here with you. All will be well," he said, but his voice wavered, exposing his true fears.

A silent tear escaped down Luna's cheek. She looked down at the baby with smudges of a milky substance covering her. She tried to memorize her daughter's tiny features as she simultaneously willed the placenta out of her body.

The massage was intense, so much so that Sol pulled off his tunic and took the baby, holding it to his own naked chest. Luna gritted her teeth, fearing this was the end for her, as it had been for her mother.

No, not like my mother, she told herself. Her baby would live. She was not ready to die; she had so much she wanted to tell her daughter, so many things she needed to show her. Luna cried out in pain, feeling the pressure. Suddenly, a warm flow came out of her body. She looked down and saw the dark red and purple.

"Am I going to die?" Luna asked Dalila, feeling terrified.

"No, this is what we have been waiting for. This is good news." Dalila comforted her as the afterbirth was released then she placed the placenta in a bowl after making sure it was complete.

The umbilical cord had already stopped pulsing, so Akiiki tied it off near the baby's body, just as they had done for Asim. Sol handed the sleeping newborn back to Luna, Dalila offered him the knife, and he took it. Sol looked at Luna, and she nodded her readiness before he cut the white cord. Dalila took care of the placenta while Akiiki helped to clean Luna and get her comfortable in bed.

Alice stood to the side, watching them work and staying out of their way. She was surprised and amazed at the kindness and attention Sol and his family had given to

Luna. She had attended several Barden births, but none of them had come close to this level of care. She had always looked down on the process of birthing as a punishment women must endure, but watching her niece have such an empowering birthing experience showed her that women were chosen by the gods to bear this task not because of their weakness, but because of their strength. She saw that birth could be an entirely different experience where the mother had the power to make her own choices and give her permission instead of having others take the rights to her own body away from her. Birth could be something women could do and accomplish rather than have done to them.

"Alice?" Luna asked from the bed where she lay comfortably with Sol on one side of her and the sleeping newborn bundled on her chest in a blue linen.

"Yes?" Alice said, wiping the tears of joy that fell from her eyes.

"Thank you for coming," Luna said, meaning it wholeheartedly.

"You are most welcome, Luna, but I must be the one thanking you and Sol and his family for allowing me this experience. I will be forever grateful," Alice said, bowing her head to Dalila.

"You are family." Dalila nodded her head.

"I will take my leave and let you rest. I will come by again soon, if that is agreeable to all of you?" Alice asked as she headed toward the door.

"Yes," Luna answered as the others nodded in agreement.

After Alice left the house, Bomani came to knock on the door with little Asim. Bomani wore him against his chest in a wrap so he wouldn't crawl away. Asim needed to nurse and had held off as long as he could without his mama, so Akiiki sat to nurse him before they left together. Dalila said her goodbye and promised to be back with healing food and more tea.

"Thank you for sending for Alice," Luna said.

"You are most welcome," Dalila said as she nodded her head and left.

Luna was sad to see the people that had become her family leave, but she was also glad for the solitude with her new little family. Sol wrapped his arms around Luna and their daughter, basking in the euphoria of all they had just been through with each other.

"What should we name her?" he asked.

"I know the perfect one," she replied.

CHAPTER 26

In the month that followed the birth of Luna and Sol's first born, they stayed close to their home. On the days the spring rains didn't come, they walked the beach together hand in hand with their newborn wrapped snugly to one of their chests. They kept the baby close enough for them to kiss and take a deep inhale of the newborn smell off her little head, which was covered in thick small curls. Luna spent her time relaxing and healing, and tribeswomen brought them meals. Healers came to massage her and the baby with herbal salves. Sol started working on a project he didn't want to tell her much about, and that piqued Luna's curiosity. So, she simply enjoyed getting to know the new person who had joined their family.

When the difficult nights came with the crying newborn and sore nipples from nursing, Akiiki or Mama Dalila came to help and offer guidance. Luna had become close with Akiiki, and sometimes they would walk the shoreline together, wearing their babies and having conversations about life and motherhood. Luna was grateful for the kindness and acceptance the Net tribe, especially Sol's family, had shown her the past six months of living amongst them.

The baby's naming ceremony had gathered every single Net tribe member to the clearing where they celebrated the solstices. The early summer flowers had already begun to bloom, filling the meadow with a sweet aroma. The weather was warm, and the wind blew softly, making the event comfortable for all who attended.

When it was time to begin, Dalila called Sol and Luna to the front with their one-month-old. She picked up the baby from Sol's arms, smiling and kissing its forehead.

"This is the newest member of our tribe," Dalila started, and the crowd clapped and murmured their thanks to the goddess. "This is a special day, because we welcome not only this child to our community, but also the child's mother, Luna." More clapping and happy murmuring amongst the people. "My son, Luna, what name have you chosen for this child?"

Sol looked to Luna for the answer.

"Zora."

"I present to you my granddaughter, Zora. The meaning of this name is 'when the night meets the day, making dawn, creating twilight'," Dalila finished.

The tribe members smiled and clapped again, verbalizing their welcome to their newest members. Luna looked around at the large crowd, seeing her aunt at the front. Gannon had been invited to come along with Alice, but

Luna was glad she hadn't gotten her hopes up that he would.

The naming ceremony continued with both Luna and Sol promising to do their best to raise the child with kindness and gentleness so she could become a contributing member of their tribe. Feasting began after the short ceremony, and an altar was set up to thank the gods with gifts representing the five elements: earth, air, fire, water, and spirit. Some of the tribe members brought gifts for the family, such as handmade items from their crafts, a live chicken, and a rabbit. Sol had even carved a smooth wooden disc for Zora to chew on and grip.

Zora slept through most of her ceremony but started sucking on her balled fists, signaling her readiness for her mother's milk. Sol left Luna alone to nurse amongst the crowd while he went to get them a bowl of food to share. Luna held her milk-filled breast so it didn't cover Zora's nose while she suckled, and she smiled when her daughter's tiny hand gripped her own.

"Luna?"

She looked up to see Layla walking up to her wearing a light yellow wrap that accentuated her curves and her usual chunky turquoise jewelry.

"Yes?" Luna asked, not sure what to expect.

"My gift for Zora." Layla held out a closed fist.

Luna hesitated only momentarily then opened her hand below Layla's. Layla opened her fist and a beautiful crystal necklace dropped into Luna's palm.

"For clarity of mind," Layla explained.

Luna pulled her hand closer to take a better look at the white crystal attached to a black braided cord.

"It is beautiful, Layla. Thank you," Luna said, and she sincerely thought so.

Layla smiled genuinely at Zora and nodded her head before she left.

Sol returned with their food, and they enjoyed it together. He helped feed Luna bites as she nursed Zora. Luna realized this would be her life now, and she was glad for the partnership. She was the happiest she had ever been in her life, and she would enjoy it while the moments lasted.

Another month went by as Sol and Luna prepared for their hand-fasting ceremony. She had decided she wanted to have the celebration by the sea at dusk. The tribe prepared another large feast, lit torches, and prepared a large fire on the beach.

Luna wore a dark purple wrap that was embroidered with white runes and symbols at the edges. Her tribal tattoos were almost fully visible, and her hair was blowing freely in the salty breeze. Luna wore the simple purple shell necklace Sol had given her and her own crystal pendant hoop earrings. Akiiki had helped her paint her face with blue paint: a line across, below her eyes, and a thinner one below it. Luna nursed Zora before handing her to Akiiki then they opened the door of the house that had become hers.

The music started with drums beating slowly. The tribe members stood and parted for Luna to walk through them to where Sol stood waiting by his mother. He was excited that the day had finally come. Although he and Luna had been living as a couple already, he was impatiently awaiting the time when he would get to be hand-fasted to her. He watched with anticipation for any sign of Luna. Finally, she opened the door and walked down the stairs he had built for her with his own two hands. Akiiki followed behind her with baby Zora, but his eyes were glued to the beautiful Luna making her way toward him as she chose to bind her life to his.

The pace of the drumming increased as she got closer, matching his own heartbeat. A host of other instruments joined the drums as Luna reached the end of the large crowd of Nets and Dabney tribe members who had come to witness their joining. Luna reached him, maintaining eye contact the whole way.

Luna's body burned from the intensity of Sol's gaze. She was happy to see the ardent love in his features and to experience the desire it stirred within her. She knew she wanted to spend every day of the rest of her life with him. She reached him, and he held his hands out to her. Luna took both of his hands and stood to face him.

Dalila stood to their side, facing the crowd. "Sol and Luna have gathered you all here today to witness their willingness and desire to be hand-fasted together." Dalila weaved the cord around their hands silently before continuing. "Relationships are about living in the present moment together, facing whatever life brings together as partners. Do you have anything you wish to say to each other?"

Sol started, "Luna, I promise I will give you the best of myself. I promise I will be there when you need me. I promise to love you until the end of time itself. You are the air in my lungs, the fire in my body, and my inspiration. I promise I will take care of you and protect you with all I have. I promise to be your friend, your lover, and your husband. I give you myself out of my own free will."

Luna waited a moment before responding. "Sol, I promise to love you and take care of you. I promise to be there for you as well. I am proud of the man you are today. I promise I will do my best as your partner in life and as your wife. I join myself with you out of my own free will."

Dalila announced, "Sol and Luna, you are bound together. May the goddess bless this union."

Everyone in attendance clapped and cheered as Sol and Luna sealed their promises with a kiss. Sol's warm mouth left Luna eagerly looking forward to their night together after the celebration for their first time as husband and wife.

Luna and Sol turned to face the cheering crowd as the sunset lit the sky with orange and purple hues. The waves crashed onto the shoreline with the receding tide. Akiiki held Zora out to Sol, Bomani by her side, holding baby

Asim. Sol took his daughter in his arms and kissed her cheek. The baby's brown eyes were open, and her face was alert, looking at the crowd of loud adults making so much jubilant noise. Sol tapped Luna's shoulder, motioning behind her. Luna turned to see Aidan with Layla at his side, already measuring up his chances. She seemed to be giving him a hard time, and Luna saw Aidan rising to the challenge.

Alice was there, wishing the couple health and happiness, and Luna went to give her a hug before she left. Alice was happy to hold Zora, running her fingers through her curls as the baby cooed. The feasting and dancing began, and the night was full of laughter and merriment. When the stars were fully out, Sol came over and took Luna's hand with Zora in his other arm over his shoulder.

"I have a surprise for you," he whispered in her ear.

Luna smiled, curious, and followed him away from the crowds toward the river that separated the Barden tribe lands and that of the Nets. Luna saw Alice and Gannon standing on an object in the middle of the river, and she looked to Sol in a panic.

He squeezed her hand. "All is well," he promised.

When they approached, Luna could see the beautifully crafted bridge and realized it must be what Sol had been working on in secret for the past month. The sight of her father brought anxious flutters to Luna's belly. She held tight to Sol's hand and continued on, stepping onto the bridge to face her father as he stood next to his sister.

"Is that my granddaughter?" Gannon asked, breaking the silence.

"Yes it is," Luna answered.

Gannon glanced over to try to get a better look at Zora, and Alice approached.

"May I?" she requested.

Sol let go of Luna's hand and passed the sleeping Zora to Alice, causing the baby to stir awake.

Alice brought Zora over to Gannon, who seemed too afraid to touch the baby at first. He looked to Luna and then to Sol, seeking approval. Sol nodded his head, and Gannon took the baby, holding Zora to look at her face. Luna saw the unsure hardness of her father's weathered face soften into a smile.

"She looks like you did when you were born with the curly hair," he said softly.

Zora reached out and grabbed his braided beard, and they all let out a small burst of laughter, helping to lighten the tension among them.

"I asked Alice to send for you to meet me here, because I want to start to get to know some of your tribe, beginning with you and your family, Sol. I agree that this bridge was a good idea," Gannon said.

Luna could see the words were hard for her father to speak. She was completely shocked to hear them at all.

"You have changed your mind?" Luna asked.

"No, *you* have changed my mind. I have come to realize that life is too short to waste time making decisions out of hate. I lost Bale, and now I am losing you. I want to know my granddaughter, Luna." Gannon said, looking to Luna and then back to Zora.

"Thank you, Father," Luna said.

"Take care of my daughter, and my granddaughter," Gannon told Sol, handing Zora back to him.

"I will," he promised.

Gannon nodded his head before he and Alice went back to the Barden village.

Luna looked to Sol. "What…how did you…?"

Sol smiled and put his arm around Luna. "This is my gift to you. I built the bridge because I hoped one day we would be able to put it to use. I spoke to my mother and Alice, and they arranged for Gannon to meet us here. Loss of those you love can shift things and put them into new perspectives. Your father is trying to find whatever joy he can in the life he has left. He still has a long way to go, but having him experience us and our culture will help with that. I still don't trust him, but I know you still mean something to him, and so does our daughter."

"Thank you, my love," Luna said, meaning so much more than the simple words could convey.

"Now, let's go back and enjoy this night to celebrate *us*," Sol suggested.

Luna kissed him, and he pulled her closer. They stood in

the middle of the wooden bridge Sol had built to cross the divide and link her tribal land to his. They were wrapped in each other's arms, Zora between them, falling back to sleep.

Luna released Sol enough to whisper into Zora's ear. "Wake up, baby bear. Wake up. Tonight is the beginning of the rest of our lives together."

THE END

CHARACTER LIST

Luna: main character (Roman goddess of the moon)

Sol: main character (sun – Spanish)

Gannon: Luna's father (Celtic)

Terra: Luna's mother (goddess of the earth)

Dalila: Chieftess of the Nets (gentle – Egyptian)

Jabari: Sol's father (brave – Egyptian)

Akiiki: Sol's sister (friend – Egyptian)

Bomani: Sol's brother-in-law (warrior – Egyptian)

Ata: Sol's younger brother, oldest twin (Ghanaian name for firstborn twin)

Atsu: Sol's younger brother, youngest twin (Ghanaian name for second-born twin)

Layla: Sol's love interest in his tribe (born at night – Egyptian)

Ama: healer woman in Net tribe (Ghanaian name for a girl born on Saturday)

Asim: Akiiki and Bomani's son (protector/guardian – Egyptian)

Bale: Dabney tribe's chief (living near castle wall)

Aidan: Bale's son (like a fire – Celtic)

Thomas: Barden tribesman

Zora: Luna and Sol's daughter (dawn – Slavik)

TRIBES

Barden tribe: Luna's tribe (from the valley of barley – Celtic)
Net tribe: Sol's tribe (the divine mother – Egyptian)
Dabney tribe: third tribe (White settlement – Celtic)

GODS AND GODDESSES

Isis: Egyptian goddess of women and fertility
Neith: Egyptian goddess of war and hunting
Ceres: Roman goddess of agriculture
Thor: Norse god of thunder
The Green Man: The idea of the green man was developed in several different ancient cultures and evolved into a wide variety of examples. It is known as a symbol for rebirth, the cycle of growth each spring, and the changing of the seasons.

THANK YOU

Thank you for reading this novel. We hope you are emotionally satisfied with Luna and Sol's love story.

If you enjoyed reading this novel, please leave an honest review on Amazon and share it with your friends and family.

To receive email updates about future novels, give-aways, and more, visit the website below to join our newsletter today.
www.amkusi.com/bookfans

To contact us, use the email address below.
amkusinovels@gmail.com.

Thank you again for reading Luna and Sol's love story!

Cheers,
A.M. Kusi

ABOUT THE AUTHOR

A. M. Kusi is the pen name of a husband-and-wife team, Ashley and Marcus Kusi, authors of *Our Bucket List Adventures* and *Questions for Couples*.

We enjoy writing love stories that have a strong female protagonist, are emotionally satisfying, and have a happy ending.

Find more about our novels and sign up to be notified of new releases at **www.amkusi.com**.

Happy reading!

www.ingramcontent.com/pod-product-compliance
Lightning Source LLC
Chambersburg PA
CBHW032158180726
48284CB00001B/94